11/15/16

Warmest best wishes.

Ronald L. Brown

THE LEGACY

THE LEGACY

A Novel by
RONALD LAWRENCE BERN

NEW YORK 1975

Library of Congress Cataloging in Publication Data

Bern, Ronald Lawrence, 1936-
  The legacy.

  I. Title.
PZ4.B5224Le [PS3552.E7257] 813'.5'4   75-23341
ISBN 0-88405-116-1

To my Elaine,
with love

1

The funeral home had been a stage for the town's comings and goings throughout the day. The strongest, the social elite and the rich, had come, mostly early on with easy words ready for the family. They were the doctors in the town, the lawyers with good practices, the merchants, the bank officers, the presidents of the cotton mills and their wives, and the fading remnants of the "old" families whose positions were assured for a few more years in the town's regard until, one by one, they would lose the old once-white houses that told the town who they were.

The lesser people came, too. Farmers and dairymen with whom the old man had traded cows, store clerks and barbers, mill hands driven from the land and into town, salesmen and bank tellers and the old Greek who had drawn him a cup of coffee at 7:45 every weekday morning for the past 23 years. Figurative hats in hand, most clearly embarrassed, they paid halting respects and left quickly.

The only constant presences in the room were members of the family.

"Come look at Papa," his mother had said. "He looks so peaceful, David."

It was early morning, and he sensed rather than felt her hand on his arm, so lightly was it touching him, and yet there was about it an urgency, drawing him toward his grandfather's body. Although he had arrived almost an hour earlier, he had been careful to avoid the quadrant of the room in which the body was displayed, feeling a deep sense of foreboding at the thought of looking down at the old man's face or even brushing against the casket. It was not that death was strange to him, or frightening. He had seen it at close range before. It was that the death of this particular old man was strange and the prospects of a world without him even stranger. About his grandfather's death and even the funeral parlor, there was a sense of unreality, which he knew would be gone the instant he looked down into the ruined face.

As his mother edged him through the assembled mourners and respects-payers and curiosity seekers, as they skirted the wall clotted with rafts of white gladiolas and roses, David wanted nothing more than to turn and walk away. But that, he knew, would require explanations no one would understand. So he moved forward, joining the short line to the coffin.

The dozen or so people ahead of him looked briefly into the casket and, satisfied, moved on, and in an awkward, shuffling gait, David moved with them. At first he saw the fabric of the dark-blue suit, then the shirt and the skillfully knotted blue tie, then he was staring down at the face itself.

David's first thought was the skill with which the undertaker had molded the flesh into an attitude of quiet repose, had sewn the lips into an expression resembling a pleased almost-smile, had neatly closed the eyes, had turned from public view the ravaged jaw, cut away in years beyond David's memory, neatly concealed now in silk and shadow. The tallow-colored deathbed skin had also now disappeared under the rougebrush.

He stood looking for some time at the still form, the forehead, the nose and mouth, and nothing happened to him. He was neither wracked with grief nor was he stunned, as he had expected to be. Instead, his mind dealt only with the excellent job the undertaker had done.

The line behind him grew longer as he stood, rooted, fascinated with the face, feeling a twinge of guilt that he could be, at that moment, thinking other than reverent thoughts.

He might have stood longer had not his mother gently tugged his sleeve and nodded forward.

"Didn't he look peaceful?" she asked as they slowly passed the flower stand below the coffin. "Did you see how he looked?"

"Yes, ma'am, he did look at peace," David answered absently. Then, she began to cry again, and he put his arm awkwardly around her shoulder.

"The last thing on earth he ever said was, 'where's the boy' ..." she sobbed. "You knew that, didn't you, David ... that you were his last thought before he died?"

"I know," he answered gently, his hand patting her shoulder.

Then a well-wisher was talking to her, and she stopped crying.

2

"Miss Rachel, I'm sorry as I can be 'bout your daddy. This town'll never be quite the same without him," Dr. Jimmy Holden said.

She nodded gratefully, thanking him and reminding him that her father had always said he loved Doctor Jimmy, and assuring him that the whole family was grateful for what he had done to make his last days easier.

Seeing Dr. Holden talking to her, others drifted toward Rachel, knowing that Dr. Holden would find the right words to put Rachel at ease.

David stood a bit apart, appraising the well-wishers with curious objectivity. As the doctor said a last few words to Rachel, Jack Clinton and his wife stood by, uncomfortable, not knowing quite what to do with themselves until they could extend their own condolences. Finally, the doctor moved away, and the Clintons were talking to her. A few words were exchanged out of David's hearing, and then Clinton's wife leaned forward stiffly to embrace Rachel. They had known each other for more than 40 years, David knew; had gone to the old East Whitfield Street School together as children. Yet neither had ever before entertained the remotest idea of hugging, even this formally, before.

David turned away to watch others coming into the room. The September sun had climbed higher outside the shrouded windows, and people seemed to enter the room a bit more langorously, to move by the coffin and around the room with slower paces. Beads of sweat now stood out on their brows and upper lips as they entered the funeral parlor. The first rings of sweat began to appear at the armpits of summer suits. The carefully powdered faces of the ladies seemed to droop in the poorly air-conditioned chamber.

Few people made overtures to David. They had come prepared to offer sympathy to the old man's wife and his children; somehow, the grandchildren didn't count. One man, the manager of a dry goods store on State Street, did try to strike up a conversation about bass fishing at the lake, but David only made a distracted answer and moved away. Others spoke in passing, a few murmuring condolences, and he answered them with quiet courtesy.

In the moments he stood alone he was conscious of disembodied bits of whispered conversations, unconnected with speakers or listeners, floating free around him, and he listened without concentration.

". . . never be another Isaac Shulman," a voice behind him said.

"My azaleas were the best this year they've ever been," another said to his left.

". . . an' just look at her," another hissed. "She's not even cryin' and there lies her pore daddy dead and gone."

". . . bet it was a million or more he left his kin . . ."

3

"My momma's gettin' on right poorly herself . . ."

David continued to listen, disinterested in who spoke the words, thinking absently about the ways people come to look at death and talk about life.

"This fire and theft policy is the best the company has ever offered, and if you'd like me to, I'll . . ."

". . . all's I got was a 55-acre allotment for 400 acres of land. Ain't hardly worth buying seed an' fertilizer, you ask me," one farmer told another.

"It's got to where even if the government lets you put a crop in the ground, ya can't find good niggers to chop an' pick it anyway," the second answered.

"Well, Jake's a good boy. I remember a boxing match I saw him in where he hit another boy so hard he like to . . ."

"I can just send you the forms, and you . . ."

"Never been to a Jew funeral before; you ever been . . ."

Now the voices all began to run together.

"Could be closer to five million. . . . I took a covered dish to Mrs. Shulman's house, poor thing, but she was in bed and. . . . He was a good'un; his word was good as airy a contract ever wrote on paper. . . . I have to clean behind her; she thinks she's too good to get on her knees and scrub the floor. . . . You hear the one about the three niggers in the jungle that. . . . Rachel is the best of 'em, far as I'm concerned. . . . Then you add a half a cup o' sugar an' three eggs. . . . Ol' Aaron was a good ol' boy till he got them crazy notions about sending niggers to white schools. . . . Any more rain an' the weevils gonna take us over. . . ."

Finally David shut them all out, watching instead of listening, moving off to the quietest part of the room across from the door. Minutes passed, and hours; new faces came, mumbled the same embarrassed, self-conscious words to members of the family, and left to be replaced by others. Still David stayed, barely conscious that the faces were changing. His father had come over sometime earlier, suggesting that he go home, but he had answered that he would like to stay on a bit.

Thoughts flickered through his mind like feathery images from a poor projector, a jumble that he made no real conscious effort to bring into sharper focus.

Who did that old man really love, he wondered. I never saw him kiss a single soul, not Grandma or Mom or any of the grandchildren. Why was that? I must have been his favorite if he died calling for me. But did that mean he loved me? That feeling I carried for him since I was old enough to remember; what was that? Love or fear or

4

respect or what? Nobody was ever tougher than he was, or stronger
. . . he showed the town . . . what?

At that moment the questions were wrenched loose, the
thoughts ripped apart, by a shriek that assaulted the once steady,
even lapping of voices and rendered them silent—a wail transported
from a different place and time and dredged up from the depths of
human sorrow.

He whirled to see his grandmother slipping to the ground at the
foot of the casket, with hands reaching out to help her. Even as he
rushed across the room, David was conscious that the shriek and the
pitiful, open sobbing that had now replaced it were terribly out of
place. In the town, people were expected to hide their grief, to wrap
it in quiet respectability, to cloak it in decorum. Men never cried,
"quality" women only occasionally and even then with quiet dignity.

As his grandmother was helped into the next room, the wail
seemed to hang suspended in the air—audible to David long after its
last echoing died; almost as if only another Jew could hear it, feel it,
through some special sensory perception conceived and nurtured in
their common heritage of suffering, as only a dog can hear high
frequencies.

Now he shuddered, feeling a cold chill creep across his chest and
shoulders. In a strange way he sensed death in the room for the first
time. The wail of Baila Shulman was, to him, the final punctuation
mark on Isaac Shulman's life. The old man was dead, and the wail had
cut away the unreality of it. He was dead because his wife Baila had,
alone among them all—the strong and the meek, the family and the
other mourners, the people who came out of respect and the ones
who came out of curiosity—given expression to an unknowable grief
that said it was real. And so made it real.

For a moment David reacted with embarrassment to his grandmother's breach of genteel manners. Then he disliked himself for
having allowed himself to feel ashamed. But still the wail—the single,
piercing, wounded cry—rang in his ears, painting pictures on the
mirror of his subsconscious: of ancient Hasidim in curled earlocks
huddled under their prayer shawls; of unspeakable poverty and
crowded huts on dirty streets in Russia, in Poland, in Austria, in
Hungary; of pushcart vendors in tiny Russian shtetls and in lower
Eastside neighborhoods in New York, haggling with old women over
the price of a piece of fish for Friday night's dinner; of stinking holds
below decks in rusting ships, crowding immigrant upon immigrant
together for crossings, their faces turned to the bright promise in the
West with Sh'ma Yisroayl ringing from the rotting docks they had
left behind.

David shook his head to clear it of the sights and sounds, glancing around him as he did. At first, all he saw were the people nearest him craning their necks toward the chapel where his grandmother still wept in small, choking bursts, and he despised them for their grossness. Then he saw Marcie, her dark hair framed in floral wreaths, her hand resting lightly on her father's arm. She was looking directly at him, and when he spotted her, he was conscious for the first time of the yarmulke he wore on his head.

Against all logic, David had not expected to see her there; in truth, he had hoped she would not come. There would be, he knew, so much at the funeral that would emphasize their differentness, and he was not ready for that. Not yet.

So for a moment, he simply stood and stared. Sensing his feelings, Marcie whispered a quiet word to her father and walked toward him.

"David, I'm so terribly sorry," she said, ever so gently touching his hand. "I know you must be crushed."

To his astonishment, he saw that her eyes were brimming with tears. He took her small gloved hand in his and thanked her for coming. Then with self-conscious clumsiness, he asked her why she was crying.

"Because I know how much you loved him," she said, "and so I loved him, too."

David felt a roaring sensation in his ears, a drawing of the muscles of his jaws, and his eyes began to sting. He knew that for the first time in many years, he was about to cry, and he turned away. Marcie understood, and so she simply stood by him for the several moments it took him to regain control, to refocus his mind.

Then he felt her tug at his arm, and he turned to see his grandmother walking with great dignity toward the door. Excusing himself, he walked over to her and placed himself in her path. Her son, his Uncle Jake, who loomed large at her side, seemed slightly annoyed that David had stopped their progress, but his grandmother's eyes brightened when she saw him.

"Oi, David," she said, "mein life is over."

She seemed so tiny, dwarfed by Jake and the towering, arched ceiling of the room and the ascending wreaths behind her. And so terribly alone.

David gathered her into his arms, murmuring to her that her life was not over and that she musn't believe that it was.

Soon she was gone, walking the rest of the way with her head held high, the grand lady Isaac Shulman had made her.

When David returned to Marcie, her father was standing with her.

"She's a remarkable woman," the girl said softly. "You must be very proud of her."

David nodded, reaching as he did to shake her father's outstretched hand.

"I'm awfully sorry," the older man said. "All of us are going to miss him, David."

"Thanks, Mr. Stevens. I really appreciate your coming and bringing Marcie."

The three of them stood together for a few more minutes, talking uncomfortably about his family and the funeral, and then Stevens suggested to his daughter that they should leave now. As they started to walk away, she turned, whispered goodbye to David again, and then left him.

His eyes followed them across the room, watching the infinite grace with which she walked, the slender legs seeming to glide her along without disturbing the upper portions of her full body. At that moment he realized that he had not said one word of endearment, nor had he even hinted with words that she meant anything more to him than any other townsperson paying a courtesy call.

He might have hurried after her to say something more, but as she turned the corner of the room toward the outer door, he spotted, for the first time, old Lucy, standing still as a stone in the vestibule outside the room, against its farthest wall. As he moved across the deeply carpeted floor toward her, he thought to himself how very black and small she was. Indeed, her blackness was emphasized by the unrelieved whiteness of the walls and flowers that framed her. She was old and a little bent under the burdens of work, age, and race. For 35 years she had washed Mr. Isaac's shirts and scrubbed his floors, and now she had come to say goodbye.

She was crying—standing in the hall in a torn coat, an old hat of Baila's perched on her head, her skinny legs sticking out of a pair of shoes that had belonged to his sister, Jennifer—whimpering to herself quietly so as not to bother any white folks. David took her arm and started to lead her into the main room that held the casket, but she hesitated.

"Ain' 'posed to be no colored folks in dere, Missa David," she said.

"You aren't colored folks, Lucy. You're family."

"Well, didn' nobody ax me to come down yere nor to no funeral neither," she sniffed.

"I'm asking you," David said. "God knows, you got more business being here than most of these people."

As they began to move into the room, he added:

"If we all weren't so stupid, we'd have sent a car for you. I'm sorry, Lucy."

"Needna sont no car. Lucy didn' mind walkin' fur as she had to t'say goodbye to Missa Isaac."

Several women in the room appeared to be annoyed that a black woman was being brought among them, looking at her with disdain and moving away as she approached. But David glared and they quickly shielded their annoyance.

At the casket Lucy cried out and fell back on him slightly, but the cry was muffled and turned in on itself.

"You all right, Lucy?"

"Lawd, God," she moaned. "Lawd, Missa Isaac. . . ."

David put his arm around her thin shoulders and helped her into the chapel and to a pew. She cried for a moment and suddenly, almost hysterically, she jerked her head around toward him.

"Ol' Lucy no 'count. Ain' got no time to be cryin'. Gotta take care o' yo' Grandmomma. Where she, Missa David? Where yo' Grandmomma?"

For the second time, David felt his throat constrict, heard the roaring in his ears.

"Grandmomma's all right, Lucy. Go ahead and cry. After all these years, you got the right." Almost choking on his words, he crooned over and over to the little black woman: "You got the right."

Finally, she too was gone, maybe to church, David thought, or wherever worn out old black people go to cry out their grief.

All of them were gone—all but David Harris and his grandfather, Isaac Shulman.

David crossed the empty chamber to the casket and for a long time stood looking at the rouged face with the peaceful expression. All about him was silence, heavy and oppressive. Time began to run together in his mind, so fleeting and richly varied were the images that crowded together, flashing, tumbling, rushing to be delineated into thought and memory.

And he remembered.

2

The last strains of the "Shadow" theme faded from the big console radio in the Harris's living room, and the announcer for the local station cut to a commercial for the Somerset Ice and Coal Company.

"Remember, it's a long way till Spring, and you don't want to get caught some cold night without. . . ."

David tuned the commercial out of his mind, savoring in its place the Shadow's unfailing ability to win; to outsmart, outrun, outfight the men in whose hearts evil lurked, as he had again tonight.

"So just call 1299, that's 1299, for prompt delivery. . . ."

He could do that: he could outsmart and outfight evil people—he knew he could, at least someday when he was older, he could. He felt quite heroic at that moment; he and the Shadow, standing together, as they had only a few minutes ago, against the forces of evil that lurked everywhere, forces only he and the Shadow could divine.

"You're warm in the winter, cool in the summer. . . ."

Then the commercial ended, and David waited for the thrill of the creaking door, that inevitable Friday night radio sound effect that heralded the "The Inner Sanctum." As he waited, lying on the floor in front of the radio as he always did, he looked at the big RCA Victor white-and-black, spotted dog staring quizzically into the horn of the old-fashioned gramophone, wishing he had a dog like that. Maybe for Christmas this year he would be surprised with a puppy of his own, but he doubted it. Since his little cocker spaniel, Chesty, had gotten run over by a car, his parents didn't seem to have much interest in getting him another dog.

He heard scraping sounds in the cellar over the even tone of the announcer's voice, and he knew his father was shaking down the grate in the coal furnace. Every night and again every morning before the rest of the family woke, his father would put on his old gray sweater and go downstairs to stoke the furnace and get the fire going. As he listened to the scraping sound, David thought how much he would hate to have to tend that furnace, especially in the mornings when it was cold and damp in the cellar. But his father never seemed to mind; at least, David never heard him complain about it.

In a few moments the scraping sounds stopped, and David knew that the cinders were shaken down and his father would be shoveling coal into the furnace with the short, sturdy shovel he kept in the coal bin.

Then the spine-tingling creaking of the Inner Sanctum's door filled the room, with the scary voice of the announcer hinting at the terrors that lay behind that door, terrors David wondered about many times but never heard described, because Inner Sanctum came on the radio at 6:30 Friday night, and on Friday nights at 6:30 he and his family had a regular appointment across town.

His mother's voice announced that the time had arrived.

"David, get your coat, honey. It's time to go to The House."

As he zipped up the front of his short, wool jacket, David thought how he really didn't mind too much leaving "Inner Sanctum" to go to The House, particularly since his cousins would be there.

Outside, David and his sister Jennifer huddled together in the back seat of the dark-green 1940 Ford. It was already dark outside, cold for early December. Even inside the car, their breath smoked.

It was nice to snuggle against Jennifer. David didn't mind at all that his parents were delayed for a few moments in the house. When he heard the back door slam, he looked out of the window to watch Ben and Rachel coming toward the car.

"Davey," Jennifer asked, "do you think Daddy looks like Ronald Colman? Aunt Nell says he does."

David thought for a moment. "No, I think Daddy looks only like Daddy. Nobody else."

Not that he didn't think his father was handsome. He seemed to David to have a face made only for smiling, the quick, brown eyes exactly like his own, and a regular, even nose. His moustache, which scratched or tickled the children when he kissed them, was dark brown, just like his hair, and always neatly trimmed.

What David was proudest of was his father's strength. He had been a weightlifter before he was married, and, as David had heard his mother say many times, he was as "strong as an ox." David loved to hear stories of the fights his father had had, and sometimes he showed the boy the jagged scars in his back where he had been stabbed years before and almost killed. He was going a little bit to paunch and had started doing exercises every night to get back in shape.

"Too much easy living," he would grunt as he did pushups in his bedroom on the gray rug.

David would watch every night, sitting in the rocker without talking, not wanting to break his father's concentration. With each pushup, the muscles in the sides of his arms and in his back and shoulders would contract and bulge, relaxing as he went down toward the floor again. It seemed to David that the exercises would be good if his father wanted to lose weight in his arms and shoulders, but he could never see how they would help him lose any pounds in his waist.

One morning, he asked his mother about the exercises, and she laughed.

"The main exercise your father should work on," she said, "is not pushing up, but pushing back—from Ruth's hot biscuits and sweet potato soufflé."

He liked it when his mother laughed. The corners of her blue eyes crinkled in a special way that pleased him. His mother liked the color of her eyes, so much so that she surrounded herself with blue things—furniture, clothes, jewelry, even the Buick they had before his father bought the Ford. Her hair was as black (as Ben described it) as "the darkest tips of a crow's wings," and she kept it clipped close in the very latest style. She was pretty, everybody said that, and David liked to hear them say it. She complained about being a bit overweight sometimes, but Ben would only smile and call her pleasingly plump, causing her to make a funny face at him.

They were joking about something as they got into the car; Rachel first, with Ben holding the door, then Ben back around on the driver's side. David could tell his mother was happy by her light step and the way her voice lilted as she talked.

"I just love this crisp, cold weather," she said to the children. "It always puts me in mind of a cold, winey mountain apple, just ready to take a bite of."

As his father backed the Ford out of the driveway, David wondered why it was called "The House" instead of, say, "Papa's house" or "Papa and Mama's house." All of the members of the Shulman family in Somerset lived in their own houses. But when any of them referred to *The House,* they clearly and unmistakably meant the large, forbidding house on South Main Street where Isaac Shulman received his family on Friday nights, his children and grandchildren arrayed about him like a king's court, his wife Baila serving in mostly silent adoration.

David's grandmother was allowed to speak on Friday nights, but only about limited subjects. For example, she could talk about cooking, about how little her maid, Lucy, managed to get done, about the grandchildren's grades in school or how much they had grown. But she was never allowed to comment on any world affairs or business matters or any events that took place outside of her actual daily life. Sometimes she would begin, but Isaac would always interrupt her in the same way. He would start to laugh, a tolerant, patient little laugh, and say, "Baila, please . . ." And she would fall silent.

Friday nights were for men talk, although all of the women, and occasionally some of the older grandchildren, sat on the stiff couches and chairs in the big parlor and listened. Mostly Isaac and David's father talked—about business and livestock—and told Jewish stories.

Uncle Jake, the oldest of David's mother's brothers, sometimes talked about football or a good bull he had bought or a fellow he had whipped when he was in college. When Uncle Aaron was there, he sat quietly, sometimes smiling, most often looking beyond the room. David's youngest uncle, Irving, always came into the room when they arrived, sat for a few minutes—usually talking quietly to David's mother—and then left the room to go upstairs.

When his grandfather spoke, David listened carefully. Sometimes he tried to maneuver himself into a seat near his grandfather's left side. This gave him a clear view of his grandfather's jaw, which he never tired of looking at. Most of the jaw was gone, cut away in an operation years before, and in place of the flesh and skin and whiskers and bone of a regular jaw, there was a deep hole with a piece of skin plastered over it.

The truth was, David always wanted to see it closer than he got the chance to so he could figure out how it worked. But he was afraid that his grandfather would catch him staring at it, so he only stole quick glances at it and then looked away.

What he couldn't figure out was how his grandfather ate food, because it looked as if the entire jawbone was cut away. It would be hard enough for him to chew anyhow, since he had lost all of his teeth because of the operation. But if the bone was cut in half, David wondered, how could he work his lower jaw up and down? Maybe the jaw being hinged on the other side of his face was enough to make everything work; David didn't know.

Under the piece of scarred, pinkish skin that covered the hole, there was always something moving when his grandfather talked, and David wondered about that, too.

Every Friday night David would try to get into position to look at the hole more closely without his grandfather catching him, until finally one night Jennifer told him it wasn't nice to stare at Grandpa's

12

jaw, that it might make him feel bad if any of them just stared at it and that he probably wanted everybody to pretend that it was just like anyone else's jaw, and if David stared at it, it would just remind Grandpa that he didn't have a normal jaw like everyone else's and make him feel awful. So David tried to stop staring, but he kept on wondering how his grandfather could eat and what the little thing was that moved under the skin when he talked.

David was sure his father liked to go to The House on Friday nights, since he always laughed and joked with Isaac Shulman, whom he called "the governor," and Isaac Shulman seemed to talk mostly to him. As they drove along South Main Street, through the middle of Somerset, David planned what he would do at The House after he had kissed his grandmother and his aunts and shaken hands with the men and greeted his cousins. Tonight, maybe he would explore upstairs in the recesses of the back rooms. If he was lucky, maybe Uncle Irving would show him his stuffed animals and the cured skins he had packed away in the big steamer trunk in his room.

"Well, here we are again," Ben said, as he eased the Ford behind Uncle Jake's Chevrolet.

Rachel felt a prickling annoyance at the way her husband said *again,* as if Friday night at The House was a chore. For her, it was an unalloyed joy, because it brought her together with all the members of her family, but mostly because it brought her together with her father, who liked Jennifer and his other grandchildren, but beamed at David, who, because he was the oldest grandson and a smart, quick boy, was his favorite, and therefore Rachel's proudest accomplishment.

She started to comment on Ben's "again," but then decided to forget it. In a few minutes she would be home, a thought that struck her as she headed up the walk, for The House was more than a Friday night institution for her. It was, and always would be, home, regardless of where she lived with her husband and children. If she had reflected further on this thought, she might have begun to feel an uneasy sense of guilt. But the brightness of the light in the entrance hall was crashing around her at that moment, greetings were being called out, and her father was there, across the long parlor, waiting.

Behind her, David and Jennifer waited to enter for the several moments it took Rachel to kiss her mother and greet Jake's wife, Rebecca. Then they were inside, being prodded forward by their mother to go "say hello to Papa."

As always, he sat at the far end of the big sofa to their left as they entered the room, with the "children" gathered in chairs and on sofas around him. As they entered, he continued to speak without interruption, and all of the others listened intently.

When David approached him, the old man paused for a moment and turned his attention to the boy.

"*Nu, Dovidl?*" he said, thrusting out his hand. David took his hand without answering and felt the accustomed pressure of the old man's grip. Slowly the pressure grew without another word between them, until the pain showed on the boy's face, with Isaac Shulman beginning to laugh, mostly because the boy worked so hard at not giving up, laughing a high-pitched cackle that always came with the handshake, which lasted until the boy was on his knees, biting his lip, refusing to beg to be released as the other grandchildren would have.

Ben watched this ritual without comment, as he did every Friday night, understanding that this was the old man's way of demonstrating affection for the boy. Jesus Christ, he thought, how crazy can you get? To have to show love with pain. He knew the old man would not really hurt the boy, that in a moment he would release the small hand and that would be the end of it. For a moment, Ben felt pride in the fact that David would not cry out or beg as the other children did, and in the same moment, he realized that his feeling was as crazy as the old man's, and he felt embarrassed.

For the old man, shaking hands with his grandchildren, male and female, was a substitute for kissing them. He had never kissed any of them, not even as infants, nor had he ever kissed one of his own children. To shake hands, though, was entirely appropriate to him, and to crunch the small bones of the hand together when the boy took his gnarled hand was more than appropriate; it was, strangely enough, very satisfying—in ways the old man never would have admitted.

"*Nu, Dovidl,* is it enough?"

The boy winced but refused to reply.

"Enough, is it enough?"

Still the boy, now on his knees, held out. And then it was over, the old man laughing and turning his attention back to his audience.

He had just begun to tell a story about his childhood in Russia —in fact, the story of his own birth—and, as always when his grandfather told the strange stories from so long ago, David found himself listening in rapt attention.

There was something about the stories—and the strange aura that came over his grandfather when he told them—that was both frightening and fascinating. Although David did not understand it, there was about the old man a kind of mysticism that lived and glowed in him only when he talked about Bogdanya, the tiny village of his birth in eastern Russia, and about the ascetic rabbi of Bogdanya, his father—the boy's great-grandfather—whose wisdom and hateful sternness had long since merged into a single trait in Isaac's mind,

14

and were the only legacy he had by which to remember and revere his father.

David had missed the beginning of the story, and, as his grandfather talked, he forgot to look at the scar, forgot his cousins, forgot the old leather-strapped steamer trunk upstairs that held the animal hides. At that moment he saw only the strange light in his grandfather's eyes, heard only the words he was saying, thought only of the scene he was painting. He had listened, transfixed, for so many hours before, that the events and scenes of his grandfather's childhood, recalled so often in this room, were his most vivid first memories. In his mind, he pictured—perfectly, he was sure, beyond doubt—the rabbi at his books, his prayer shawl covering his head. He saw the sons of the rabbi of Bogdanya, huddled near the oven, also motionless, as they always were when their father was home and reading the Commentaries, having learned as babies—their teacher, Channa, their mother; their lessons a cruel slap or a boxed ear—that when the rabbi of Bogdanya, their father, was studying or supplicating God, they could make no sound.

As Isaac told the story, his oldest grandson listened intently, conjuring up in his mind the rabbi's lips moving silently as he read in the dim lamplight. A tall and powerful man, the rabbi dwarfed the table at which he sat; the book almost disappeared in his hands. His beard, full and flecked with gray, covered his collar and flowed across his chest like a shawl; the long earlocks curled into it and seemed to disappear.

"Ah, what a father," Isaac recalled proudly, and indeed, who would not have envied him his distinguished parent?

After all, wasn't his father the learned rabbi of Bogdanya, the leader of all the Jews in the village, the most learned man of all the elders? Was he not the most respected man in the entire Jewish community? Had not this man, his father, been the voice of wisdom that settled all disputes?

The wisdom of Mordecai Shulman had indeed been known among Jews as far away as Pinsk. No man, it was told, ever went away dissatisfied with his decisions, regardless of the settlement. The spring before, a man had been given the coveted seat of his father by the eastern wall of the synagogue over his brother's claim, yet the brother had seen the wisdom of the decision and gone away at peace. This man had been awarded a disputed goat, that man a droshky, this one a business.

On the afternoon Isaac was born (the time Isaac was now describing to his family), even as Channa had begun to grunt with the first pangs of childbirth, the elders of the town had assembled in his room to hear with him the pleas of two litigants.

15

Moisha the boxmaker, a wretchedly poor man, had died, leaving only a thin cow behind him. The two sons of the boxmaker had both laid claim to the cow, glaring at each other through red-rimmed eyes, even as the first *Yortseit* service was ending.

"It is mine by birthright," the elder son, Nachum, had cried angrily.

"No, it is mine because my need is greater," the younger brother, Beryl, had contended.

And so the argument had gone for days, until finally the litigants had been shepherded into the rabbi's house.

As was his way, he listened gravely to both sides of the argument, hearing Nachum first. Although the presentments lasted well over an hour, only once did he interrupt, bringing his great hand sharply down on the table.

"Shaa!" he called into the next room, angered at Channa's moaning, which was proving to be a distraction. (In the next room, Channa bit her lips, tore at the straw mattress on which she suffered as the pains became more frequent, and did not make another sound.)

"The cow legitimately belongs to me," Nachum said, "because I am the oldest son and the legitimate heir to my father's estate."

"What need have you for a cow?" his brother appealed. "You have a rich dowry, a good business, God be praised. No one in a hundred versts has not heard of your fine Pesach wines. What is the need?" There was no envy in the man's voice as he recited the list of his brother's riches. But still, the older brother was unmoved.

"I want the cow because it is rightfully mine, and that is reason enough," Nachum replied shortly.

On they talked, presenting this argument and that, and the rabbi merely listened.

Finally, Joachmin the shamus prompted the younger brother: "Tell the rabbi of your need," he said to Beryl, "and let us hear his judgment."

As he spoke, Beryl almost choked on his misery. "My wife, Pesha, goes about in rags, trying, God bless her, to make a sabbath meal from water and a chicken neck. My children, honored rabbi, live on crusts of black bread. Hunger stalks my house like Haman himself," the younger brother cried out.

"If I had the cow," he continued, "how things would change. There would be milk and cream and cheese for my children, maybe a little left to sell. Oi, with God's help, maybe even a little piece of fish for *shabbes* . . . a whole shirt for little Ezriel."

Then, near weeping, he could say no more. Looking about him, the rabbi decided that he had heard all of the relevant evidence. He cleared his throat twice.

16

Huddled behind the stove, the rabbi's sons awaited his words in gathering suspense. Such a dilemma, Avrum, the first born, thought, is impossible of solution.

"Reb Nachum," the rabbi said to the older brother, "it is my understanding that you want to own the cow because its ownership would give you satisfaction in that it is your legal right. Is that not so?"

"It is as the respected rabbi has said it," the elder answered.

"Reb Beryl, you want the cow because it can give your family food and sustenance. Is that correct?"

Beryl nodded his head vigorously. "Only I and our Almighty know the wretchedness and the need of my household."

The shamus and the others pondered how they might decide, how they might strike a balance between legal right and moral right. But before any of them had reached a decision, the rabbi was pronouncing the settlement.

"The matter will be settled in this way, may it please God," he said. "You, Reb Nachum, the eldest, shall have the cow, to keep in your shed, to feed and care for, and to prize among your other possessions. And you, Reb Beryl, because of your need, will have the fruits of the cow. The milk will be yours, and all that derives from it. And the manure will be yours, too, for it is also the issue of the cow, and Reb Nachum's shed must be cleaned by your hand."

Joachmin the shamus had to restrain himself from laughing out loud, so clever and so just was the rabbi's decision. Nachum's birthright and Beryl's need would both be satisfied with one cow.

As the men began to file out the doorway, Chiam, the rich man who occupied the seat in the synagogue nearest the eastern wall but for the rabbi's, congratulated the rabbi on his wisdom and each brother for having won his plea.

After bidding each man goodnight and God's blessings, the rabbi closed the door and returned to his bench, donning prayer shawl and phylacteries, and beginning to read from the Zohar. From their positions at the stove, Avrum and his younger brothers, Uri and little Motel, heard their mother's choked screaming. Soon Shaindel, the midwife, hurried in, knowing somehow that the time was come, and her mumbled prayers and instructions and soothings and pleadings filled the two rooms of the hut.

Within minutes the frightened boys heard the strange, hollow, slapping sound, time after time, and finally, they heard the pitiful, thin wail as Itzrok Shulman, fourth son of the rabbi of Bogdanya, drew his first tiny breath of air.

Such as it was, Isaac told his audience, the spark of life now burned in Itzrok Shulman, a tiny, sickly baby who would somehow manage to live and come to this place, thousands of miles away, to tell how it happened.

The story was over, but still the rich, vivid images filled David's imagination, and he continued to ponder them. The scratching of his father's match against the brick fireplace brought him back to the present, and he was visibly startled.

Seeing his reaction, Isaac began to laugh:

"See, Dovidl, things were different then. Harder. No fancy hospitals and doctors and a big *tsimmes* about having a baby. My father got mad because my mother dared interrupt him with a groan of pain when she was trying to birth me in the next room, all alone."

Then he laughed again. But the strange light was gone out of his eyes; the spell was broken; and David went upstairs as soon as he politely could to look at the skins.

For most of the rest of the night, the men talked about things David didn't understand. As he drifted in and out of the parlor from time to time, he heard his grandfather discussing the Jews in Europe, about how they must be fleeing by the thousands.

"In the name of common decency," his father said at one point, "in the name of humanity, I can't believe Roosevelt and Churchill will just stand aside and let Hitler destroy the Balkans and then Europe. It doesn't make sense."

"What would you do?" Jake asked him. "Go to war?"

"We may have no other choice," Ben answered him.

There seemed to be a growing anger in his voice, and David left the room to look for Jennifer and their cousin, Linda.

When he found them he gravely informed Jennifer that "we might go to war," not really understanding what that meant. Linda started to giggle at him, but Jennifer stopped her.

"I'm going to pray tonight that we don't, Davey, and maybe you can, too."

3

The next morning broke cold and overcast, and David woke early. Turning comfortably under the blanket, he considered going back to sleep; then he remembered that it was Saturday.

The room was still partially dark. No sunlight streamed on the wall behind the edge of the drawn shade and the drape. For a moment he studied the framed picture on the wall above his chest of drawers, wishing, as he often did, that he could be a part of the colorful English hunting scene, mounted on horseback behind the racing foxhounds, dressed in a fancy red coat and high, black, riding boots.

In a few minutes, he knew, heat would begin to come up through the pipes, and soon after that, Ruth would be in the kitchen baking biscuits and frying eggs. He would get up then, he decided, when the house was warmer, but for a little while he would snuggle deeper in the delicious warmth of the heavy wool blanket.

Every Saturday was precious to David. If it rained, as it probably would today, he was disappointed but not badly, for rainy Saturdays usually meant having Jennifer all to himself. Together they would play endless Monopoly games, listen to "Let's Pretend" and the other Saturday morning radio programs, lick the mixing spoons as Ruth made cakes, and invent clubs and contests and games to play.

Once in a while Saturdays meant—as his father had promised the night before that this one would—spending the morning in the company of men at the Harris Mule Company.

David never experienced a treat that surpassed in pure pleasure a Saturday morning at the mule barn; first, because he was admitted,

19

almost as an equal for those few precious hours, into the world of grown men, and second, because the stories he heard there about fighting and shooting and hunting were incomparable in excitement for a five-year-old boy.

Without question there would always be a crowd of farmers at the barn, regardless of weather or season, because Saturday was a day no self-respecting South Carolina cotton farmer worked. It was almost a matter of honor not to work on Saturday, even if the cotton hung ripe in the bolls and a rainstorm was sure to strike first thing the next morning.

On Saturdays farmers came to town in mud-splattered Fords and Plymouths and pickups and once in a great while in mule-drawn spring wagons. The center of Saturday morning social activity was Somerset's three mule barns. During the week the farmers might come to one of the barns to trade mules, cattle, or horses; but on Saturday they came to talk and sometimes to take a pull on a pint of bourbon when their throats got dry.

Winter Saturdays were David's favorites—the colder and rainier, the better. On warm, sunny days the farmers were likely to drift in and out of the barn's hall, talking in groups of two or three and looking over the livestock in the big, straw-floored stalls. But when it was cold and raw they would all come inside, gathering up chairs in a circle in the office—close to the potbellied stove which glowed red and drew steam out of their wet brogans and the uncuffed legs of their gallus overalls—and tell stories.

Brax and Thomas would always be there, too, not in the circle, of course, but leaning against the wall. It was expected that they would be there, as (it seemed to David) they had always been. They had worked together at his father's barn since before he was born: Brax, huge and copper-colored, his handsome face always ready to break into a smile over strong, white teeth, as outgoing as Thomas —smaller, older, and infinitely blacker—was shy. Nobody would laugh harder at a joke, nobody would slap their knees with more hilarity, than Brax and Thomas, almost, it seemed to David, as if that were the price of admission they felt they had to pay. Only the white men talked, but Brax and Thomas were allowed to listen and laugh when they wanted to at the white men's stories and jokes.

No obscenity was permitted, but David was only vaguely aware that this prohibition was taken by the adults as a matter of course because of his presence. Sometimes the talk around the stove made his heart pound and his imagination soar, particularly talk about shootouts and other kinds of violence. But more often the talk had to do with mules and cows, with trades between this one and that, with land and field hands and weather.

20

When the farmers talked about their land and their crops, they did so with a strange, crushed resignation, an acknowledgment that the bargain they had struck with life was an unequal one: they could only plow the land, plant the seed, spread the fertilizer, chop the Johnson grass, poison the weevils, and hope. If the weather was right they could bring in a good crop, maybe even two bales of cotton or more to the acre. But with any sudden excess of bad weather in late spring or summer, they might find themselves looking down the double barrels of disaster. In hours or even minutes, a year's work, a year's security, and maybe even the land itself could be gone, leaving behind it only a soul-numbing sense of displacement and failure.

David had seen such a time in August the year before. The cotton stalks had stood in rich flower, tall and straight and full of bolls just beginning to burst. The weevils had been tolerable that year, the weather wet in early spring, hot and dry from May to August—perfect cotton weather. In nearly every farmer there was a quiet, understated elation, since the two previous years had been lean ones, with rain in September spotting the cotton.

"Reckon your young'un 'ar could've made a bale an' a half this year," Mr. Lee Ross had said to David's father.

"Ever' white man an' nigger in the county's got a bale and a half shore as it was in the gin."

The Harris farm was more than proof of Mr. Lee's confidence, its 150 acres of cotton perfect in all respects, tall and well developed, every stalk loaded with healthy, ripening bolls. Not even the low edges where the quick summer rains ran off showed spotty growth. To a cotton farmer it was the prettiest picture imaginable.

Then one afternoon, a hailstorm seemed to blow in on the tail of a lightning bolt, the bastard child of nature's summer excess and a dirt farmer's luck. First lightning rent the heavy afternoon, walking across the land like an evil old goat, setting brush fires and killing grazing cattle. The sky grew dark, and out of the darkness came the wind—at first a pleasant, cooling breeze, then suddenly a landlocked gale, shattering chinaberry and pine trees with its force. And on the wind came the hail: freakish chunks of ice fired like bullets by the wind, killing everything in its path.

In seven minutes it was over—only seven minutes of ice, whipped across the western edge of town on an August afternoon. In its wake lay a kind of desolation few had seen before. The cotton crop was destroyed. Not that the bolls had been shaken off the brances or the branches torn from the stalks. All of it—leaves, flower, branches, bolls, and stalks—all of it was gone, swept away, it seemed, by the wrath of God.

21

Ben and David rode out to the farm in silence. When they passed the fields at Jim Altman's place, David thought at first that his memory was playing tricks on him. He thought the fields had held cotton and corn just the day before; now they were entirely barren.

They rounded the bend by Jackson's Store, and their own fields came into view. Only then did David begin to understand what had happened.

Ben caught his breath sharply. He slowed the car and parked on the shoulder of the road. As they walked into the field, he kicked a few rapidly melting hailstones. For a long moment, he stood without speaking, only shaking his head slowly and looking out across his land.

Finally he put his hand on David's shoulder.

"Look at it good, son. You may never see its like again."

"Where did it all go?" David asked.

"Cut down, a whole crop cut down as smooth as a combine cuts wheat, and blown away. Makes you realize how puny man really is, David; how little he can do when the hand of God is raised."

"I'm sorry, Dad."

"I am too," Ben said with a long sigh. "But it's not a major tragedy for us. We have crop insurance, and that'll pay part of the damage. The ones to feel sorry for are the poor devils who aren't covered—the ones whose lives depend on this crop."

Then Ben thought of Buck Mason. Buck would be standing in his fields now, too, just down the road, surveying the damage. But for Buck it would mean the end. Without this crop he wouldn't be able to meet his mortgage payments. He would lose the 55 acres of land he had struggled so long and hard to hang on to, the 55 acres that set him apart from other Negro farmers, that gave him position and prospects that other black men working white men's land could never hope for.

"Come on, David," Ben said, "let's go over to Buck's place."

Ben drove slowly, grimly fascinated by his own ruined fields. He would have to check the damage to the buildings and the "cropper" houses on his place and get them repaired. He would have to put in a claim for insurance payments. Maybe he would have his hands sow peas in the cotton fields, since the fertilizer was already in the ground anyhow and the peas would make a quick cash crop. He'd talk to the county agent when he got back to town, to find out whether peas were the best crop.

But first he'd talk to Buck Mason. Ben spotted Buck standing in the field nearest his old ramshackled barn, his head bent, not moving. As Ben drove into the yard a chicken squawked and ran out of his path, but Buck paid no attention. As if deafened by the hailstones slamming disaster against his tin roof, he heard nothing. All he saw were the battered matchsticks that had been fine four-foot stalks of cotton a few minutes before.

As the white man and the boy approached him, he finally heard, turned, and touched the brim of his old felt hat in an automatic gesture of respect.

But he said nothing.

"Looks like you got hit mighty hard here, Buck," Ben said.

"More'n I kin stand, Cap'n," the Negro said. "I finished dis time, sho."

"You had rough times before," Ben said.

"Not lak dis, no sir, not lak dis here. Crop gone plumb to hell."

"Maybe you can make another one. I'm thinking of sowing peas on my place. Maybe a crop of peas can be made before the frost."

"Cain' even do dat, Cap'n. Got no seed . . . no money to buy none; lightnin' kilt my mule. Cain' do nothing now. Ol' Buck finished."

Then his massive shoulders began to tremble and finally to shake. He had worked so hard and so long to get up the first payment on his place, had struggled so to keep it, and now God Himself had taken it away from him. Tears traced a path down his creased face.

David felt a surge of pity and tears began to gather in his own eyes. Then his father was speaking again.

"Don't cry, Buck. I don't want to see you lose this piece of land. Hell, you deserve to own it. Let me see what I can do."

Buck stared at Ben, a look of mingled hope and hopelessness on his face. He was still staring after them as Ben eased the car out of the yard and back onto the paved road.

"He's a good Nigra," Ben said, more to himself than to David. "He deserves better."

"What can you do, Dad?"

"Not sure yet, son," he answered. But David knew that his father already was figuring out the steps he would take.

Back at the mule barn in town, Ben called Brax.

"Put a good mule on the truck," he told his top hand, "and then drive over to the Ansco store. When you get there, Mr. Martin'll have seed peas and lime. Drive'em out to Buck Mason's place—you know, the place west of mine—and drop'em off. Tell Buck I said there's no use wasting the fertilizer he's already got in the ground, and if he gets those peas in the ground in a hurry, he'll make a cash crop. Tell him I'll see him later."

As Brax drove the big stake-body truck out into traffic, Ben went into his office where he found Isaac Shulman talking to several farmers who had not been hit by the hail.

"Did the storm git to you?" one asked Ben.

"Yes, it hit particularly hard out my way. Lost everything standing in the fields, every boll, leaf, and stalk. I never saw anything so desolate in my life. You just have to see it to believe what that Goddamned hail did. How about you fellows? You get hit?"

"Naw, I was lucky. Passed within a half mile of my place and never blowed off a boll. Pete here wasn't touched, neither."

"You carry crop insurance, don't you, Ben?" Isaac asked him.

Ben smiled. "Yessir, Gov'nor. I been paying crop insurance premiums for 12 years now without ever so much as interrupting my agent's lunch. But he'll get a call before today is out."

Ben picked up the telephone directory, intent on finding the agent's number. Then he decided that could wait.

"You boys know old Buck Mason, the Nigra's got that little place west of mine? He got hit hardest of anybody I know. Hail took his crop off and lightning killed his mule. I went over to see his place and me and Dave here found him standing in a field, crying. He's worked awful hard to buy that little place, and now, with his crop gone, he's going to lose it."

"I know Buck," Isaac said. "He's a pretty good nigger; used to work as a blacksmith years ago till he saved up a down payment. I'd hate to see him lose that place."

"I'm going to help him some; already sent him a good mule and seed peas to make himself a quick cash crop. But that won't be enough to pay his mortgage through the winter."

"Who holds his mortgage?"

"The Building and Loan, I think," Ben answered.

Jim Dean, one of the farmers, spoke up. "Be a good chance for you to add to your farm, Ben. His piece used to belong to the old Fowler place anyhow."

Ben shook his head. "No, I don't want it that way. I really feel sorry for Buck."

"Seems to me," Dean said, "some white man's always helping that nigger. Hell, Lee Ross combined his whole grain crop last year, and Joe Landon musta give him fertilizer and seed 10 times since he got that place."

"I hear tell," Pete Broyle said, "that Buck is real friendly with all the highfalutin niggers in Somerset. How come that nigger doctor Penn or the undertaker ain't runnin' out there with nothin'? Hell, that undertaker got more'n me and Jim and you put together, Ben!"

" 'Em niggers'll make theirselves scarce now," Dean cut in. "Ain't never been a nigger that'd help another one. Never!"

"Ben," Isaac said quietly, "I'll call J.P. over at the Building and

Loan and see what can be done about the mortgage. Meanwhile, here's $50 to help old Buck out now."

Dean watched Isaac take five $10 bills out of the big wallet he carried. As Ben laid them on his desk, the farmer reached for his own wallet and a $10 dollar bill—not out of liking for Buck Mason but because of a sense of white man's responsibility which, if called on to do so, he could not begin to articulate.

"Well, Mr. Isaac, that's right white of you. Reckon I'll just sweeten the pot a tad," Dean said.

Other farmers came and went, and by the end of the afternoon, Ben held $140 which he and David delivered to Buck before they went home for supper.

As they drove east on Drake Road toward home, Ben told David: "You see, son, in the South, the best friend the Nigra has got is the white man. Don't ever forget what you saw today. What I did, what your grandfather did, what all the rest did—was done not because we had to but because we wanted to. It was done out of caring for another human being who also happens to be a Nigra."

It had been a good lesson, one David was not likely to forget. He thought about it as he sat in his chair near the stove, perhaps because Mr. Dean and Mr. Broyle were there in the barn together again.

Although it was just after nine, the barn was already crowded with visitors. Brax already had gone twice to Doc Carey's veterinary office on the other side of the barn for extra chairs. Outside, the wind whipped the cold rain into sheets, and the streets were all but deserted. The crowd around the stove was particularly jovial, laughing and whooping at the jokes and stories.

When Mr. Lee's turn came, he told about a black woman who went to the sheriff's office to report that her husband was missing.

" 'Yore man done run off with some old fan foot, that's all," Lee said, mimicking the sheriff's voice.

"But two days later she come back, threatenin' to call the FBI in if the sheriff didn't hunt fer him. So the ol' sheriff said he'd look aroun', and sho nuff, he found him—at the bottom of a shallow swamp pond. Had about 400 pounds of loggin' chains wrapped around him. An' when they derricked him up, ol' sheriff said: 'Ain't that just like a nigger, tryin' to steal more'n he can tote off!' "

Everybody laughed except David. He was embarrassed for Brax and Thomas, and he glanced sidelong at them. But as usual, they were laughing loudest of all.

Then the laughter stopped abruptly. As David turned, he saw all eyes fastened on the door, open now and framing an old man. He was as tall and straight as a Georgia pine. His hair was white and full, and heavy, white eyebrows topped cold, steely gray eyes. For a moment the man stood in the doorway, the moaning wind announcing his arrival through the still-open door, then he took several steps forward. As he did so, Thomas and Brax ran out of the office as if the demons of hell were licking at their heels.

How strange, David thought. Why were they running that way?

He took a closer look at the old man who was wearing very old-fashioned clothes but apparently not old ones. He had on a black frock coat, a high, celluloid collar with a black, string tie, and a large-brimmed, white hat.

The old man took off his hat and nodded slightly to David's father.

"Good morning to you, Mr. Harris, sir. Might I join you gentlemen at the fire?"

Ben was on his feet instantly.

"We'd be more than honored by your presence, Mr. Jessup, sir."

After a few minutes by the fire, during which the conversation was more subdued because of his presence, the old man spoke again.

"Mr. Harris, my throat is a bit dry. Would you be kind enough to summon one of your niggers to run an errand for me?"

Ben called Thomas who reluctantly appeared in the doorway, clearly preferring to stay out in the rain rather than take one step over the threshhold. When Ben indicated that Mr. Jessup wanted him, Thomas was seized with a fit of shivering that had more to do with fear than with his wet overalls. His eyes rolled; he seemed to blanch (as much as a coal-black man can blanch) as he turned to face Mr. Jessup.

"Thomas, take this money and go to Mr. White's whiskey store. Fetch me a pint of Old Granddad bourbon whiskey. And see that you get back with it in a hurry."

Thomas took a tentative step forward, then another, stretching out his arm as far as it would reach. Finally he had the money in his hand. Then he turned and ran out the door. A few minutes later, he was back. Wet to the skin, he still knocked on the door, waited to be called in, and approached the old man with the greatest deference.

As soon as Thomas had given the bourbon and the change to Mr. Jessup, the black man turned and darted back out into the rain to the accompaniment of snickers from some of the farmers. Jessup offered the bottle around the circle before tipping it up for a long draught; then he lapsed into silence, smiling only slightly at the stories the others told.

The morning passed and finally the last of the farmers was gone. As Ben locked up the barn, David could contain himself no longer.

"Dad, what happened this morning? I mean, when that old man came in. What was the matter with Thomas and Brax? I never saw 'em act that way before."

Ben grinned and ducked into the Ford, David close behind him. As he cranked the car, Ben explained.

"My boy, you just saw a living legend. That was Mr. Theodore Jessup. He was a baby during the War Between the States and a boy during Reconstruction. When he was about 18, he and his father and two brothers had about built back their ruined plantation, almost killing themselves in the process. One day, riding his fields, he told one of the hands to chop another section of cotton instead of the one he was working. Seems this was a particularly mean Nigra who hated all white men in general and the Jessups in particular. Tension had been building between the hands and the Jessups anyhow, and this time the spark was struck to the powder keg. The Nigra looked Mr. Jessup square in the eye and called him a white son-of-a-bitch. As the story goes, Mr. Jessup reached for his pistol, then stopped himself and said: 'I should kill you where you stand, but I won't. Instead, you go get every nigger on this place who feels like you do, arm yourselves and meet me and my brothers on the covered bridge in one hour. By God, we'll settle this once and for all.' "

Ben drove into the driveway of the house and switched off the engine. But instead of opening the door, he turned to David to finish the story.

"In one hour Mr. Jessup and his brothers stood at one end of the bridge, each with two loaded revolvers. And a whole gang of Nigras, armed with shotguns, rifles, and pistols, stood at the other end. The firing commenced. When the smoke cleared, the Jessup brothers were shot all to pieces, but they refused to fall. Thirteen dead Nigras lay at the other end of the bridge, the rest having either run or dragged themselves off. When the doctor came to the Jessup place, he said it was a miracle any one of the brothers could stand on his feet down there, much less all three, shot up as they were. But it was pride that made their backs stiff and their legs hold, son. Just stubborn white man's pride."

"But that was so long ago," David said. "Why are Brax and Thomas still scared of him?"

"Well, you know how superstitious Nigras are, son. The original story had him killing 13, but over the years the story grew and by now I reckon old Thomas would tell you he killed 1,300, with another one every month or so since, to stay in practice. Besides, the talk is that he still carries one of those pistols he used that day on the bridge, and that doesn't make the Nigras in this town feel any easier about him."

Once in the house, David wondered if Ruth would be scared of Mr. Jessup, indeed, if she had even heard of him. But he thought it better not to ask.

4

"Now that old blue jay up there in the hickory tree is the most devilish bird in the woods," Ben said. "He'll chase a little song bird out of its nest and break its eggs just for the fun of it. Isn't that something?"

Jennifer clucked and decided she would never again think a blue jay pretty.

Then David was gesturing overhead.

"Hey, look at the squirrel on the wire," he called.

Above their heads, balanced as delicately as a circus performer, a big gray squirrel tripped across the telephone wires.

"Boy, I sure would love to catch him for a pet," David said.

"Don't ever touch a squirrel, Davey," Jennifer warned gravely. "My teacher said that their teeth are so strong and sharp from breaking hickory nuts that they can cut your finger right off with one bite."

For a moment David stood trying to envision his hand with a finger gone, folding the end joint of one finger under and looking at it.

"Boy, I bet that would hurt . . . if a squirrel bit off your finger, I mean."

"I wouldn't like to find out how it would feel," Ben said, "and I wouldn't like you to find out, either."

They walked for a moment in silence, then Ben asked David if he had told Jennifer what happened at the mule barn the day before.

"Nosir," he said, and then he told his sister about how Brax and Thomas had run out into the rain when Mr. Jessup came in.

"You should have seen him, Jen. He was really scarey looking, 'bout seven feet tall with a big hat and funny-looking clothes and these mean-looking eyes. And a gun, Jen. He was carrying a gun, only you couldn't see it. An' even Brax was scared of him. You shoulda seen it!"

"I don't think it's very nice for anyone to go around scaring people," Jennifer said, "and I don't think Mr. Jessup is a very nice man."

Ben chuckled and stroked the back of Jennifer's head.

"Sounds like you've got Mr. Jessup classified with the blue jay, darling. But I think there's a pretty big difference. Mr. Jessup doesn't mean to scare anybody. It's just that people are naturally afraid of him because of something that happened a long time ago—even before I was born. And you know how terribly old I am."

He loved to joke with the children, particularly about the impending time when he would be old and gray and entirely dependent on their goodwill for a hot meal once in a while. But Jennifer would have none of it.

"Daddy, please don't start that again. You'll have David crying and it will ruin our walk."

"You're right," Ben nodded. "Let's forget about Mr. Jessup and get on over to the radio booth."

As he often did on quiet Sunday mornings, Ben had set out with the children for a walk to the campus of Somerset College, a collection of old brick buildings surrounded by a broad expanse of well-tended grass, pines, and water oaks. The objective of these walks was always the same—a small radio station which transmitted Sunday programs from broadcast offices in one of the college buildings.

When they arrived, several other people had already gathered to watch and listen to the announcer, who worked in a glass booth and waved and smiled at the children between the records of church music he played. Today the announcer seemed in a particularly good mood, and as soon as Ben and the children walked in, he printed a note which he held up to them.

It said: WHAT'S YOUR FAVORITE SONG?

Jennifer read the sign to David.

"Tell him the Shadow song, Daddy," the boy said urgently.

"The what song, son?"

"You know, the song they play when the Shadow comes on the radio. That song."

"Davey," Ben said patiently, "all he plays is church songs. He wants to know what our favorite church song is."

Ben started to chuckle. "Jennifer, you think he has a recording of 'Hatikvoh' or maybe 'Adon Olam' back there?"

Jennifer said, "Oh, Daddy," in exasperation, but she was laughing, too.

Ben printed PEACE IN THE VALLEY on a sheet of paper and held it up to the glass. The announcer signaled OK and started looking through the stack of records behind him. Then the commotion started in the back offices of the studio. First, loud voices were heard, like the beginning of an argument, and then a man came running toward the announcer's booth, holding a long piece of yellow paper in front of him and yelling at the top of his voice.

David was frightened. As he dashed to get out of the man's way, he could make out only two words, *War* and *Japs*.

He heard his father mutter "Oh, my God," and felt Ben's hand on his shoulder, pushing him toward the door. Then they were walking fast across the campus toward home.

"What was the man yelling about?" David kept asking. "What's the matter?"

For a while, Ben didn't answer. Instead, he urged the children to try and move more quickly.

Finally, in a tight, grim voice, he told them.

"It's war," he said. "The Japanese have bombed our ships at Pearl Harbor and now, God help us, we're at war."

David had never seen his father look so worried and upset. He started to query him further, but Jennifer stopped him.

"Davey, I don't think Daddy wants to talk right now. Let's see if we can see another squirrel on the wires between here and home."

Although he would not have admitted it to them, David didn't see why war was such a terrible thing. In fact, he was quite excited by it, particularly since he was in on a big secret before most of the grown-ups in the town knew about it.

As the weeks went by, nothing happened to change his point of view. There were parades down Main Street. Men he had met in his father's barn gave speeches in the square at the foot of the Confederate statue. Exciting music and newscasts poured out of the radio.

Wade Douglas, a tall boy who lived with his parents down the street from the Harris family, was the first person he knew personally who got a uniform. Wade enlisted the day after David heard the news about the war, and within a few weeks, he was home from basic training at Camp Jackson, wearing a khaki army uniform with bright brass buttons and shiny boots. When David saw him, he was walking with a pretty blond girl down Oakland Avenue, even taller and straighter than he had been the year before when he starred on Somerset High's basketball team. David had seen Wade hundreds of times, but this was the first time he remembered seeing him with a girl. He wanted to run up for a closer look at Wade's uniform and would have without giving it a second thought if the girl had not been there. Instead, he just watched them pass. Wade was too engrossed in his conversation to notice David, and the girl never took her eyes off Wade's face.

As they neared the corner, Rachel came out into the yard and put her hand on her son's shoulder.

"Did you see Wade, Mom?" he asked excitedly. "Didn't he look great in his army suit?"

Rachel shook her head slowly.

"He's just a baby. Hardly 18 years old. And now he'll be going off to war."

As they watched Wade and the girl slowly make their way toward the Douglas home, they saw Ben driving up Oakland Avenue in the Ford. Wade waved happily at Ben, and Ben returned his wave.

"He ain't no baby, Mom. He's a soldier."

"David, for heaven's sake, how many times have I told you not to say *ain't*. The word is *isn't*, and unfortunately he is, too, hardly more than a baby, certainly too young to go off to some horrible place thousands of miles from home to get hurt or maybe even killed."

"Wade won't get killed," David said confidently.

"I hope you're right," his mother said. "He's always been such a sweet boy."

As the months went by, more and more boys they knew—boys like Wade Douglas—appeared in uniform, home on leave to spend a few quiet days with their girl friends and families, all seeming somehow a bit taller than they ever had been before, a bit prouder. And then they would be gone again.

To most of them, war was fun, all wrapped up in flying flags and marching music, in smiles from pretty girls and pats on the back from the coach, the high school principal, the mayor if they chanced to see him, and their fathers.

David heard the music, and when he was very lucky, he even got to hear stories about basic training from the boys in the neighborhood home on leave. In his excitement he couldn't understand why his mother seemed so sad.

One afternoon he burst into the house, looking for Jennifer. He had just seen Bobby Coleman home from boot camp, wearing lieutenant's bars on his Marine uniform. When he ran into the living room, he found his Uncle Jake talking quietly with his mother. Their conversation ended abruptly when he entered the room, and Jake got up to leave. Rachel hugged Jake and kissed him, and the big man looked embarrassed. Then he chucked David under the chin with his fist and promised to bring him a Japanese sword when he came home.

That night David asked Jennifer why their mother was crying. "Is it somethin' I did, Jen?" he asked.

"No, Davey, it's that Uncle Jake is leaving for the navy in the morning, and Mom's scared he might get hurt."

The first boy in Somerset to be killed in the war was Tommy Creighton. He had just turned 18 when he enlisted; four months later he was machinegunned to death at a place called Corregidor.

An army lieutenant and a corporal came to the fine old Creighton place on Webster Road to tell Tommy's mother that he had been killed in action.

As the months passed, in Somerset as in towns all over America, there were more lieutenants in olive drab cars with large white stars on the doors, weaving their way from one painful scene to another. The poorer people gasped when they came and cried. Somehow that made it easier for the young officers. But the "quality" people like Mrs. Creighton held themselves erect—remote, somehow, from what they heard and now knew—waiting to regain the privacy of their rooms before they cried.

As the military cars made their way down the quiet streets with greater frequency, the last glamour of the war wore away. No more marching bands paraded on Saturdays. Gold stars began to appear in parlor windows, and the newspaper carried growing numbers of pictures edged in black—of children who were yesterday's basketball stars, football players, boys who milked before they came to school, boys who laughed, boys who held their girls and whispered in the darkness. All hurried into death in some place far away, now brought to a common fraternity of unseeing eyes and lips that never again would frame a laugh—dead.

As each young man's family received a caller at their door—or when the numbers became unmanageable for the War Department, a telegram—the town flinched, convulsed, and asked why.

5

Ruth didn't like it, not even a little bit. But there wasn't anything she could do, so she would just have to make the best of it. She would try, she knew that, and maybe she would even smile with the family. But as sure as this was Monday morning, she was going to feel sick in her heart all day.

"Will, you get outn' that bed and get yo' clothes on. You wanta get fired agin?!"

Ruth's husband Will rolled over under the quilt and snuggled down into the pillow, still half asleep.

"You hear me, Will Simmons?" she harangued him. "You ain' nothin' but a lazy, good-for-nothing nigger . . . all you'll ever be. Git up, you hear?"

Now Will was sitting up in bed, rubbing his eyes. Across the room Ruth was slipping into her starched, white uniform.

Will grinned at her.

"You sho is good lookin' to be such a mean gal," he said. "How come you to be so snappish this mornin'?"

"Ain' snappish. Now stop yo' sweet talkin' and get outa' that bed. It's comin' on seven o'clock."

"Git me some breakfast, then," he said.

"Git yo' own breakfast," she snapped. "I ain' studyin' bout yo' breakfast."

For a long moment, Will glared at her, then he started to laugh.

"Now I knows what it is. Yo' l'il ol' boy gonna start school this mornin', an' you done got yo'self all riled up over it. Ain' that it, Ruth?"

34

"Ain' no such a thing," she snorted. "What I care? Havin' him go off to school jus' gonna make my work easier, tha's all."

But that wasn't so. The thought of David starting school filled her with a numb, aching feeling. Now she was losing him, losing David, who was hers. Now she would work every school day in a quiet house, the one person she loved most in the world across town in a school room with a bunch of trashy little younguns and a teacher who didn't care a thing about him, maybe him running in the street after a ball or getting hurt on the playground or walking in puddles of water and catching cold; being away from home all those hours with nobody to look after him properly, and her all alone in the house, cleaning and baking and washing clothes and watching the clock until two o'clock every day, lonesome and miserable.

Will was grumbling about breakfast when she left the house, but she didn't bother to make up with him. On the bus she took her accustomed seat in the back next to the the last window. As the seats around her began to fill up with other maids bound for north Somerset, she avoided conversation.

When the bus stopped at Marshall Street, she got off and walked at a slower pace than usual toward the Harris house. Consumed by her feeling of loneliness, she noticed neither passersby nor barking dogs nor cars that slipped by in the warm September sunlight. Finally she was at the house and in the kitchen, her kitchen, as she had long since come to think of it; for the moment, she lost herself in planning her day. She had polished David's white shoes and pressed his tan shorts and jacket the day before. So she decided to make him a special breakfast. Mr. Ben was up and around, running the water in the bathroom. He would want coffee as soon as he came in, so she put on the coffee pot first, shaking a pinch of salt in the coffee grounds to make it just the way he liked it. Then she carefully measured out the flour and eggs and milk for wheatcakes—David's favorites—and cut thick slices of the sugar-cured ham Miz Rachel had brought home the day before. As the wheatcakes were cooking in another pan, Ruth broke eggs in melted fat and in the oven she heated the cinnamon buns she had baked the day before.

When Ben came into the kitchen Ruth was pouring a cup of coffee for him, and he greeted her pleasantly, as he always did.

"Good morning, Ruth, that sure smells good."

"Mornin', Mr. Ben. I got some sweet rolls in the oven, nice and hot. You want one with yo' coffee?"

"No, thanks. I believe I'll just have some coffee till the family comes in to breakfast."

For a moment he sipped his coffee reflectively.

"Well," he said finally, "this is a big day around here."

35

"Yassuh," Ruth said quietly.

"Hard to believe, isn't it, Ruth? I mean, that David is starting school. Seems like just yesterday we were bringing him and Miz Rachel home from the hospital. Now here he is, starting the first grade."

Ruth was close to tears, so she said nothing. Ben understood what was happening, sensed how she was feeling, so he tried to cheer her up.

"With that little scamp out from under your feet, you'll be able to get things done a lot easier," he said. "Why, I don't know how you ever get a cake baked, what with him hanging around to lick the pan and the spoons and asking a thousand questions."

"Never bothered me none," she answered quietly. "I always like havin' that boy roun' me."

Ben understood then that nothing he said would make her feel better, so he lapsed into silence, drinking the fragrant coffee and thinking his own thoughts.

Rachel and Jennifer came into the breakfast room together. For Jennifer, too, it was the first day of school, but this was an accustomed matter; they had watched her go off to school on first mornings for four other Septembers.

"Well, look at your princess," Rachel said to Ben. "Doesn't she look gorgeous?"

Jennifer, pretty and leggy as a newborn colt, was wearing a carefully pressed blue-and-white, voile dress with puffy sleeves.

"All the women in this family are beautiful," he said as he leaned forward to be kissed by his daughter.

"Fifth grade," he said, shaking his head. "You're just getting to be an old lady."

Jennifer was about to reply to her father's kidding when David came in, rubbing his eyes with one hand and trying to tuck his shirt into his short pants with the other. Instantly Ruth was across the room to fix his shirt. For a moment she worried with the collar, then she smoothed out a few imaginary wrinkles in his shirt and stood back.

"My, my," she said, "aren' you the big grown-up man, goin' off to school an' leavin' Ruth here all alone."

"I'll be back early, Ruth. Then we can play," he answered her gravely, and she quickly turned away toward the dishes in the sink.

The children left with Ben in the Ford, and Rachel stood in the doorway, waving, with Ruth just inside behind her, watching the car disappear down Oakland Avenue. Rachel had at first thought to go with him the first day but then decided against it. After all, Jennifer would be with him; she would show him where to go and what to do.

It was hard enough seeing him go off this way.

"Maybe I should have gone with him," she said to Ruth.

"Yessum, maybe," Ruth said, her voice quavering. And then she was gone, back into the kitchen.

As she ran her bath, Rachel tried to remember the last time she had seen Ruth so shaken. As she slipped into the steaming water she decided that not since the first time she had seen the girl, more than 10 years ago, had she seen her in such a state of agitation.

Ruth had shown up at the back door, terrified, thin to the point of emaciation but still pretty, a scared little girl of 16, the color of heavily creamed coffee, dressed in tatters.

She was speechless when Rachel first opened the door, but finally she managed to force out the words.

"Ma'am, I sorry to bother you. But . . . but. . . ."

"What is it, child?" Rachel asked.

"It's that . . . I . . . I so hongry, ma'am," she stammered. "I . . . I. . . ." Then she looked down at her ragged shoes and could say no more.

"Come in, then," Rachel said. "Let's get you something to eat."

She guided Ruth into the kitchen, indicating that she should sit down at the breakfast room table. She found cold chicken and potato salad in the refrigerator, and she put them on the table, along with some leftover tomato salad. The girl began to eat, self-conscious and embarrassed; it was obvious that she was famished, yet after she finished the first of the three pieces of chicken, she stopped eating and instead stared at her plate in silence.

"What's the matter, child?" Rachel asked. "Why don't you eat more?"

With a great mustering of courage, the girl pleaded: "Ma'am, my mamma ain't had nothing to eat in three days 'ceptin' some grits. I wonder. . . ." She broke off, too embarrassed to continue.

Hunger was no stranger in Somerset in the winter of 1932. The less fortunate in every town and city in the country struggled merely to survive. But in small southern towns like Somerset, the poverty had taken on a particular quality of grinding, soul-numbing hopelessness. There were no bread lines in Somerset, little CCC or WPA work for the poor whites and none for the blacks. Old, black women sat on the sagging porches of their shanties, puffing rabbit tobacco in corncob pipes and staring out at nothing. The play of their grandchildren was sadly dispirited, their fathers long since having abandoned them for other towns and unfulfilled glimmerings of restless hopes.

Beans and grits were cheap, but they weren't enough to live on, and the nickels and dimes the white people paid for a load of wash, scalded in front-yard iron pots and ironed to the rhythm of breaking backs, didn't buy enough of these even if they were. The scrubbiest turnips, the most wilted collard leaves, had been rooted out of back-yard gardens and were gone. Hunger stalked the "black bottoms." The songs black women crooned to their babies, sucking at dried-up breasts long after they should have been weaned, were as sad as the wailing chants of their forebears chained in the holds of dark, gloomy ships—songs without hope—more the moan of the condemned than the songs of the African plains.

"Hush, honey, hush, honey, hush, doan' cry . . . hit gonna git better bye an' bye. Ol' man comin' home to stay. . . . Hush, honey, hush. . . ."

The white people in the town said "no niggers are hungry; no quality white folks would ever turn a hungry nigger away from their back door. Why, just last week, I brought a strange farm nigger right into. . . ."

But the message hadn't reached the black bottoms. Even if it had, there were those who wouldn't, or couldn't, beg.

Of course there were whites who were genuinely kind—hundreds of them—who went to the shanties with baskets of food when they heard of particularly bad situations. But most waited in their kitchens, feeling vastly Christian when they handed out cold biscuits and table leftovers to the few who knocked at their back doors.

"You want to take something to your mama, is that what it is?" Rachel asked the girl.

"Yessum, please. I know you thinkin'. . . ."

But Rachel interrupted her. "You go ahead and eat your fill. We'll have plenty for your mama when you're through."

After the girl had eaten, Rachel discovered that her name was Ruth. They talked for a few minutes, and Rachel sensed about her a manner she liked.

Her maid had left her several days earlier, with a bus ticket to Atlanta clutched in her hand. Rachel had tried to dissuade her, but Leola had persisted. She was, she said, "goin' to 'Lanta to find my man," a sad delusion against which she had saved for a year.

"He may be anywhere by now," Rachel had pleaded.

"No'm, I hear he in 'Lanta," Leola said patiently, "an' I goin' t' find him."

She was adamant, and Rachel had worried all night after she left, tossing sleeplessly, worrying about what would become of Leola.

As Ruth was about to leave, a bag of food clutched in her hand, Rachel interrupted her profuse outpouring of gratitude and apologies.

"Would you like to come to work for me here, Ruth?" she asked.

Ruth's eyes widened, her voice quavering in excitement.

"Could I, ma'am? Really, could I? Lord, I sho' be the hardest workin' gal. I doan' know much 'bout cookin', but I kin learn quick. I kin do the washin' and clean a house good as anybody. I be happy to work just for food, dat's all I needs, an'. . . ."

Again Rachel interrupted.

"No, that wouldn't be fair. You come to work here tomorrow morning bright and early and I'll give you your food and enough for your mama and pay you three dollars a week."

Ruth began to cry. She started to hug Rachel and then caught herself, started to speak and couldn't.

The next morning at six, the family was awakened by a gentle but persistent knocking at the back door. It was raining, and Ruth had walked three miles without a hat or coat—huddled in a croker sack cape—to get to work. No one knew how long she had been standing at the door when Ben finally heard the knock.

When Jennifer was born in August, Ruth took the baby into her heart as if she were her own. But four years later, when David was born, she felt even more affection for him. Ruth didn't love Jennifer less; she just loved David more. He was the baby, *her* baby, in the custom of the South; this was understood, even taken for granted, by everyone in the Harris household.

In many ways Jennifer and David and Ruth all grew up together.

And now, this morning, with David off to school for the first time, they were separated, and things would never be the same again.

David did not understand this. For him, school was a wonderful adventure. His teacher, Miss Trudy Workman, had taught Jennifer and years before, his mother. She was the oldest teacher in the school, and many said she was the best. She had almost infinite patience. Every new school year delivered into her charge a whole class of children who would be hers for nine months—who would make up for the children she had never had—and she thought this a reasonably fair bargain with life.

At recess the first day, David played kickball with boys and girls he had never seen before. On his second try, he kicked a home run. As he rounded the bases, his instant best friend, a boy named Benny Layton, was excitedly cheering for him. Running, shrieking with joy, ducking the throw and scoring the run for his team, David was the happiest he had ever been.

Miz Trudy, as she had been called by two generations of Somerset children, decided almost immediately that she was going to like David. During the morning of the second day, she had, as was her practice on mornings of second days of school years, begun to probe gently to find out what her new charges knew.

Of all of them, David knew the most. He could say his alphabet perfectly; he could count to 100 by ones and tens; he could even do simple addition and subtraction.

"Where did you learn arithmetic?" she asked him.

"My sister, Jennifer, taught me, Miz Trudy," he answered.

"Are you going to be as smart as Jennifer was in my class?" she asked him.

"No, ma'am," he answered without so much as a second's hesitation.

At this, Miz Trudy began to laugh—a good, hearty, honest laugh that made the children feel good.

"How do you know you won't, David?" she asked finally.

" 'Cause, ma'am, nobody's smart as Jennifer," he answered gravely.

After school that day, Miz Trudy went to the A&P to do her weekly grocery shopping. At the meat counter she met Rachel Harris. The two women exchanged friendly greetings, and Rachel asked the teacher about David.

"I declare, Rachel, that child might just put me in danger of violating my first rule of teaching."

"What's that, Miz Trudy?"

"My rule about not having a teacher's pet. He's just as smart as he can be, and such a little gentleman."

"I don't remember your feeling in danger when you taught me," Rachel teased.

"Lord, Rachel, don't remind me how old I'm getting. Besides, it wasn't you that put all this gray in my hair. It was that Jake!"

They laughed together, remembering Jake in their own ways.

"I know he was a scamp," Rachel said. "But you know, I always loved him better than just about anybody. There's a goodness about that boy that people don't see under that gruffness of his."

For a moment they were quiet, then Rachel told the teacher that Jake was in the navy now, shipped out heavens knows where. But if she knew Jake, he would probably have managed to get himself right in the thick of the fighting. "You know, Miz Trudy," Rachel said gravely, "I pray for all the boys every night, but I say a special prayer for Jake. He never did learn how to run from a fight. I know it sounds silly, but I think deep down that's what worries me the most."

The older woman patted Rachel's shoulder and tried to cheer her up. "Now Rachel," she said, "you know that scoundrel's too mean to get hurt. And if they get him mad, big and strong as he is, there's just no telling. . . ."

She was cut off in midsentence by a man rudely shoving his shopping cart between her and Rachel, almost knocking over Rachel's cart in the process. He was slightly stooped, his black hair starting to turn gray. His seedy suit fit poorly, as if he had lost weight and neglected to take his pants to the tailor to be taken in. Still standing between the two women—as if he were unaware they had been talking—he pondered the selection of poultry in the meat case. Finally he picked up a skinny frying-size chicken and deposited it in his cart.

Rachel and Miz Trudy were momentarily taken aback. Seldom had either seen such an impolite performance in Somerset, certainly never by any man who had the slightest pretensions to being a gentleman.

Rachel found her tongue first.

"You might at least say excuse me," she said to him.

He was already backing his cart away from them when she said it, and he looked back at her with a sneer that showed a crooked row of yellow teeth.

"Yes, ma'am, Mrs. Harris, ma'am," he said sarcastically. Then he was gone.

The two women stared after him in surprise. He knew they were staring at him, and he was glad.

It had been a hard day for him, and he had no patience for any bitch smart talk, particularly from a Jew bitch like Rachel Harris. She didn't know him, he was sure of that, but *he* knew *her* all right. She was the daughter of Isaac Shulman, the big Jew in town, and her husband was a Goddamn mule dealer who thought he was as good as a Christian ... maybe even better ... with his Christian name and his big bank account.

But he wasn't. He wasn't any better than that Greenberg prick editor he had talked to that morning. Well, the Goddamn Jews had shit on him for the last time, all the Greenbergs and Cohens and smartass Harrises—all of them. She wasn't going to show him up, no more than any other son-of-a-bitch Jew was. No siree, never again.

At the checkout counter, he took the chicken, loaf bread, the small cans of corn and beans, the RC Cola, and the Moon Pies out of the cart as quickly as possible, impatient to be out of the store.

"Afternoon, Mr. Luker," the cashier said. "Nice day, ain't it?"

Luker ignored him, paid the check after adding it again behind the machine, and left. He had work to do.

That night, in his furnished room at the Rice House, Elmer Luker sat down at his battered old Royal typewriter and began to write. His stomach hurt from the drink of Old Stag he had taken and the greasy chicken he had cooked for himself on the hotplate. He typed a few words, crossed them out, typed a few more, and finally, he gave in to the pain in his stomach.

With an angry jerk he opened the door to the cupboard where he kept his groceries, reaching for the yellow box of baking soda. Then he ran some water into a glass, mixed in a spoonful of the baking soda, and walked, half hopping, around the room until he felt the gas in his belly bubbling up into a substantial belch. Then he felt better and returned to the typewriter.

Ordinarily, writing was hard work for Luker. Unlike some of the more naturally gifted reporters for the *Somerset Daily Democrat*, he had to suffer to get a story—even a lousy, four-graph news story— down on paper and edited to the point of being acceptable.

He was in the newspaper business because of an accident of perception. As a boy he had thought of himself (for no particular reason except that it made him feel good) as a writer. That perception had never left him, kept alive through failure after failure in writing by a desperate need to be "somebody," as well as an unfailing ability to blame his failures on forces beyond his control. When anybody would listen, he still talked about the novel he was writing, even though it stung him when some people snickered.

Working for the *Democrat* was a frustrating experience. He wanted more: the *Atlanta Journal*, at least, maybe even the *New York Times;* but he never seemed to get a break.

During his spare time Luker wrote articles, essays, and short stories which he sent, with high hopes, to magazine editors. At first he had sent them to high-paying magazines such as *Colliers* and the *Saturday Evening Post*. But as one rejection slip followed another, he readjusted his sights, aiming at ever-smaller journals and publishers. Always the same results: a cold, form-letter rejection, without one personal word of encouragement scrawled at the bottom.

That morning, he had called the editor of a small review from which he had received a rejection slip the night before, a fellow named Greenberg. He had begun talking quietly, so the others in the news room wouldn't know he was using the telephone for private business. But soon he was screaming.

As the phone clicked dead in his hand, he became conscious again of where he was. Everyone was staring. Hughes, the city editor, made a wisecrack. He snarled a comment back at Hughes, drawing his lips back in a curl over his rat-like teeth. Then he turned back to his typewriter. As he did, it popped into his head all at once, clear as a bell. Of course, for Christ's sake. It had been there right in front of his nose all the time and he hadn't had the brains to understand it: you gotta be a Jew to get published by Jew editors and Jew publishers or even to get on a decent newspaper. The bastards owned them, too; they owned every Goddamn thing. That's what it was. You had to be a sheeney. Lots of writers used pen names. You never saw a name like Goldfarb or Weinstein, but the editors knew who they were just the same.

Luker had always hated the Jews, just as his father had hated them. He had learned early about their greed and immorality and obstinance. But he had let it go; had left them alone as long as they left him alone.

But now things were different.

How many Goldfarbs and Moscowitzs and Cohens must have rejected him over the past years, with their anonymous, hateful rejection slips. By God, if he had sent his stuff in signed Mel Lazar or Isaac Shulman or Mort Levine, it would have been published. The no-good Jew bastards. He would get even now for a lifetime of slights and insults.

As he began to type, the words came easily, easier than they ever had before. The copy seemed to leap out of him, well-turned phrase after well-turned phrase.

The piece was begun out of spleen, without aim, without any particular thought of publication. It was late when he started, and after two hours of work, his eyes started to get heavy and he had to put it aside, even though he was feeling a gathering sense of excitement about it.

It was good, really good. The next day he could hardly wait to get out of work so he could get back to it. For four straight evenings he wrote, cut, edited, and polished it. Finally, on Friday night, it was finished. The next morning he showed it to Braden, a photographer at the paper who frequently made fun of Luker's writing, sneering about prizes and best-selling novels.

"Another Pulitzer Prize winner, Luker?" Braden asked sarcastically.

"Just read the Goddamn thing."

Luker watched the photographer's face carefully as he read the 12 typewritten sheets and saw what he had hoped to see: an expression of growing concentration, a slightly raised eyebrow that meant he had registered a point, a look of surprise.

"Christ, Luker, this stuff is dynamite," Braden said. "Honest to God, I didn't think you had it in you."

Billy Partain, a sportswriter, came by, and Braden called him over. "Billy, read this copy," he said, handing the sheets over to the genial ex-football player without identifying its author.

When Partain had finished reading the article, he was equally enthusiastic.

"Man, who wrote this?" he asked. "Nobody around here?"

"Luker here wrote it," Braden said. "I guess the old boy's not bad after all."

It was good. Braden said it. Partain said it. And as it circulated around the editorial offices of the newspaper, several others came over to say it again. Suddenly, by God, after all these years, he was a writer.

"Why don't you show it to Mr. Hopkins?" Partain urged, "Hell, maybe it'll be published. It sure oughta be."

Luker's heart leaped at the thought. Christ, wouldn't that be something, to publish it right there in the *Democrat.* That would rub the nose of every Jew in Somerset into the dirt where it belonged. Everybody in town would look at him differently, just like Braden and Partain were looking at him now. Maybe he could even get some stuff without paying for it for a change.

But Hopkins was the publisher, and he had to worry about advertising. The Jews all had stores and they all bought ads; he would probably be afraid of offending them. Besides, maybe Hopkins liked Jews. For all Luker knew, Hopkins might entertain 'em in his home every night.

Partain was looking at him, waiting for an answer.

"Naah, I don't think so, Billy. I wrote this for a magazine published up in Arlington," he lied. "I kinda promised the editor, and I wouldn't want to disappoint him."

That night Luker thumbed through his well-worn *Writer's Guide,* looking for a magazine he thought would take the piece. One after another, he wrote down the names of magazines and then crossed them out. None of them would be fair enough to buy the piece.

He would think about it, he decided, and set the piece aside. Meanwhile, he would write more.

Every evening for the next three weeks he hurried home to his typewriter and his notes. For his second piece he dug deeply into his files, pulling out the best stuff and stealing it freely, tacking thoughts and paragraphs together with the simplest bridges. Nobody would ever know he was stealing; the stuff had been published years before. And after all, he wasn't really stealing; he was *researching.* What had the article said in *Writer's Digest?* If you copy from one writer, it's plagiarism; if you copy from three writers, it's research.

His files made him look brilliant. The copy he wrote was tightly edited, even intellectual; the words were well chosen and scholarly. He referred to books published in England, Switzerland, and Germany, to articles published in intellectual digests in Greece, France, and Spain, to mainstreams of thought skipping across cultural and national boundaries—all as if they came straight from his own erudition.

He produced a third piece and a fourth, all with the same sense of joyful creativeness. Each time he completed a new one, he would take it to Braden, now his friend and critic, and each time Braden would tell him how fine his writing was.

"This one's even better than the other three, Elmer," Braden said of the fourth piece. "If I were you, I'd let Hopkins see it. Hell, he doesn't like Jews any better'n you do."

"How do you know?" Luker asked cautiously.

"I've heard him say so a hundred times. You know, I go to the same church he does, and sometimes we talk on Sundays about the war and all. He hates Jews. Just last week, he told me that if it wasn't for the Jews, his boy wouldn't have to be working up in Washington; he could be home writing sports like he wanted to."

"Are you sure?" Luker asked tentatively, his mind now racing with possibilities.

"Sure I'm sure. Hell, I wouldn't throw you a curve on something like this, would I?"

On Monday Luker allowed Braden to show the four articles to Hopkins. An hour later, Hopkins sent for him.

When he entered the pine-paneled office, Luker was terrified. Maybe he shouldn't have let the pieces get into the publisher's hands. Christ, he had been fired before for trying too hard; maybe it would happen to him again. He needed this job. Where else was there to go? Hopkins was probably going to chop him up for trying; that's what they had all done.

The publisher was on the telephone, looking angry. Luker felt out of place in the plush leather chair across the desk from him. Oh, God, he pleaded silently, not again. Please, dear Jesus, not another firing.

Finally Hopkins finished the conversation and put down the receiver. For a long moment, he just looked at Luker; then he smiled.

"That stuff of yours is good, really good," he said simply.

"I'm glad. . . ." Luker began, but Hopkins cut him off.

"It's mighty seldom that we see any kind of creative writing around here," he sighed. "I pay out a lot of money every week, Luker, you know that? And I don't see much creativeness or much thought for my money. These bastards are too glad to clip the crap off the wires and set it . . . the easy way, that's what they're all interested in."

Luker made no comment, smiling encouragement instead. How good it felt to hear Hopkins put the others down. Like that bastard, Hughes, chopping up his copy every day. And Rutledge, always so superior just because he had a column, and Dunlap, who couldn't write his way out of a wet paper bag, lording it over him because Dunlap got bylines.

Hopkins poked a wet-ended cigar in his direction. "But you, Luker; you've written some excellent stuff here. And I'm gonna publish it. What do you think of that?"

"I think it's great, Mr. Hopkins. I really. . . ."

Hopkins cut him off again.

"It's not going to be easy. The Jews in this town are gonna squeal like stuck hogs. I might even lose some advertising because of you."

Again Luker was stuck for a response, but Hopkins supplied his own.

"But I don't care. An' you know why I don't care, Luker? Because what you've written is the truth. And I believe in the truth."

Hopkins had already worked it out in his mind. He would use the pieces as Sunday features, one a week, on the editorial page, under Luker's byline. That way he could spread them out. If the heat got too bad, he could always fire Luker to show the town where his true feelings were. But he doubted that the Jews would make any real trouble. Hell, Jews were always scared of their shadows; none of them would dare stand up to Walton Hopkins. If a couple of them wanted to withdraw their advertising, let them. They'd have to come crawling back; there wasn't any other place they could advertise. And they'd think of their business before they thought of their honor; if they didn't, they wouldn't be Jews in the first place.

"Is this all you got, Luker, or is there more?" he asked.

"I'm writing another piece right now, Mr. Hopkins," Luker answered. "And with a little time, I could write a hundred more of 'em."

"Well, you take the time," Hopkins said. "I'm gonna run these as Sunday pieces and that'll give you a month's lead time to catch up. I want more, and I don't want you to think about another thing but a backlog of these articles. You understand?"

"Yessir," Luker said. Hopkins dismissed him with a wave of his fat hand.

That night, Martin Stoker, the Linotype operator, refused to set type for Luker's articles. The night editor, Robert Gaines, was called to the back room, and Stoker told him he wouldn't do it.

"Some of the Jewish folks in this town are very good people," Stoker said. "Do you know what this trash would do to them, Bob?"

Gaines read the first page of the first article and nodded his head.

"Mr. Isaac Shulman is the best friend my daddy ever had," Stoker continued. "I know every one of his children. I played football with his boy, Jake, and now he's off somewhere, maybe dead already, fighting in the war. And Mr. Isaac's second boy, Aaron, just got his draft notice, and he'll be gone soon, too. Hell, they bleed, too, and die just like everybody else, and it isn't right to do this to their people while they're somewhere fighting a war for us. It just isn't right, and I'm not going to be a part of it."

Gaines agreed.

"You're right as rain, Martin. No doubt about it. But that article's gonna get set whether you set it or not, and you know damn well if you don't, somebody else will."

"Well, at least it won't be on my conscience," the typesetter said.

But the editor persisted. "You know it's supposed to go on the editorial page, don't you, Martin? That means it's supposed to be the opinion of one person, the person who wrote it, not the fellow who set the type for it or the one who copyedited it."

"I don't care," Stoker said stubbornly. "I'm not gonna set it; even if it costs me my job, I'm just not."

Gaines admired Stoker's guts, wishing he had as much himself. The article would create very bad feelings against the Jews in town, he knew that, and that bastard, Luker, and Hopkins must know it, too. But the editorial decisions of this kind were made by Hopkins, not Gaines, and he had worked too long to get this job to lose it now.

The next morning, Sam Atkins, the day Linotype operator, set the type. Stoker was fired. On Sunday the article ran in the top right-hand corner of the *Democrat*.

The headline read: "Murderers of Christ."

6

Ben was pouring a cup of coffee when he heard the thump of the Sunday newspaper hitting the front porch. It was a sunny fall morning, the kind he liked best, with the leaves outside the kitchen window turning to reds and golds in the crisp, sweet morning air.

Rachel and the children were still asleep. For a moment he sat stirring his coffee distractedly, wondering why, after all the months since Ruth had started getting Sundays off, he had never quite gotten the knack of making a good cup like she did.

Then he went out for the paper, deciding as he did to take the family for a ride up to the mountains that afternoon. The trees would be beautiful now in new autumn colors. Maybe he would stop at a cider stand along the way and buy a jug. As he stooped for the *Democrat*, he chuckled at remembering how David always drank cider on their rides up the country with absolute confidence that he was on the way to getting stone drunk.

By the time he returned to the white breakfast room table, Ben had unfolded the paper and started to read the lead article. Absently he reached for the pack of Camels in his shirt pocket, struck a match, and inhaled the first drag of the day.

The front page was full of war news. The lead article quoted Roosevelt's speech, promising that the turning point had come in the war. Another article farther down the page described American victories against the Germans in Algeria, where U.S. troops had been fighting all week shoulder to shoulder with the British and the free French.

Christ, that's good, Ben thought. The late summer of '42 had been bleak enough, what with Rommel sweeping across Africa into Egypt, the Eastern front crumbling, and American shipping going down all over the Atlantic. By God, that British general, Montgomery, had finally shown the Germans they could lose last month at El Alamein. Now maybe the Allies were on the high road to whipping those sons-of-bitches.

Ben wished he were in the thick of it. Hell, he was as strong and healthy as any of them. What did it matter that he was 42? It frustrated him to sit in his kitchen, reading about the war and knowing he was too old to go. Particularly a war like this one, with half of Europe on fire, torched by a maniac who had to be stopped before he crushed the world under the treads of his tanks.

Ben ground out his cigarette in the glass ash tray on the table, poured himself another cup of coffee, and continued reading Roosevelt's speech. He had heard it on the radio the day before, but he read it carefully anyhow; when it jumped to an inside page, he opened the paper and followed it.

Opposite the end of the speech was an article about a boy from Somerset who had been killed accidentally by a shell on an artillery range at Camp Campbell, Kentucky. Ben shook his head sadly at the irony of a boy dying like that, out on a practice range where some damn fool probably jerked a lanyard on a field piece without an "all clear," or maybe because some other damn fool had given the signal without clearing the piece properly. Ben pictured the 18-year-old boy cut to pieces and bleeding out his life in the sandy soil of Kentucky, for nothing, nothing at all; his body a broken monument to somebody's carelessness, still now, the boy having died without even a chance to get into the war and lose his life for a reason, even if it is a lousy one.

Wearily Ben lit another Camel and turned to the editorial page. A headline, "Murders of Christ," drew his attention immediately to the lower half of the page, and he began to read Elmer Luker's first article. As he read, his rage grew, mixed with a terrible, sinking feeling in the pit of his stomach. He read it through, following the tortured logic with which Luker "proved" that the hands of every Jew, living or dead, were stained with the blood of Jesus Christ, how every Jew throughout all time had been personally responsible for the commission of history's most obscene crime.

When he had read the last word, he began to read the article again, more slowly, trying as he read to understand why Hopkins, the publisher, would do such a thing to the Jews in Somerset and wondering at the same time what the repercussions would be. Halfway through, he hurled the newspaper across the room and walked out into the back yard. The day was less glorious now. The leaves were

49

just as brilliant, but now, when Ben looked at them, he saw only that they were dying. It was a time when things were dying everywhere, he thought bitterly. Leaves on the trees and fine young men and innocent women and children in a dozen countries—and now, that dirty, no good son-of-a-bitch Hopkins had apparently decided that things weren't bad enough, so he had stepped up to the plate and hit a Goddamned home run against the Jews of Somerset County, who had never done a thing to him but buy advertising in his newspaper and vote the straight Democratic ticket he so ardently promoted.

The article was devastating. If anything, the four words printed neatly in italics under the last paragraph were, to Ben, even worse: *First of a Series.*

Ben backed the Ford out of the garage and drove aimlessly for a while, his knuckles white on the steering wheel. The town was just beginning to stir, to eat its eggs and grits and get ready for church, and most of all, Ben thought, to open its Sunday newspaper.

Somewhere, he knew, a preacher would be changing the text of his sermon. Elmer Luker, whoever that was, had given him a new text—for more than one Sunday. Now it was all right to say it in church—*look, it says right here in the newspaper.*

Ben drove for over an hour, through the center of town, out to his farm, back through Vernal Mill village. As he passed the familiar landmarks, the stores and the houses, the churches and the factories, he could think only of how the *Democrat* was being received this morning, how in some of the houses he passed—too many of them —the people would be too ignorant not to be influenced by Luker's article.

Finally he headed the Ford north toward home. Because he didn't want to disturb the children, at breakfast he acted as if nothing had happened. But as they were dressing in their rooms for the ride to the mountains, Ben discussed the article quietly with Rachel, who had read it with her coffee.

"Decent people won't be persuaded by that garbage," she told him firmly. "It's just the trash that gets stirred up by this kind of thing, and they don't really matter very much anyhow, do they, Ben? I mean, in any real way?"

Throughout the afternoon Ben tried to share her feeling. But all he could feel was an aching sense of displacement. For years now he had loved this town, had worked to make it his, and now suddenly he felt as if it no longer belonged to him, nor he to it. He was no longer Benjamin Harris, a citizen of Somerset, South Carolina. He was only a Jew in an alien place, as, he knew, Jews throughout history must always have ended up being.

Rachel fell asleep easily that night, breathing lightly on the pillow beside him. But Ben lay staring into the darkness, wishing he could somehow rationalize things the way she could, to know unfailingly that everything would turn out all right. Maybe it *would* be all right, he thought, but it wouldn't happen by itself. The words *First of a Series* burned in his mind. There would be more—of what?

His stomach hurt now. He quietly slipped out of bed to get a glass of milk.

When he finally fell asleep, he tossed restlessly, dreaming scattered snatches of dreams about roiling, yelling mobs and a pistol that wouldn't fire.

The next morning David and Jennifer were dressed for school and eating breakfast when Ben decided they should stay home from school for the day. Jennifer wanted to know why.

"I just think it would be a good idea," he told her quietly. "And I want you both to stay in the house with your mother and Ruth."

Ben was tight-lipped and, Jennifer thought, a bit pale. She could tell he was terribly upset, so she didn't ask any more questions.

When he left the house Ben drove past the barn and down to Lazar's Department Store, to talk to Mel.

Mel Lazar had lived in Somerset for 40 years and was one of the elder Jewish statesmen in the town. He was also the major Jewish advertiser in the *Somerset Daily Democrat,* a fact Ben hoped might count for something.

As he walked through the front door, Ben was not surprised to find some of the others already there. Hy Goldstein, who owned the Music Box, was talking quietly with Mel's son, Al, and Nate Rosen, who ran the liquor store on the square. Morty Levine, the shoe salesman, was distractedly examining a display of men's blue work shirts.

When Ben walked in, the group coalesced around him and got down to business.

"I kept the children home from school," he said.

Morty nodded and said he had kept his Sarah at home, too.

"A fine thing," Nate said, "to have to hide our children in this day and time."

Mel Lazar grunted as he heaved his heavy body up from a chair.

"Why would Hopkins do such a thing to us, that's what I want to know," he wheezed.

"More important is, where does it leave us and our families?" Nate answered.

"Rachel is convinced that the intelligent people in Somerset won't be moved by this business," Ben said.

"She's right. Most of'em won't," Morty Levine answered. "But they won't raise a finger to quiet down the ones who are, neither."

51

"Morty's right," Al Lazar said. "This afternoon, a bunch of *goyim* we all call our friends will play golf out at the Country Club and say to each other that it's just a pity that the newspaper leaned on the Jews yesterday. But that's all they'll do."

At that moment, Isaac Shulman burst into the store, fury written all over his face.

"I called that *mamzer*, Hopkins, on the phone," he said angrily. "When the secretary heard my name, she said he wasn't in. So I drove over to his office, and when the secretary said he wasn't in again, I walked by her and there he was in his office, the fat *shtik drek*, stuffing his mouth with food at his desk."

"What did he say to you?" Mel asked.

"Nothing," Isaac raged. "Nothing. He wouldn't say a word. I told him I was a representative of the Jewish people in this town and that we wouldn't stand for any more such ignorant, traitorous articles. And he had the nerve to turn his back on me and walk out of the room."

Isaac sputtered with rage. "On me! That trash treating me like a common nigger! A nobody!"

"Mr. Shulman," Hy Goldstein said softly, "I'm sorry about your affront. But I'm more worried about the safety of my family and about my business. These articles could start a pogrom in this town."

"Maybe not a pogrom," Ben said, "but at least a hell of a lot of *tsores*. Some Jews down in south Georgia had a thing like this last month. I heard a house was burned before it was over, and a couple of Jews I used to know in Augusta were beaten up by a mob. My brother called and told me about it a few days ago."

Shaking his head, calmer now, Isaac spoke to the group.

"This thing has got to be stopped before it goes any further. Look, Mel, you and some of the others spend a lot of money advertising in the paper. Why don't you call, as a representative of the Jewish advertisers, and threaten to cancel all future ads if such articles appear again."

"I got a feelin' it ain't going to help, but I'll try," Mel grunted. He disappeared into his office, and the men started to relax. But one look at Lazar's face when he reappeared told them their brief feelings of relief were unjustified.

"Well," he said angrily, "that son-of-a-bitch didn't even want to bother speaking to me. But I insisted, so he came on long enough to tell me he didn't care what I had to say. Then he hung up."

Rubbing his knuckles, Ben said he'd "love to go over there and beat hell out of that son of a bitch."

"That's all we need," Isaac said. "Tomorrow morning there'd be a picture of the *mamzer* on the front page of his paper, showing his bruises, and a story about the Jews beating him. Then we would catch hell."

"What's all this talk about beating?" Morty asked. "Listen, maybe there won't be no more articles. Maybe they got it out of their craw now. Maybe he'll start to think about what Mel said and stop the next article."

Maybe.

The Jews in Belgium were saying maybe Hitler only wanted to deport German Jews. Maybe he'd leave them alone. In reeking cattle cars crossing the German frontier, Jews huddled together against the freezing cold and said maybe the resettlement camps wouldn't be so bad. In Warsaw the Jews were saying maybe. Maybe being pushed together in the ghetto would be as far as it would go.

Maybe.

In the winter of 1942 *maybe* was a word Jews all over the world substituted for a sense of confidence and security.

"Maybe," Morty Levine said, and some of the men in Mel Lazar's store felt a little better.

7

On Wednesday, three days after Elmer Luker's first article appeared in the *Democrat,* David Harris was accosted on the playground by a boy in another first grade class.

"You killed Christ," Billy Gradison said flatly.

"Who?" David asked.

"Christ," the boy repeated.

"No, I didn't. I didn't kill nobody. I'm only six years old."

"Yeah you did, too. All the kikes did. I know it."

"How d'ya know?"

"My momma told me. You callin' my momma a liar?"

"No, but. . . ."

A whole new phase of David's life and education had begun. Endless repetitions would follow, but he did not know that as he stood in the yard at North Jordan Street School, facing the hard-set, freckled face, the clenching and unclenching fists, of Billy Gradison.

In the late afternoon, as Ben sat in the living room with his son, there was a look of sadness, of faraway resignation, of another place and time in his eyes.

"Daddy, what does *kike* mean?"

The warning signs had been there for weeks, Ben thought. Even before the editorial in the *Democrat.* Mumbled conversations between old friends that stopped self-consciously when he walked into the bar at the Elks Club; editorials in the newspaper before Luker's which questioned, albeit subtly, the "real" causes of the war in Europe; sermons in the churches with such titles as "Christians at War."

54

Father Charles Coughlin had softened them up for the last 10 years with his radio programs, Ben reflected bitterly, and Henry Ford hadn't helped much with his *Dearborn Independent*, in which he revived, and gave new credibility to, the "Protocols of the Elders of Zion."

The war gave all the simmering prejudice and hatred a focus and a reason—"the Jew War," as it was called by growing numbers of rednecks who had, as a way of life, always needed to find a scapegoat for everything that was uncomfortable, unexplainable, or frightening. For generations the niggers, the yankees, the Supreme Court, and more recently, the liberal establishment and the eastern press had sufficed neatly to explain away their troubles and forgive their incapacities.

This war was different, though. American boys were dying in places whose names they couldn't even pronounce—and for what? Niggers had nothing to do with it. Neither did yankees, any more than southerners did, or the courts or the newspapers. Then slowly, silently, a consciousness began to form. *Of course, it's those greedy Jews in Europe that got Hitler goin' in the first place. Our boys are dyin' ten thousand miles from home to save a few money-grubbin', Christ-killin' Jews. It ain't right, you hear me? It just ain't.*

"But what about the good Jews here in Somerset?" some asked.

"Fuck'em," the answer came back; "it's their fault, too."

"Daddy, what does *kike* mean?" the boy asked again, stirring Ben from his momentary stream of thought. Ben looked at his son with a swell of compassion. Putting his hand tenderly on the boy's head, absently stroking his dark hair, Ben began to talk. His words came haltingly, each carefully measured. "Dignity," "heritage," "suffering," "courage," "survival," "ignorance," "pride," and "rights" were some of them. He realized that he wasn't explaining it very well, at least not so a six-year-old child could understand. But he could find no other way to explain it except in the context of thousands of years of Jewish persecution, suffering, and survival— thousands of years to which he and now his son were direct lineal heirs. There was tenderness in his voice, but when he came to the end, unavoidably it took on a hard edge.

"Two ways . . . both hard," he said. "You can turn your face and walk away, or you can fight them. Either way, son, your mother and I and Jennifer will love you and respect you just as much."

"What did you do when you were little?"

"I fought, son," Ben said, "but I don't know to this day whether it was the right choice or not."

"Teach me to fight, daddy," the boy said.

And the die was cast.

"We always been accused of killing Christ," Mel Lazar told his son. "What's new about it? Calm down. It'll blow over, you mark my words."

"So we had a couple bad days of business," Hy Goldstein said to his wife. "What does it mean? Maybe we're being oversensitive."

"See, Ben, I told you it wouldn't make any difference to the good people," Rachel said. "What does it matter if a few ignorant fools get stirred up?"

"Jesus Christ," Ben exploded. "How can you say that . . . that it doesn't matter? It matters one whole hell of a lot, to me and to you and to every Jew in this town, and God knows, to your son. He had a fight yesterday afternoon at school, Rachel, and he may have another one tomorrow and the day after that—and I can't do a thing to stop it. The worst part is, he doesn't even understand why it's happening to him. It's not his doing, and it's a cryin' damn shame, and if nothing else comes of all this, that makes it *matter* terribly."

For the moment they both sat in silence.

Finally Ben spoke again, this time more softly.

"He asked me to teach him to fight, and I did. Did you know that, Rachel? I taught him how to hold his hands and how to lead with his left and how to hit other little children in the face so he could get it over with fast. Isn't that just beautiful . . . me having to tell my son how to hurt other children before they hurt him first? Isn't that just a beautiful state of affairs?"

She hated the thought of David fighting, and tried to force it out of her mind.

"He'll be all right," she said finally. "At least, thank God, he's little. What if he were older . . . old enough to. . . ."

Her voice trailed off. Ben knew she was thinking of her brother, Aaron, who would be heading back to Camp Jackson in a matter of hours. He had finished his basic training two weeks before, and now —today—he was finishing his leave.

"He's going this afternoon," she said almost in a whisper. "Maybe he'll get sent to Africa. Maybe he. . . ."

"Maybe he won't get sent overseas at all," Ben interrupted. "There's plenty of boys who never leave the states, too, you know."

Kind, gentle Aaron. It was hard for Ben to imagine him with a rifle in his hands, in some godforsaken hole in the ground at the ends of the earth, killing and maybe even being killed. Unaccountably, he remembered a story Hemingway had written years before about the Spanish Civil War. It said that if the Italian mamas knew about the different kinds of vultures on the African plains that attack any animal when it's down—birds that start with a man's eyes and face, to rip out the flesh even if he's not dead yet so long as he hasn't the

56

strength to roll over on his stomach—that they would refuse to let their boys go over there and fight, and the war would be over. Ben remembered thinking when he read it that Hemingway had written the piece with an interesting combination of ornithological fact and romantic nonsense, because the world over, mamas had cried and wrung their hands and prayed to their gods for their sons, but they had never once managed to stop them from killing other women's sons or being killed by them, any more than Baila Shulman could stop the killing of her son or his killing other boys, if that was in the cards —and they never would.

Ben liked Aaron; the thought of his going started a gnawing feeling deep in his stomach. Every time he had thought about it during the past few weeks, he had been haunted by a dark premonition that Aaron would never come home again, a feeling stronger than he had about any other boy he had watched march off in this miserable war that he was five years too old to fight in himself.

The few days of Aaron's leave had been spent quietly, much of the time at home. Ben offered to drive him back to the camp after his leave was up, but Aaron had said no, he would ride back on the bus like everybody else.

At the bus station, Aaron's pretty blond wife Nell clung to him and cried. Baila and the other women kissed him, wished him good luck, and gave him foolish pieces of advice.

The last to arrive was his father, who drove up alone in his Buick only a few minutes before the bus was to depart. Aaron was reassuring Nell again that he would be all right when his father walked up to the bus platform and called his name.

For a long moment, the two men stood looking at each other; then the bus to Camp Jackson was announced, and time was gone. Aaron leaned forward toward his father, perhaps to embrace him or even to kiss him, although he had never kissed him or been kissed by him before. Even as he began to move slightly forward, he knew he would be refused, but the need to wrench some sign of caring out of Isaac was so strong in him that he didn't care. He was saying goodbye, perhaps for the last time, and he wanted more than anything else for his father to relent. He wanted it so much that his wanting overruled his sure knowledge that he would not—perhaps could not—and so he leaned forward to embrace Isaac even though it couldn't happen, because Isaac Shulman couldn't let it happen.

The older man merely reached up with one powerful hand and clamped it on his son's shoulder, holding his arm straight between them.

Aaron stopped trying to reach for his father then and stood straight, looking into his father's eyes for some sign that he was loved by him and that it mattered that they might never again be together.

"Goodbye, Papa," he said. "It's time."

"Be a man, Aaron," Isaac said. "Above all, be a man."

And that was all he could say. Abruptly he turned and walked away. Another man on the platform recognized him and nodded.

"Evenin', Mr. Isaac."

But Isaac Shulman was gone, his back disappearing into the gathering dusk on Creighton Street.

Soon the bus was gone, too, and Aaron opened the magazine he had bought and tried to forget that his father had searched his heart and could only find an admonishment for his son to take away with him to the war.

Ben stood staring after the bus, wondering how Aaron must feel about what his father had said. What, in God's name, did a war give you a chance to be except a man, Ben wondered.

"Explain that to me," he said to Rachel in the car. "What kind of a thing was that?"

But Rachel only shook her head and stared out of the window.

"Look, the Christmas decorations are starting to go up on the square," she said finally. "It's going to be such a sad Christmas this year."

8

Elmer Luker's second article did not take notice of Aaron's leaving for the war, any more than it recognized that Jake Shulman, whose past athletic glories had been trumpeted on the sports pages of the *Democrat* under such headlines as "Shulman Scores Fifth Straight Knockout to Lead ACC" or "Shulman Standout in Georgia Game," was somewhere in the Atlantic on a ship identical to the scores already cut to pieces by German submarines, if not already himself in a watery grave, or that tens of thousands of other Jewish boys were leaving or had already shipped overseas or were dead.

In 31 neatly set column inches of type the article explained away nearly 20 centuries of history, finally getting to the present and the heart of the war issue, articulating the darkest suspicions of the ignorant, putting into words and into what appeared at first glance to be logical sense what they already had dimly begun to believe on their own.

The article placed the cause of the war directly on what it called the "International Jewish Conspiracy." A sidebar caption promised that this article and others to follow in the series would demonstrate the ways in which world Jewish aims were being furthered by the war, and would expose the methods of war profiteering by which Jewish manufacturers were getting rich and the connection between the war and the ultimate Jewish plan for world monetary control.

The United States is involved in a cataclysmic struggle for survival. At this writing, thousands of American boys—the flower of this nation's young manhood—lie dead, many buried in foreign soil. The crime of this war is that the fight in Europe is not their fight; the issues are unrelated to them or the country which sent them to their deaths. Like pawns on a global chessboard, they have been pushed relentlessly forward by an unseen hand that would not let them stop short of the bitter, dark earth.

Even as this atrocity continues, sane Christian people throughout the world ask—Why? The question is heard on the lips of little children, left fatherless by this war. It is sobbed into the pillows of mothers and wives bereft of their sons and husbands. What twisted aims can this anguish and pain serve? What Godless, demonic force has caused the blood of so many innocent young men to be spilled on foreign soil?

For an answer, they have only to think for a moment, indeed to look around in their own towns, to realize what force has maneuvered America, and the world, into war. Clearly and beyond a shadow of a doubt, the blame rests on the International Jewish Conspiracy, which throughout modern history has been demonstrably well served by Christian wars, in which another Jewish war profiteer won a fortune for every boy who fell. Adolf Hitler, now condemned by our government in Washington, understands this lesson of history well, and has moved to stop the Conspiracy, once and for all. But for our intervention, he might be successful.

What he strives to do is make the world safe for white Christians to live together in peace and brotherhood; to guarantee a thousand years of peace on earth. But the Jewish interests in this country have seized upon this opportunity and pressed Roosevelt, himself always maneuvered and controlled by Jewish money sources in the Northeast, to move to war.

For whose benefit is this war being fought? Is there a single purpose it can serve for this country? Is territorial expansion in the Philippines or a foothold in Africa a reasonable objective? Do we, as a nation, stand to gain any objective at all?

The answers are clear if we will but heed them. The Jewish pocketbook fattens while its owners wade in the blood of the Christian world. . . .

Paragraph by paragraph, the article continued, giving historical precedent for its thesis, incorporating quotes from the Bible, the surest reference source in South Carolina, and to urge the local citizenry, in the interest of their sons, their husbands and fathers and brothers, to make their voices heard, to condemn the "conspiracy" and bring it down.

60

The article hit the Jews of Somerset like a streak of hot summer lightning, deeply wounding some and terrifying others. Over the next few days following its publication, even the most optimistic of them could not fail to recognize that the town was changing, in large and small ways, perhaps in ways that would never be forgotten.

The signs were everywhere.

Mrs. Gordon Daniels, Baila Shulman's neighbor and friend for 40 years, was stiffly formal to her at the food market. Aaron Shulman's wife was not called about the weekly bridge game she had played in every Thursday for three years. Hy Goldstein's daughter, Joan, was called a dirty Jew by another girl at school. Sarah Levine was troubled by obscene phone calls. Al Lazar, who would leave for the navy in less than a month, was called a "Goddamn draft dodger" by a former classmate.

Of all the Jews in Somerset, the one who suffered the most overt and unremitting pressure was David—the only Jewish boy in the Somerset school system. For the first time in his life, he was beginning to experience a bitter sense of aloneness. He was too young to rationalize the difficulties he suddenly confronted, and this made them all the more painful to him.

On the Monday after Elmer Luker's second article, David was called a kike by a friend he had played with on Oakland Avenue many times before, and David knocked him down. On Tuesday another boy in his class pushed him into a fight.

As the days passed, the boys at North Jordan Street School found there were several words they could say to force David to fight them: "dirty Jew," "kike," "mockey." Even the word Jew itself could be hurled—and understood—as an insult.

David hated the words, the resignation he felt, the short, heart-thumping walk to the bushes on the North Jordan Street side of the playground.

He would hit David on the shoulder—whatever his name was that time, Billy or Bobby or Michael or Ross—or in the stomach or chest, because that's where six-year-old boys hit each other.

All the while envying him his lovely Christian anonymity and his blond hair and the big, safe church he attended with his parents every Sunday morning, David would hit him back then, in the face —hard—like his father had taught him to do. Usually once was enough, but sometimes he would have to hit the boy three or four times before it was over.

David hated the fighting. Each time, he silently prayed that his adversary wouldn't make him hit him again, and usually he didn't. Instead, he would scream at David through the blood, tears, snot, and defeat: "You did too kill Jesus," or "I'll git you tomorrow, you wait an' see," or "the Jews did too start the war," or "wait till my brother gits aholt of you."

And it would be over.

Until the next time.

And then another boy would say one of the words.

He knew just where to hit them, and he wasn't reluctant to hit hard. So he always won. But that only made things worse.

The other Jews in Somerset heard of his fighting; a few were proud of him, but most felt embarrassed or threatened.

"What is this, your son beating up all the other children?" Mel Lazar asked Ben. "We need this on top o' all our other *tsores?*"

"What do you want him to do?" Ben shot back. "Let the little bastards wipe their feet on him?"

Lazar persisted with his usual ghetto logic.

"Whoever heard of a Jew behaving in such a common fashion . . . beating another child every day? I tell you, Ben, it ain't good."

"And I'm tellin' you, by God, he doesn't have any choice. You think I like him having to go through this, Mel? You think that?"

Lazar shrugged and walked away.

In bed that night, Ben cried for his son. It was the first time Rachel had ever seen her husband cry. It began with a quiet conversation in the dark.

"Why does he have to go through that kind of pain . . . every single day?" Ben asked. "Why can't those little *mamzers* leave him alone?"

"It's what they hear at home," she answered quietly. "At supper they hear their fathers tell their mothers that the Jews are responsible for the war and for killing their god. And I guess they feel heroic the next day when they fight David."

"The worst part," Ben said, "is that he's all alone."

For a long moment there was silence between them, and Rachel sensed that Ben was struggling.

"If only I could fight it for him," he said haltingly. "He's so little, so . . . so. . . ."

Then he began to cry, silently at first and then with deep, convulsive sobs. It was difficult for him to cry, but there was no helping it, so total and bitter was his anguish.

"It's . . . just . . . that . . . he's so . . . so little," he choked.

Rachel patted his muscular shoulder, trying to comfort him. She had already cried her heart out during the past few days, thinking of her baby, her little one, bravely facing not one child alone, but all of them, his fists cocked, ready, crushed by the jeers of the others and watching a fist start toward his belly.

"Cry, darling," she crooned to her husband in the darkness. "Cry all the pain out of your heart. It's all right . . . it's all right."

In the next room David lay sleeping, having already said his prayers, in shame, secretly begging God to make him like everyone else.

"Please, please, dear God, I've been different long enough. Make me like everybody else." But apparently, God was busy with other matters.

And the next day it started all over again. On the playground at recess time, he heard them saying what their parents told each other, what Elmer Luker wrote for them, what their neighbors and older brothers and friends, and in one or two instances, what their preachers said.

"Says right in the Bible, clear as day, 'at Jesus was murdered by the Jews."

"If it wasn't for them stinkin' Jews in Germany, there wouldn' be no war now."

"The Jews here ain't no better."

"No . . . no . . . that's all wrong," David tried to tell them. "Look, my Uncle Jake is in the navy fightin' like everybody else. My Uncle Aaron. . . ."

It didn't help. Nothing ever helped.

Even as David prayed to be unnoticed, even as his father sobbed out his bitterness, the pressure was growing in the town.

"You have to admit, it's a Jew war, Ben. Everybody knows it," Charlie Bolt said at the Circle Diner over his coffee.

"What the hell is that supposed to mean?" Ben answered hotly. "Is Hitler destroying Czechoslovakia and Hungary because of the Jews?"

"Well, maybe not directly. But hell, you know the Jews in Europe are the real cause of it, Ben. I don't mean you, but. . . ."

Seeing the muscles in Ben's jaws tighten and the veins begin to pop out on his neck, Bolt stopped in the middle of his thought.

"That's very nice of you, Charlie, to concede that I didn't personally start the war. After all, you've seen me almost every day for the past 10 years, so I couldn't be much of an international Jewish agent."

For a few moments he sipped his coffee in angry silence, but Bolt wouldn't leave it alone.

"Surely, Ben, you're not tryin' to tell me the Jews have nothin' to do with it," he said.

Ben exploded.

"They have a lot to do with it! A lot! They're being slaughtered by the thousands and their bodies are getting in the way of the tanks and making the Germans mad," Ben sputtered. "It's hard to drive over all those dead people!"

"Now wait a. . . ."

But Ben interrupted Bolt, getting to his feet as he did so. "You better quit while you're ahead, Charlie. We may have been friends for a long time, but if you say one more word . . . just one more . . . I'm gonna break your Goddamn jaw!"

Bolt grabbed his check, shot a furious look at Ben, and walked indignantly toward the cash register.

"Goddamn Jews," he muttered to himself in the safety of the diner's vestibule. "None of 'em any fuckin' good. None of 'em."

The next afternoon David had to whip Martin Bolt, Charlie's son, behind the bushes on the playground.

Martin had started it in a new way: "Goddamn Jews are all alike . . . none of 'em any good."

9

In his pine-paneled office Hopkins paced as Luker settled himself into a plush leather chair. Finally the publisher stopped and poked his cigar at Luker.

"Luker, I'm gettin' a lot of heat to stop your articles," Hopkins said.

Luker's heart sank. Oh God, oh God, oh dear Jesus, it's gonna all fly out the window now, he thought. All of it.

"Where's it comin' from, I mean, the heat?" he asked timorously.

"Where the hell you think? From the Jews. Christ, they're squealin' like a bunch o' stuck hogs. Threatened to cancel their advertisin' first, and God only knows whatall else."

Luker tried to look directly at Hopkins' face, but he couldn't; his eyes were stinging. Instead, he looked at his scuffed shoes, then across the room and out the window.

The bastards. The no-good bastards. They're doing it to me again. They're cutting me off. Oh, those miserable dirty Jew kike sheeney mockey bastards. . . .

He wanted to ask Hopkins what he meant to do, but he didn't dare, because asking the question might hurry Hopkins into a decision he hadn't made yet.

". . . a lot ridin' on this thing, Luker," Hopkins was saying. "You probably don't know it, but there's been talk of puttin' me up for Publisher of the South next year."

Still Luker didn't speak. Instead, he nodded his head slightly, trying to force what would look like a confident grin onto his face.

Wearily Hopkins dropped into a side chair near him. The wrinkles in his flacid face worked around his mouth as he chewed the fat cigar. He dug one finger under his shirt collar and tugged to loosen his tie.

He liked the sound of his voice, the authoritative way it rolled when he made his pronouncements. He hesitated for a moment to lend drama to his next statement, wishing there were a better audience than this limp piece of crap, Luker.

"But you know somethin', Luker?" he said finally, "maybe there's more at stake than that. Maybe somethin' nobody's mentionin', somethin' called freedom of the press. An' maybe such a thing as free enterprise. By God, I never backed away from a fight before. . . ."

His voice trailed off; he shifted the cigar to the other side of his mouth.

Hope flooded into Luker, bringing with it an overpowering sensation of relief. He could feel his guts start to unwind, the tightness start to dissipate in his jaws. But Hopkins hadn't said it yet, not for sure.

"You mean. . . ." he started uncertainly.

"Yeah, that's right, Luker," Hopkins said, cutting him off. "I made up my mind. Your articles continue. Hell, I ain't gonna be pushed by the Jews in this town, an' they might as well know it."

Luker didn't know how to express his exuberance, so he simply walked across the room and grasped Hopkins' soft hand, a foolish grin on his sallow face.

"Keep it up, Luker. Give 'em hell. You might just wind up with a regular column out of this."

As Luker walked back to the city room, visions of grandeur filled his head. His mentor, settled in leather and rich pine, had other thoughts: the same thoughts that always occupied his mind—power and money. He had tasted power before. He had put two mayors in office, had sent one of them to the U.S. House of Representatives and kept him there. He had put three state senators in office. One had died in office; the second, the dumb son-of-a-bitch, had gotten himself shot, but the third had a long memory, so it didn't matter too much. They all knew where the real power was, and by God, he could make 'em snap to any time he wanted to.

In the week that followed the first Luker article, hundreds of postcards and letters had flooded in, some requesting as many as 50 copies of the day's paper that carried it. The switchboard, by actual count, had taken more than 500 telephone calls, almost all of them congratulatory to him and the paper. Toward the end of the week, calls came in from as far away as Texas and Florida, all in the same

66

vein. That dumb ass Luker didn't begin to know how good a thing he had stumbled over.

Hopkins was thumbing through some of the letters the paper had gotten when his desk phone rang.

"A Mr. Harris for you, Mr. Hopkins," his secretary said.

"Which Harris?"

"Mr. Ben Harris."

Hopkins' first reaction was to say he wasn't in, as he had done with most of the other Jews who had called. Then on a whim, he decided to talk to Harris.

"Yeah, I'll talk to him."

There was a click, and he heard Harris's voice.

"Mr. Hopkins, this is Ben Harris calling."

"Yeah?"

"I'd like to come over and talk to you. Would you have a few minutes to see me sometime today?"

"Nope, 'fraid I'm gonna be busy all day."

"Well, what about tomorrow?"

"No, my calendar is full up."

With growing impatience, Ben asked if they could meet in a week.

"I'll be busy then, too," Hopkins replied flatly.

There was a momentary silence, and then Ben said in a hard, even tone: "Someday this is gonna be over, by God, and Hopkins, you're gonna pay."

"Are you threatening me?" Hopkins asked.

"It's not a threat. It's a promise!"

Then the phone went dead in the publisher's hand.

For a moment, fear clutched at Hopkins. Harris was a different kind of Jew, a tough bastard.

Then he snorted at his own foolishness. All Harris had to do was raise one Goddamn finger and his ass would be mud. He would have the cops all over him.

"You wanted the first mail, Mr. Hopkins?"

The copy boy was peering through the open doorway, a sack of mail in his hand.

As soon as the boy left, Hopkins pawed through the stack, finding many requests for multiple copies of the issues Luker's articles had appeared in. There were hundreds of them, and Hopkins took particular pleasure from the ones postmarked the farthest distances away.

"Sweet Jesus," he chortled. "Now ain't that somethin'?"

On Saturday night the town's lone night-duty squad car answered two calls. The first was a report of vandalism; someone had thrown a brick through a front window at Lazar's Department Store.

"Just kids havin' theirselves a good time," one of the policemen concluded.

Two hours later the car got called to a cross-burning on South Willow Street. This time, the night reporter for the *Democrat*, tired of hanging around the station, went along for the ride.

At Brownlee Street, the cop riding shotgun turned on the siren.

"Gotta let them ol' boys know we're comin'," he said to the reporter, who grinned. It was, after all, standard operating procedure. Everybody knew the Klansmen were just a bunch of "good ol' boys" out to raise a little hell.

"South Willow," the driver said over the siren's wail. "Ain't no niggers on South Willow. Reckon what the hell's goin' on?"

"I dunno," the reporter said. "Guess we'll see in a minute, though."

"Better slow it down a little, Charlie," the other cop said. "Don't want to run up on them boys gittin' their cars out."

The car slowed, but the siren continued to pierce the night with its pulsating, imperative scream.

When the car finally arrived, the cross was beginning to sputter out, and neighbors were standing in their yards, watching, some of them in bathrobes, the legs of their pajamas showing underneath to the ground. A few of the women wore curlers or bandanas.

One policeman busied himself kicking the cross over, while the other knocked at the door of the house. He had to knock several times before it finally opened a crack.

"You call us?" he asked bruskly.

"Yes, sir," the face in the crack replied.

"What's your name, sir?" the policeman asked, taking out his report pad and pencil.

"Morton Levine."

On the way back to the station house, the reporter pulled a half pint of Old Stag out of his coat pocket and offered it around.

While the other cop took a long drag on the bottle, the driver spoke over his shoulder to the reporter.

"Gonna write a story, are you, Billy?"

"'Bout what? Bunch of kids havin' a little fun with a few sticks and matches. Nothin' to it, far as I can see."

On page 7 of the *Democrat* the next morning there was a story about a break-in at Dr. Williams' cabin out at the lake. On page 12 there was a report of a car theft in Robertsville. On the back page, the mayor warned against writing on the walls in the restrooms at City Hall. But the cross-burning at Levine's house and the breaking of Mel Lazar's big display window were not mentioned.

The editorial page in the Sunday edition was different. The Rev. Dr. Robertson Crater's column, for the first time in years, was moved to the bottom half of the page. In the top right-hand spot where the doctor's column usually ran, Elmer Luker's third article was featured under the headline, "Blood of Innocence."

Luker kept the top spot on the editorial page for weeks running. It pleased him greatly that he, Elmer Luker, was the "top" columnist at the *Democrat*, as he now referred to himself with growing frequency, and that he had displaced a column that was syndicated to "God knows how many newspapers around the country."

Hopkins felt Luker's stuff got better each week. By the seventh Sunday article, he was already considering clearing out the storage room near the men's toilet and fixing it up as a private office of sorts for him. Hell, it wouldn't cost him anything, and the way Luker was generating money and excitement for the paper, it sure couldn't hurt.

The tone of the seventh piece particularly pleased Hopkins. It quoted freely from the Old Testament and various historical texts, working to prove the essentially warlike nature of the Jews, to demonstrate the centuries-old thirst for blood which now was being satisfied vicariously as white Christians died for them in the war on which they fattened their bank accounts.

> Despite consistent claims of peacefulness as a people, how peaceful can people be who began the Christian epoch by brutally killing the Prince of Peace Himself, the blessed Jesus Christ of Nazareth?
>
> At Jerico, and again at the city of Ai in the land of Canaan, at Midian and at Mizpah, at Jabesh and Samaria and Jerusalem, the Jews slew tens of thousands of men, women and children, laid waste their fields and cattle, destroyed whole civilizations. Throughout the era described by the old Testament of the Bible, the Jews washed their history in the blood of those who refused to believe as they did, and gave the historical lie to any claims to peacefulness that they or their descendants might ever make. It was only after wading in the blood of generations. . . .

Hopkins knew that most of Luker's stuff was a bunch of unmitigated crap, but he also knew his readership and the temper of the times. And he knew what worked. In the past few weeks the circulation of the *Democrat* had increased by more than 25 percent, and the mail sacks of requests for subscriptions and reprints continued heavy. Hell, he didn't have anything against the Jews, not really. They'd never gotten in his way before, and he even had a grudging admiration for a couple of them like Mel Lazar and Isaac Shulman who had come to Somerset with nothing, accumulated money, and built a place for themselves and their families. But the fact was, they had never before been important to him one way or another. But now things were different, because now he had stumbled onto something, something damned good. He was saying things in his newspaper that people all over the country wanted to read, things nobody else had the balls to publish. It might be the beginning of a brand-new kind of power base, one with national implications, and that was just what he had been looking for all these years. This just might be the ticket —*his* ticket—into affairs that would ultimately reach well beyond having a Congressman and a lousy state senator or two in his pocket. The big time, by God, where he'd belonged all the time. Losing a few dollars in advertising and pissing off a few Jews was a small enough price to pay for that.

He poured himself a half of a water glass of bourbon from the square-cut glass decanter on his side table and swished it around while he thought about it.

Wonder where Luker gets that stuff about Midian and Jabesh, he chuckled. Som' bitch is probably stealing it word for word from somewhere, but nobody else seems to care, so I sure don't.

Across town, at Isaac Shulman's house, Mel Lazar slammed his thick hand against the newspaper.

"What's so damned miserable about it is there's nothin' we can do but let it happen," he said.

Isaac Shulman sat in his customary place in his parlor, and his son-in-law, Ben Harris, sat on the couch opposite him.

"We're gettin' a little taste of what kind of hell the Jews're catchin' in Europe right now," Isaac said reflectively. "Just a little."

"Well, one thing's for sure. It's gonna get worse before it gets any better," Ben answered. "I think we have to be ready for whatever comes."

"What's that mean, 'be ready'?" Lazar asked.

"I think we should arm ourselves," Ben said, pulling a Smith & Wesson detective model .38 pistol out of his coat pocket. "I know it's not much of an answer, but it's as good as any I can think of right now."

"You're *meshugeh ahf toit,* Ben, you know that?" Morty Levine exclaimed. "If you had been me a few weeks ago, with 50 or 60 drunken *goyim* in bedsheets in your yard, yelling and burning a cross, what would you do, shoot 'em all?"

Ben shook his head gravely. "No, Morty, I wouldn't have. But I know this. If one of the bastards had stepped into my house, he'd have been a dead man. That's the option a pistol gives me that you didn't have."

"Listen," Isaac Shulman broke in. "We're here to talk about stopping violence, and you're talking about makin' it worse. We gotta stop Hopkins and that other *mamzer*, Luker. None of the rest of 'em mean anything."

"Isaac's right," Mel broke in. "So what now?"

Joe Klein, who had remained silent the whole evening, finally spoke.

"I think Arnie and I can get to somebody important in Washington. Maybe some pressure from the government on Hopkins would stop this thing."

"How you gonna do it?" Mort asked.

"Well, I can't guarantee anything. But my brother-in-law in Washington is a labor lawyer with good contacts in Congress. Maybe he can get Arnie or me into the right place."

The next morning Joe Klein and his brother, Arnold, were on the Southern Railroad's early train to Washington, a briefcase carrying the past seven Sunday editions of the *Somerset Daily Democrat* on the seat between them.

When they returned on Wednesday afternoon, Joe told Isaac Shulman that he thought they had gotten the job done.

"I guess we won't know till Sunday morning," he said quietly, "but I believe it may be OK."

Three days later, just as the pressman was locking up the Sunday paper, the switchboard operator buzzed Hopkins' office with a call from Washington.

He had been expecting a call from somebody up there—maybe with a request to serve on one of the war advisory boards . . . maybe the one on war information or something. What with him keeping a Democratic Congressman up there to vote Roosevelt's bills—almost entirely by his own efforts, if the truth were known—it was time a little dividend or two got paid somewhere. Past time.

There was a clicking on the line and then a woman's voice said crisply:

"Mr. Hopkins?"

"Yes, this is Hopkins."

"Hold the line, please. Mr. William Fairfield calling from the State Department."

"Yes, Ma'am," Hopkins said, smiling at the thought of talking to Billy Fairfield again. As the phone clicked, Hopkins thought to himself how smart Billy was. Little old Barnwell boy. Worked his way up from rewrite man on the *Charleston News and Observer*, right up to assistant to the secretary of state. Just by knowing the right folks at the right time.

His thoughts were interrupted by the strong, southern-accented voice at the other end of the line.

"That you, Hop?"

"Hello, Billy. How ya doin'?"

"Not bad. Keepin' mighty busy, though. How 'bout you?"

"I'm in good shape. What can I do for you, Billy?"

There was silence for a moment; then Fairfield cleared his throat.

"Hop, I had a call from Bernard Jacobs this morning. He called to talk to me about you . . . asked me to get in touch with you."

Hopkins was startled. Christ, Bernard Jacobs. One of the president's top advisers. One of the four or five biggest men in the country. Calling about him. Must be something big. Maybe. . . .

"Why, Billy," Hopkins started, "I'm mighty flattered. . . ."

"Hold on, Hop, till you hear what he said," Fairfield interrupted.

"Seems like a series of articles in the *Democrat* got called to his attention," Fairfield continued softly. "Articles written by a fella named Elmer Luker. Mr. Jacobs wants 'em stopped, Hop. Stopped today."

Hopkins was stunned. "But, Billy, I . . . I. . . ."

"Let me tell you just what he told me, Hop," Fairfield continued. His voice was lower now.

"Said you can stop 'em quietly now and nothin' will be done to you. But if you choose not to stop 'em, he said he's gonna bring the entire weight of the administration down on your head—beginnin' with the Justice Department."

There was a long moment of stunned silence, and William Fairfield, a smart kid from Barnwell, South Carolina, who had worked his way up in the State Department by knowing when to talk and when not to, waited for Hopkins' answer. He had known all along exactly what Jacobs was so exercised about. In fact, he had copies of the Luker articles spread out on his desk in front of him then. Hell, he didn't blame Jacobs or any other Jew for being furious, but there was no reason to let on that he knew. Someday he might need Hopkins. Never could tell about. . . .

"Listen, Billy, I didn't mean any harm by publishin' those coupla articles."

"Well, Hop, I reckon Jacobs didn't see it that way. You wanta hear what he dictated to my secretary . . . what he said I was to tell you?"

There was an embarrassed silence again, so Fairfield glanced at his notes and began again.

72

"Said to tell you, Hop, that right this minute, Jews by the tens of thousands are being hauled together like animals in cattle cars all across Europe, that the most informed opinion here in Washington holds that Hitler's ultimate idea is to murder every one of 'em.

"Said that thousands of young American Jews are fighting and dying across both oceans . . . a few of 'em from Somerset County, an' a lot from South Carolina.

"Said for me to ask you if you think they're part of the Jewish conspiracy you seem so determined to eradicate. Said to ask you, Hop —an' I'm just relaying the message, God knows, embarrassing as it is—said to ask you if you are so blind or so stupid or so insulated from reality down there that you can't see the world is being washed in Jewish blood?"

Hopkins started to answer, cleared his throat, and Fairfield interrupted him one last time.

"Hop, you might as well hear the last of it. He said for me to ask you if you really think the Jews need any more punishment . . . an' I'm readin' here again . . . any more punishment from an arrogant, hate-ridden, son-of-a-bitch like you?"

Fairfield didn't like having to say it, but he figured he had better let Hopkins know just how outraged Jacobs was, and he couldn't figure out any better way of doing it than to say exactly what the senior presidential adviser had told him.

"I don't deserve all that," Hopkins said finally in a low, choked voice. "God knows, there's no more patriotic man in South Carolina than me, Billy."

"I know, Hop, I know," Fairfield said in a soothing voice, all the while feeling hypocritical as hell, because he felt like Jacobs did. He had seen the same reports coming out of Austria and broadening sectors of central Europe that Jacobs had.

"I don't know what to do," Hopkins added, but both men knew precisely what he would do.

"Hop," Fairfield said, "I'm sorry as I can be that I had to tell you all this. You an' me, we been friends a long time. But, Hop, I know Jacobs pretty well now, an' I know how hardheaded he is. If I were you, I sure would cut off those articles. An' I'd do it quick!"

For another few moments he tried to console Hopkins, then they said goodbye.

For a full minute Hopkins sat in stunned silence, still holding the phone in his hand. Then he bellowed through the wall for his secretary.

"Tell the press room to shut down the run . . . right now," he blurted at the startled woman, "and send somebody in here from the city desk."

When the *Democrat* appeared on the town's doorsteps the next morning, thousands of disappointed readers looked vainly for Elmer Luker's column. In its place was the Rev. Dr. Crater's column. A wire story on growing war shortages was pulled out of the page-7 form and slugged into the editorial page form to fill the hole. And on page 7 a picture feature about the schoolboy patrols in the city schools was run to make the page. The feature carried pictures of several dozen boys in white belts and red hats, crossing younger students at their posts. One of the patrol boys in the largest picture was David Harris.

10

Within several months the town ostensibly returned to normal. As Hy Goldstein put it, the *goyim* "came back," buying guitars and sheet music and clarinet reeds as if nothing had happened. After a while Mel Lazar and the others began placing advertisments in the *Democrat* again, grudgingly, but with the recognition that there was no other place to advertise. Ben Harris unloaded his pistol and put it away.

The jagged cut in the town that had briefly separated the gentiles and the Jews had scabbed over. But like a fistula, secretly eaten deep in the flesh and hidden, the wound remained; it could only heal slowly, from the inside out. In the stores and restaurants and on the streets, casual conversations between the Jews and the Christians had about them the slightest edge of unease, the pervasive hint of forced joviality. The handshakes seemed a trifle overhearty, the smiles a bit too quick.

"In time this will all blow over," Rachel said, and for the most part, she was correct. Certainly appearances could lead to no other conclusion. But what she could not know, what none of them could know, was what was happening behind the smiles, around the dinner tables, behind doors closed to them.

The children were a barometer of the adult mood; they had less guile in such matters, were less restrained. Gloria Lazar was quietly dropped from a social club and from the high school annual staff. Sarah Levine's longtime best friend refused to answer her telephone calls and snubbed her at school. Barbara Silverstein was unexpectedly blackballed by the Cotillion Club. Jennifer was slapped after school one day by two older boys who called her a Jew bitch and laughed as she ran away, crying.

David was the best barometer of all. On two consecutive days, several boys ganged up to pull him down and hold him while others hit and kicked his stomach and back.

But then, the ethic of the time, which held that "two on one is nigger fun," prevailed.

And so the groups only jeered, at least once or twice a week finding a lone champion of the white, Christian cause, another little gladiator to be cheered and encouraged in his brave, lonely struggle against whom? Against the kid . . . what's his name . . . David, ain't it?

"Yeah, David Harris."

"He's different from us, ain't he?"

"Yeah, it's his people wants to hog up all the money in the world, and. . . ."

"Naw, that ain't it, I mean, 'bout the money. His people's the ones that started the war."

"You mean his folks, the ones that live up there near the Welborns? How in . . . ?"

"Naw, that's dumb. Not them, I mean his real people . . . the Jew people, all over."

"Oh, the Jew people. That's his people?"

"Sure, he's a Jew, ain't he?"

"I dunno. Reckon he is. He don't look like a Jew, though. How you know?"

"It don't matter what he looks like. He is, an' that's what matters. Killed Jesus, too. Said so right in the newspapers. My momma read it to me."

"He's a real smartass. Thinks he can whip anybody."

"Can't whip me. Can't no Jew. . . ."

"Say, whyn't you show him after school? All you gotta do is call him a name and he'll fight."

"What'll I call him?"

"Just say, 'You're a dirty Jew!' That always gets him."

"Reckon I will. Ain't that somethin', 'bout killin' the Lord Jesus."

"Hey, boy, you're a dirty Jew."

Behind the bushes on the playground, the two boys squared off, surrounded by nine others.

As it always did at such times, David's heart pounded. This new kid was tough-looking, maybe a little fat, but big, with heavy arms and legs and a big chest. The whitish scar on his chin made him look mean. David had dreaded this inevitable moment since the kid had first come to the school in September. Now here he was—not so much angry as hurt, because being alone never stopped hurting—putting up his guard against a tough fight he had no heart for.

As he closed with the boy, David quickly glanced around at the other faces. As always, the eyes avoided his, the faces fixed in attitudes they thought appropriate to the occasion, attitudes between excited smiles and sneers, all urging on the new kid. Just one of 'em, David thought desperately; why can't just one be for me, just this once.

The other boy raised his hands, cocky, confident, for the crowd's benefit. But his knees felt weak, and his stomach began to heave. How had he gotten into this, anyhow? This boy was probably tough . . . probably knows everything there is to know about fighting, probably. . . .

"I'll give you one chance to take back what you called me," David said. "I don't have nothin' 'ginst you. If you want, you can take it back."

The kid was giving him an out. He probably isn't even a bad kid. Desperately the boy thought of and discarded half a dozen possibilities. But it all came down to one thing: he was the new kid, he was the biggest kid in the class; if he took it back, he'd be lower than whale crap on the bottom of the ocean.

As he hesitated, buying a few seconds of time, a call rang out behind him.

"Come on, Brad, don't listen to that Jew stuff."

The voice hurried him beyond further thought. Swallowing at the lump in his throat, the boy said, "I ain't takin' nothin' back," and sent a fist aimed at David's stomach with all his strength, carrying his hopes that it would land and the thing would be finished.

David neatly slipped the punch and swung. The other boy saw the fist coming through the air just before it landed, giving him time to turn but not enough to duck or dodge. David had aimed at his jaw, but instead hit the new boy on the nose.

Even as the searing sensation spread across his cheeks, he heard the crunching, snapping sound of the cartilage that formed his neat, even nose. As he felt the pain in his face, the blood was already trickling down Brad's face and onto the front of his shirt. As David felt the snapping under his knuckles, he stepped back, frightened as he had been once before when another boy had begun to bleed. Haltingly, as if asleep, Brad hung in stupefied indecision, putting his fists down, putting them half up again, then giving up as the blood and snot coursed down his chin, and starting to cry.

The others glared at David in silence.

"I didn't mean to hurt him," David said.

But no one answered him, no glance or nod or sympathetic look.

They were walking away, one muttering, "you couldn' expect no better from a Jew."

When David got home the phone in the hall was ringing. A frosty woman's voice asked for his mother, and David handed her the receiver.

"Hello. Yes, it is. Yes. He what? Could you repeat that? Hold on a moment, please.

Placing her hand over the mouthpiece, Rachel turned to her son.

"This is a Mrs. Jorgenson, David. She says she is calling from the emergency room of the hospital. She says you broke her son's nose . . . that they're going to sue us."

Oh, God, David thought. Now I've really gone and done it. Now I've dragged Mom and Dad into it.

"I didn't mean to hurt him," he blurted. "Honest I didn't. It's just that we had a fight and he turned his face wrong and I hit him on the nose instead of the jaw. I couldn' help it, Momma. He called me a name and I had to."

"What name did he call you," she asked quietly.

"A dirty Jew, same as most of 'em."

There was a determined set to Rachel's jaw as she removed her hand from the mouthpiece.

"Mrs. Jorgenson, David tells me he hit your son in a fair fight which your son started. He says your son called him a 'dirty Jew.' "

David watched his mother's pretty, cupid's-bow mouth purse as she listened in concentration, straining to get some hint from her face as to what she was hearing.

Then she said goodbye and hung up.

"I'm sorry, Mom. I really didn't. . . ."

But his mother interrupted him. "Don't apologize, David. The boy's mother said what you did to him was nothing compared to what she was going to do when she gets him home." Then she smiled and held out her arms to him. When she pressed his face against her ample chest, she felt the need to say more.

"They're not all bad, honey. Just a few that make all the others look that way."

Secretly Rachel was proud of her son, as she had been proud of Jake years before. But she couldn't admit it to him.

"Anyway," she said, "where does a little *shtarker* like you come to break people's noses?"

Then he was sobbing. "I'm still sorry. I don't want to hurt nobody. I didn't want to fight that boy. It's just that they won't leave me alone, Momma, none of 'em, they just won't."

Rachel hugged him tighter, smothering the pain.

"It's so hard, Momma, when everybody's against you."

"My poor *tottalie,* my poor little *tottalie,*" she murmured. But that was all she could do. She couldn't promise that things would get better nor could she personally intervene. It would just have to wear itself out. Tonight, in the privacy of her room, probably after Ben had fallen asleep, when all was still and God might have the best chance of hearing, she would pray for David. To start with, just one little friend so he wouldn't feel so terribly alone. God could change things; Rachel was sure he could. As long as she knew this, she wasn't helpless; she could pray.

The next morning, as he walked past the furnace room toward class, a deep voice startled David.

"Boy, you sho wha'd him good."

Blake, the janitor, had watched the fight.

"One lick, and dat all it taken. Ain' dat sompin, a little bit of a feller lak you."

"I didn' want to," David said. "Blake, I don't want to hurt nobody. That's the truth."

"Sometime in dis ol' worl', you don' git yo' druthers. Den you gotta do de bes' you can."

David watched the broad smile crease the coffee-colored face.

"Ever'day, I watches dat ol' clump o' bushes; dat right, ol' Blake always watch. An' when you whips another'un, I jist smile all over."

Putting a massive, gnarled hand on David's shoulder, Blake shook his head for a moment, thinking about the one little boy who was always in the bushes alone against the others.

"You gonna be fine, boy. Ol' Blake know."

Then he went back into the furnace room where he endlessly stoked the huge coal burners, and David felt a little better.

11

In the winter of 1943 the people in Somerset began to sense that the war was turning around. Corregidor was in the past now; so were El Alamein, Bataan, and Guadalcanal. Outside the churches, in the stores and mills and plants, in the restaurants and schools, people talked about places called Bougainville and Tunisia and Guadalcanal —places they had never heard of, never cared about before, but now cared about deeply, fervently, because their sons, husbands, brothers, and friends made them important with their blood and, in some cases, with their deaths.

There were victories now, where earlier there had been only defeats. But victories, the town learned, took their toll, the same way losses did. It was hard, awfully hard, to get happy about a battle the newspaper or radio said the Allies had won when you knew it had cost the life of someone who lived down the block.

It was an uncommonly cold winter in Somerset. The Bermuda grass was beaten and gray on the lawns and side lots, and the last dead leaves on the water oak trees were driven down by the wind and the cold, slanting rains, so that now only the trunks and branches stood bleak and bare against lowering skies.

Henry Merrill, Jr., Dr. Merrill's only boy, was killed in January. His picture appeared on the front page of the *Democrat*, showing him in his naval officer whites shortly after he was commissioned. Under the picture was a story about how his ship was sunk by enemy submarines somewhere in the north Atlantic. The picture and story were printed in a black frame. Dr. Merrill didn't see any of his patients for a while, just staying home in the big frame house on

80

Carter Road with Mrs. Merrill and not taking any calls or seeing any visitors.

Another Somerset boy died the same day, a runty boy named Jimmy Sanders, who had black stumps for teeth and outsized hands on scrawny, bony wrists. There was no picture of Jimmy in the paper, just a small notice in the column, "News about Our Boys in Service," that he had been killed in action in Africa.

When the telegram came in the afternoon about Jimmy, nobody was home to sign for it, since his mother and his father both worked the second shift at the mill. So Charlie Singleton, who lived in the mill house next door, had to sign the book and go to the mill with the yellow envelope whose meaning by now nearly everybody in the town knew.

All the way to the mill Charlie tried to figure out what he would say to Sanders. They had drunk liquor together, had argued a time or two, but they generally got on OK, he thought. He never put nothing into that little old boy, nohow; maybe he wouldn't take on so bad.

Charlie wanted to give the telegram to Sanders' wife and let her tell Sanders. But he knew he wouldn't do it that way. Reckon the best I can do, he thought, is just find Sanders and hand him the envelope and maybe stand there while he looks at the telegram and maybe not, depending.

As he entered the mill the noise of the slubbers and the twisters, the pickers and the looms, rolled over his thoughts and eased them. Looking down the long rows of twisters, he saw the girls in scarves and overall pants, putting up ends. He chuckled to himself when he saw Margareet Ramsey, who had come running by him spraddle-legged and hollering that afternoon when he was working the second shift. When he grabbed her to find out what the matter was, she had jerked away from him wild-like and finally had fell down on the tar and gravel path with a bunch of women around her that wouldn't let no men get close, and her hollering all the time till the doctor come there, and after a minute, him sending into the mill for a hammer and everybody wondering what he done with the hammer until the next day, when the story got around. Seemed Margareet had got a mite horny settin' out in the water house toilet, smoking all by herself, and had taken it into her head to give herself a little relief, and the next thing she knowed, the Coca-Cola bottle she was using formed a vacuum from being shoved in and out and grabbed onto something up in her, and when she had come running spraddle-legged out of the water house, that bottle was hanging onto her stubborn as a mud turtle. Right smart of the doc to figure out that bustin' the bottle would unvacuum the bottle, Charlie had thought at the time, and still did. Charlie remembered asking Sanders just how far he thought that bottle ever got up that sweet thing, and remembering that, he had to remember what he had come to the mill for in the first place.

Sanders was doffing a bolt of cloth when Charlie found him. He stood aside until the bolt was on the cart. Then Sanders saw him.

"Hey, old boy, what you doin' over yere this time a day?"

"Got somethin' for you, Sanders. Reckon it ain't too good." Sanders grinned at him.

"When you ever had anythin' good fer me, you ol'. . ."

Then the smile faded, for Charlie was drawing the yellow envelope out of the bib pocket of his overalls. Sanders knew instantly what it was.

His hand trembled as he tore the envelope open. His mouth set in a grim line, for a moment, and then broke after he had unfolded the scrap of paper and started to form the words. For a long time his lips moved soundlessly around the words, some of which he couldn't make out, some he could, but all of which, together, he could understand.

Finally he looked up at Charlie.

"Says yere my boy Jimmie is dead."

Clumsily Charlie put his hand on Sanders' thin shoulder.

"I'm sorry, Sanders, sorry as I can be."

For a long moment Sanders gazed off toward the picker room, into space, seeing none of the life and motion beyond the scrap of yellow paper.

Then he mumbled something, which was lost under the sound of the looms, that Charlie couldn't hear.

Charlie's hand was still on his shoulder. Ever so gently, he shook him, afraid to shake him hard lest he start him crying, but needing to know (later he would wonder why he needed to know, but he would never come up with an answer that made sense) what Sanders was saying.

Now Sanders said it again, louder, but still faint against the whine of machinery.

"I said he went off from 'yere never knowin' I keered anythin' fer him, an' I did. God's truth, I did, Charlie. He'uz a ugly little ol' boy, an' he hung around the house a right smart, but I . . . I . . . loved him anyways. He 'uz mine . . . my boy . . . don't you see it, Charlie?"

"Shore I do. Shore I see it clear as light," Charlie said, and then they were walking down the row of twisters to find Sanders' wife and then go home.

After a few days Dr. Merrill and his wife received the pastor of the First Presbyterian Church in the library. They got down on their knees with him on the thick, white rug and prayed for Henry, Jr.'s deliverance and talked quietly afterward about life and death. The pastor was quietly reassuring, positive that God had a scheme for all living things and that Henry, Jr. had been gathered to His bosom in the fullness of youth for a purpose. When he left, Barbara Merrill cried herself to sleep and her husband drank two glasses of 12-year-old bourbon and knew things would be all right.

Sanders went to the Holiness Church on Sunday and when the preaching got hot, fell out in the aisle and rolled on the floor, kicking and howling like a dog.

All around him people were moaning "amens," believing that Sanders was speaking in tongues. But Sanders was screaming not in tongues but in pain and guilt, for he had let that little old runty boy go off without ever telling him that he meant anything to anybody, least of all his daddy, and now he was dead and it would always be too late. "Praise God," the preacher sang out over Sanders' screaming, and the others echoed him. But even after he was calm again, Sanders couldn't do it, couldn't even think of God—only that lonely little old boy he had let go off to die without anything to take with him to maybe make the dying a little easier. Praise God.

It was a busy time in Somerset for God and preachers. God loomed larger in Somerset than ever in February 1943, for it was a time when everything seemed to be dying, and God is where you have to go to learn to live with death.

It was a comfort that God was everywhere around them that winter. They could hear Him in the songs their niggers sang as they made their beds and scrubbed their floors. He wheezed out of beer-joint juke boxes as newly saddened drunks pumped nickels to salvation via the Carter family or the Blackwood Brothers. God's own legends were painted on big rocks along all the roads into town, all promising that God or Christ was truth everlasting, that He or They could be trusted with the heaviest burdens, that the day of reckoning was at hand.

God was lettered in white on the neat, black signs in front of the Baptist, Presbyterian, Lutheran, Methodist, Holiness, and yes, even the Catholic Church. God was in the schools. Every day began with asking the blessings, "in Christ's name, amen." God was on the radio; on Sundays there were almost no programs other than sermons.

Most particularly, God was in the revival tents. Somerset was an important stop on the revival circuits. Regularly, in the open land surrounding the town, sweaty men under hot, smoky canvas pulled at their collars and wrenched at their black coats as they breathed the sulphurous smoke of hellfire and damnation and foretold with utmost certainty the fate of sinners unrepentant; smiling only when the fear or the hysteria finally clutched the audience beyond endurance; and stumbling, halting, moaning, they came forward for their Christian absolution, or, for the faith healers, as the sinners sick in body and spirit came, or were helped, down the rough aisles for the laying on of hands.

"Heal," the sweating, exhorting man of God would cry, "heal, in the beloved name of Jesus Christ . . . let the healing power of God's love flow into this twisted body . . . HEAL! HEAL!"

"Lord, this ain't a bad man . . . just strayed from Your path. But he ain't really bad. He's beggin' Your forgiveness and Your lovin' peacefulness to flow over these twisted legs. He's beggin' to bear witness to Your great goodness . . . to let the healing power of Your love make him whole agin."

Shouting, begging, sweating, Brother Martin or Brother Wayne or whoever he happened to be this time would look out of the corner of his eye at the audience, caught in the magic of the moment, mouths agape, knowing that the Lord Jesus Christ was performing a miracle right before their eyes, knowing beyond any uncertainty of weather or boll weevils or mortgages at the bank. And exultation would enter his work, for now he had 'em, for God and for himself, and a wave of joy would sweep over his own self.

"Heal! as Thou madest Lazarus straight to take up his pallet upon his back and walk! Heal!" the voice going low and then peaking in intensity with each "heal," confused bits of scripture mingling with the present reality, this stinking, tobacco-stained cripple on homemade crutches, the gallus overalls stiff with sweat and clay, the old chambray work shirt frayed at the collar, the breath stinking of rotted teeth and yesterday's corn liquor—hardly a fit temple for the spirit of God, but necessary, because the hysteria was rising in his rheumy eyes, the kind of hysteria that could make a man forget his arthritis or lumbago long enough to walk down the aisle without his crutches, not falling until brother-whatever-his-name-was could make the collection of souls and wrinkled dollars, the forthcoming of both helped mightily by the miracle of healing and of Christ's work, and leave.

A moan would start somewhere in the audience and become a scattered wave, breaking over the red necks of the sinners in the front rows. Even before the stink-breathed cripple started, the moan would begin, the impending miracle being anticipated and known even before its evidences.

Cry, you sinning, smelling son-of-a-bitch, the preacher would think, for tears were necessary in the scheme of things, and he would start 'em, had to start 'em.

84

"Are you feelin' it? Feelin' the love of God washin' over your pore crippled body, brother?" this said with a benevolent smile, a half step back, hands on the sinner's forehead and behind his greasy cowlick.

A rapt, hypnotic stare was all he might get back the first time, so he would have to help with the feeling, too.

"I feel it, I feel it good, now," he would say in his most joyful-noise-unto-the-Lord voice, "I feel it, like heat flowin' through my arms and into this pore crippled body."

The moaning would increase, and the likker-drinking sinner in his hands would yield, starting with a low voice that got higher with each exhortation from the healer.

"Oh Jesus, sweet Jesus, I feel you in my back."

"Say it, brother. Bear witness to the people!"

"I feel hit. Hit's like lightnin' heat through me. I feel hit . . . the healin'."

Now the tears would come, and the voice would climb to a near scream.

"Bear witness," the healer would repeat, louder now, wanting the scream, wanting the voice to break out loud, wanting the man to exult to the audience, to prove his mission and the healing power that Christ had put into his, Brother Martin's or Brother Wade's, into his hands; the power that brought the people down the aisles to him for healing and saving and for making the brass collection jar fuller than it otherwise would be—to continue his mission of healing to the sick in body and spirit.

As the crutches dropped away and the farmer still stood, he had them, and with a beatific smile he could muster only on these occasions, he would look out at the shifting, stumbling mass, raise his hands, and begin the first of his six or eight, "Praise the Lord's," each more intense and fuller in hope and salvation.

"Praise the Lord!"

Praise the Lord, Christian soldiers, Praise the Lord.

For as long as he could remember, David had seen these big tents going up or coming down around Somerset. Several times his father had been asked for the use of his fields, but somehow the tents always went up somewhere else. David always wondered what was said, what happened, in the tents at night, when the crowds gathered and the flaps were let down. And then in the spring of 1944 he got a kind of glimpse inside, not into a real tent meeting, but into the *meaning* of a real tent meeting, at the picnic grounds of Towanee State Park.

It was a perfect day. A light breeze played in the big oaks and pines of the park. The air was fragrant with new grass and flower smells; the blue jays and mockingbirds were singing and shrilling at the picnickers spread out over the grounds.

David sipped cups of cold Towanee Country cider his father had bought at a roadside stand. Jennifer teased him about getting drunk. Ruth had prepared the basket, and David was sure it was the finest picnic lunch in all of Towanee Park.

"Um, best potato salad ever tasted," Ben chewed. "Best."

Jennifer giggled and picked at a chicken wing. Slowly the plates of chicken and salad and biscuits diminished, until no one could eat another bite.

Then Ben lit a cigar and stretched out on the grass with a deep sigh of contentment. Jennifer helped her mother clear the plates and cups, and David wandered off toward some other picnickers he saw nearby, hoping for a game of catch.

Before he got to the other children, however, he was intercepted by a gray-haired woman who stared into his face with a look that made him feel uneasy.

"Wadn' you with 'em people over 'ar?" she asked.

"Yessum, thos'r my folks."

"Name of Harris, ain't it?"

"Yessum," David replied, wanting very much to be away from her.

"Yo' granddaddy's Mr. Shulman, ain't he?"

"Yessum, that's right."

"You know who I am?"

"No'm, I don't."

"I'm Preacher Morgan's wife."

David mumbled that he was glad to meet her, as he had been taught to do, but nothing could have been further from the truth. Actually he wanted only to back away from her and run back to his family. Not that he knew her nor even her husband, even though the preacher enjoyed a certain reputation in Somerset for his fanatical fundamentalism. No one was more righteous, straight, or zealous in the pursuit of the lambs strayed from the fold. And no one in the town's recent memory—at least no one in a church pulpit—had gone on record more vigorously against the niggers, the atheist yankees, the Jews and the socialists, than Preacher Morgan.

The town was certain he had a first name, but few had ever heard him called other than Preacher Morgan. As well as the story could be pieced together, Morgan had been a cotton mill hand, working twister frames on the third shift of a mill in Greenston, when he had

86

gotten "the call." As he told it, he was hot and tired, having drunk strong drink the night before, so he went out to the water house for a soft drink and a cigarette. After he took the first sip of his Coca-Cola, he reached for his sack of Bull Durham and papers to roll a smoke. Then, as he would explain with hushed awe, a voice called out to him: "Don't smoke that cigarette. It's poison to your body."

He thought one of his coworkers was joking with him, but when he looked outside the water house, no one was in sight. Outside now, the voice called to him again.

"Morgan, leave your paths of evil and walk to God."

"Huh? Who's there?"

"Morgan, preach the gospel of Christ. Carry the word to the sinful. That is why I put you on this earth."

As Preacher Morgan told the story, the voice was ghostly and deep, and it faded with the last few words and was gone.

He fell down on his knees, right there in the mud behind the water house, and cried like a baby.

"Cryin' with joy! Joy! Feelin' the warmth of Christ flow over me like River Jordan. Feelin' the peace in my heart," he would shout from his pulpit. "Joy! Tears of joy! Puttin' my hand in the hand of God, that's what I 'uz doing', and feelin' Joy in my heart."

That was the story of his call. Hardly a Sunday went by in his little Baptist Church that he did not repeat it or some variation of it.

"Feel it with me," he would exhort his 30 or 40 wilted congregants, sweat pouring down his great, flapping jowls, staining the front of his shirt, spreading slowly in rings at the armpits of his black suit. "Feel the healin' warmth of our blessed Lord Jesus, Jesus, Jesus Christ, feel it down in your hearts; get the joy down in your hearts, brothers and sisters, open yourself up an' let it flow in; let it root out your troubles an' your sin, let it push the poisons out of your bodies, that clean, pure love that Jesus is a yearnin' to give you."

Another sermon for which Morgan was appreciated concerned the killing of Christ.

"Forgive them, Lord, for they know not what they do," he would begin, proud of the ring in his voice when he recited scripture. "When he was hangin' on the cross, hurtin' an' dyin', the Lord Jesus Christ begged God his Father to forgive the very Jews 'at nailed in the nails in his pore hands an' feet, 'at cut his side and put him up 'ar to die."

Here he would pause for dramatic effect and then go on.

"An' you know what? Mos' of 'em never even heard his words. They 'uz too busy throwin' dice for his robe, th 'onliest worldly possession he had. An' when God seen that, he cast a mark on the

Jews an' set em wanderin', never to have no homeland agin. An' even on the Third day, when He rose up outa the grave, the Jews wouldn't believe He was th' Son o' God, and so. . . ."

And on he would preach, his face shining with pride, preaching the sweet gospel. Occasionally he moved one of his congregants, but none ever as deeply as he moved his wife. As he spoke, she could feel the power of Jesus in her veins, feel the love throbbing in her skinny, shriveled chest. Morgan had not had intercourse with her in a long time, over three years now, had told her that he couldn't be "botherin' with things of the flesh no more" and that she would have to "give her body to Christ now 'stead of wantin' to roll around in lust like regular folks," now that he was a minister of the gospel.

It was enough for her. She could feel it in her heart and body— the love, like heat spreading through her, as she described it. As time went on, she became more crone-like, more shriveled, grayer. And in her eyes, the heat showed.

To gain sympathy, Morgan told people—especially young women—"not to tell nobody, but my wife ain't right in the head, pore thing."

"Don't go to no regular church, do you?" Preacher Morgan's wife asked David.

He looked down at his shoes, scuffed them in the dirt, and said, "No, ma'am. We go to a synagogue."

"What I thought," she said. "You know what? I jus' love the Jew people."

"You do?"

"Sho, I do. Jesus was a Jew, you know. I ain't forgettin' it, no siree Bob, I ain't."

Now he wanted even more to walk away, but he could not; there was no opportunity.

"You know wha's gonna happen to th' Jew people?" she asked him.

"No, ma'am, I guess I don't."

"You oughta know, so I'm gonna tell you. One'a these days, ar's gonna come a Antichrist, an' half o' all th' Jews in the world is gonna get up an' folla him. Gonna believe he's the true messiah. But he ain't gonna be, and they gonna folla him anyhow, and fer punishment, they gonna die by the millions, just like it's wrote in the Book, a slow an' painful death, writhin' an' a shriekin'—men, women an' little chillun. Over the whole world, they gonna die, an' Jew blood's gonna run thick an' deep through the streets, right up to th' wagon rim."

David shuddered with the images of his parents and Jennifer and himself covered with blood, falling and screaming. Now her face was contorted with ecstasy, and David began to be afraid of her.

"Says right in th' Book, jus' that way," she said. "But you know wha's gonna happen then?"

"No, ma'am."

"Then," she said, her crone's face beaming, "the true Christ's gonna come. 'At's all I'm livin' fer, you know, th' time when Christ comes."

As she spoke, her eye lids fluttered and closed over her eyes, her face inclined heavenward, her wrinkled, pale skin trembled around her mouth, her lips spread in an ecstatic smile.

"Well, when He comes, the other half o' the Jews gonna recognize Him and folla Him."

"And they're going to go to heaven?" the frightened boy asked her.

Her ecstacy quickly fell away.

"Naw, they ain't nothin' o' th' kind. They gonna die, too, a painful, slow death, all of 'em, ever last one, with mothers wailin' for their babies lyin' dead on the groun', and keelin' over theirselves, an' once agin blood's gonna run in the street right up to the wagon rim and finally all the Jew people—ever last one—will be dead."

"But why?" David asked plaintively.

"Cause you got the word right 'fore yo' faces an' you still turn yo' backs on Jesus. So yo' people gotta suffer. But they's hope, don' git me wrong 'bout that. Them first, the ones that follow the Antichrist, they gonna burn in the fiery pit for all time and forever. But the other ones 'at rise up and folla the true Christ, they gonna burn for only seven times seven years, an' then they gonna be purified an. . . ."

"Excuse me, Mrs. Morgan. May I borrow my son back for a few minutes?"

It was Rachel, who had seen him in the clutches of the preacher's wife and come to rescue him.

"Why shore, Miz Harris. I'uz jus' tellin' your boy here how much I love the Jew people. Always have. Jesus was a Jew, you know, an. . . ."

"We're all very grateful for your love," Rachel interrupted. "Now please excuse us. My husband is waiting."

Walking back toward Ben, Rachel noticed a shudder pass over David's thin shoulders.

"What did she say to you, *tottalie?*"

"She said all the Jewish people were gonna die a horrible way," he answered gravely. "She said we were gonna shriek and scream and our blood. . . ."

"Shh, don't ever repeat such foolishness, David. Everybody

knows she's crazy as a loon. I've never heard such nonsense. And for her to tell a child that! Good Lord!"

David felt better. But still, what if—just by some chance—it was true? Momentarily, his family racked in death throes flooded into his mind again, and then his mother was saying that it was time to cut Ruth's apple pie, and it was over.

Late that night David lay alone in his room, watching the light play tricks on the wall as it filtered through the breeze-stirred apple tree outside his window.

How come, he wondered, there was nothing so positive and sure about what was going to happen in his own church? He thought about that for some time in the darkness.

"Praise the Lord," David intoned into the night-blackness, in the little prayer he had learned in Sunday school, "who gives us this blessing and our sustenance."

12

Among the chosen delegates of Christ in Somerset, none were so persistent, so shrill in their absolute rightness, than the prowling young men, dressed in dark, cheap suits, who walked the streets every Saturday night, carrying their bibles, their pamphlets, and their gospels of Christ. They were, they believed, the chosen, called appointees of God and the Lord Jesus of Nazareth, touched by His hand and by so being touched, chartered to save the heathen hordes, the unfortunate souls wandering in bewilderment, all as yet unwashed in the blood of the sacred lamb.

Behind them this night was the Middleton Theological Seminary, where Monday morning they would reveal their victories over Satan in the classroom. Ahead of them in the shining future was a life of soldiering in the army of Christ.

They were easy to spot and avoid, traveling as they did in pairs, the ubiquitous bibles carried uneasily at their sides. But if one happened around a corner on the square and nearly collided with them, the avenue of graceful escape was cut off. In their earnestness and zeal they were somewhat pathetic; in their ignorance and rigidity, they were appalling. Yet common courtesy forbad turning on one's heel and walking away. So the Jews in Somerset, when trapped, usually stood politely and listened, answered the first few questions, and tried to find a way to edge away.

Their simple preparation for gathering souls to God's eternal bosom was enough to persuade the sharecroppers and mill hands. But the few biblical verses and the rehearsed evangelical pitch they were taught as freshmen at the seminary weren't enough to enable them to gather converts to Christ—and stars for their respective crowns—among the recalcitrant Jews.

Ben was invariably annoyed at their clumsy arguments and their persistent ignorance and rigidity, but like the others, he tried to be polite when the seminarians visited themselves upon him.

One summer evening, as he emerged with David from the Palace Drug Store, carrying a quart of peach ice cream, two of them were waiting on the sidewalk outside, their eyes already fixed on him.

"Evenin', brother," the first said.

"Evenin'," Ben answered.

The second young man fixed him with thick-glassed, myopic eyes, ignoring David.

"Brother, we're on a mission of grave importance, an' we'd like to talk to you. We're here to bring all sinners out of darkness into the light of Christ."

"Well," Ben said lightly, "you've sure got your work cut out for you in this town. Now if you'll excuse me. . . ."

"Wait," the myopic one said, "wait jus' for a minute. Have you yourself given your heart to God?"

"Well, yes, in a manner of speaking, I have," Ben said.

"What do you mean, a manner of speakin'?" the first one asked.

"It's just that I believe in a great, universal God, and yes, I have given my heart to him," Ben replied.

"You mus' be a Catholic, talkin' like that."

Ben could feel the ice cream soaking through the cardboard carton and into the paper bag, so he decided to end the encounter quickly.

"No, I'm a Jew."

The two crew-cut students appeared shocked, both seeming to feel the urgent need to retire for a moment to dig out the Seminary Instructions for Street Conversion sheet and discuss strategy. A Jew. Here was a big one. Boy, if you could convert a Jew, wouldn't that be something to tell Dr. Palmer and the others. A Jew. Unh, unh. But what do you say to a Jew? Hadn' been nothin' said about Jews, least not 'bout savin 'em.

The first young man, flushing through crusted, acne scabs and whiteheaded pimples, spoke first:

"Brother, you're in danger of eternal hellfire. It says right in the Bible that. . . ."

"What Bible?" Ben asked curtly.

"Why, *the* Bible. Ain't but one real Bible."

"Not true," Ben answered. "There are dozens of bibles; the Old Testament, the New Testament, the Torah, the Koran . . . dozens of 'em."

"They's only one true Bible, and it's the way and the light, an' ever word of it truth . . . not like those others," the myopic one said, now rather unsettled by this Jew's blasphemous question.

"You ever read any of the others?" Ben asked.

"Sure, I did. Read a right smart of the Old Testament in 'Bible Study.' "

"Well, what's wrong with that Bible?"

"Nothin', ain't nothin' wrong with it. But it's the New Testament talks about Christ, the savior—not the Old Testament."

He paused for a moment, looking to his partner for support, and got only a despairing look.

"Why, you people don't even believe on the Christ. What do you know, anyhow."

Ben had enough.

"Listen, I have a container of peach ice cream that's about to go to waste, and I have to go. But just for the record over at the seminary, yes, I do believe in the historical existence of Christ, and I believe he has been a strong civilizing force in a world that needs all it can get. As far as his being the messiah—no, I don't believe that, and I'm not likely to anytime soon. Most of all, I believe that everybody ought to be free to believe in anything they want to, from Christ to Buddha to a water oak tree."

Then he left, carrying his now sodden bag carefully away from his side, his son beside him feeling very proud.

For a long moment, the two students stood in silence, watching Ben and David as they disappeared in the haze of Main Street's old-fashioned streetlamps.

Finally, when the one with bad eyes could see him no more, he spoke:

"What's he talkin' about, a water oak tree?"

"Dunno. Jew talk, I reckon."

"Nothin' else matters much if he don't believe in Jesus." Slowly he removed his thick glasses and wiped them absentmindedly on a handkerchief that had once been white. "Boys howdy, I wish we coulda got *him*. Wasn't no way, though. Jews don't know nuthin'."

As they began to walk back toward their car, the acned one stopped short.

"Say, ain't that nigger over 'ar got a likker bottle stickin' outa his coat? Le's go over an' get him right with Christ."

"Wait a minute," the myopic one demurred. "Mr. Palmer never said nothin' 'bout savin' no trashy niggers."

"C'mon, anyhow. That nigger ain't gonna give you no smart mouth like that Jew did. Be good practice for savin'."

"Aw, all right," his partner said, his glasses now back on his nose.

"But I don't see the point to it. Everybody knows can't no niggers get in heaven." As he spoke, he squinted ahead of him, the light just good enough for him to see his partner grip the startled old Negro on the shoulder.

"Uncle, I got a important question for you. Is your heart right with Jesus?"

The half-drunk old man didn't know how to respond to this young white man with the strong grip already hurting his skinny shoulder. Oh Lawdy, he thought to himself, must is a preacher, and he done caught ol' Claud wid a pint in his pocket.

For a long moment, he just stared, pulling his cap off his head and looking down at his shoes. Then he admitted that his heart wasn't "zactly right wid blessed Jesus," and in moments, to the enormous satisfaction of his youthful tormentor, his nigger was in tears.

"Nawsuh, ole Claud ain' no count; drinkin' an' gamblin' an' whuppin' de ol' 'oman. But I loves Jesus, dat for sho; can't nobody say no different, neither. Not 'bout ol' Claud, dey can't. Members when my mammy usta not never miss a meetin', an' her in de YPI an' everythin', usta take us younguns to de church down roun' Lownsville an' den. . . ."

The tears coursed down the grizzled black cheeks now in earnest, and the Negro halted his panegyric of youthful rectitude to honk several times into a brownish-red handkerchief.

"Belie' me, reveran suh, come tomorrow mornin', I gonna be in church wid de ol' woman; gonna git right with Jesus, sho' as dis here is Sat'dy night."

The acned one fixed him with his iciest, most preacher-like glare.

"You gonna give up your drinkin' and your womanizin'?"

"Yassuh, sho I is," and for emphasis, he blew his nose again into the handkerchief.

"What 'bout that bottle there?"

The old Negro thought a moment before he answered.

"Ain' gonna drink hit; gonna take hit home an' put it on de shelf an' look at hit to remin' me to stay shut ob de devil's ways, das what I gonna do."

"Uncle, you ain' lyin' to me, are you?"

"Nawsuh, Lawdy, nawsuh. Wouldn' lie to no preacher, 'ticularly no class white folks preacher. Do, de Lawd'ud strike me wid a bolt of lightnin'."

"Prove it, then."

"How I gonna do dat, suh?"

"If you ain't lyin', take that bottle and break it right here on this curb. Put the devil away from you, jus' like it says in the good book."

"Please, sah . . ."

"Now! Me an' Jesus need you to do it now!"

Reluctantly, the Negro pulled the pint out of his tattered coat. Lord, how he hated the thought of breaking it after saving for it all week, and after just taking one little drink of it to boot. Wasn't much else an old darky had to look forward to besides a little drinking on Saturday night.

Now the second preacher-to-be began to feel involved. Seeing the religious fervor mounting in his friend, he felt envious. He hadn't done a thing, hadn't brought one soul to Jesus in the four months since he registered at the seminary. Maybe he could get a little of the credit, even if it was only a sorry old nigger they were saving.

"Come on, uncle. At this very time, Jesus is lookin' down on you, longin', yearnin' to have you come to Him. But you ain't goin' no-wheres long as you befuddle yo' mind and spirit with strong drink, 'cept the fiery pit, to burn in eternal damnation. Break that bottle for Jesus now, uncle, and walk yo'self straight to God."

His face was shining and his voice rose as he spoke until it was shrill, further frightening Claud and moving him inexorably toward the crashing of the bottle. Finally, with resignation, he did as bidden, looking up as he did so to get some benediction, some commendation. But even as the amber liquid seeped away into the dirt and trash of the gutter, the two seminarians were walking away.

Slowly he sank to the curb. "Lawd sho am hard on de ol' nigger," he muttered, "sho am hard."

Around the next corner the two students encountered a group of teenage boys emerging from a pool hall.

Already warmed to his task, the myopic one was prepared, ea-ger, needing to move quickly to speak first, ahead of his partner.

"Boys," the newly confident one said, "that pool room is nothin' but a den of iniquity. You better get right with Jesus right here an' now. Now you know, just like it says in the Bible, that. . . ."

But the largest one cut him off with a contemptuous gesture.

"When I want to talk 'bout Jesus or anythin' else, I'll go see me a real preacher, not no snotnose seminary student."

The others laughed, following him down the street toward the movie house.

"Don' feel bad," the acned one said. "The Lord's work is hard." But even as he spoke, he felt smugly superior. After all, hadn't he just brought that nigger to Christ, even got him crying? Maybe he'd concentrate on niggers from now on, he thought, at least till he was told not to.

"Wonder where the nigger street is in this town?" he asked the other one.

13

In his second year in grammar school David learned to hate September and December.

"Where were you yesterday, David?" the teacher asked.

What could he say? They were all looking at him. He paused a long moment, embarrassed, trying to think of a good way to say it.

"At our church, Mrs. Marchant," he finally replied in a faint voice.

"What were you doing at church, David?"

Please, please, they're all listening, he pleaded with his eyes. Don't make me say it. You know what I was doing there. Please don't make me say it out loud.

Those words didn't—couldn't—come out.

"Yesterday was a holiday, ma'am."

"What kind of holiday, David? I'm sure the class would like to know."

"A religious holiday," he said quietly, trying to keep the words away from the others, at least from the ones in the back of the room.

"What, David? Speak up. I can't hear you."

Please. Don't do this to me, his eyes said.

"It's a religious holiday," he said more distinctly.

"What's the name of the holiday? she asked.

His face hot with embarrassment, David said he couldn't remember.

"If I'm not mistaken, it's Yom Kippur," she instructed the class. "I believe that's the Jewish day of atonement."

Then the snickers started. Out of the corner of his eye, David saw the others exchanging winks, nodding, grinning, and gesturing toward him.

"Jew." "Kike." The air was thick with the words, but only David could hear them.

"Isn't it the day of atonement, David? Does that ring a bell?" she persisted, "or is it the new year?"

Please stop. I'm only seven years old. I can't stand what you're doing to me.

"Day of atonement, I think,"

And for that year, September was over.

In a way, December was just as bad. Every year, the class sang Christmas carols for weeks before the holiday. David learned them quickly. He liked the melodies. But there were words in them he felt it sinful to say. He thought it would be wrong for him to say, "Christ the Lord," or even the word Christ.

> Oh come let us adore Him,
> Oh come let us adore Him,
> Oh come let us adore Him,
> _____the Lord.

Could they tell, he wondered. Everyone was singing. Could they tell that one voice, his own, out of 25 had not said "Christ?" He was almost sure they could.

On Friday, the day before Christmas holidays began, Mrs. Marchant called him up to the front of the room to lead the class in carols. When she called his name, he felt a sinking sensation in his stomach. Slowly he walked to her desk, wishing he were anywhere else in the world but there.

They will find out for sure, he thought miserably. They'll catch me not singing all the words.

But he fooled them. He mouthed the words, moving his lips to form *Christ* and *Savior* without actually saying them. Nobody said a thing to him that afternoon; he was happy to see the green Ford pull up to the school a few minutes earlier than usual.

"Hiya, buddy," Ben called out. "No problems today, eh?"

"No, sir. Everything was fine," he answered.

It was a chilly day. David pulled the collar of his jacket up around his neck. For a few minutes they rode in silence, Ben debating whether to tell him that his Uncle Aaron was right in the middle of what was shaping up as one of the biggest battles of the war. He decided not to.

"What are you and Jennifer planning for Christmas?" Ben asked.

"I dunno, Dad. We're gonna buy some presents tomorrow morning, I know that. An' I want to get some food and candy and stuff for the kids out on the farm, if we can."

"Sure, you can. Do it every Thanksgiving and Christmas, don't you?"

"Yessir, I like doing it. 'Specially when we hand out the candy."

"Well, I think it's real nice of you and Jennifer to want to share what you've got with other people who aren't so fortunate."

"Yessir."

Then they lapsed into silence again.

Ben was worried about his son. There were too many times now when he seemed content to sit quiet and alone, drawn into himself and his own thoughts. He had been such an outgoing child until the problems at school began. Now, no matter how he and Rachel and Jennifer worked to cheer him up and help him get through, he seemed more and more desolate and lonely.

David's reticence to talk about his fights at school and his other problems with the children and the principal bothered Ben. If he could just talk it out, just get it out of his mind. But apparently he couldn't, no matter how easy Ben tried to make it for him.

Those idiotic bastards at the school didn't make things any easier, punishing him repeatedly for fights he couldn't do anything about. The problem was, he always won, which marked him as being in the wrong somehow, as if he were a bully. But Ben would bet his last dollar that David never started any of those fights; the boy hated the whole thing much too much for that.

He had straightened out the principal several months before. David had been whipped with a ruler for fighting, and when Ben found out, he drove directly to the school, ready to fight himself. When he entered the small office, the principal glanced up from his papers and appeared to go a bit pale.

It had taken very little conversation to convince the principal that he had been wrong.

"If what you do here is whip children with a ruler for doing something wrong, then I guess I can't object too much if David gets a whipping that he deserves. But he will not be whipped again by you or anyone else for fighting when there's nothing else for him to do," Ben said angrily. "Is that clearly understood?"

"There are other ways for boys to settle . . ." the principal started, but Ben cut him off.

"You know that, and so do I. Now you just let the children in this school know it, and maybe explain to 'em how it's done. Then maybe they'll leave my son alone. But until they do—until they stop taunting him and insulting his religion and mine, I have instructed him to beat hell out of every one of them he has to. Is that clear? Every one.

On my instruction. And if that won't fit in your system of rules and values, you've got two choices—either make them leave David alone, or deal with me. But whipping my son unjustly will not do. I won't have it. And I believe you'll find that if you persist, dealing with me will be a lot more difficult than with a seven-year-old boy."

Ben turned and left then, and the principal did not whip David again. But he did reprimand him, time and again, and made him stay after school to wash blackbords. His teachers weren't much more understanding, as far as Ben could see; but David took the pressure, stuck it out, and got quieter.

Christ, if there were just something he could do, Ben thought for the thousandth time. Just something. If there were some way he could find the boy one little friend who would stick by him—just to support him, so he wouldn't feel so lonely all the time.

"There's Joe," David said quietly, and Ben stirred out of his thoughts to look toward the sidewalk. He knew who David was referring to, even which side of the street to look at, for Walking Joe always followed the same route in the afternoon, from some indeterminate place to his destination in the middle of town. Walking Joe —bent, earnest, gray in all his aspects. David had never heard him called anything other than "Walking Joe." Occasionally children walked along behind him, chanting:

"Walkin' Joe, ol' Walkin' Joe; walkin without no place to go!"

Who had first said those words, Ben always wondered. Whose father among the children who followed him, as a child himself, had first chanted at the bent back of this solitary man? Out of what well of unkindness—out of what callous heart—had those words first sprung?

"Walkin' Joe, ol' Walkin' Joe; walkin' without no place to go!"

Yet always he walked on, undeterred by the meanness of the children; by rain or cold—always walking with the same slow gait to meet another empty afternoon.

"Where is he always walking to, Dad?" David asked.

Ben sighed and shook his head slowly. The light turned green; as he put the car in gear, he told David the story he had heard.

"There are lots of different stories about Joe, son," he said. "The one I hear most often begins a long time ago, when Joe was a young man just like any other young man, with the same hopes and dreams and feelings. Seems he met a young girl, visiting some kinfolks from up north, and he fell in love with her.

"They were together every minute they could be, and he proposed marriage. She accepted. At the end of her visit, on the old C&WC railroad platform in the center of town, Joe said goodbye to her, standing there in the station for a long time watching the train, and finally, even the smoke, disappear in the sky.

"The story goes that she had promised to come back in two weeks, with all her clothes and some stuff to set up a house when they got married."

Ben paused to light a cigarette, and David waited for him to continue.

"Wellsir," Ben said, "it's told that on the appointed night two weeks later, Joe walked to the station to meet her. The old sidewheeling C&CW locomotive screeched to a halt in the station in a spray of sparks and smoke, and people started to get off the train. A lot of women got off but not the one Joe was looking for. So he just naturally figured she had missed the train somehow, and he came back the next night and the next . . . walking to the station each night, still believing. But she didn't come."

Ben braked for a stop sign.

"See, David, Joe just never lost faith. Every night he went to meet that train, believing she would be there."

"But where's he goin' now?" David asked.

"Well, in a way, that's the saddest part of all," Ben answered. "Years ago, the C&WC closed the train station here in Somerset. That meant no more passenger trains would stop here again. The station went to wrack and ruin, all grown over with weeds and windows knocked out, but Joe just kept coming at the same time every afternoon, just standing there in the weeds, holding his hat and waiting for the train."

"Can't anybody do anything to help him?" David asked.

Ben thought a long moment before he answered.

"I don't think there's anything to do, son. See, Joe only has one thing in his life that's important to him, and that's the dream that someday that girl will be back. Sure, it's a bit faded, the dream, I mean, and not too logical. But it's his dream, something he can hope for whether the trains run or not. Now what could anybody do for him except maybe convince him she's not coming? Seems to me it would be awfully unkind—taking his dream away. It's all he's got."

David thought about Joe and his dream all the way home. As he and his father got out of the car, he said quietly:

"Poor old Joe must be awful lonesome."

Ben nodded and stroked the top of his son's head.

"You get lonesome much, David?"

David looked up at Ben and then looked away.

"In school sometimes," he said, "but not when I'm with you."

Ben started to answer but couldn't find the right words. So he simply stroked the boy's head.

Inside the house, Rachel and Jennifer were listening intently to a news broadcast on the radio.

"Hi, Mom, we . . ." David started.

"Shhh," Rachel held up her hand for silence.

David realized there must be something special about this broadcast, so he sat down to listen.

". . . in heavy fog, a strong German force led by Field Marshal Von Rundstedt attacked a thinly held American front in the Belgium Ardennes sector. Heavy fighting is reported all along the line, with the weather favoring the attacking German forces. Allied forces are reported to be regrouping under General Bradley for a counter-attack. Meanwhile, on the Eastern front. . . ."

Rachel turned the radio off and for a moment sat numbly, looking out the window at the bleak, leafless trees.

"What's the matter?" David asked. "Is something the matter?"

Jennifer walked across the room and whispered that Uncle Aaron was there where all the fighting was going on and that mother was worried about him.

101

14

Isaac Shulman was seldom seen without a black cigar clenched between his teeth. It was a trademark with him. He removed it only to eat and sleep—laughing around it, talking through it, until one day in early 1929 when a sore developed between the lip and the lower right gum of his mouth. Smoking became uncomfortable, and he began carrying the cigar clenched in his teeth unlighted. The sore grew, and finally he dropped in to Doc Braden's office.

Doctor Matthew Braden, the family doctor for many years, was uncertain and evasive.

"Isaac, the fact is, it could be a lot of things. Could be some kind of gum disease, could be an erupted abscess, could be. . . ."

"I don't want to know what it *could* be," Isaac interrupted. "I want to know exactly what it is . . . exactly. Now either you figure it out or send me to someone who can."

For a moment the doctor was silent, glancing down at the letter opener he held in his large hand.

"That's just the point, Isaac," he said. "What it could be—and what it most likely is—is cancer. That's what I was getting at."

"Doc, if it is cancer, what happens?"

Isaac fixed him with his gray eyes, leaving no room for compromise in words, euphemistic phrases, some other way of saying *death*.

"If it's cancer, Isaac—and remember, I can't say for sure that it is—well, if it's cancer, you're probably gonna die."

Isaac felt dizzy. He felt the floor of the room tip and dip and saw the light bulb in a strange, hazy perspective.

102

"Die, huh?" he said. "So Isaac Shulman is gonna die."

"Now, Isaac, I didn't say that for sure. I said . . ."

Isaac held up his hand to stop the doctor.

"I'm not so anxious to die, doctor. Someday I may not mind, but not now. I'm not ready. And if I want to live, what is the best thing to do?"

"There is a clinic up in Rochester that's run by two brothers," Doc Braden said. "They've been doing some wonderful things. If you like, I'll make the arrangements."

"Wire them," Isaac said, "tell them Isaac Shulman is coming."

When he left Somerset for Rochester, Isaac did not know whether he would ever see it again. Therefore he said his goodbyes carefully. On the way to the train he carefully studied every tree and rock and building, every face along the dusty streets, every stone in the road, as if remembering them would bring him back to them, or at least as if remembering them would give him something to have in his mind while he was dying.

He drove slowly with his son, Aaron, in his big Packard, acknowledging the greetings grandly, remarking to himself that he had built that building, that he had helped that white man or that *schvartza* who waved as he passed.

Like his father before him, Isaac had wanted most in life to reproduce himself. Lately he had thought that Aaron might come the closest, so he had chosen him to take to Rochester and the hospital, and perhaps to be the one to bring his—Isaac's—body home. In Jake, his eldest, he found part of what he subconsciously sought. Jake was strong, physically and in spirit, and he was fair and honest. But the primary quality, the intellectual thread that bound Isaac's life together and gave it dimension and meaning, was, in his opinion, largely absent in Jake. Undeniably Isaac had thrilled to his son's accomplishments in the boxing ring, on the football field, the track, and the ringing basketball courts where he starred. He had loved the compliments that came to him because of Jake, loved even more the headlines in the newspapers in which the name Shulman loomed large. But a few months after his last college football game was over, Jake was already being discussed in the past tense. "You know Jake Shulman," they would say, "the one who used to play ball over at the college. He was really something!"

Then there was the youngest son, Irving, who moved through his life like a shadow. As powerful as Jake was, that's how physically weak Irving was. The boy seemed only to want to make peace with life, quietly, on whatever terms he could get. Isaac wanted more of his sons: wanted them to want to conquer life like he did, to drink it and surround it and force it into their spirits, to taste it in vitality and victory. But Irving seemed only to want to avoid it.

Once when he was 13, Irving had disobeyed Isaac, sending him into a towering rage. An old mare that had pulled the buggy years before had gotten to be a useless nuisance, finally pulling up lame in her stall. Isaac had said the mare would have to be shot. When Irving begged for her life, Isaac ordered him to stay out of it. But Irving quietly took her out of her stall and hid out in the woods with her for two days. Jake found him there, cold and hungry, and urged him to come home. When they arrived, Isaac was waiting with a razor strap.

"You disobeyed me," he said to the frightened boy.

"Papa, I . . ." the boy started, and then he could say no more. Frozen with fear, he stood helplessly, wincing but without crying out, as the strap rose and fell. The sounds of Isaac Shulman's grunts as he wielded the leather were the only sound above the faint whistling noise it made as it cut an arc in the air and the cracking sound as the strap tore into the boy's legs and buttocks.

"I'll teach you to—" and again the strap landed.

"Papa, please don't. . . . please," Rachel sobbed, "please. . . ."

But the strap was already up and over his shoulder again, the boy growing distant in his look, more removed from the pain even as the strap fell.

". . . no son of Isaac Shulman will . . ."

Baila threw herself, pleading, at her husband's knees.

"Isaac," she screamed, "you're killing him."

"Get away," he roared. "He's not going to disobey. He's not, do you hear me, Goddamn it, Goddamn it . . ."

Now Rachel's arms were around her younger brother.

"Hit me, then, Papa, if you need to hit anymore. Hit me. At least I can feel it . . ."

"You'd defy me?" Isaac roared. Wheeling around, he saw the others, frozen with fear.

"You, Jake . . . you think . . ."

Then he stopped, because the rage was gone.

As he turned back, a vestigal part of the rage rekindled, for Rachel still stood before him, shielding Irving, staring at him without dropping her eyes, challenging him. His hand tightened on the black, molded handle of the razor strap, the muscles flexed in his right arm, but only for a moment.

"Get out of my way," he said to Rachel. "Get the hell out of my way."

"You can't hit him anymore, Papa. He's not strong like Jake. He can't take the punishment. Let him alone . . . please," she said, choking, pleading. For the first time in her life, she was challenging her father, and she was terrified; but there was nobody else, so she stood, unmoving, until the fires banked in his eyes, the razor strap slipped to the floor, and Isaac Shulman turned on his heel in disgust and left the room.

Slowly, like a staged tableau, they came apart, with Irving at their center, slumping now to the ground. Gently, Jake pried Rachel's fingers from the boy's arm, lifted him, and carried him to his bed upstairs.

Only then did Rachel's sobbing become audible, growing in choked intensity. It was more than Irving she cried for; it was the loss of innocence for them all, and the fall from grace of Isaac Shulman, whose hand was made for the handle of the razor strap but who had swung it too hard and too many times that night for life not to change for all of them.

Irving lay in a coma-like state for 24 hours, mumbling and crying out intermittently. Rachel did not leave his bedside. She patted his hands and stroked his thin arms whenever he roused himself, to reassure him that someone was there.

When he finally came to, he looked around the room, softly illuminated by eerie, full moonlight cast in shadows through the pecan trees outside the window and saw Rachel, exhausted, dozing in the high-backed chair near the bed.

"Rachel," he called softly.

She was instantly awake.

"Yes, Irving, I'm here," she said.

"Rachel, I had a bad dream. I dreamed that I was dying and Papa made me go on living. It *was* a dream, wasn't it, Rachel?"

"Hush, now," she said. "We'll talk about it in the morning."

"No, let me tell you. In the dream, I was getting away from everything. I was really happy. I was going somewhere . . . I don't know here . . . but I knew when I got there, I would be as strong as everybody else. I was almost there; everybody would be happy. Even Papa. And then Papa came up and stopped everything. I kept trying to get out, but he wouldn't let me, and I begged him. I told him if he would just let me go, if he would just let me . . . that I was doing it for him, anyhow. But he was too strong, and he kept saying, no I couldn't, and I couldn't get by. I wanted it so bad . . . I even fell on the ground and tried to crawl through his legs. And I begged, and he stood there saying no, and then the door closed . . . it was a big iron door with a heavy lock that turned and shut out the light, and then, Rachel, and then . . . there was no place to go anymore."

A strange light glowed in his eyes as the boy pulled himself up on one elbow, and then he gasped.

"Rachel, I hurt so much. Why do I hurt so much, Rachel? What happened?"

She did not answer, but only eased his head back to his pillow and murmured to him that he would be fine.

From that night on Irving moved through the house like a shadow, seldom speaking unless spoken to, avoiding contact whenever possible with anyone but his mother, Rachel, and Aaron. He seemed content only when alone and working in quiet pursuits that he devised. Gradually the upstairs of the house filled with carefully wrought model ships and stuffed animals. Hour after hour he would sit with a piece of wood in his hands, slowly turning it, nicking it with a knife, while a great barn owl he had mounted watched over him with unblinking, yellow eyes.

As the train pounded north, by rotting shacks standing out clearly in the bright night, by black stands of loblolly pines and picked-over cotton fields, Isaac sat quietly, remembering and regretting the night he had whipped the frail boy. Peering out the train window, he felt time slipping, and as he closed his eyes for a moment, space and time ran together. The piece of wood being slowly nicked by the knife was not in Irving's hand but in the hand of Isaac's brother, Motel. It was not him, Isaac Shulman, raging, but Isaac's father, and not in Somerset but in Bogdanya, not in a fine house with pillars but in a wretched hut with dirt floors, not Jake frozen in fear and horror but his brother, Avrum, as the strap whistled through the air and slashed into unresisting flesh.

Then time slipped back into perspective, and the dizziness went away.

Beside him, Aaron dozed lightly, his mouth slightly ajar, a book still open on his lap, loosely held in his hands. Aaron was softer than Jake, only a bit smaller. His face was full, with a square jaw and a strong nose. Always there was life in his eyes, interest, a kind of cognition that pleased Isaac. His hands were well formed, the nails carefully pared and cleaned. Not hands made for fighting but for holding books.

Aaron was smart, in an open, honest way, Isaac thought, as he gazed at his sleeping son. When the boy had prepared for the trip, Isaac noted with pleasure that he had packed books with his clothes.

Maybe, Isaac thought. Just maybe.

He did not want to sleep. Soon, he reflected, he would be sleeping through eternity. Now he must see and feel all he could. So he sat through the night, peering out at the countryside that slipped by.

106

Only once before had he made this trip and then in the opposite direction, a peddler's pack of goods at this feet, traveling to an uncertain future and an unknown destination, a pregnant wife still suckling their first child behind him in the back room, facing the toilets on Hester Street in New York.

But then he had life. He had the strength of a bull. He had everything before him. And now? A stinking, festering sore, eating into his flesh.

As the train clattered through the foothills of the mountains near the North Carolina line, as it slid by the little farms along the right of way, Isaac sat and stared.

At the clinic Isaac Shulman began by insisting on the truth, without elaboration, which he got.

"The cancer is widespread," the doctor said, "and the surgery very complex. There are a number of possible complications. We'll have to cut across a number of blood vessels. When we get inside, we may find necrosis in the carotid artery or the subclavian vein. And even if you survive the surgery, we may not get it all. That's the truth, Mr. Shulman, all of it."

"What are my chances?" Isaac asked.

"We'll do everything we can, but the chances are, it won't be enough," the doctor said. "There are limits to what we can do; unfortunately, we only know how to perform surgery, not miracles."

Carefully the doctor studied the face of the little man across his desk, watching for signs of faintness. But his attention was not rewarded with so much as a flinch, not one tic of a facial muscle nor the remotest sign of blanching. Only interest, almost as though his face was a problem looking for a solution rather than, in all probability, the signs of a death sentence.

"Miracles? Miracles, I don't expect, doctor."

Isaac did not like the idea of the knife and the bone saw and the cut arteries any more than he would have liked to be hoisted by his heel tendons like a steer by the big *shvartza*, Blue, who worked in his slaughterhouse and have the sharp knife brought across his throat. But he would not flinch, not in front of this doctor—or anyone else.

"Do you want to operate today, doctor?"

"No, not now," the doctor said. "There are other things you need to get done first. First, you need to have all your teeth extracted, then give the gums a few days to heal. So you have time."

"And how should I spend this time?"

"Well, Mr. Shulman, if I were you, I believe I'd go home to South Carolina and get my affairs in order and try to be with my family."

"Anything else?"

"Yes sir, there's one other thing. If you have a God, Mr. Shulman, pray to him."

Now Isaac managed to smile.

"I thought God was a forgotten piece of superstition to you modern scientists."

The doctor surveyed the tough little man. "Believe me, Mr. Shulman, if you survive, it will be because God willed you life."

"That means I have a chance to live?"

"Yes, I believe you do. But not by my hand alone."

Then the doctor left. For a minute or so, Isaac sat without a different thought than about the ticking of the watch in his vest.

The train ride back to South Carolina seemed endless to Aaron. He looked out the window or read most of the time. His father wanted no conversation; he simply told Aaron what the doctor had said and lapsed into long silences.

Back in Somerset, Isaac settled his accounts, appointed Jake and Aaron co-executors of his estate, updated his will. Rachel was surprised, the first night he was home, to find him in prayer shawl, yarmulke, and phylacteries, *davening*, occasionally tapping his breast with his right hand in the ancient sign of repentance.

"Papa, what. . . ." she started, but a stern look silenced her. For the first time in many years he was again the son of the rabbi of Bogdanya, pouring out his supplication to the God of living things, as he had learned to do so many years before.

As the doctor had ordered, Isaac next visited the dentist, suggesting that he send his other patients home; that he had a long, tiring job for him to do.

"I want you to pull out my teeth, doctor."

"Which ones, Mr. Shulman?"

"All of them," he said firmly.

As he spoke, the dentist was examining Isaac's mouth.

"But your teeth are perfect, Mr. Shulman. Set in like iron. No bone loss. Perfect. I wish mine were as good."

Somewhat impatiently, Isaac repeated that he wanted them pulled, explaining that his doctor had ordered it done.

"Well," the dentist said, "I can pull several at a time over a period of weeks. That way, it won't be such a shock to your system."

"All, please. Now!"

"Then I'll schedule an operating room at the hospital. Under a general anesthetic, I can. . . ."

Isaac interrupted. "I don't want to be put to sleep."

The dentist, a small man with thinning hair and large gold-rimmed glasses, slowly shook his head.

"You mean, Mr. Shulman, you want me to take a pair of pliers and pull out a mouthful of strong, healthy teeth with you fully awake in this chair?"

Before Isaac could answer, the dentist continued:

"You may be able to stand it, but I don't think I could."

Isaac chuckled slightly and reached beside the chair for his valise.

"I figured that, doctor. Get two glasses; I brought some anesthesia for us both."

With that, Isaac produced a quart of 12-year-old bourbon.

The dentist sent his other patients home, and he and Isaac matched drink for drink, neat, from paper cups. When the bottle was empty, the dentist wrenched out the first tooth, the upper right wisdom tooth, and Isaac only grunted from the pain. Then the dentist rocked the molar beside the bloody hole back and forth until it, too, could be wrenched free. Sweat began to pour down the dentist's forehead, and he paused to sponge it off before grasping the third tooth, hoping all the while that Isaac would faint. But he did not, and when the last of his teeth lay in a thin mixture of blood and water in the tray beside him, Isaac rose, spat, washed out his mouth, and walked unsteadily to his car.

For the remainder of the time he had at home, Isaac busied himself with matters of business, extending leases on the properties he owned, instructing Jake on the management of the slaughterhouse, explaining to Aaron how the livestock business should be run. Always a realist, he even planned for death. But to Baila, he spoke of life. Only Baila had ever seen softness in him. To the rest of the family and to the town, he was cold as steel. But Baila knew the gentleness in him. She had touched it many times, as she did again now as the last few hours flew before Isaac was to depart.

Embarrassed because of his raw gums, he had held back from her, spending their time together with the phylacteries strapped on his arm and head. Now, in the dead of night, she whispered to him, urged him, drew him into herself. Afterwards she spoke in a hushed voice.

"My Itzrok, my teacher, without you there is no sun in the heavens for me. You know that?"

"I know, *shainkeit,* I know."

"Then you'll come back to me?"

"I'll be back, *Shaineh Peshe,* I'll be back."

From somewhere down the darkened train corridor, Isaac Shulman heard the high, brittle sounds of a woman's laughter, and even as it died away, he strained to hear it again. The sound had somehow traveled beyond the rushing wind and rattling wheels, had been encapsulated in a draught of will and carried to his ears alone in the dark night of the northbound train.

In his mind Isaac slipped in and out of time sequence as blithely as the laugh slipped out of the car and into the noisy void of wind and wheels. Every sound, every moan of a sleeping passenger, every thought that rushed through his consciousness reminded him of other times. Even the laugh, whirled by him in a whisper and gone into the darkness, reminded him of other laughter, of inexplicable, tear-stained, gut-wrenched laughter of Delancy and Allen streets, and yes, even Hester Street, 30 years ago.

As he had plodded the streets with his rags, as he argued with this poor Jew or that one about a tattered coat, even as he climbed the stink-ridden steps on Hester Street, all about him he had heard laughter.

The ghetto had rocked with the jokes of the Jews. No matter how mean life became for them, the Jews could be counted on to make a joke. They laughed at the rich Jews uptown who wouldn't spit on them; they laughed at the Irish cops who stood on their necks; they even laughed at the sweatshops where they swapped their health, their youth, and their eyesight for a few pennies a day. But mostly they laughed at themselves—at their own aspirations and conceits, even at the way they ran from the anti-Semitism that blossomed around them like foreboding callow lilies in the spring.

Sometimes they paused in their laughter. As the older Jews watched their sacred orthodoxy disappearing in their children, watched them accepting socialist ideals and secular philosophies, saw their sons cutting their hair and donning short jackets, they paused in their laughter. But only temporarily.

As he thought back, Isaac recalled that he alone seemed not to laugh. Where others found humor, he found bitterness. Where others spent their energies dreaming up *vitzl* for the entertainment of their friends, Isaac planned and scrambled and plotted for the next day and the day after. To the ones who laughed, it seemed to him, the ghetto was a home; to him it was a jail. To him, the bustling and the laughter were an affront.

Almost from the first day he had realized that values in America were crazy and bleak. Importance was weighed in terms of acquisition. Money meant position, power, status; affairs of the mind meant nothing. The Jew who had made a few dollars could and did laugh at the Talmudic scholar from his home village who would not have walked on the same side of the street with him a few years earlier. In all of this Isaac Shulman was a nobody, just as Baila's father said he would be. All his reading and study were less important by far than his ability to sell his rags. He was always bitterly conscious of this as he went about the streets of the ghetto, wheedling other poor Jews to buy a used shirt, a worn overcoat, a patched pair of trousers that were his peddler's stock in trade.

He, Isaac Shulman, with all his reading and study, a nobody, a five-foot six-inch *nebechel* with a head full of arguments no one was interested in, a tattered coat the focus of his life.

Not that he was alone. Among the old men in rags, looking like nothing more than beggars as they picked their way through the littered streets toward some sweatshop where, say, ladies' girdles were made, was frequently a brilliantly accomplished scholar, perhaps an author or a Hebraic translator, with volumes of unpublished commentary littering the cramped room that was his home. He too was a nobody in this America, this strange new place where the poverty and heartache were no less real than in the villages the Jews had fled.

Any Jew who arrived with $50 was a rich man; more than half of them set foot on American soil as Isaac had, with no money at all. Still they came, and with them came the straining of the ghetto's boundaries, the breaking and mending of them, until finally it covered a square mile. The uptown edge was at 14th Street, the eastern and western boundaries the East and Hudson rivers, the hard frame the Italian neighborhoods to the east and the Irish to the west.

At the center old men and women remembered the green meadows, the clear sunshine, the clean snow of their Russian *shtetls* —wistfully gazing east—but few returned. At their feet was a broad ocean, and across it, growing anti-Semitism, Cossack raids, conscription in the Tsar's army for their sons. So they wore out their lives quickly, at the needle trades day and night or behind their pitiful pushcarts of vegetables or umbrellas or, like Isaac Shulman, their stocks of worn-out clothes. And they hoped.

The headlamp of the train pierced the darkness ahead, lighting the lonely ribbons of steel, the long stretches of pine, oak, and hickory. It caught the startled gazes of the night creatures—deer, raccoon, opossum, which watched from the brush beyond the roadbed. And Isaac dared to hope.

A funny thing, hope, he thought to himself. A funny thing. Hoping is for when things get bad, wanting is when they get a little better. He could almost laugh at this, but there was the sore in his mouth, growing bigger and making laughter harder than it had before.

Aaron stirred in his sleep, the book sliding from his hand to the floor. As Isaac bent for the book, he looked carefully at his son, appraising him as he might a steer in his slaughterhouse.

A good boy who read books. A good start.

111

The train whistle, moaning its one-note dirge, brought with its sombre tone another thought: who would say Kaddish for Isaac Shulman?

He felt a sudden urge to awaken Aaron, to teach him the simple words of the Kaddish so that he at least would be prepared. The words tripped across the front of Isaac's mind: *Yisgadal, v'yiskadash, sh'may rabo.*

Then he realized there would be time enough for the Kaddish. So instead of waking his son, he gently covered him with the blanket that lay across his knees. As he did so, he was somewhat surprised at this disposition to gentleness. Where had it been, he wondered briefly, when his children needed to be gentled rather than savaged? His hand always seemed to hold a strap instead of a small hand.

The thought was hateful—and new—to him. So he put it out of his mind. Under his breath he cursed the darkness outside. He would have liked to see the countryside.

Yisgadal, v'yiskadash, sh'may rabo . . . yisgadal, v'yiskadash . . . the words continued to bound across his mind. They were not hard words to learn; he would remember to teach Aaron in the morning.

15

That Isaac survived the surgery was a source of elation among the surgical staff at the clinic; that he proved a difficult recuperative patient was a source of continuing aggravation. His face was tightly bandaged, his mouth clamped closed by the gauze and tape.

The third morning after the operation, his doctor was making the rounds when a nurse ran up to him.

"Mr. Shulman is unwrapping the bandages," she cried, out of breath. "Some of the packing has already fallen out. I couldn't stop him. Please hurry. . . ."

When the doctor arrived, Isaac was staring in horror at his face —or rather, at what was left of it. The right side was little more than a bloody excavation. What the surgeons considered a work of art was to Isaac the embodiment of nauseating ugliness.

Moving his jaw, now hinged only on the left side, was grindingly painful. To move his tongue, of which a piece had been removed, was even worse. The surgeon and the nurse, momentarily immobilized, stood staring. Sweat poured down Isaac's forehead as he struggled to make the words:

"Why . . . din . . . le . . . die?"

Then, mercifully, he collapsed, unconscious.

When Isaac returned to Somerset his lower face was still heavily bandaged, and it remained so for months. Gradually, his speech grew more intelligible; the pain diminished and the wound healed. But still the bandages remained, night and day. For the first time Isaac began to understand the extent of his own vanity. He knew he could not forever remain bandaged, yet he preferred to delay the time

113

when he would have to reveal his ugliness to Baila and the town.

At night, when he changed the bandages behind the locked bathroom door, he would carefully examine the scars for signs, not of healing but of rawness. As long as there was any sign of rawness, he reasoned, he had a legitimate excuse to keep the bandages on.

In the spring the last rawness disappeared, but still the bandages remained. Then one morning, the decision to remove them was taken out of his hands. He was standing in a cattle auction ring in Atlanta, bargaining for a particularly fine jersey milk cow, when a gate to a cattle pen was inadvertently opened. A black Angus bull, apparently angry at having been penned up, rushed the ring and charged the first man he saw. Jake, who saw the bull bearing down on his father, started to run to intercept it, shouting as he ran. But he was too far away; the best Isaac could do was sidestep the horns.

When the bull hit him, it was with a glancing blow of the shoulder. It sent Isaac skidding across the manure-littered floor of the ring. Frenzied with anger, the bull turned to charge him again. Bellowing like a bull himself, Jake threw himself across the last few feet of the ring and onto the bull's horns. With incredible strength, he stopped the bull, wrenching its head violently over and down and throwing it to one shoulder.

As the bull lay panting, his tongue lolling, Isaac was helped to his feet, stunned but unhurt. It was only after he had been helped to a chair and given a glass of bourbon that he realized the bandage was gone, lost somewhere in the straw.

"Jake, look at me," Isaac commanded.

"Yessir, Papa, I'm looking at you."

"No, not into my eyes. Look at this part of my face, here where the cutting was done."

Slowly Jake forced his eyes to focus on the hole in his father's face. At first he felt like retching, but he managed to control his stomach. It seemed to him the whole jaw was gone, with the hole thinly plastered deep into the face with a sickly piece of mottled, pink skin.

"What do you think, Jake?" his father asked, his voice like steel.

"Wh . . . wh . . . wh . . ." Jake began to stammer.

"Cut out that Goddamn stuttering and answer me," Isaac commanded. "You're a man. Look at my face and tell me what you think of it."

Jake yearned to be released from the necessity of answering. He knew he couldn't frame the words as slickly as Aaron could or in the consoling manner that Rachel would do it. Even Irving could do better, he thought miserably.

"It ain't too pretty, Papa," was the best he could manage.

114

To his amazement, his father began to laugh.

"Is that all, Jake? That it ain't too pretty? That's not so bad."

With that, he turned up the glass of whiskey, and Jake felt a second urge to retch as he watched something move inside the scar.

Gradually Isaac's family and Somerset grew accustomed to his scar. Baila shrieked and cried the first time she saw it and then spent months trying to apologize to him. The town leaders—the mayor, Mr. Goodman at the bank, and the others—were too smooth to let their reactions show. To each he addressed a specific question about the scar, wanting to get the subject discussed and done with. To a man, they acted as if they had barely noticed.

Each time, he would smile and feel good for a moment. Then he would think to himself how smooth they are, those *goyim*, grudgingly admiring their ability to lie.

None of his grandchildren ever knew him with a whole face, so they grew up imagining him always to have been scarred. David, the third of his grandchildren and the oldest male, pondered for hours how he chewed, talked, spat. Finally, he decided to ask his grandfather, since no one seemed to want to discuss the subject with a five-year-old boy.

After supper one Friday night, Ben dutifully bundled the family into the Ford and drove to The House. When they went inside, Isaac crushed the boy's hand in his powerful grip, laughed, said the boy seemed to be getting a little stronger. Then the adults were talking, the conversation carried as usual mostly by David's father and by Isaac. There was no chance to ask him about the jaw.

David wandered through the house for a while, pausing upstairs to inspect the huge barn owl and the other birds and animals his Uncle Irving had mounted. Downstairs again he briefly considered sitting with the adults and when he got the chance, asking his grandfather about the jaw. But he sensed that his grandfather would be angry, so instead, he drifted into the large parlor across the hall from the room the adults occupied.

At the far end of the darkened room, there was a box of matches on a table. David felt a strong urge to strike one. He hid behind the couch where he was sure no one would see him. Hardly had the match flared, it seemed, when a powerful voice carried across the room to him like a slap.

"Dovidl, come here!"

He was terror-stricken. He paused, hoping that somehow his grandfather would be distracted. But again the command rang across the expanse of the two parlors. Slowly David approached the couch, looking as he did for Jennifer. Then he remembered she was upstairs talking to Uncle Irving. His parents seemed to be angry; their faces gave him no encouragement. He felt naked and alone.

"Were you striking matches?" his grandfather demanded.

For the first time he could remember, David started to respond to an adult with a deliberate lie.

"No sir, I wasn't striking matches. I was . . ."

Then he caught himself. "Yessir, Grandpa, I'm sorry. I was . . . I. . . ."

His grandfather interrupted him.

"Lying is worse than striking matches. Don't you ever lie again in my house. You know that big razor strap I keep upstairs? I'll wear it out on you. You understand?"

David understood but was too frightened to answer. Finally the old man nodded gravely that he could go. He ran upstairs as fast as he could to find Jennifer.

16

More than anything else, David wanted not to cry. He could feel the tears welling up in his eyes, and his throat hurt from trying to swallow the lump there. There was a drawing sensation in his jaws and behind his ears. He knew that if he let himself go for just a second, he would start to cry and probably not be able to stop.

It wasn't that he was afraid to fight Joe Billy; it was just that he was so disappointed at having to.

He knew what had happened. He had heard part of it when he was hanging up his jacket in the cloakroom. Billy Crane and the others had called Joe Billy names because he was David's friend, called him yellow and a Jew, although they knew he wasn't. Finally it was too much for him.

At recess Joe Billy told David he was going to whip him after school.

"But why?" David had asked.

"Why don't matter," Joe Billy answered.

"But aren't you my friend?"

"Naw, being your friend's too much trouble."

They were the only words the two boys exchanged until after the bell had rung and they were getting their coats.

"David, I . . ." Joe Billy started, then he stopped.

"Yeah, Joe Billy? What . . ." David's stomach was turning over with the hope that maybe this time, just this once, things would be different. But Joe Billy just shook his head and started toward the playground.

It was over quickly. David let Joe Billy swing first, still hoping

117

that he wouldn't, and Joe Billy caught him by surprise with his left hand, his fist glancing off his shoulder and grazing his chin. It didn't hurt; David was still willing to let Joe Billy go, but the others were around and jeering at him, and he knew he couldn't. Joe Billy looked surprised that David hadn't hit him immediately. He was confused, so he hesitated before taking another shot. David stepped in and hit him harder than he meant to, right on the mouth. Joe Billy stepped back, looking terribly hurt, and a trickle of blood started down his chin from the split in his lower lip.

Quit now, David thought desperately. Come on, Joe Billy, quit so's I don't have to hit you no more. I never wanted. . . .

He couldn't avoid the next punch—Joe Billy caught him square in the stomach, doubling him over. Now Joe Billy came at him with both fists. David was out of choices. He stepped back and then quickly forward, hitting the other boy in the stomach and then in the face again. This time Joe Billy went down on his hands and knees and started to vomit. The others muttered and moved away. David squatted down beside Joe Billy to see if he could help him. There was blood mixed in with the thin yellow vomit, and only when he got down close did he realize that Joe Billy was crying.

"I'm sorry," David said. "You made me do it, Joe Billy, but I'm still sorry."

"Git on away from me," the other boy choked. "You just git on."

There was nothing left to say, so David got up and started toward the spot where his father always parked the car after school, arriving a few minutes later than the other fathers, because it was too hard for Ben to watch the lonely little figure in the corner of the playground behind the bushes, fighting another child he didn't want to fight.

All the way up the worn concrete steps from the playground, David looked down, saddened by the sure knowledge that Joe Billy, too, was now his enemy. He was very much alone. He wasn't going to cry, he knew that, because the fighting had taken something out of him that made him want to. Now, for some reason he didn't understand, he didn't want to anymore. But he was still sad. Maybe he would always be sad, he thought, because maybe there would never be another Joe Billy that at least let him hope.

When he looked up he was surprised to see his grandfather's Buick parked at the curb rather than his father's Ford. His grandfather had never come to the school. As he approached the car, he was afraid something had happened to Ben.

"Nu, Dovidl?" his grandfather said, in his usual greeting to his oldest grandson.

David hesitated for a moment, not sure what to do. His grandfa-

118

ther pushed open the door and waved him into the car.

"Hi, Grandpa. Where's my father?"

"I told him I would come for you today," Isaac said. "I wanted to."

When they shook hands, Isaac neither squeezed David's hand nor laughed as he usually did, nor did he immediately put the car into gear.

"I saw you fighting that other boy," his grandfather said softly. "You whipped him."

"Yessir," David answered miserably. "I always whip them, every time. They don't know how to fight good."

"And why were you fighting, may I ask?"

"Same old reason," the boy answered. " 'Cause I'm Jewish, and they aren't."

The old man started the car and pulled away from the curb. David glanced at the scar in his jaw and then looked away toward the houses slipping by.

"Do you fight much, David?"

"Yessir. 'Bout every day now."

"And do you like it, the fighting?"

"No sir, I don't. I don't want to hurt nobody, but they keep making me."

Isaac stopped the car at a red light and momentarily fixed the boy with a stare.

"Would you change it if you could?" he inquired softly.

"I don't know what you mean," the boy said. "Change what if I could?"

"Change being Jewish to being gentile?"

David thought for a long moment. He started to answer, and then stopped, then started again.

"Well, sir, I . . . you see. . . ."

"Be careful to tell the truth, Dovidl, to me and to yourself," Isaac said. "It's a big question."

Finally David forced himself to tell the truth.

"I know it isn't right, but to tell the truth, I would if I could. It's just so hard. . . ."

"That's what I thought," the old man interrupted. "That's why I came over here."

They rode in silence for a few minutes.

"There's no other way you could feel, Dovidl. I knew that. What do you know about being a Jew? What have you ever been taught or seen or learned that could make you feel any other way? Nothing."

"But you're a Jew," Isaac continued, "and you do have to fight, or run, so you might as well begin to understand what it is you're

119

fighting for. What a Jew is. What it all means to you and me and all the Jews in the world. It means something, Dovidl, the fighting and the bleeding; it means more than you know. The fight back there with that boy is of a piece with thousands of years of history, except the difference is that you didn't run, you didn't fall down; you made the other one fall down and then you walked away a winner. That's where it's different, Dovidl, and believe me, it's a good difference. But you got to understand what it all means so you can understand the importance of it."

David listened, fascinated and surprised. He did not know his grandfather had ever been told about his fights, and now he seemed to know all about everything. Even better, he seemed to be proud about it, rather than mad.

The old man said nothing else until he stopped the car on the dirt road that crossed Ben's farm.

"Pick up a handful of that dirt," his grandfather told him.

David picked up a clod of the clay soil that grew his father's cotton and wheat and crumbled it in his fingers.

"That's your father's soil, Dovidl. He owns that soil and all the land around us here."

"Yessir, I know," the boy said.

"Do you know that in some places, Jews aren't allowed to own land?" Isaac asked.

"No sir."

"But a Jew can own land here. That's something important," Isaac said. "In Germany Jews can't own land. They've been chased out of the universities, and the synagogues are being burned to the ground, so they don't have a piece of their own land to stand on or a place to learn or even a place to pray on *shabbes*.

"What I'm saying is that being a Jew isn't constant, that it changes in meaning, depending on where you are and when you're there.

"It's happened all over the world, Dovidl, the land being taken away and the schuls being burned, for thousands of years, and the men have been killed, just like they're being killed in Germany now, and sometimes their women and even the little children. But there are still Jews everywhere, and there always will be, because we refuse to give our oppressors the satisfaction of dying out and because they always need somebody to hurt."

Now Isaac's voice grew angry.

"That piece of dirt in your hands, Dovidl, that means it's different here, because your father owns it and so far, nobody said he had to give it up. Maybe they never will. But the *mamzerim* in this town

120

also know how to hate, just like the *mamzerim* have always known. That's why you have to fight.

"But if you could change being a Jew and because it's hard, you did it and became something else, or if I did or your father or any of us around the world did, we would be saying that nothing in the past was worthwhile, that all the Jews who didn't run or change got murdered for nothing—and that would be bad."

"I know it's hard for you, and it ain't going to get easier for a while. What you have to do is try to understand what it all means, that the best way to live with the trouble is to be proud that you're a Jew.

"And why should you be proud? Because we are better than our murderers, Dovidl, more moral, more human. We prize learning. We know how to respect something more than guns and muscle and force. Better because we have the Talmud and the Torah, because our strength comes from intelligence and from God."

David tried to give the appearance of understanding every word his grandfather was saying, but both of them knew he didn't. So his grandfather began to talk in a different way.

"Let me put it this way, Dovidl," he said. "You're an eight-year-old child in America, in a town where your family lives and some of us are respected and in some ways, even feared, and still, you have a tough time just going to school. Is that correct?"

"Yessir," David answered.

"Well, this is a bad time, because of the war and because some ignorant fools blame us for it, just like they have always blamed us for things we had nothing to do with. When the war is over, things will get better, but deep down, the feelings won't ever change. We would like to believe different, but we have too much history to prove us wrong.

"So if they have an excuse sometimes later, here or in Atlanta or in New York or in Paris, it will be rough again. What we have to do is remember what we are, and why they feel the way they do—and most important, what it is about us that lets us survive in dignity and pride.

"We're better, you understand that much, Dovidl, that we're better than anybody else, if only because we have died by the millions for the right to keep on being what we are, to keep the Torah and our sense of decency and our faith. It would have been easy for us to disappear somewhere back in time, to just give up and say to hell with it—I can't take it anymore—and lose our faith and our identity. But we didn't and we won't."

The old man regarded the boy for a moment in silence.

121

"You don't run, do you, Dovidl?"

"No sir, I never did."

"That makes me proud," Isaac said. "When you stood up to that child on the playground awhile ago, when you knocked him down and only then turned and walked away, you made me proud of you. It isn't the Jewish way, not as it's always been in the past. But maybe someday soon it will be. Maybe someday Jews won't run anymore. Maybe it's my grandson who stands for that new way."

He turned then to walk back to the car, and the boy followed him out of the field. Suddenly it felt good to be David Harris.

For Isaac Shulman that was the end of it. He had done what he could to show the boy that it all had meaning and that he could feel some sense of pride about the fighting and the loneliness. The rest would be up to David.

In a way, Isaac had given David a considerable gift that afternoon. As the old man intended, the boy now had a rationale that made it easier to cope with the cruel events crashing in around him. Not that he had to fight less or that he could feel even slightly less isolated. But now he had a new response that made him feel somehow more decent and respectable.

"You're a dirty Jew," the old challenge would be called.

"I'm proud to be Jewish. Wanna make sumthin' outta it?" David would now call back.

It was a new battle cry, and David felt good about it. He still hated the fighting, and he still let the other boy take the first swing. But it was different now—better. He started to like the feeling of winning.

Through the long, lazy summer days of 1944, David tried to forget the fighting and the insults, and Jennifer helped him. Ben brought home a pony named Red for the children, and Rachel took them swimming almost every afternoon at the lake. They invented games to play: Jennifer became Nioka, queen of the jungle, or a fabled fairy princess, or Nancy Drew, girl detective, with David ever her faithful consort and companion. Far away from the bushes on the North Jordan Street School playground—continents and centuries away in their imaginations—they laughed together, rode horseback, plunged half-terrified from the tower at the lake. And David forgot.

Ben and Rachel sat by the radio every night at six to hear the war news, but Jennifer usually pulled David away, to another room or out into the yard, to work puzzles or curry Red or just to talk.

It seemed to them that the summer would never end. Then one morning, very suddenly and with what seemed to David to be very little warning, it did end, and they were back to school.

"Maybe it'll be different now, Jen. You think it might?" David asked gravely.

"Oh, I hope so, Davey. I hope so more 'n anything."

For the first few days of the third grade, things did appear different. Not that he was accepted. He was largely ignored by the other boys as they went about the business of settling down for another school year. But at least nobody called him out to fight.

In the third week of school David had to miss a day to attend Rosh Hashonah services. The next day, when he returned to school, several boys began to bait him.

Oh, God, he thought miserably, not again. Please, not again.

But his prayer availed him nothing, any more than the ardent prayers he had said the day before in the little synagogue over the grocery store had availed him. It was coming now, he knew, and it was just a matter of time before it happened.

David was quiet at supper that night, and Rachel gently probed to discover what was bothering him. She noticed something different about him as soon as he came home from school, but he wouldn't talk about it. She didn't push him, preferring to let him choose his own time.

As she frequently told her own mother, she was dedicated to two ideas in rearing children: a child needed love and a child needed freedom. With enough love, Rachel said, a child could develop the sense of security he needs to use freedom wisely. With enough freedom, the child wouldn't feel smothered by the love.

"Do what you think is right," she told her children. What she left unsaid was that if they made a mess of things, she, Rachel Shulman Harris, would be there to pick up the pieces.

Finally, as she was putting him to bed, David blurted out:

"Momma, I'm the only kid in the school that doesn't have a friend. The only one."

She soothed him as best she could, told him in her most reassuring voice that everything would be all right, and finally, when he felt better, he fell asleep.

"Not a single friend. A lone wolf; that's what he called himself. God, isn't that a miserable way for a little boy to have to feel?" she said to Ben as they lay together in the darkness that night.

They talked for nearly an hour about what, if anything, they could do. Finally Ben said, "we can't force them to be his friends. All we can do, Rachel, is be his friends ourselves . . . I mean, even more than we have been."

The crickets outside the window sang their early fall night songs, and for a long moment, they lay listening to them.

"We've given him all the love in the world already," Rachel said gently.

"It's not enough," Ben answered. "He needs more . . . more than love. He needs friends, too."

They both fell asleep, pondering the problem. When Ben awoke, he decided, even before he opened his eyes to the bright sunshine of a new day, that he would begin with David in the outdoors, that he would be his best friend on the lakes and rivers and in the woods of Somerset County.

If they could go fishing and camping and later, hunting, together, Ben decided, it would be better for the boy.

He would have to teach himself about the outdoors as he went along, at the same time he was teaching David. Most of the farmers he traded cattle with were outdoorsmen, he thought. Perhaps they would help. Maybe Sam Perry.

Suddenly Ben was eager to be up and about. He had much to do that day, and more before the weekend came.

On Sunday David wolfed down his lunch, eager to get on with the afternoon.

"Don't eat so fast, David," his mother said. "There are plenty of fish in the lake. They'll wait for you."

Ben grinned. "David," he teased, "I understand Mr. Gilmer is wondering who invaded his bamboo patch. I hear it just about disappeared."

"I only cut down a few," the boy responded. "You see, I wanted. . . ."

"Daddy's just teasing you, Davey," Jennifer said. "To be honest, I can't figure out how you cut down the first one with that dull old pocket knife of yours."

"Apparently," Rachel said, "he used something else for part of the job. Like my good butcher knife."

David squirmed and looked at his plate.

"Sure is a nice day for fishing."

Ben took the last sip of his iced tea, then pushed back from the table.

"Well, son, let's go get 'em. What do you say?"

David was up like a shot, kissing his mother goodbye, hugging Jennifer, promising Ruth he would bring some fresh fish for dinner, and then running out to the garage to get their tackle.

He had cut and trimmed a large assortment of cane poles. He dragged all of them out to the car. Ben had stopped by Bradshaw's sporting goods store for a few small hooks, floats, and split shot and a length of black, nylon line. These had been dumped into a cigar box. Thomas had completed the equipage by digging a coffee can full of worms.

After selecting the two smallest poles, Ben shoved the butts through the front window and against the back seat and tied the poles to the radio aerial of the car. Then they were off.

Ben felt good as he turned off Main Street, heading east toward the lake. He felt that this was the beginning of a new stage in his relationship with his son. They would be spending many hours together in the years ahead, fishing together and just being friends.

"There's the lake," David sang out as the spillway at the lake's lowest end came into view.

"Let's fish there, what d'ya say, Dad?" he asked.

"I don't know, son. Let's have a look first."

At the spillway, in the roiling water just below the dam, a lone figure—an old, colored woman—fished with a long cane pole. As Ben stopped the car, the cork on her line dipped sharply and she jerked out a tiny bluegill bream.

"See that, Dad? She got one. Let's fish here, please."

"Wait a minute, son. Let's see how she's doing."

They walked over to the old woman, who was dressed in a patched, gingham dress bleached nearly white and an old bonnet which, Ben surmised, must have seen much service in cotton fields.

"Howdy, Auntie," he said.

"Evenin, Cap'n."

"Doin' any good?"

"Yassuh, I catching a few."

"Any to keep?"

"Yassuh, dey in de bucket."

"Mind if my boy has a look?"

"Nawsuh," and to David: "Honey, you go 'head an' look all you want. . . ."

In the bucket were about two dozen silver-dollar-size bluegills. Suddenly the obliging cork went down again and the woman added another, if anything, even smaller, fish.

"Auntie, time you cut the heads and tails and fins off those fish, there won't be much left to cook, will there?" Ben asked jovially.

"Yassuh, dey good. I grinds 'em up an' makes salmons outa 'em." As she rebaited her hook with the tail half of a redworm, Ben wished her good luck and headed back up the bank toward the car.

"We gonna fish here?" David asked anxiously.

"Well, son, those fish were awfully small. What do you say we try for some bigger ones down the lake a piece?"

Noticing David's disappointment, Ben promised that if they

were unsuccessful, they could come back there and fish, and David felt better. In a few minutes, Ben drove the Ford into the Babcock property and headed for the dock Dr. Millege had described as a fair place to take a boy fishing. As David ran out on the dock to look at the water, Ben rigged up the poles with the black line, pinched on sinkers with his teeth, and tied on hooks.

"Here's the way you bait them," he showed his son. "Run the hooks through the worm at least three times, and be sure the point of the hook is covered."

Ben threw the first line out, and together they watched the spiraling circles radiating away from the point where the float rode the surface. It was a warm, windless, autumn day, perfect for cane pole fishing and being together. As Ben rigged the second line he found that he could scarcely watch what he was doing, so anxious was he for David to catch a fish. There was no doubt in his mind that something important was happening in both their lives that day. They had always loved each other, had been as close as a father and a little boy could be. Ben had taken David and Jennifer swimming many times, as well as horseback riding, picnicking, blackberry-picking, and hiking. But here he was today on a fishing trip with his son —the two of them alone together in the woods, on the water, surrounded by the greatest majesty God had ever created, feeling close to each other in a way that was impossible indoors.

"Come on, baby, grab that worm and go," Ben pleaded silently with the fish. "Give the kid a break, will you. Come on and take it."

But the circles disappeared and still no fish came, nor did they come to the second line when it was thrown out beside the first.

Ben studied David carefully. The boy was hunched down on the dock, down on one knee, intent on the float—the thatch of brown hair, as usual, in disarray, the dungarees, as always, wearing out at the knee. What one noticed about David, particularly at times like these, was his hands. They were always busy, fussing now with the set of the rod, picking up the worm can and putting it down again, opening and reopening the cigar box.

More time went by, and still no fish broke the quiet. The sun was high over the water now, and Ben guessed maybe the fish were feeding deeper.

"Lemme move the floats up, David. Maybe that'll get the bait down to where the big ones are."

He moved the floats so the bait would settle a foot deeper in the water; he recast the lines and warned David to watch them carefully.

Even as he spoke, Ben looked beyond the boy to the floats. Suddenly one disappeared in a swirl of water.

"David, grab that near pole," Ben yelled. "There's a fish on."

Ben had expected to catch sunfish, if anything, on the dock, but this didn't look like a sunfish to him. Although he hadn't been fishing in many years, he remembered that sunfish—even the big bluegill bream—tended to peck at the bait or to grab it for a short run and either let go or come back close to the surface, causing the float to pop up and down. This float had simply disappeared; even as David scrambled for the end of the pier to grab it, the bamboo pole was starting to move.

Then it was in the boy's hands. Ben could see that he was dealing with a good fish.

The green pole bent from the tip back to the middle, and the line sawed back and forth in the water.

"Easy, son," Ben called. "Don't try to horse him. He's a big one. Just play him and tire him out."

David hung on, working hard to gain on the fish. Then, with a sudden cracking sound, the green bamboo pole split halfway down its 12-foot length. Ben grabbed at the part above the butt section to keep the fish from getting too much slack line.

"Grab it here, son, and keep fighting him."

Now David had less than seven feet of slender, green, uncured bamboo between his hand and the line, with half of the pole dragging awkwardly below. But he hung on. Gradually the runs of the fish became shallower and shorter. Finally he was hauling a four-and-a-half pound catfish up over the side of the dock.

As it hit the planking, the catfish began to flap desperately. Abandoning caution, David threw himself on it.

Finally Ben managed to convince him that the fish was subdued and all his. David got up slowly, eyeing the fish suspiciously, awaiting some new burst of activity. Ben disengaged the hook from the tough mouth with come difficulty and slipped the tip of the cloth stringer through the fish's gill and mouth.

"Look at him, Dad, look how big he is."

David's eyes were shining, his voice ringing with excitement.

"I guess it's the biggest fish in the whole lake. Ya think they'll put my picture in the paper?"

Ben grinned with pleasure. What an incredible accident, he thought. Everyone knew that big catfish were caught at Braden Lake almost exclusively on the bottom, with some kind of stink bait like mullet or chicken guts, and mostly at night. Everyone knew that the best you could hope to do with a worm and bobber, fished close in to shore in the middle of the day, was a few bluegills. Everyone, that is, but his son. David actually believed you could take a dime's worth of line, tie it onto a worthless, green, bamboo pole, and catch a four-and-a-half pound catfish.

"Boy, wait'll Mom and Jennifer and Ruth see this baby," David said. "Wait'll Grandpa sees it."

"They'll all be mighty proud of you, son," Ben said, a silly grin on his face. "They'll say you're some kind of a fisherman."

In the excitement, they had forgotten about the second pole. David went over to check on his catfish, which was now swimming lazily in the water on the long stringer. After cutting away the splintered section of the pole, Ben baited David's hook again. Then he noticed the other cork dive, bob under and pop back to the surface.

"Grab the other pole," he called, and David had his second fish —a skittering, scrappy bluegill that had swallowed the small, number 10 hook. David soon had the bluegill on the stringer beside his catfish. And Ben knew that he had discovered a new dimension in both his and his son's lives. He had a fisherman on his hands now. His son had found a friend—his father.

Before the sun set, the two of them had taken six more big bluegills. Heading home in the car, David was the happiest Ben remembered seeing him, chattering away about fishing and the next time they would go out together to the lake.

"Together" was what it was all about, Ben thought. Together with his son.

17

David could scarcely remember a time when there hadn't been the war. The bitterness, the urgent news broadcasts on the radio, the deaths and injuries to men he knew in Somerset, the dreariness of it was all of his memory.

His mother changed right before his eyes, growing sadder and more nervous as month followed tense month. In the afternoons it seemed that Jake's wife, his Aunt Rebecca, or Aunt Nell, Aaron's wife, was always at his house, crying, occasionally even screaming, with his mother trying to calm them and reassure them that their husbands—her brothers—would come home safely. Sometimes Ben wondered (at least subconsciously) whether they weren't there to punish Rachel for having a husband at home while their men were overseas, and he grew increasingly impatient with them.

"They're making you a nervous wreck, and I want it stopped. Christ, I don't see how it helps them to tear you to pieces every day!"

"They need somebody, Ben. I'm the strong one. It'll be OK," Rachel would answer. And the next afternoon, one or both of them would be back.

By the time Jake got home the war had gone on too long for welcoming committees and bands for returning heros. Only his parents were at the train station, with Rebecca and Jake's two-year-old daughter, Linda, and Ben and Rachel.

They all knew he had lost his left arm. First, the navy had wired them, then Jake had written it in one of his infrequent letters. But none of them—least of all, his mother—was prepared for the uniform sleeve neatly pinned up from the elbow.

As Jake stepped onto the train platform, tall and thin in his whites, Baila gasped "Oh, mein God" and fainted. Ben caught her and tried to hide her from Jake.

Rachel tried to conceal her tears as she walked quickly toward her brother. Jake kissed Rebecca and with his right arm swept Linda, whom he had never seen, up to his chest. Baila, now revived, hugged her son and cried. Everyone but Isaac pretended that the sleeve wasn't pinned up, that they hadn't noticed his loss. Rachel kissed him while Ben clapped him on the shoulder and told him how good it was to have him home.

Isaac stood a bit apart, waiting. Then Jake clasped his father's hand.

"Hello, Jake," Isaac said simply.

"Hello, Papa," Jake answered.

"Does it hurt?" his father asked.

"Not anymore."

"Well, at least it's over now," Isaac said.

"Yes," Jake said slowly, "it's over."

For over a month Jake had been in the hospital, thinking his life was over. Everything he had ever done that gave him joy and distinction required two arms, required him to be a whole man—the boxing, the football, everything. Maybe it would have been better if the shrapnel had killed him. Then, slowly he had begun to think maybe there was more to life—in a larger sense, more than doing the things that brought joy to his father first and secondarily to himself. He would find a way to live with one arm, by God, and to hell with it.

"No more headlines for Jake Shulman, eh, Papa?" he said.

"It doesn't matter," Isaac answered. For a second or two he clasped Jake's right shoulder. Then, without another word, he turned and walked away to the car.

Through the long winter of 1945 Jake sat in his living room, mostly alone, anxiously reading the newspapers, listening to the radio, brooding over how he would live in his new world.

With the coming of spring he went to work, building a cattle business of his own, now busy and determined. There was about him a new softness and a sense of compassion; for, having taken the winter to think, he discovered that he could think and what he thought about was other people. Even as his new barn took shape Jake began to pay more attention to the shattered men at the Veterans Hospital in Springfield, a 30-minute drive from Somerset. By the time the warm stirrings of April were upon the land, he was a familiar figure in the mental wards there, bringing small gifts and encouragement to the boys who had been broken in ways that could only be

130

healed slowly, with understanding and caring.

The end of the war was near. The death camps at Belsen and Buchenwald and Auschwitz and Dachau had now been liberated, their pitiful rolls of walking skeletons freed, and the grim task of bulldozing the burial grounds begun. In three camps alone—Majdaken, Treblinka and Oswiecim, in Poland—more than 6,000,000 men, women and children had been murdered in gas chambers. Half the Jews in the world lay dead, cremated or buried in common graves, the transportation and body disposal problems having been solved with typical German scientific efficiency.

Most of Europe was a smoldering ash heap. In the spring of 1945 Hitler shot himself and joined the 30 million people who had fallen victim to his paranoia and his visions.

The *Somerset Daily Democrat* confidently predicted that soon, the remaining Japanese forces would be destroyed and Japan would surrender. The summer dragged on, but the fighting continued in the Pacific. Then on August 6, a single bomber released the first atomic bomb to be dropped on a military target. The casualties at Hiroshima were approximately 78,000 dead, 10,000 missing and 37,000 injured, not counting those who were to suffer later from exposure to gamma rays.

The *Democrat* hailed the explosion as "the final lesson the Japs needed to force their surrender . . . a classic demonstration of ultimate American superiority in the science of warfare . . . the single blow that will keep America safeguarded from attack for five generations."

A newspaper in Japan reported:

"Many were killed instantly, others lay writhing on the ground screaming in agony, from the intolerable pain of their burns. Everything standing upright in the way of the blast—walls, houses, factories and other buildings—were annihilated, and the debris spun round in a whirlwind and was carried up into the air . . . every living thing was petrified in an attitude of indescribable suffering. By the evening the fire began to die down and then it went out. There was nothing left to burn. Hiroshima had ceased to exist."

A new chapter in the immorality of war had been written, and its sequel was inscribed three days later, when a second atomic bomb destroyed Nagasaki.

The war was over.

In September Aaron came home. He had not been wounded, but he had changed in many ways. He had new ideas about justice and decency, new, radical ideas born in a muddy foxhole, fostered by the intensely personal reactions he experienced as he watched other men share their last cigarettes, exhibit the most incredible kinds of courage and sacrifice, kill other men, as he himself had killed, or cry over their buddies' torn, still bodies.

"Some sense, some progress has to come out of all this. It can't have been for nothing," he told Ben soon after he got home.

The two men knew that Aaron would have to leave Somerset.

18

Old Blake picked up the claw hammer and, grinning as he always did the first day of school, clanged it against the black bell. It was the 32nd year he had rung the first bell—announcing that another summer was gone, that school was in, that for the first strange day old friends and new ones would be thrown together to size up their new teacher and each other, as well as what the new school year would be like.

Blake particularly liked the littlest ones. Many a lost six-year-old had been comforted by the gentle old black man, soothed and then guided to the right classroom.

"Doan you worry none, honey. Ol' Blake gonna git you right when you needs to be. Wha' dat teacher name? You know? All right, now. Hush now, ain' no need to cry no mo'."

"But I. . . ."

"Hush up, honey. Doan you worry none 'bout yo' doan know her name. Come on, now, we go see de principal. He know."

How many, Blake wondered. How many scared younguns I gentled down the first day?

Now the children were surging around him, the older ones chattering excitedly with their friends, the younger ones walking uncertainly in directions they had been told to go.

"Hello, Blake," a voice behind him called.

Turning, the hammer still absently held in his hand, Blake saw David Harris grinning and waving.

"My, my, ain' you growed?" Blake said. "Mus' a been a head over de summer, looks lak to me."

133

David was tan after a summer in the sun.

"Dem boys betta' not fool wid you this y'ar," Blake said, showing the gold in his front tooth when he grinned. "Do, you' gonna wha'em good, big as you got."

David nodded and headed through the crowded front hall of the old, yellow school building.

Wish Blake hadn't said that, he thought. He had spent the summer hoping it was over, not talking or even thinking about it. Now, maybe because Blake said it, the trouble would start again.

A summer had gone by now; the war was over; there wasn't a reason for trouble. Please, Lord, let them have forgotten.

In the classroom he was pleased to see that three of the boys were new in the school.

Maybe, he thought. Maybe.

Their teacher was Miss McGraw. As the second bell rang she walked into the room, put her books on her desk, and wrote her name on the board.

"My name is Miss McGraw," she said, as the buzz of talking quieted. "Welcome to the sixth grade at North Jordan Street School."

Her voice was soft and slightly tremulous. She was scared to death. Her first class, her first school year as a teacher. So much depended on how she handled the first few contacts with the children. Must be pleasant but firm, efficient, confident, in control from the first moment.

Her teaching methods course notes reminded her that some order, some arrangement of things in a consistent way the children could learn, would make it easier.

First the roll.

"Mary Allen," she called.

"Here, ma'am"

The little, blond girl with the freckles . . . must remember . . . the little blond. . . .

"Billy Clark."

"Present."

The boy with the straight nose and the glasses. The boy. . . .

"Sarah Cramer."

When she got to the H's she looked up at David Harris with particular interest. She had been through all the children's records. All had a few notations here and there, but the Harris child's record was a mass of entries.

His former teachers had written that he was bright, sensitive, sometimes intellectually lazy, frequently working below his potential. Not surprising entries. A challenge to a good teacher. But the entries had also noted with remarkable frequency, reprimands and

134

punishment for fighting with other children. One teacher had written: "persistent troublemaker who does not respond to punishment."

As she looked at him (allowing herself the luxury of an extra moment more than she had studied the others), Marjorie McGraw decided that this child needed her most, and she would give him all she could. Not that it could fail to complicate her life even more. But it was not for the perfect children—the Sarah Cramers, with perfect grades and universal teacher affection—recorded row on row, year after year, without flaw or exception, that she had chosen to teach. It was for the David Harrises—the children on whose lives she could have a real and lasting effect.

After classes were over she talked to David's first teacher, Miss Trudy Workman who had for many years made it her business to take new teachers under her wing the first day of school. For awhile they exchanged pleasantries about the school and their new charges. Miss Trudy looked troubled when Marjorie asked her about David.

"He's a good child," she said. "A sturdy, good boy who deserves everything you can give him."

Then she was silent, gazing out the window at the lower-level playground where a few children still lingered to talk.

"I taught his mother, his uncles, and his sister. And I taught him. So many years. . . ."

The newcomer didn't want to offend Miss Trudy with too many questions; particulary, she didn't want to be thought of by her as a new, "modern" educator with a head full of frivolous new ideas about how to handle children. But the older woman made her feel so at ease.

"Why is his record so full of disciplinary notations?"

Miss Trudy's wizened mouth turned down in a frown, and she tossed her gray-white hair impatiently.

"Because some of our teachers don't have the sense or the understanding of a dominicker rooster!" she said. "That child is Jewish—comes from one of the best families in town. David just came along at the wrong time, that's all. An accident of birth, you might call it, that he was born and lived almost six years and then, the December before he started school in my class, the Japanese had to bomb Pearl Harbor and get us into a war."

"I don't understand," Marjorie McGraw began.

"Well, listen, then," Miss Trudy interrupted. "There was a wave of anti-Semitism that swept this town when the war started, like it did in lots of towns. It's not that Somerset's any worse than other places. It's just that it's not any better."

Shaking her head sadly, she told the young woman how too many people in the town had blamed the Jews—maybe because they had to blame someone and couldn't think of anybody else—and David Harris, when he entered school in 1942, was the only Jewish boy in the entire Somerset school system.

"As much as I love them," she continued, "there's nothing as cruel as a six-year-old child. They deviled him and called him names that I guess they learned from their parents and from each other—and one by one, they made him fight them.

"I watched him day after day, one lonely little boy, hurt, scared, out there by that big bush near the fence. I tell you, it was the saddest thing."

"But that was in the first grade!" Marjorie said.

"No, unfortunately it went on beyond the time when there was any reason except the fact that he always beat them, and they couldn't let it be. Not here in Somerset, South Carolina."

"There was anti-Semitism in New Jersey, too."

"But what you didn't have in New Jersey," Miss Trudy said, "was little southern boys striving to grow up and be *southern* men. That's all a southern boy is, Marjorie, a little embryonic southern man. What they get first—I don't know how—is an odd sense of honor, some kind of code that makes them kill each other when they grow to manhood down here, and inadvertently kill themselves, for the most trivial reasons. Our southern menfolk—they're not like other men. There are lots of interpretations you could put on it, and I'm sure you will. Maybe it's because they never quite grow up. Maybe because they're the last men left who care about honor, whether they confuse it with other things sometimes or not. Problem is, their sons get the code before they have any kind of sense of justice to go with it."

"And David?"

"Near as I could tell, he committed two great sins. One was being different at the wrong time; the other was refusing to run or turn the other cheek like his people—if you've read your history— are supposed to do.

"Some of his teachers have paddled him and made him do extra work for fighting. But that's because they've not had the sense to understand that there isn't a blessed thing he can do about it. School's a bad place for children to learn about adult stupidity and injustice, don't you think?"

"Miss Trudy, do you think it will be over this year, I mean, for David?"

"I hope so, child. But if it isn't, you try to help him. Will you do that?"

"Yes, you can count on it."

As Miss Trudy left the room Marjorie wondered if someday she would be talking to a young girl just out of college, staring out through rheumy old eyes, intent on teaching the lessons the girl's school had neglected to teach her.

David was made a school patrolman again, and every day at 12:45 he buckled on his crossed, white patrol belt, put on his red hat, and went out on early patrol to help the children from grades one through three across North Jordan Street.

It was the third week of school, and David had begun to allow himself to believe that the trouble was at last over.

As the other patrol boys walked by him toward their posts, he grinned and greeted them, and each spoke back. Willie Tripp was the last to pass. As he walked by he suddenly and without warning swung his fist at David, catching him just under the left ear with his knuckle. A sharp pain knifed through David's head, stunning him. Then Willie Tripp was saying something to him, but David couldn't hear him. Holding his hand over his ear, he shouted back at the other boy, but he couldn't hear himself either.

David was terrified. Oh God, Oh God, I can't hear anymore, he thought. I'm deaf . . . please. . . .

He was yelling that he'd get the other boy when he came off patrol, but he couldn't hear himself at all. and he watched Willie Tripp disappear toward Calhoun Avenue.

Why? why? he wanted to yell. Why did you have to go and do it? It hurts, and I never did nothing to you, nothing. I can't hear, and oh, it hurts.

But he only yelled that he would get the other boy. At least he *thought* he yelled it, because he couldn't hear what he was yelling.

Then the smaller children were at the crossing. He numbly did his job, seeing the children talking and laughing, but hearing only a distant ringing in his ears. A car went past, then a truck, then he heard a slight sound. Gradually the sound grew larger until he could hear again. But the pain still knifed through his jaw and the back of his head, and he felt a fury he had never felt before.

Willie saw it, sensed it, when early patrol was over. He knew David had to get even. He tried to detour, get away, but David stalked him, cut him off, finally trapped him in the bicycle rack, wanting for the first time ever to punish another boy, to make him pay for the pain and the injustice. David aimed his punch at the boy's jaw, right where he had been hit, but missed because Willie turned his head, and hit him squarely on the nose instead. Almost instantly, the front of Willie's white shirt was covered in blood, turned as red as David's fury had been, and the anger left David. But for the first time, he was glad. He saw no reason to apologize or care. Willie was standing there, dumbly, as his pants began to stain. It was beautiful

137

to David, a sight he would always remember, because Willie Tripp had hit him when he was smiling and saying hello, and that was more wrong than any other had been.

He waited for the call from the principal's office. When it came he told Miss McGraw what happened—this time not taking the blame as he had so often in the past—and she went to the office with him to intervene in his behalf.

Willie was there, still in his bloody shirt. While the principal heard David's side of the story in the next room, she admonished Willie.

"Do you go to church?" she asked angrily.

"Yes, ma'am."

"Which one?"

"Primative Baptist," he said.

"Don't they teach you it's evil—a sin—to hate other people because of their religion?"

"No, ma'am, I never heard nothin' about it."

"Well, it is, and if you haven't heard it, I'm telling you now."

The boy looked puzzled.

"I don't hate nobody because of no religion," he said. "Who said I did, anyway?"

Marjorie was impatient.

"Nobody said so, but you must. Actions speak louder than words, you know."

The boy looked at her blankly, the blood clotted under his nose.

"Well, I don't," he said slowly.

"Then why did you hit David?"

Willie wanted to blow his nose, but he was afraid it would start to bleed again, so he sniffed lightly, then a bit harder, before he answered.

" 'Cause he's the toughest," he finally said.

"What does that mean, 'he's the toughest'?" she asked.

"He thinks he can lick anybody, Miss McGraw. And he's always bein' a smart aleck, an' I wanted to show him."

What had Miss Trudy said, something about southern boys straining to be southern men, something about a code?

"And when the other children pick fights with him?"

"Same thing," the boy said slowly, uncertainly. "There's names you can call him to make him fight you, but I don't know why they make him so mad."

"You mean to tell me," the young teacher said, "that if you could whip David Harris, it would be kind of important, because he's the toughest boy. And that the boys start fights with him because of that and not because of his church?"

138

"Yessum, Miss McGraw. I don't even know what church he goes to."

As David came through the door to the outer office, Marjorie suddenly understood what all the others had missed, because nobody else had ever asked the right questions. It wasn't that David was Jewish anymore; that had only been what started it years before. It was that he always won. He was like some caricature of a child's western drama—a top gun—taunting the confusing, developing sense of manhood of the other boys around him.

Of course!

It wasn't that the other boys were inherently bad or even unjust. They were only doing what they thought they had to do in order to fulfill some pathetic, distorted sense of masculinity they couldn't articulate or even understand.

Willie was on his feet now, waiting to be called.

"Willie, come in here," the principal said.

"Yessir," he answered, and as he walked by David, he paused and stuck out his right hand.

"I'm sorry for what I did," he said slowly. "It was stinkin' an' I'm sorry."

David stared at him without moving.

"I'd like to be your friend if it's OK," Willie said, pushing his hand out farther.

David took his hand and shook it, and as the boys stood there, clasping hands, a strange sense of elation came over David.

"I'm sorry I busted your nose," he said, his voice rising. "I really am."

"I know," the other boy said. "It don't matter anyhow. I had it comin'."

Marjorie explained it to David outside the classroom. She felt excited, as if she had made a discovery. And David understood part of the idea, and he liked it—and himself.

19

Nell pleaded with Aaron not to make the speech, but he would not be dissuaded. Finally, in desperation she called Rachel.

"Have you heard what he's going to do, Rachel?"

"No, I don't know what you're talking about, Nell."

"He's planning to give a speech tomorrow at the annual memorial service," she said. "He's going to get up there and say that this town and the country mustn't forget that black boys died in the war just like white boys did . . . that if they're good enough to die for the country, they're good enough to eat at any restaurant and go to any school and ride anywhere they want to on any bus or train, just like any white person."

There would be trouble, Rachel realized. Maybe very serious trouble. The time wasn't right for this kind of talk from anyone, let alone a Jew, even if he would be wearing his uniform and even if he did have three rows of battle ribbons on his shirt.

"Have you tried to reason with him?" Rachel asked.

"Oh, Rachel, I begged him all this morning. *Begged* him! Lord, he could get killed!"

For an instant the horrible irony of what could happen—Aaron being shot to death on Main Street in Somerset after coming through the entire war alive—flashed into Rachel's mind.

"Nell, take it easy," she said. "I'll call Papa."

She located Isaac at the Elks Club and quickly outlined the situation over the telephone.

"You can't let him do it, Papa," she said finally. "You know what it could mean."

There was a pause, then her father answered.

"Aaron's a man, Rachel. He'll do what he feels he has to do."

"But, Papa. . . ."

"I don't agree with it, but I won't try to stop it. I don't want you to, either."

The speaker's stand at the memorial service was decorated with red, white, and blue bunting. The invocation was given by the Rev. Ernest Hart from the First Baptist Church, who offered a long prayer for the dead, in which he pronounced their cause, and that of the nation, to be right, and promised that the boys who had fallen had been gathered into the bosom of Christ and would spend all eternity in the heavenly paradise He had prepared for them.

The mayor spoke next. After a brief, mostly nonpolitical speech about the fineness of the people of Somerset and the fineness of the boys they had raised to go over there and fight to protect their freedom and democracy and the American way of life, he read the roll of those who had died, accompanied by the muffled, muted trumpet and drums of the Somerset American Legion Post. Next a man in his dress marine uniform, sitting in a wheelchair, came to the speaker's post. The mayor lowered the microphone for him, introduced him as the town's most decorated war hero, and the only one who had been awarded the Congressional Medal of Honor. The crippled marine spoke about the war and how Americans had shown the greatest courage ever seen on a battlefield in all the history of the world, and how the U.S. had whipped the Germans and the Japs into the kind of destruction and surrender that would contain their military ambitions for a hundred years.

The crowd cheered wildly, the drum and bugle corps struck up the Marine Hymn, and children waved flags and struggled to get a closer look. Then Aaron came to the microphone, looking handsome in his dress khakis. Adjusting his glasses, he took out the notes he had made, glanced at them, and put them aside. He spoke in a low voice, beginning his speech with a story about a soldier in Belgium whom he had scarcely known, who saved his life and the lives of four of his buddies by throwing himself on a live German grenade. The crowd tensed, enjoying the story, because they had not been there and therefore had to live the excitement of the battlefield vicariously, and for some reason, the boys who had come home still didn't like to talk about it. But this Shulman boy—Isaac Shulman's son—didn't much seem to mind. Just think of it, I mean, what it takes to throw yourself down on a grenade knowing it was gonna kill you, rather than trying to get away. . . .

"I never even knew his name until after the grenade had gone off and cut him to pieces," Aaron said. "It happened so quickly, and

141

then, when it was over, we rolled him over and saw what was left of his dog tags and found out at least the name of the man who had given his life to save ours. His name was Johnson, and he was black. We were all white, but that didn't appear to make any difference to Pfc. Willis Johnson who died without making a single sound, without saying a single word to any of us, but instead, gave his life so we could live."

The crowd was stunned, listening in hushed surprise as Aaron developed his plea for social justice, for equality for everyone in the society, but mostly for Negroes, for equal rights in education and at the polls and in stores, because all of them together, white and black, Protestant, Catholic, and Jew, people of Spanish and Polish and Italian and Russian and yes, even German, extraction, had gone over there together to get a job done, and in doing it, had earned the right to respect and dignity and opportunity. They had earned it with their courage and determination and lives, and by what they had done, had strengthened this system of government that guarantees equality under the law.

There was a polite scattering of applause when Aaron sat down. After a naval officer from Somerset had spoken, Rev. Hart gave a closing prayer, and the town's second, and last, annual memorial service was over.

The crowd surged around the platform to congratulate the speakers, but as Aaron came down the wooden steps, most of the men and women turned away to let him pass, unapplauded and uncongratulated, to walk alone to his car on the other side of the town square.

As his father had predicted, Aaron had done what he had to do. He didn't care what the town thought of him. He wasn't afraid of what might happen. He had worn out his fear somewhere in Belgium three years ago. He laughed in the telephone when he received a threatening call, telling the caller to "go to hell" and hanging up. The following night, he frightened away a small group of Klansmen who came to burn a cross on his lawn. Most of the Klan members had refused to participate—even though they freely admitted they hated the nigger-lovin' Jew bastard—because he was a soldier just home from the war, and that somehow earned him one more chance. But seven members, after the meeting of the Klavern, decided to go anyhow, and after liquoring up on moonshine for three hours, nailed together two four-by-eights and wrapped them in gasoline-soaked rags. At 4:00 A.M., they quietly slipped out of their cars, sneaked onto Aaron's front yard, and began to dig a hole for the cross. But before they could get it set straight, a double blast from a .12-gauge shotgun echoed out of the trees along the driveway, and a strong voice told them to freeze.

"Those were double aughts," the voice said out of the darkness, "and I aimed them over your miserable fucking heads." There was the distinct sound of a double-barreled shotgun breaking and two more shells sliding into the tubes.

"The next load will be gut high, and killing."

The Klansmen stood frozen, the cross seated at a crazy angle in the half-finished hole. Then the voice started to laugh.

"You wouldn't make a pimple on a combat soldier's ass—not one of you," the voice said. "Now you've made me waste two perfectly good shotgun shells, and I want a little souvenir for 'em, so you just slide off those sheets and stack 'em up neatly on the lawn."

Terrorstruck, the seven men did as they were told.

"How does it feel to have your faces hanging out where anybody could see you?" the voice asked. "You like it?"

No one answered, so Aaron gave them a disquisition on cowardice, particularly theirs and the entire Ku Klux Klan, while they stood in humiliation and fear of the shotgun. Then he told them to run, by God, run like the rabbits they were—and they were running and falling down his lawn to the echoes of his laughter, until they were in their cars and safely away.

The following week Aaron moved to Charlotte, North Carolina where, he told Ben, he thought he might be able to get something done for the Negroes and maybe even the Jews.

"It's just no use trying here," he told Ben as he said goodbye. "Besides, I might make things bad for the family. In Charlotte there are a few other people who feel like I do."

Ben grasped his hand, wished him luck, and watched his car disappear north.

For the next few weeks Somerset pretended that Aaron's speech had never happened. At least the pretense was made whenever any members of his family were within earshot. But privately, "that nigger-lovin' Jew" was discussed frequently and bitterly.

David had not had a fight in school in five months, since he busted Willie Tripp's nose back in September. It had been a good time for him; he was the happiest he had been since he could remember. Then one afternoon as he was finishing patrol duty, he found himself surrounded by a crowd of boys from his class and from the sixth grade.

"You love niggers, don't you, boy?" one leered at him.

"Huh?" David said, bewildered.

"All th' Jews loves niggers," another said.

"Yeah, Jew girls screw niggers, too," a third chimed in.

"Your sister like niggers?" another boy asked.

He was the one David hit first. Then they were all hitting him, and he went down. Several boys piled on top of him, hitting him, and another boy kicked at his head. Then suddenly, one fell backward, then the other, wrenched clear by a pair of hands at the back of their collars. The third boy who had been kicking him stopped, surprised, and then he went down, shoved hard by a boy named Bobby Brock whom David scarcely knew.

"What the hell . . . ?" one boy started.

Bobby Brock wheeled around to face him. "He ain't done a thing to you . . . none of you. You got no right to be beating him like that. Takes a bunch of cowards to gang up on one boy."

David scrambled to his feet, tasting blood in the corner of his mouth. He didn't understand what was happening, but he was immensely grateful for it. He could ask questions later.

"Any one of you want to fight him, that's a different story," Bobby Brock said. "But not all of you . . . not while I'm around."

David pushed it.

"I'll whip anybody here who wants to fight like a man," he said. "Anybody."

No one in the crowd moved.

"What about you?" David asked one of the boys who had been on top of him. "You want to try?"

The boy hung his head.

"Well, do you?" David insisted.

"Naw," the boy said.

"You?" David asked another. "Any of you."

No one stepped up. David stood beside Bobby Brock, glowering, strangely elated, wanting now for one of them to take him on so he could show this kid Bobby his stuff, but the boys only looked down at the ground and began to drift away.

Finally, only David and Bobby stood together.

"You didn't have to do that," David said.

"I know. I wanted to," the other boy replied. "It wasn't fair."

"Thanks. Thanks a lot," David said. "I couldn't whip all of 'em alone."

"It's OK," Bobby said.

"Say, you want to come over to my house sometime?" David asked.

"Sure, I'd like that."

Then the green Ford pulled up in front of the school, and David turned to leave.

"So long," he said to the boy.

"Yeah, so long," he replied.

"Maybe tomorrow . . . I mean, about coming over to my house?" David asked.

"Sure," Bobby smiled. "That'd be real good."

In the car David talked excitedly about his new friend, and Ben beamed as he drove toward home.

They both sensed that something important had happened, and they were right. Bobby Brock—because he was fair above all else, because his sense of right and wrong transcended his sense of belonging to the group, because there was in him a bright curiosity about another boy the others said was different—had made a statement by what he had done and what he had said to David on the school grounds. He had said that David was no longer alone.

The next afternoon he rode home with David and Ben, and the boys spent the afternoon in the side lot playing baseball. Rachel interrupted the game twice to serve them lemonade and cookies, and, as she told Ben that night, she had to restrain herself from interrupting more often, so pleased was she at David's happiness.

"A friend," she said to Ben, "it's such a simple thing, such an automatic thing, for children to have friends. And yet, it's been so long in coming for David."

Her voice trailed off as she gazed out of the window into the moonlit flower beds beyond the apple tree.

"Bobby invited him over to play on Saturday," Ben told her.

"I went to school with his mother," Rachel said "You know her, Ben. Ruby Brock. We used to see her downtown having lunch at the Hot Shoppe from time to time."

"Oh, sure. I remember. Yes, she seems an awfully nice person. She's married to a good fellow, too. Old Harrison Brock. He's an executive at Vernal Mill. I play a hand of cards with him from time to time at the club."

"David told me Bobby stepped into a fight yesterday to help him. That takes a lot of courage."

"It does, Rachel. I believe he must be a fine little boy. I just hope he and David stay friends, that it doesn't get too tough for him to be David's friend, I guess, is what I really mean. It's awfully hard to stand against the crowd, and that might be what he'll have to do."

Rachel looked at Ben quickly.

"Oh, Ben, I hope not. I hope this terrible thing is about over now."

On Saturday the weather drove the boys inside the Brock house and as the slanting sheets of rain drummed against the windows, they played Monopoly and told ghost stories. For Bobby it was just another rainy Saturday, but for David, it was a terribly important day.

In December Bobby announced that his mother was setting a place for David at Christmas dinner and that there would be presents for him under the tree. There always seemed to be a place in Bobby's house, and in his life, for David, and in David's for Bobby.

The world had changed for David. Bobby Brock had made it change.

20

"A book, eh, Dovidl?" Isaac Shulman said. "I always see you with a book in your hand."

"Yes sir," David answered. "I like to read."

The old man seldom spoke to his grandchildren on Friday nights, beyond acknowledging their greetings, but he noticed what they did and heard a surprising amount of what they said. He was always listening for something, watching for something without realizing quite what it was.

"What is this book?" he asked the boy.

"*Huckleberry Finn*, Grandpa."

Isaac lightly took the book out of the boy's hand and opened it to a middle page, musing over a paragraph.

> . . . about daybreak I found a canoe and crossed over a chute to the main shore—it was only two hundred yards—and paddled about a mile up a crick amongst the cypress woods, to see if I couldn't get some berries. Just as I was passing a place where a kind of a cowpath crossed the crick, here comes a couple of men tearing up the path as tight as they could foot it. . . .

Isaac read on a little way, then closed the book.

"Is there value in reading such a book?" he asked the boy.

"Yes sir, lots," David replied. "Jennifer says it's one of the greatest novels ever written by an American."

David paused a moment, looking down at his shoes.

"Besides," he added, "a book kinda keeps you company when

147

you don't have anybody to play with or anything. 'Specially a book like this."

Reading was a gift from Jennifer. Before he could read himself, she had read to him for hours on end, sharing with him the things that interested her, as she always shared everything with her brother that she thought had value. When he entered school she helped him learn to read faster, and then spent hours in the library, looking for simple books that would interest him. Her task took on a new urgency when the loneliness had gathered about him, for she could not be with him all of the time. The bookshelf in his bedroom reflected her taste in books. The older books were the series by Clinton W. Locke, the Hardy Boy mysteries, and individual books she had found for him like *Starbuck Valley Winter*, his favorite, and *The Little Lame Prince*. When he was 10 she introduced him to adult fiction, carefully and with great forethought. The first of what David called his "grown-up books" was a novel she had found quite accidentally, a little-known one by John Steinbeck, *To a God Unknown*. Jennifer had read *Grapes of Wrath* and *Of Mice and Men*, and when she went back to the library, she discovered *To a God Unknown* without having heard of it in school. When she took it from the shelf, she noticed that it had been checked out only twice since the library had bought it. This piqued her curiosity, so she took it home and read it.

"I've been looking for a book to start David on—I mean, a book that will get him interested in more serious kinds of literature," she told her mother. "And I think I found a good one to try."

Rachel looked at the title page thoughtfully.

"Don't you think Steinbeck is a bit advanced for a 10-year-old, Jen?"

Jennifer shook her head slightly, in a little gesture that her father always liked, because it made her pretty chestnut curls toss around her face.

"I don't think so, Mom. This isn't like *Grapes of Wrath*. It's a small book, kind of easy, and it tells a story about a man who owns a cattle ranch, about how he loves his land. I think David feels the same way about our farm. He's around the barn a lot with Daddy and around cattle and men who raise and trade them, so I think the book would be special to him. I'm not sure. I just think it would."

"Well, why not give it a try. Let's see."

David approached the book gingerly, setting it aside for several days, unsure. But Jennifer had been correct; as soon as he had read the first 10 pages, he was hooked. At that moment, a whole new world opened up him. Soon he would be reading more of Steinbeck, Hemingway, and Mark Twain, C.S. Forester, William Bradford Huie, and Robert Penn Warren.

148

"It's good," his grandfather said. "Jewish hands were made for carrying books, Jewish heads for studying them."

Then he was talking to Jake and Ben. David went quietly into the breakfast room to read. But Isaac wasn't paying much attention to his conversation that night. He was thinking about David with a book in his hand, about his own father, the scholar, and about himself.

The rabbi of Bogdanya sat at his bench, his head covered by a prayer shawl like an ancient. In front of him the Book of Piety fired his imagination and sent his senses reeling. Oblivious to others, the rabbi read aloud, starting in a whisper to himself, then louder until Channa could hear him through the wall.

As he intoned the Hebrew words, a tiny, unnoticed witness sat, watched, and listened as if hypnotized.

As long as his father read, Itzrok would sit and listen—hour after hour—without once diverting his gaze.

"Mama, it's as if he understands every word," Avrum once said.

"Don't be foolish," Channa scolded. "He's two years old, and you already have him understanding the Talmud. Is that the kind of nonsense you learn from the other boys at *cheder?*"

But still she wondered, too, and watched, as her Itzrok, the crippled baby on whom she focused all of her pity, sat and listened. Even the slightest mutterings seemed to be a source of fascination for the baby. Only when his father was away from the bench did he grow restive and begin to cry.

Hourly, nightly, with all her strength and hope, Channa begged God to give the baby strength.

"I am unworthy in your sight, oh God," she moaned. "I am as the smoke in the air that disappears and is no more at the slightest whim of the wind. I am willing to bear all suffering for my unworthiness, if it pleases You, but I beg You not to punish my baby, my Itzrok, for my failings."

Overhearing her once, the rabbi told her sharply that she should give thanks to God for all she had and never again question His will. But still, secretly, she prayed, pleading for strength for her youngest. And she waited for a miracle.

Itzrok Shulman's world was bounded by 12 walls which surrounded the three tiny rooms through which he dragged himself.

The room he knew least about was the one in which his parents slept. More familiar was the one that held the closely crowded straw pallets on which he and his brothers slept. There was no window in the tiny room, and the crumbling walls sweated and dripped water most of the year. The room, like his parents', was always dark, illuminated only briefly at night when the lantern cast its shadows about the cracks and recesses of the ceiling.

The third room, only slightly larger than the other two, was where he now sat watching his father. A thin, gray shaft of light streamed through the room's only window, falling across his father's shoulders.

The rabbi sat huddled over the room's only table, a rough-hewn wooden top mounted on unshaped wooden legs. Behind him an ancient sofa was set against a wall. The fabric, once flowered, had long since faded into a general, threadbare gray. The horsehair stuffing was visible in several places, having thrust itself through the binding under the weight of generations of sitters. Even the wooden frame was warped; but it still accommodated the men of the village who came to hear the rabbi render his judgments.

In the corner of the room nearest the window stood the cabinet which held the house's only treasure: the rabbi's books. Each was handled as tenderly by him as if it were an infant; his sons were forbidden to touch the books or even the cabinet on pain of a violent beating.

The oven occupied the far corner of the room. There, on a scrap of rug, Itzrok would take up his vigil to watch his father study and hear him read.

He had learned to talk before his first birthday, first by imitating his brothers' sounds and words. The more he learned, the more his brothers and Channa encouraged him to learn. At an age when his brothers had barely mastered the most basic words, tiny Itzrok was articulating complex thoughts.

"How can such thoughts come out of such a tiny head?" Uri asked his mother.

But Channa only shook her head. Months passed into years, and although Channa still prayed for a miracle, the boy could not walk.

His occasional trips out of doors were made on Avrum's shoulders. Although the younger brothers cared about the little, wasted boy, they were ordinarily too preoccupied to remember him.

Once, while playing in the fields, Uri and Motel came upon Reb Yussel Zarnetsky's goat, grazing on a short rope. For a while the boys contented themselves with tearing up handfuls of sweet grass and feeding them to the goat, watching, fascinated, as the grass was turned sideways in the thin mouth, ground by the yellow teeth, and then swallowed. Tiring of this game, Uri told Motel to wait for him, then he dashed back to the house for Itzrok.

"Come, Itzrok, you're only in Mama's way. Come out and see Reb Yussel's goat with his white beard."

Since Avrum was in cheder, Uri had to move his little brother

150

himself. He was not strong enough to carry him, so he arranged a heavy sack on which Itzrok could sit and be dragged. Itzrok straightened his withered legs and announced that he was ready to go, and Uri pulled him bumping over the doorsill and along the rough, unpaved street beyond. As always, Itzrok craned his head everywhere on its skinny neck, taking in all of the sights at once beyond the walls in which he was held prisoner by his lameness. To him, the huts and sheds were marvelous, the sky a miraculous blue vault, even the streets—rutted and strewn with garbage—a sight to behold. The several thicknesses of sacking under him cushioned the bumps and stones only slightly, but Itzrok was almost oblivious to discomfort.

"So much to see," he said quietly. As they progressed slowly through the streets, the thin Uri pulling the tiny cripple behind him on a sack, heads turned; Jews who knew them sadly shook their heads and murmured into their beards; two coarse peasants laughed to each other. Uri heard the laughter and thought bitterly about it, but Itzrok only craned his neck the more, looking at the world. In the middle of the village, he became particularly excited. Here people went about their commerce, this one loading a droshky with scrap, that one carrying bags of wheat into the nogid's granary, another setting up his stall with scallions and potatoes and beets.

Through an open door the boy saw a baker pull loaves of white bread from his oven on a long, flat stick, and smelled the rich aroma of cakes.

Here Uri paused, out of breath, kneeling beside his brother.

"Here is the best place in the town, Itzrok," he said. "Smell the babka and the rugelah in the baker's oven. Just to smell it is paradise!"

"Have you ever eaten the baker's rugelah?" Itzrok asked quietly.

The older boy shook his head. "No, little brother, but someday I'll earn enough to buy all the rugelah we can eat. You'll see."

Itzrok only smiled his quiet, strange smile, then they were off again.

Near the edge of town they encountered the fisherman, Shaya, the box on his little wagon piled high with fresh fish. Itzrok stared at the gaping mouths of the carp and pickerel on the wagon. Seeing this, Shaya—normally a brutish, argumentative man—called his shaggy horse to a stop. Getting down from his seat, Shaya reached for the largest carp.

"What do you think of this beauty?" he asked Itzrok. "Has there ever been a finer fish?"

The smell of Shaya was the smell of his fish. When he came to the synagogue every morning, the other men pulled slightly away, for even the fisherman's best gabardines smelled of ripe carp. The women of the village all hated Shaya because of his sharp tongue and rough ways. Even Channa, the wife of the rabbi, was not immune to his sarcasm when she came to buy a fish. Only on the High Holy Days did Shaya seem to soften in his ways. Uri had heard his mother say that Shaya would rather leave his fish on the riverbank to rot than give one to the poorest starveling in the village. But the sight of Itzrok—pale, crippled, dragged in a sack—seemed to stir his compassion.

"Look at the teeth in this one," the fisherman said. "Did you know, little one, that the pickerel's teeth are sharp enough to cut the net?" But Itzrok did not answer. His gaze was held by the long, thin fish, dappled in fading yellow and green.

"Does it hurt the fish to die?" he asked gravely.

Shaya started to laugh, then turned serious.

"It is God's will," he answered, "that some must die so that others may live."

As the children watched the fisherman's wagon disappear down the road, Itzrok asked Uri:

"How does Reb Shaya know that is God's will?"

Uri only shrugged.

"Such large questions for such a little *boitshick!*"

Then they were off again toward the field and Reb Yussel's goat with the white beard and yellow teeth. As he dragged his burden, Uri thought of rugelah. And Itzrok thought of dead fish.

When their father was at home his sons moved about quietly, spoke almost in whispers, except when spoken to by him or by Channa. When he sat at the bench with his books, even Channa moved about on tiptoe. And when his opinions were sought by the townspeople, the children were usually banished, along with Channa, to the next room.

The quick anger of the rabbi was as familiar inside his house as was his wisdom outside it. A twisted ear, a slap was never new or unexpected to his sons; Channa had acquainted them with such from the earliest time they could remember. But for the rabbi, a slap never sufficed. When angered, he would mete out such punishment that Channa often feared he would kill the child.

Avrum bore most of the brunt of his father's rage. If he was not the direct cause of the problem, as the oldest son he should have prevented it. And blows were rained on him with open hand, fist, and strap that could be heard several houses away.

Silently and with almost infinite resignation, Avrum would stand the beating, neither questioning nor flinching. When the rabbi had worn out his anger, Arvum would walk away with as much dignity as was left him.

Avrum was a disappointment to his father. At the celebration of his first son's circumcision, the rabbi had envisioned a fine future for him, one of scholarship and learning. As celebrants sipped the tiny cups of wine and ate the fish with him, one after another had wished the rabbi the best of good fortune, may it please the Lord, for this fine son who would follow his father's example.

"With such a father," one said, "the son must be destined at least for the chief rabbinate of Odessa."

"Already one can see the intelligence burning in his eyes," another said.

"Ah, rabbi, he will embarrass the other boys at cheder with his scholarship," another told him.

All of this the rabbi hoped himself, and he encouraged the boy at his studies as the years passed. But always Avrum fell short of his father's expectations.

When he asked Michael, the melamed who was Avrum's teacher, about the boy's progress, the melamed always seemed to answer evasively.

"How do your young scholars get on this week?" he would ask.

"As always, rabbi," Michael would answer with a sigh. "Most learn like peasants; one or two give hope."

"And Avrum?"

"Ah," the melamed would say, "no boy tries harder." Or he might say, "none takes his studies more seriously." Or even, "when the others clamor out like wild animals at the end of class, Avrum stays to read or to clarify a point."

"And his progress?" the rabbi would ask.

"He is trying," was the answer, and nothing more.

When he visited the cheder, the rabbi found little more that was encouraging. The melamed would get flustered as he entered, the children attentive. The rabbi would ask to hear the boys recite, and one after another would be called to the bookstand. Some read poorly, some well. The son of Joachnin, the shamus, read with golden tongue. Avrum was never one of the better ones. So Avrum was punished at home.

"*Yold,*" the rabbi would shout. "Learn from my strap if you cannot learn from the books."

Once Channa intervened during a particularly savage beating.

"For the love of God, you'll kill him," she pleaded.

Only then did the rabbi release the nearly unconscious child, glaring menacingly at the others as the boy crumpled to the ground. Weeping quietly, Channa gathered the boy into her arms as her husband left the room.

Rocking him in silence, she felt as she seldom did the bitterness and barrenness of her own life. "A good boy," she crooned over and over again, holding Avrum's bleeding face close to her breast.

As his sons grew older, the rabbi realized that Uri and Motel would also disappoint him. Despite his bleak surroundings, Uri grew to be the happy one, managing to find humor in the grimmest circumstances. The boy was handsome, only slightly shorter than the brooding Avrum, with bright eyes, a ready smile over even teeth, a sturdy shock of black hair growing carelessly over his forehead. Uri laughed at the world: his studies, a meager meal of herring and black bread, even the slaps that earlier mirth earned him.

"He has a rare gift for laughter," Michael told his father. "He brightens the world with his smile."

"And what will my fine comedian grow to be? A cigarette-maker, a keeper of cows, God forbid?"

"But, rabbi, you yourself have taught us that the Jewish facility for laughing at our troubles has helped us to survive our persecutions."

The rabbi only shook his head and left the synagogue, reminded by the melamed of his business with Uri.

Motel, the third son, attracted to himself no pity for his slowness. Although he tried, he could not keep pace with the other boys. His mind grasped the alphabet and released it; his memory for blessings was poor, his ability for reading even poorer. He would repeat the words over and over again to himself, grimly determined to remember; but they would slip away from him like Reb Yussel's goat, leaving only blurred remnants of parts of words in their places.

"Such a good boy," the melamed would sigh. "But his memory is like a sieve."

To the rabbi, he could only say that Motel had no head for learning.

"Three fools and a cripple you've borne me," the rabbi would rage at Channa. "Three fools and a cripple."

"My husband," Channa replied, "you show such patience and compassion in settling disputes. Cannot you spare a little for your own sons?"

This only caused him to rage more, sending all of the sons but Itzrok fleeing before his wrath. But Itzrok stayed; he listened and heard.

As Avrum grew in height and strength, so did his compassion for his youngest brother. Itzrok became his pupil. With infinite patience Avrum repeated the *Alef-Beis*, the prayers, the holy chants. Itzrok's interest never seemed to waver, and he learned with remarkable speed.

154

At the beginning of his third year Itzrok surprised the family at the evening meal by reciting the *hamotzi*—the prayer over the bread—perfectly. By the time he was four, he had mastered the alphabet and was reading. At five he could recite from the Talmud, chanting with fine rhythm.

Throughout the town, the men heard of Itzrok's attainments, and many came to hear him.

"Read for Reb Yakov," the rabbi would say, and the small boy would select a passage and read.

"A miracle," Reb Yakov would murmur. "I'm hearing it with my ears, rabbi, and still I cannot believe what I hear. But surely this is something he has memorized."

"Not at all," the rabbi would answer. "Go, select something yourself and test the boy."

Then Reb Yakov, or whoever the visitor was that day, would select a passage and hand it down to the floor where the crippled boy propped himself up on one arm.

". . . other songs have been sung by a sage, but this was sung by a sage who was the son of a sage . . ." the boy would read flawlessly, and the visitor would only shake his head.

"How can he be other than a great rabbi someday?" he would ask. And Rabbi Mordecai Shulman would shake his head bitterly.

"And how will he lead his congregants? From the floor like a broken dog that drags his hindquarters?"

No longer noticed, Itzrok would drag himself to his place by the stove, his large, luminous eyes clouding over. Later Avrum would try to console him.

"Don't be hurt, little one. It is only his way. He really prizes your mind over all our strength—over all six legs of his other sons put together."

"I must walk, Avrum. I must walk."

"Don't talk foolishness," Avrum would say tenderly, smoothing the boy's hair over his forehead with his big hand. "It is not willed by the Almighty."

"Then I am nothing more than a dog that drags his hindquarters."

"You are nothing of the kind. You are a fine, smart boy who someday will reflect glory on your family."

"I must walk," Itzrok repeated stubbornly. "Avrum, help me to walk."

For days the question burned in Avrum's mind: can the cripple be made to walk? To him it was not merely a question of musculature, bone structure, and nerve endings; rather, it was a philosophical question to be approached in reading and prayer, a matter which may have its solution in the mysticism of the holy scripts as well as, or better than, the hands of the healers.

The melamed, Michael, quoted the Talmud, telling Avrum that all things were possible through God, that the best tonic for the cripple, the blind, the leprous was a deep and enduring belief in God and a righteous path in life.

Avrum considered what the melamed told him and spent many agonizing hours in the icy room behind the synagogue, pondering the texts by candlelight. Finally he decided to talk to the Jewish doctor, Reb Chaim Berkov, as well.

"Lameness can have many causes," the doctor said. "Perhaps an inherited defect, or a fever, or rickets caused by diet. One cannot know without an examination."

Avrum begged him to see the boy. "I have no money," he pleaded, "but I would work at any chore in return for such an examination by the learned doctor."

After some hesitation the doctor agreed. The next day Itzrok was brought into the examining room on his brother's shoulders.

A numbing terror swept through Itzrok's body like a cold wind. The room was small, decorated only with framed diplomas hanging on the walls. On the shelves were strange books in dark bindings, along with bottles, syringes, and tins. In the middle of the room stood a high table to which the doctor motioned Avrum. At the four corners of the table, lamps were suspended from the ceiling; they bathed the doctor's face in an eerie glow as he bent over Itzrok.

Then gentle hands were on his legs, carefully probing the weak muscles, pinching the ankles, manipulating the knees and toes. A pin pricked the bottom of Itzrok's feet, and the doctor studied his face carefully to see how he winced with the prick.

"Hm . . . good . . ." the doctor said and jabbed him again with the pin. For a few more minutes he manipulated the joints of the boy's legs. Then, satisfied, he turned away from him to talk to Avrum.

"I see no physical reason why he cannot walk. His legs are thin, weak, but the nerves are alive and the muscles functional. Perhaps he had the fever as an infant and then never learned to walk."

Joy swept over Avrum such as he had never felt before.

"And how shall he be made to walk, doctor?"

"Well, it will be painful and slow for him," the doctor said. "But his legs must be exercised. You must massage them to stimulate the muscles. It may help to soak them in hot poultices, but mostly you must work to strengthen the muscles."

Avrum gathered up Itzrok in his strong arms, thanking the doctor profusely as he did so.

As they were leaving the office, the doctor called a warning after them.

"The boy will have to want to walk very badly in order to ever do so."

That winter was unusually severe. Deep snows blanketed the frozen fields around Bogdanya. A heavy glaze of ice coated the streets and huts along Czwernieski Street and sparrows froze to death, toppling from their perches in the bare trees.

Avrum was notified that he would be required to leave for Minsk in the spring for military service. He had long ago completed *cheder*, and since there was no money for him to go to Yeshiva, he read all day in the synagogue with the other poor boys.

The study room was always cold, damp, lit only dimly by bits of burning candles. Every day Avrum took up his position at a prayer stand in the eastern corner, reading more out of a sense of obligation to his father than a desire for learning. One thought preoccupied him as he mechanically chanted the psalms: I must make Itzrok walk before spring.

He had long since admitted to himself that he was no scholar, that he would never be able to follow his father's example. In his brother, Itzrok, he had sublimated all of his own hopes. He, Avrum, would be content to be a laborer if by his efforts his small brother might someday achieve distinction. After all, Avrum allowed himself to think with pride, had he alone not tutored Itzrok from infancy, helping him develop a mind that men came many versts to marvel at?

Now he must go further; he must help Itzrok develop the proper temple in which to house such a precious gift.

But progress was slow. The night after the doctor had pronounced the legs alive, Avrum had begun, clumsily at first. He lifted Itzrok to his feet, holding his light body erect, and implored him to move his legs, to lock his knees, to move his feet, if only the slightest bit.

In the light of the stove Avrum could see the beads of sweat standing out on the boy's brow and lips as he tried and tried again with no success.

One night followed another, with Avrum massaging the calves and thighs until the muscles in his strong hands ached almost beyond endurance. Poultice followed hot poultice, until the little boy could no longer stand the pain.

"It's a good sign, the pain," Avrum would say. "It means the muscles are alive and responding."

They set an objective: that Itzrok, without assistance, would raise either foot off the ground from his prone position on his back. Together, they struggled toward this goal week after week.

"Try, try, my little one," Avrum would urge. "Try again and pray that God will help you."

And so they worked, tried, prayed for the same miracle Channa had long since abandoned hope for.

Uri, now apprenticed to a silversmith, would lighten the strain with a bright word of encouragement, a quick smile, a joke. Motel amused himself with his carving. He resented both Itzrok's learning and Avrum's lack of attention to him, so he stayed away. With his pocketknife, he carved beautiful menorahs, mogendovids, and other designs; since these attracted grudging praise from his father, it was enough.

Itzrok's legs became Avrum's life. He begged him to eat more to gain strength, gave him the best portions of his own meager meals, and bloodied a peasant man who laughed at the sight of Itzrok being drawn on a makeshift sled.

He was finally rewarded with the sight he had so longed hoped to see. As he wrapped his wool scarf around his head one morning, he heard Itzrok call to him.

"Avrum, Avrum, please come quickly. Please hurry!"

In the next room Avrum found Itzrok holding his right foot several inches off the ground, sweat pouring down his neck and staining his blouse, his pale face even whiter than usual. Tears of joy welled in Avrum's eyes, and he fought to control the emotion in his voice.

"You're going to walk, little brother. God has smiled on you, strengthened you. You're going to walk."

Then he was down on his knees, kissing the boy's head, sobbing into his hair and patting his thin shoulders.

In the synagogue that day the others noticed a change in Avrum's voice. As he chanted, his voice rang clearly and resoundingly as a bell. When he made his *brochas,* the words came alive as if the fingers of God had reached into his breast and touched his heart.

When spring came Avrum packed his few belongings—a shirt, an extra pair of pants, his prayer shawl and phylacteries, and several prayer books into a sack—and left for Minsk and the hated military service of the Tsar.

Many Jewish boys from the village had made this journey. Some never returned. Others came back in short jackets, clean-shaven, with blasphemy on their lips and "enlightenment" in their hearts. Their talk was of secular books, of revolution, of a socialist paradise in which the workers would be revered and the rich brought to their knees. But a few came back unchanged, returning to the old ways.

For several hours the rabbi sat in quiet conversation with his first born. The rabbi displayed the closest semblance of tenderness toward him Avrum could remember, as he warned him of the temptations that lay ahead and entreated him to remember his Jewish background and heritage.

"God is the central meaning in life, and the only reality for a Jew," his father said. "Lose God from your heart and you have lost everything."

Channa clung to the neck of her oldest son. She had packed hard-boiled eggs, dried figs, an onion, black bread, and a small fish for him to eat along his way. As she did so, she cried to think of Avrum in the Tsar's barracks.

Uri clapped his back, winked, and envied Avrum his experience, not the military, of course, but the freedom of traveling, of new ways, and of putting Bogdanya, choked as it was with smoke and poverty, behind him.

He gave his older brother a gift for which he had saved, a heavy woolen scarf to wear under his uniform.

"Soon you will follow me," Avrum said clumsily. "I'll save a bed for you in my barracks."

Motel gave Avrum a tiny, carved replica of their house to remind him of home, and Avrum promised to get him some brass uniform buttons in return.

He saved his farewell to Itzrok for last, for it would be the most painful to him. The boy was distraught at his leaving. Indeed, he felt he was leaving the largest part of himself locked in the small body of his brother. All of his dreams, his plans, his hopes had gone into Itzrok, whom he believed to be destined for greatness.

For months the little one had known his greatest happiness and contentment when he worked with his powerful, older brother, even when the work was painful. The prospect of life without him was almost unbearably bleak and lonely. Avrum had been his teacher, his friend, his legs, his principal source of hope and encouragement.

From the moment Itzrok had raised his foot from the floor, Avrum had approached the boy's therapy with even more intense concentration. Over a period of time they had made the ankles and knees more responsive, the muscles more accustomed to motion. As the time for departure had neared, Avrum had worked at fever pitch, sometimes forgetting the pain of the boy momentarily, as he tried to enable him to stand, believing, as he did, that if he did not accomplish this feat before he left, it would never be accomplished. Even on the night before he left, Avrum had not given up until he collapsed on his straw pallet far into the morning hours, too exhausted to continue.

Thrusting the carved model into his pocket, Avrum turned back toward the interior of the house to find Itzrok. As he turned, a thin voice called out to him: "I too have a present for you, Avrum."

It was Itzrok, standing as uncertainly as a newborn foal, on his own two legs, for the first time in his life. Avrum caught him in his arms as the boy collapsed. His voice breaking with emotion, Avrum said he would never receive a greater gift. Then he could say no more. Patting the boy's thin shoulders, as he had done so many times before, Avrum turned and hurriedly left the house.

The next year passed swiftly for Itzrok Shulman. He learned to walk and then to run. His life expanded outside the hut in which he had spent almost the entirety of his first seven years. Learning quickly became the central motif in his life, religion the highest moment. He came to know the people in the town as they pursued their everyday lives. Most were poor, underfed, clad in patched coats, frayed skullcaps, and shabby shoes. They struggled to stay alive, to put food on the table, to have a bit extra for the Sabbath—this one selling vegetables, that one stitching work clothes, another tutoring a few students.

In them, Itzrok began to see the essential, nonintellectual meaning of Jewishness. They were, he understood, not broken by their poor circumstances, not sunken by poverty into melancholy or degeneracy. Instead they celebrated Psalms, thanked God for His blessings, and rejoiced with happiness that came from their souls.

In the synagogue, when the scrolls were lifted from the Ark, Itzrok began to understand that the Jews had little other than Torah, but that Torah, somehow, was all they needed.

"Blessed be Thou who hast chosen us among all nations and given us the Torah . . ." they sang, and the song was one of joy. The historical scheme for the Jew was one of suffering, starvation, torture, even death by the millions—and still they celebrated joyously. The cup of today always seemed to be bitter for the Jew. From it he was constantly forced to drink to the dregs; yet his face always turned to tomorrow and his countenance was brightened by it.

"*Sh'ma yisroayl adonoy elohaynu, adonoy ehod*," they sang. "Hear, Oh Israel, the Lord our God, the Lord is One."

From the heart of history's ghettos, from the worst pain and suffering, from the depths of the worst pogroms, the *Sh'ma yisroayls* always could be heard, sung with exultation. All of this Itzrok Shulman came to understand to his marrow, to feel as other Jews had felt before him for generations.

Outside the synagogue, the town and the fields became his province. Once his legs were strong, he wanted to be everywhere at once, to see everything and learn everything. What other boys took for

160

granted were wonders to him. He explored the twisting streets and alleys of the village for hours. For him, walking itself was a precious experience—never a waste of time, no matter where it took him.

He came to know every store, every house, sign and vegetable stand in the village. He fixed each in his mind, attributing to it its own special significance. To a man released from prison, every stone and ditch outside its walls is beautiful; so it was with Itzrok Shulman when the bondage of his crippled legs was finally broken.

The deep snows, the warm, spring winds, the slanting rainstorms of summer—all were a joy to Itzrok. The tiniest hut, the dirty alley that twisted around it and disappeared into a hole in the ground, were of interest.

Michael, the melamed, told the rabbi that never had he seen such a mind as Itzrok's.

"He comes to me ahead of most boys I have taught for three years," he said. "Surely he will fulfill your greatest expectations."

As the boy progressed, the rabbi seemed to soften, his unrelenting, stern demeanor at home beginning to relax.

Coming home on military leave at the end of a year, Avrum had immediately noticed the difference. His father greeted him warmly, taking his son's hand in both of his, clapping him on the shoulder, and calling him "my son."

Avrum seemed taller and straighter than before. Channa called in the neighbors to see how handsome her son looked in his uniform with the rows of bright buttons and high boots.

For Itzrok every moment of Avrum's leave was to be guarded jealously. They sat together for hours, with Avrum talking of the wonders he had seen: a huge locomotive with steel wheels and a smokestack belching clouds; buildings that seemed to reach the clouds, with row upon row of windows on all sides; wide, paved avenues which could accommodate eight droshkys across; sailing vessels that skimmed the river like birds in flight. He drew vivid pictures of military life, describing in great detail the stench of the barracks, the endless drilling, the second-class citizenship of the Jewish soldiers; the unremitting cruelty of the sergeants toward them.

"For a simple ox like me," he told his brother, "the army is only barely acceptable. But you, little brother, must at all costs avoid it."

Avrum's furlough seemed to evaporate, and soon they were saying goodbye again. Itzrok tried to find words that would express his gratitude for all that had passed, but Avrum interrupted him.

"There is no debt, little brother. You are a scholar and I planted the seeds of scholarship in your mind; you have legs and I helped you find them. I see you walk, I hear you recite—what other thanks could I possibly ask? God has been kind to me.

In his 10th year Itzrok Shulman was helping other boys in the cheder, some of whom were already preparing for their bar mitz-vahs. At 12 he had progressed beyond the point where the melamed could teach him further.

All of Rabbi Mordecai Shulman's plans were now predicated on Itzrok's attending the Yeshiva at Pinsk. From his own meager earn-ings, the rabbi pinched a few groschen here, a half ruble there, against the time when his son would be ready. Itzrok, too, was taken with dreaming of the Yeshiva. What pictures he painted in his mind: ... study rooms with inexhaustible supplies of books; professors with the wisdom of the ages to share with him; other boys of understand-ing to learn with, to argue the Talmud with; a great synagogue in which to pray. . . .

He described all this to a happy Channa. She was a good woman, plain in appearance with close-set eyes, a large nose, and a square jaw. In her burned a depth of feeling for her children, but most of all, for her youngest, which overwhelmed even her sense of duty and obligation to her husband. Years before, she had accepted the defects in her children as uniquely her own fault.

"Three fools and a cripple," her husband had called them many times, and this made Channa's whole reason for being questionable in her mind. When Itzrok had shown such precocity as a tiny child, she had been given a new lease on dignity, at least a ray of hope for some fulfillment. When he had dragged himself up from the floor and begun to walk, the ray became a sudden burst of light in her life. And so it burned brightly for her now.

For hours on end she would sit soundlessly, watching him at his studies, always smiling slightly as her eyes followed the turn of a page, her ears heard the chants or simply imagined sounds that might be emanating from her son were he not reading to himself.

Itzrok was not made uncomfortable by her gaze as others might have been. He had grown accustomed to it by now; in fact, her reverence for his work was pleasing to him. He frequently read aloud for her benefit. Even the words she could not understand were music to her ears.

These were the happiest times in Channa's life. But God had not willed sustained pleasure as her lot. Her husband became ill and as the weeks passed, grew progressively worse. It had begun insidi-ously, with occasional headaches that gradually became more fre-quent.

"Perhaps you read too much," Channa suggested.

"And shall I stop reading?" her husband asked. "What then will be my life?"

So he pored over his books, trying to ignore the growing pain.

At first, a night's sleep relieved him, but gradually the pain extended into the nights, making sleep difficult. When he did fall asleep, it was restless and unrefreshing. Night after night Channa lay quietly beside him, hearing him mumble, feeling him tearing at the mattress.

The rabbi believed that God was testing his faith. He prayed that, above all else, he would be worthy in God's eyes.

"I have thought evil thoughts, done less than I might for the poor, been impatient with the ignorant, even less patient with my own children."

"What were you saying?" Channa asked gently, stirring from her sleep.

"Nothing."

"Does it hurt now?"

"Only a little. Go to sleep."

And so the nights passed. At times he felt a sudden, unexpected tenderness for his wife and the children she had borne him. At other times he could hardly endure the pressure pulsating against the inside of his skull, and he could feel nothing else. Regardless of his will and his trust in God, he felt himself sink into deep pits of depression and melancholy, so that for hours he could only sit and brood.

At other times a sudden sense of happiness and well-being would come over him, not just as he read or led services, but at the most ordinary moments.

Everyone noticed, Channa most acutely.

"How strangely our beloved rabbi acts these days," Rachmael, the butcher, said. "He seems to be a different man from day to day."

"Ah yes," sighed the shamus. "One wonders if the rabbi has not seen sights we have not been privileged to see."

Always the pain returned, throbbing at his temples, stabbing at the backs of his eyes. The doctor's nostrums, which had helped at first, soon grew ineffective. A deeply compassionate man, the doctor cursed the limitations, the inexactness, of his science, and reviewed over and over again the symptoms for possible clues that would help the man of God.

For months it remained thus, with only the rabbi knowing the degree to which the pains had grown. Finally it became so severe that he left Channa's room, even on Friday night, the night of union. He preferred to toss on the straw mattress Avrum had occupied, which was placed on the floor near the oven.

When he slept, Channa heard his mumbling, usually incoherent but sometimes quite clear. She listened to hear her own name but was always disappointed. Sensing death, she now sought some sign —even the mumbling of a painridden, restless man in his sleep—that she had not failed him and that, in his way, he cared for her.

163

Three names she did hear: God, Avrum, and Itzrok. Time after time she made out fragments of his confessions of failure in God's eyes. Of Itzrok he muttered pieces of prayers that, if it please Him, God should look down on the boy with compassion, to guide him in the paths of righteousness and the lessons of the Torah. Of Avrum he only begged God's forgiveness.

"Take a little soup," she pleaded.

"I have no appetite now," he answered.

"A little tea with a sugar cube, then, to keep up your strength."

"No, not even that."

"Let me heat a glass of milk, then."

"My stomach will only turn it back."

The rabbi had grown as frayed as his jacket, so thin that he appeared to be a skeleton covered with wax skin. He never left his bed now, and his days were filled with longer and longer periods of meditation. His many visitors were turned away with but few exceptions. Those who came spoke quietly, soon finding that they had nothing left to say other than their felicitations.

"How are you, learned rabbi?"

"I am useless now, in God's eyes. Just another mouth to feed."

"Please don't say that. All of us depend on you as our spiritual leader, our teacher."

"And how shall I lead or teach from this bed?"

"It is enough that we know you are here, that you are our advocate to the Almighty."

"Not now, but soon."

Those who came away said they had noticed a strange light in his eyes, a mystical look in his face. Weak, painridden—still, some said, a power issued from him.

"May God forgive me, it is almost as if he had already died," the shamus said.

Finally he refused further medication, concerned that his illness was robbing Itzrok's chances of going to Yeshiva. But the few rubles he had saved were quickly vanishing. No one could bear to tell him that a young rabbi from the Yeshiva at Minsk had been brought to his synagogue to lead them. The meager contents of the poor box went to Rabbi Shulman's care, but little else. After all, did not the new rabbi need sustenance? Should not he receive a few rubles to keep body and soul together?

After the first year even the gifts at Purim and Chanukah were diverted from the Shulman house.

In the second year of the rabbi's illness, Channa sent Itzrok out to work in order that he could eat. She stayed with her husband, only desiring now to attend him.

164

"A saint," she would say. And little more. And she also grew thinner and paler as she watched Mordecai Shulman's strength ebb away.

One night she was awakened by her husband's voice, stronger than it had been for some time.

"Avrum," he was calling, "Avrum, come closer so we can see you."

Channa ran into the room, only to find her husband staring into air.

"Mama, Papa," he said, "Look at Avrum, my eldest. See how straight and tall he is."

"There is no one here, my husband," Channa said, but he didn't hear her. There was a strange intensity in his face, illuminated even more by the candle burning on the table above him. His eyes were wide and hopeful, a smile played on his lips.

Then he sat up, held out his arms, began to sob.

"I have tried, Papa, but I failed in many ways."

"Mordecai, there . . ." Channa began, then suddenly realized what was happening. Her husband lay back, slipping slowly to the mattress, a half smile on his lips.

Even as he closed his eyes, he saw them still—his mother and father, standing by his bench while he read.

"I tried to . . . God, my God . . . blessed art thou . . . Avrum is a good boy . . . tell him . . . blessed art. . . ."

Now the mutterings became weaker, less coherent. Channa threw herself across her husband's legs, clinging to him.

"Don't leave me, Mordecai, please." she sobbed.

"Channa, Channa, are you there?" he asked weakly. "Tell Avrum. . . ."

A single wail rent the night air along Czwernieski Street. Mordecai Shulman, rabbi of Bogdanya, had slipped from his burdens and gone to his God.

In his bed that Friday night, Isaac lay thinking of his father. What would it mean to him that his youngest son had acquired wealth and respect among the *goyim* in Somerset, South Carolina? Nothing. Nothing at all. He had left all but the most basic tenets of his faith. He no longer *davened* every night. He ate *traif* like the crudest Russian peasant. He had allowed his own children to grow up like *shaigetzes*, with no learning or understanding of the Torah and the law, no love of scholarship, no Jewish values. Jake, the bull, who brought his father vain pride when he clubbed another young man senseless in a boxing ring or broke another's bones on the football field. Aaron, quiet and gentle, who might have been a scholar if he,

Isaac, had had time for him, to teach him as he had taught others in Bogdanya so many years ago. But he had not found time. There was the slaughterhouse to run, rents to collect, meetings of directors at the bank, the cattle business. And Irving, what of him? Was he a reminder from God that he himself had been weak in body once? That the compassion and caring of Avrum had been required for him to walk? A question posed in flesh and blood—his own—about his own ability to care? He put the discomforting thought out of his mind after awhile. As he dropped off to sleep he was thinking of his grandson, David, sitting alone in the parlor, reading a book.

21

"There ain't enough Jews in this town," Mel Fleisher said.

"What does that mean, there ain't enough Jews?" Isaac Shulman asked him.

Fleisher sighed dramatically.

"You know what I mean, Isaac. What do I have to do, draw you a picture?"

"What if each paid according to his ability? Would there be enough then?" Isaac persisted.

"I knew it," Fleisher said, throwing up his hands. "I knew it would come to me paying more than my share." He knew the argument was over, so now he would bait his old friend a bit more for the fun of it.

"This synogogue you want to build, Isaac. Why all of a sudden you got the building bug? The room over the grocery store was always good enough for us—till now."

Some of the others caught the twinkle in Mel's eye and joined the fun.

"Yeah, Isaac, what's the rush? The idea only came up last week, and now, we gotta vote already," Morty Levine said. "Why not wait awhile and think about it?"

For a moment Isaac looked across the room at Ben Harris, who had missed the joke; then he looked at Mel Fleisher and started to laugh.

"You're an old rat in the barn, Mel," he said. "Can't fool you, can I?"

167

"Nu, Isaac, what's that supposed to mean?" But he was grinning, too.

"All right, so my first grandson is being bar mitzvahed in a year, and I want him to say his haftorah in a shul, not a grocery store loft. That's such a crime?"

Before the others could speak, he continued. "You, Mel, you don't have grandchildren? You, Hy, you don't have a daughter to confirm? Or you, Mort?"

"Not right away," Hy Goldstein said.

"It doesn't matter. Soon you will," Isaac said. "Besides, it would be so terrible for us to get together like *mentshen* in a shul on Yom Kippur? Or have a decent place for Friday night prayers? Even in Russia we had a shul, even when all the Jews were starving."

"Never mind Russia," Mel grumbled. "How much is all this gonna cost us?"

"$32,000, maybe a little less," Isaac said. "I already got rough plans, building estimates, and a mortgage."

"How come you have . . ." Mel began.

"Because I contributed the first $10,000 and put it in the Building and Loan this morning," Isaac said, smiling.

The workmen placed the last ceiling tiles the day before David's bar mitzvah. He had ridden 110 miles round trip on a bus six days a week for seven months to be tutored by the rabbi; as he sang the final blessing, the look on his grandfather's face told him he had performed well. In the first row, his parents, Jennifer, and his grandparents sat together, and behind, in the second row, the rest of the family. The mayor was there, sitting with Dr. Holden and his family, and Mr. Ray Cranfield, the president of the bank, was there with his wife. It seemed to David that every important person in Somerset was there. After it was all over, they crowded around him, the men patting him on the back and the women kissing him and handing him envelopes he knew contained money.

"Boy, I'm gonna be rich," he whispered to Jennifer, and she laughed and hugged him.

"I'm so proud of you, Davey—or is it David, now that you're a man?"

"It's whatever you want it to be," he said. "Did Ruth hear me?"

"Yes, she was right in that doorway the whole time, smiling away," his sister answered.

He sought her out then, and to her embarrassment, hugged her.

"Davey," she said, "yo' sho was somethin' up there. Somethin' else. All dressed up and sayin' all that so good, jus' lak a preacher."

"I reckon he did," Lucy chimed in. "Hard to b'lieve David knowed all 'at business, an' him jus' a baby, seems lak wad'n no time,

168

visitin' his granmomma's house. Yo' granpoppa's fit to bust, he so happy today."

Then the guests were filing into the big reception room, and Ruth and Lucy were busy serving. All of the relatives and close family friends had brought covered dishes, and guests were heard to remark that the buffet was sumptuous.

David talked with his mother for a few minutes, in one of the new Sunday school classrooms, and she told him, her eyes gleaming with pleasure, how proud he had made the family, how wonderfully he had said his haftorah.

"This town will remember that service a long time," she said gaily. "Just like it still remembers my wedding."

"Seems like the whole town was here," he said.

"What's more important, David, is that everybody who is here loves you and respects this family."

"Yessum, I guess."

"You don't have to guess, son. You know it for a fact. Just look at how they turned out."

For a moment he looked down at his shoes, then looked back into Rachel's eyes. He hadn't expected to say it, but somehow, he felt he had to.

"Mom," he confided, "it was a little bit embarrassing. I mean, standing up there in front of the whole town saying my Hebrew."

"Why, I . . ."

"Tell the truth," he interrupted. "I kinda wish only the Jewish people had come."

Then he looked down again, studying the scuff marks he hadn't been able to get out of his new shoes.

She understood, but she couldn't let it drop. There was something too important to be said now. She reached out and lifted up his chin until they were looking into each other's eyes.

"It's over, David. The war is over and the anti-Semitism is over and your problems in this town are over. Everybody's let it slip into the past now. Everybody but you."

"Mom, I don't think . . ."

But she stopped him.

"David, listen to me. This is a good town. It's always been good to us. To Papa and Mamma and your dad and me and your Uncle Jake —to all of us. For a little while, things went kinda haywire when the war started, but it's over with. I know it hurt, son, but it's over now. You've just got to forget it and live your life. If it wasn't over, would all these people be here?"

"You just don't know how it is," he said quietly, his eyes downcast again.

"Yes, I do, David. I always did. I cried myself to sleep many a night because of how it was. Many a night. But all the wars are over, David. Yours, too, if you'll just let it be."

"I'll try, Mom," he said. Then he turned at the sound of the door opening.

Isaac said he wanted to talk to David alone, and Rachel nodded and left the room. David stood uncomfortably, not knowing what to say. Then his grandfather held out his hand. As he always had, he began to squeeze David's hand, but now the boy's hand was too large and strong to be crushed. David smiled and squeezed back, not hurting his grandfather's hand, but not having his own hurt, either. Isaac laughed his high-pitched cackle.

"So, Dovidl, today you are a man, eh?"

"Yes sir, I guess so," the boy answered.

"And what does it all mean to you—the service, the haftorah, all of it?"

David didn't know how to answer.

"I'll tell you what it means, Dovidl. It means that Judaism is still alive. Not just here. All over the world, Jewish boys are saying haftorahs and having their first aliyahs. What it says is that we haven't been destroyed, not all of us—and we never will be. Try as they might, the worst haters in the world—Haman, Pharoah, Hitler, none of them—they can't put out the light of our faith. You hear that, Dovidl?"

"Yes sir."

"You get a lot of gifts today, Dovidl?"

"I sure did, Grandpa."

"Well, let me tell you the greatest gift of all. You got your Jewish manhood. Keep it, Dovidl. Be proud of it. Someday, when I'm dead, you'll inherit part of my money and my buildings. You'll inherit your father's farms when he is dead. But today, you received the most precious legacy of all, Dovidl. You inherited your place in the world as a Jewish man. History gave it to you, and custom and tradition, and your God did, Dovidl. Believe it, and believe *in* it—and keep your faith. From Abraham and Isaac and Jacob and all the fathers of our fathers, Dovidl, you inherited it. Fight for it. If you have to, die for it. It's the central fact in your life; it gives meaning to the rest. It ain't so bad to be a Jew, Dovidl, not really. When it's bad is when you let yourself stop being what you are."

For a moment the old man and the boy stood looking at each other. Then Isaac's voice softened.

"Do you know the last words my mother ever spoke to me?" he asked.

"No sir, I don't."

"At the dock, as I was getting on the boat to come to America, she said: '*Abe du vest gehen nach Amerika und bleiben en guten Yid, gai gezunter hait; abe nicht, soll das shiff arunter gehen, und sollst de varen dertrunken!*'"

David could understand only one or two words, so his grandfather translated: "In English, what that means is that if you keep your Jewishness, your faith, may you reach America in safety and find happiness there. But if you are going to give it up, I hope the ship sinks and you drown in the ocean."

The boy stood looking up at his grandfather, his gaze fixed on the old man's face. What Isaac had said seemed to him to be out of context with the happiness of the day. He wondered what had moved him to tell about the incident.

"Is that what you're saying to me, Grandpa? That I should die if I don't keep my Jewishness?"

"I'm saying that you must keep your faith for yourself, not for me or anybody else. Yourself. No more, no less. That if you turn your back on it, discard it like a piece of worthless history, you'll lose half the meaning of your life."

Then he left. After a few minutes, David followed him, back into the bright room where a crowd had gathered around his father to hear his stories.

22

David heard the Ford's starter turning over. He listened as the car crunched over the gravel in the driveway. For a minute he lay listening for further sounds. Then he remembered that it was the day after his bar mitzvah, and he was up quickly and dressing.

Ruth was baking bread. The aroma drew him into the kitchen.

"Hi, Ruth," he said.

"Mornin', Mr. David."

"Mister? What's this mister business?" he asked.

"Well," the maid teased, "yesterday you became a man, din' you? Don' I gotta call you mister now?"

"Now, Ruth, you know better'n that. I'm just the same old David I always was."

"Well, leas' I'm gonna pour you a cup o' coffee like a man, 'stead of no half a cup wid' milk in it."

"Well, I guess I do deserve somethin'," he replied.

As she served the coffee Ruth could not resist stroking the back of his head, as she had always done since he was a baby.

"Honey," she said softly, "wad'n nobody at d' church prouder'n I was yestidy. Nobody."

"Did I do good, Ruth?"

"Soun' to me jus' lak a preacher," she said. "Could'n nobody have done no better."

Grinning, David sipped his coffee and thanked her.

Lowering her voice to a conspirational whisper, she said:

"Wouldn' be s'prized do yo' mamma an' daddy got a special somethin' for you. Would'n be s'prized one bit."

"What is it, Ruth? D'you know?"

"Wouldn' be right to say. Reckon you gotta wait an' see." She would say no more.

Throughout the day David dropped broad hints to his mother, but she refused to take the bait. By suppertime the suspense was unbearable. Several times, he thought of calling Jennifer, who was visiting a friend across town, to see if she might know. But each time he resisted the temptation.

As they were finishing Ruth's lemon pie, Ben suggested a little ride after supper to cool off.

Rachel, smiling, said it sounded like a good idea. Ruth looked at David and winked.

For nearly half an hour, Ben drove slowly through the country, making small talk with them. Finally, in the most casual fashion, he turned on Trager Road, then turned again up a long driveway to a big white house set back in a grove of water oaks and chinaberry trees.

"Let's drop in on the Maxwells for a minute. Just to say hello," he said.

But now David knew, and his excitement rose. Burt Maxwell raised bird dogs, the finest English setters in the county. This had to be his surprise: a setter puppy.

After Ben and Maxwell had exchanged stories about Angus bulls, and Mrs. Maxwell had served iced tea and cake, Maxwell mentioned that he had an eight-week-old litter of pups and wondered if David might want to see them.

David and the others went out to the back porch together, through the elegant, old-fashioned kitchen with its shelves of preserves and fruits in mason jars, and its oak table that Burt Maxwell's grandfather had built himself 75 years before, living in a four-room shack that had gradually grown to this gracious home as crops had been made and Maxwell wealth had been made with them.

As they walked to the porch, Rachel told David that their special bar mitzvah present to him was the pick of this litter of pups. David hurried his pace, thanking his parents and the Maxwells profusely as he did so, wondering how on earth he would choose one pup from the litter, since all English setter pups were equally beautiful.

But the choice turned out to be easy. In fact, he had barely reached the pen when she made the decision for him. She was all head and feet, and, as if she knew with certainty when he walked into the kennel that she rightfully belonged to him, she went right to work to draw David's attention before her littermates could divert him. While her brothers and sisters lolled and dozed and tumbled in the wire box, she seemed to have only one interest: David.

173

She pressed against the wire, tail working furiously, eyes appealing, head cocked. She followed David down the length of the box, pausing when he did, scrambling once more when he moved, clutching the wire and appealing with her soft eyes. When he picked her up for the first time, she sealed the bargain with her tiny pink tongue, wildly licking his face.

Actually he had always wanted a male puppy. But he never so much as lifted another puppy out of the pen. He turned to his parents and said that that was the one he wanted.

Burt Maxwell took the puppy and examined her with a critical eye.

"She's not a bad pup," he said, "but there are better dogs in the litter."

"What do you mean by *better?*" David asked suspiciously.

Maxwell held the pup's muzzle between the palm and fingers of his left hand and explained that her underjaw was a bit shallow and that her muzzle was slightly pinched.

"Her markings could be better, too," he said. "Look at that big male pup over in the corner and you'll see what I mean."

Without a doubt, the other puppy's markings were almost perfectly symmetrical. But David was already committed. "He's beautiful, Mr. Maxwell, but there's something about this one that I like a lot better. Besides, I don't plan to show her. I just want to hunt her."

Rachel, understanding, intervened. "Burt," she said, "I don't know the first thing about bird dogs, but I do know David. He already loves this puppy, and no other dog on earth will ever be as beautiful to him." She smiled at David and nodded. The pup was his.

From that moment on, Rebel preoccupied him. There was no limit to the things he found to do for her. First he fixed up a strange and somewhat less than elegant accommodation in the kitchen—an old, legless crib, stripped with cardboard to keep her from wandering out between the bars.

He spent hours just pondering the various kinds of diets most likely to promote her health and well-being. Whether to include an egg in her breakfast, or a tablespoon of grits was a momentous decision. And his concern for training her was considerably greater than it was for such irrelevancies as school work.

In the weeks that followed he made a nuisance of himself to every adult who had ever raised a pup and would talk to him about it, asking questions beyond counting.

He made even more trips to the library than usual; his interest now centered on one small section: half of one shelf of mystery and erudition—on the care, feeding, training, and handling of dogs.

The weeks passed. Rebel continued to occupy much of David's

time out of school, and an alarming portion of his concentration during classroom hours. When the bell signaled the end of the school day, he raced home to her.

It was the best time of his life. Bobby Brock was his friend now, his close friend, and that made all the difference. They were in the same eighth grade class, and several times in school, when boys had started to call David names, Bobby had stopped them.

"If you fight him, you're gonna have to fight me too," he said to Billy McKinna, and Billy had backed away.

"You didn't have to do that," David said later.

"I know I didn't. I just wanted to, that's all," Bobby replied.

Bobby was a good athlete, better than David. They played tennis and baseball together, and football when the weather turned cold.

Rebel was growing rapidly now, and Bobby helped David train her with a pigeon whose feathers they had clipped. David ignored no training hint or suggestion, no matter how fanciful or tenuous. He was sure his work with her would pay off during the bird season.

"Look at her, Bobby," he said one afternoon. "Look how she works so careful around those weeds—just like a field-trained dog."

"We'll see when the birds are flying," Bobby answered. "That's when my daddy says a real bird dog can shine, and all the rest forget their manners."

David was asked to play in baseball games now, just like every-body else, and to go to the tennis courts and swimming and on camping trips at the lake. Slowly a part of his bitterness began to fade. He began to forget what it had been like before. Once, in a crowd at the lake, he heard the word "Jew" and abruptly turned around, expecting a fight. But it was only a man telling another that he was trying to "jew" a car dealer down on a price. David didn't like it: briefly he considered saying something about it, but he decided against it and dived into the water instead.

Bobby heard it, too. Later, as they sat drying off in the sun, he said the men didn't mean anything by it.

"It's just an expression, Dave. Forget it."

During the summer David became an outdoor sportsman, under the careful tutelage of T.S. Bragg and Sam Perry. Early in the spring he and his father were invited to fish with the two men. They had gone to Buzzard's Roost with them, and later, Oakrun Lake and Lake Greenwood, to fish for bass and big crappie. When the water got warmer they fished together with mullet and chicken guts, for catfish in the rivers and ponds closer to home.

Sam Perry was a strong, gentle man who knew the quiet dignity of working with his hands in the soil for a livelihood. Sam had been a farmer for most of his 60 years and the hours he had spent following a slow mule had given him time to reflect on the good things in life. Not the least of these was the pleasure of fishing, an enterprise he went about with remarkable expertise.

His younger friend, T.S. Bragg, had been raised on a farm but now was given to tinkering with automobiles. T.S. almost matched Sam's fishing talents and may have exceeded him as a hunter. T.S. could "turn a pack of his beagles on a dime," Sam would say, "and git 'em to give you nine cents change."

Sam and T.S. taught the Harrises everything they knew about the woods and waters around Somerset.

" 'At boy's got fishin' patience," Bragg was fond of saying, "like he was born with it. Never seen the beat."

Several afternoons during the summer, Bragg stopped by to work with Rebel, and David anxiously awaited his opinion. "Looks good," Bragg said, "looks like a born hunter to me. We'll git her out with my old dog come bird season, an' then we'll see all we need to see."

In August, when the weather was too hot for fishing, Perry and Bragg decided to introduce Ben and David to "grabbling," a local and somewhat dangerous way of catching catfish. The main feature of the sport was that the fisherman walks along in the river and feels under hollowed out rocks to catch the fish with his bare hands.

David was a bit apprehensive on this first trip.

"How can you tell the difference between a small catfish and a big water moccasin, if you have to grip 'em underwater as soon as you feel 'em?" he asked.

"Reckon you'll find out sooner'n you want to," Perry chuckled.

"Well, what do I do when I find out?"

Sam regarded him whimsically and said: "Son, you just do what comes naturally!" Sam Perry was never one to waste words.

Their first time was a perfect day for grabbling: the sun was up and the river was down. Ben nosed his Ford to a stop close to the riverbank, at a spot where the ruts he had been following gave way to a tumble of blackberry vines and scrub pines.

Sam opened the trunk and took out an old wooden crate. Its contents included a dozen Pepsi Colas, a bag of fresh, vine-ripened tomatoes, and several large cantaloupes he had picked in his garden at sunup. He carried the crate a few steps into the bushes and called David. The boy found him bending over a small shaded pool, fed by a spring that bubbled over a mossy rock.

"Feel that water, boy," he said.

The water was surprisingly cold. As Perry slipped the fruit and soft drinks into the water, he said, "This here's our 'frigerator today.

That water'll have our drinks and stuff nice and cool when we're ready for 'em."

Then they were in the river and starting to work the rocks for the main course.

"We take one rock at a time," Perry explained. "First, me and your Dad will set this net downstream o' the rock so the current washes through it. Then you and T.S. reach up underneath the rock and catch what you can with your hands. What you can't reach, you "joog" with that hickory rod. That'll run the fish out. Then the net'll catch what you can't."

Bragg told David to go first. He felt gingerly underneath the rock. But when the first catfish came in contact with his hand, he forgot all caution. One clamp of the fingers and he had him—the first fish of the day.

Each rock in the river produced fish, and one seemed to be more fun than the next. Soon, Bragg took one side of the net so Ben could work the rocks with David. Fish after fish was deposited in the "croker sack" Bragg wore slung over his shoulder.

As the morning wore on, David discovered for himself the most pervasive liability of grabbling: a catfish spine jammed into the finger joint.

The sun moved higher. When it was almost directly overhead, Sam called to Bragg: "Hey, T.S., what've we got?"

With some difficulty, Bragg lifted the sack, now one quarter filled with fish.

"We've got a good many more'n we'll need for fryin'," he grinned. "David, you reckon you might know what to do with a mess of fried catfish and hushpuppies?"

No one had to wait for his answer. The morning of working against the river's current had made all of them tired, thirsty, and most of all, ravenously hungry.

Perry was already getting out his old, iron frying pan as Bragg and David headed for the little stream below the spring to clean fish.

David's pocketknife, which had seen more duty whittling slingshots than catfish, was inefficient, even in the soft skin of his first fish, and he paused to watch how it should be done. Bragg reached into the sack, took out a fish, and cut a shallow slit behind the head and then down the belly. Then he jerked the knife sharply down the length of the fish, skinning it with one motion. Two or three more flicks of the hand and the fish was gutted, the head and tail removed, and Bragg was washing the meat in the cold, clear spring water.

Most of the fish were small, averaging about a quarter pound, which is just right for frying. As David worked slowly on a particularly small one—trying without much success to emulate Bragg's deft motions, he heard about catfishing.

"Before we're through fishing together, boy, I'll teach you 40 different ways to catch catfish—one of 'em more fun than the next," he said. "We'll jug for 'em out at the lake, we'll catch 'em on trotlines in the river, we'll telephone 'em up at Lake Trinton, an' then we'll go down to Santee and hook'n line some granddaddy fish on mullet and chicken guts."

Cut. Slash. Cut. Wash. And another fish was ready for the pan.

"An' when it comes to eating catfish," he said, "why, we'll eat catfish till we can't hold anymore. Then we'll eat a few more apiece anyhow just to make sure they hold us till next time."

Cut. Slash. Cut. Wash.

"I don't think I'm bein' much help," David apologized, holding out the mangled fish he had been carving. At this, Bragg took David's knife and honed the edge on a sharpening stone he carried in his pocket.

Meanwhile Ben had gathered a triple armload of sweet pine and oak branches and built a good fire for cooking catfish. Bragg nodded in that direction and told David: "It's just about as important to learn how to cook fish as to catch 'em, so you better get over there and watch how Sam does it."

When David reached the fire, thick, white slices of fatback were already sizzling in the pan. He gathered a few extra sticks of firewood, and soon the smell of frying pork filled the air. Sam winked at David's father and said, "Ben, I reckon we better fix 'hat boy a sandwich 'fore he starts gnawing on his boot."

"We always bring along a few pieces of store-bought bread for just this kind of emergency," Perry continued as he fished a piece of streak-o-lean out of the fry pan and made a sandwich.

Nothing had ever tasted better, David thought as he thankfully nodded between bites. Perry rolled catfish in a cornmeal mixture and gently dropped the pieces into the sizzling fat. As the skillet filled he began making hushpuppies out of the cornmeal and dropping them into the fat around the fish.

Wiping his pocketknife clean, Perry sliced cold tomatoes and cantaloupe, recently retrieved from the spring, to be eaten with the fish. Then the first of the fish were ready to eat, and the fishermen gathered around the fire.

The fish were crisp and golden brown on the outside, with meat as white inside as fresh-picked cotton. David bit into the first one, and the meat flaked and crumbled off of the central bone, juicy and tender as the tomatoes from Sam's garden. Every time the skillet yielded one batch, Sam rolled a half-dozen more and slipped them

178

into the fat. The hushpuppies were light and crisp, and just as the last one would disappear from the platter, a new batch would be coming out of the pan.

Their pace finally began to slow down a bit. Bragg told David how hushpuppies got their name.

"In the old days," he drawled, "a fellow never went anywhere 'thout his hounds—even to a fish fry. And the racket a bunch of hounds can set up with fish a'fryin' is enough to pop a man's eardrums.

"Of course, they couldn't feed fish to the dogs for fear of 'em getting bones stuck in their throats. So for a long time, they just had to put up with the racket.

"Seems one day a fellow was rolling fish in meal and the howlin' got particularly on his nerves, so he wet down some meal, rolled it in little balls, and dropped 'em in the fat to fry. When they got brown, he fished 'em out and threw one to the nearest hound, saying 'hush, puppy.'

"The idea worked so well that other folks started doin' it, and finally one day, seeing how much the hounds liked 'em, a fellow bit into one hisself. And from that day to this, we been quietin' ourselves down with hushpuppies as well as our dogs."

By the time the story was finished, they were all stuffed. They just sat for a time around the fire, sipping boiled coffee and enjoying the sights and smells of a Carolina afternoon in the summer.

It felt good to David, all of it—the warm sun and the full belly and the company of good men. Most of all, being with Ben was a joy to him. But Sam and T.S. were also his friends, and back in town, Bobby Brock was waiting for him. It was the best of times.

23

David couldn't remember a time when he hadn't dreaded Jennifer going off to college. Even as they had grown older—past Saturday mornings together huddled by the radio, past the times when he needed her to teach him, even past the times when she was his only friend and companion—the prospect of her leaving filled him with an empty, aching feeling.

When the moment finally arrived, they stood together on the train platform in Greenville, saying goodbye.

"Davey, the University of Alabama isn't the end of the world," she said. "I'll be home for lots of holidays and all summer long, and maybe you'll come down and visit me at school."

"Sure, Jen. Sure I will!"

"I'll show you off to all the girls; I'll tell them 'this is my handsome brother, Mr. David Harris,' and they'll all envy me. You'll see, Davey. We'll be together lots of times."

"Jen, I . . ."

"What, Davey?"

"I jus' want you to know the luckiest thing that ever happened to me was you, Jennifer."

"It's the other way around, Davey," she said. "Listen to me. I never told you this, but I believe you're going to do something—to be somebody—real important. Believe that, honey. Believe in yourself, and it'll happen. I know it will."

Then she hugged him, very tight, kissed him, and was gone. David watched the train disappear to the south, then rode home in silence in the back seat of the new Buick. His parents chatted lightly about Jennifer growing up and how well she was bound to do at school, what with her brains and good looks.

Ben dropped Rachel and David off at home and drove on to the barn. For a while David tried to read, but he couldn't concentrate. Finally he put the book aside and went outside to sit on the patio. He was conscious only of his feeling of loneliness until he felt a nudge at his elbow. It was Rebel.

"Hiya, gal. Hiya," he said, stroking her lightly on her head and back.

"She's gone, Rebel. Just you and me now that Jen's gone," he told her. "Boy, I'm gonna miss her like anything."

She seemed to sense his sadness, her big luminous eyes never leaving his face, her muzzle working against his hand, to be stroked.

"She's the best, know that, gal? The best. The prettiest. The smartest. The best. Gonna be mighty empty around here with her gone."

The big setter licked his face, and he hugged her and petted her flanks.

"We'll just have to make do," he said.

The boy and the setter were still sitting together on the front step when Ben came home from the barn.

As David started across the lawn to the car, his father opened the trunk and took out a long, flat cardboard box.

"Got a present for you, son. Call it a kinda delayed bar mitzvah present."

The box was surprisingly heavy.

"What is it?" David asked, his hands beginning to work at the wrapping.

"Well," Ben said, "seems to me that Doc Blocker and Mr. Sam Perry and the other fellows you been bird hunting with might need a little help knocking quail down, seein' as how they're not gettin' any younger."

The box came open just as David realized what Ben meant. The little Stevens .20-gauge single gleamed in the wrapping, its barrel a deep blue.

"Oh, it's beautiful," David said. "I can't believe it."

"We didn't think your .22 would do too much good when Rebel starts to find birds," his father smiled. "You've hunted without a gun long enough."

Dr. Herbert Blocker, Sam Perry, and several other hunters in Somerset had been inviting David into the field with them for two seasons now, teaching him how to handle dogs and hunt quail. He had fired Dr. Blocker's shotgun a few times but never on a covey rise. But now. . . .

Rachel came out on the patio, smiling at David's surprise.

"Thank you, Mom an' Dad. Thank you so much."

"Just be careful with that thing," his mother said. "That's all I ask."

In the next several weeks he fired five boxes of shells at tin cans his father threw out over a field for him, taking Rebel along each time to get her accustomed to the sound of the gun. It was the last step in her training, and she reacted well, never flinching after she had heard it a few times.

David had given her all the training at home that he could. Now only a real test—of her nose, discipline, and instincts on a live covey of birds would tell. The days dragged in September and October; then, finally, one day early in November he took her into the field.

She was too young to hunt seriously; he knew that. But the bird season was still a month away, the quail were reasonably unwary, and he could restrain himself no longer.

When she streaked into the field ahead of him, his heart was in his throat. After all her training, Rebel romped like the most undisciplined scoundrel ever bred of a bitch.

What would happen if she busted her first covey? Where was her breeding and training? Why was she scampering with such abandon when this lespedeza patch had to be full of birds?

Then it happened. Suddenly she slowed her gait, raised her muzzle and tested the air, took several awkward, straight-legged steps off to her right, and froze stock still. Her head was down, her tail was down; she hunched over as if she had stomach pains. But she was holding rigidly on her first point. To David she was the most beautiful sight he had ever seen.

"Easy, girl. Good girl," he whispered as he walked up to her and on by into the lespedeza. She trembled from head to tail with excitement. As he tried to get his own trembling under control, the first bird rocketed from the cover, followed by the rest of the covey in singles and doubles.

Not a stink sparrow or a rabbit or a field lark, as he had feared. It was quail! Bobwhite! Partridge! And his pup had dropped rock, stock still at her first covey.

Though her form had been less than classic, his heart surged with pride. The books hadn't said very much about what you were supposed to do with your pup the first time she finds and holds a covey of quail. But at that moment he couldn't have cared less. He swept her into his arms and rolled over and over in the field with her, hugging, kissing, and praising her all at the same time.

The days dragged until Thanksgiving, but it finally arrived, and, with it, the bird season. Then they were in the field in earnest. Her tender age notwithstanding, the good blood in her veins and whatever discipline he had instilled showed again and again. He and Ben hunted her alone and occasionally with older, more finished dogs, and not once did she embarrass him. Even Dr. Blocker—a bird dog man all his life—was surprised at the "stanchness" with which she held a point.

As the season passed, David's love for her deepened. She was his friend, his companion, his greatest source of pride. On several occasions he overheard men in town talking about her—about her form and her nose and this or that covey she had found at eight months after older dogs had hunted the field and quit it.

At the end of the season Dr. Blocker, appraising her performance, offered his best setter, Big Tom, for stud when they were ready to breed her. "Now that will be a litter of pups," he said.

In the summer Jennifer came home with three friends from the university, and the Harris household rocked with fun. Hannah, Jennifer's roommate, almost immediately proposed marriage to David. His face and ears reddened as he pretended not to hear her. She called him "husband" all summer, and he loved it. They swam together, and fished, and laughed until tears came to their eyes, because the world seemed golden and made for happiness.

24

In August, a few days before David's 15th birthday, Rebel threw her first litter of pups. David found her early in the morning, lying exhausted on the clean, cedar shavings in her house, proudly nursing her litter. He picked up one of the puppies, held it against his cheek, feeling its warmness and softness. Rebel watched him out of the corner of her eye, calmly, he imagined, not afraid that he would hurt her pup or take it away. Very gently he replaced it at her teat and ran inside to tell his parents.

Within days Dr. Blocker, Sam Perry, and a dozen more bird hunters who had seen Rebel work dropped by to look at the pups and make small talk.

"Any one of them pups gotta be some kind of dog, bred of that Rebel of yourn and Doc Blocker's Tom," Mr. Mayfield said. "Be pleased to buy one, if they ain't all spoke for."

David didn't relish the idea of letting any of the pups go, but he knew he would have to, and since Mr. Mayfield kept a good kennel of setters and treated them well, he was promised a pup.

Dr. Blocker got the pick of the litter. He chose a big, male pup with a black patch over one eye. In eight weeks they were all gone and David was richer by $485. He could have made more had he not given two of the pups away—one to Mr. Perry, who couldn't afford to buy one, and another to Mr. Bragg, not that he couldn't, and wouldn't, have paid, but because he had taught David to love bird dogs and bird hunting to begin with, and now David could pay his debt with the gift of a puppy.

In the fall she was back in the field with him, eager to hunt, faultlessly staunch on point, now a polished bird dog. At the end of a day's hunt, he spent hours grooming her, gently picking the cockle burrs and beggar lice out of her long coat.

"I declare," Rachel said smiling, "I believe you love that dog better'n anybody in the family." But even as she said it, she was stroking Rebel's head affectionately.

"She's a lady, Mom," he replied gently. "A real lady. She deserves to be loved."

She roamed the area freely, a familiar and welcome visitor at neighbors' houses—at every one it turned out, but one.

David had just come home from school one day when the phone rang. When he answered it, he heard the accented voice of Nate Greenberg, a neighbor only recently moved to Somerset from some place in Pennsylvania.

"You own a black-and-white dog, one with long hair?" he asked.

"Yessir, I do," David answered.

"Well, she just ran across my front yard," Greenberg said, a hint of hostility in his voice.

David waited for him to continue—to say, perhaps, that Rebel had committed some uncharacteristic breach of good manners. But silence followed silence.

"Mr. Greenberg," he finally asked, "did she harm your flowers or anything?"

"No, that ain't the point," he snapped. "I don't want anybody's damn dog in my yard. And that includes yours."

"But she always runs loose in the neighborhood, and she doesn't hurt anything," David protested. "She's the most gentle, easygoing dog there is. . . ."

"Maybe you didn't understand me," Greenberg cut in. "I don't want her in my yard, and, by God, I'm not going to have her in my yard. The next time she comes onto my property, I'm going to shoot her."

The words shocked David, sending his mind spinning, grasping for something to say. Years of genteel indoctrination blocked his instinctive reply. He is an adult, David's training and upbringing said. You don't speak disrespectfully to an adult. But training, struggling with instinct, lost.

"I wouldn't do that if I were you," the boy said slowly.

"And what's going to stop me?" Greenberg asked.

"Meaning no disrespect, sir, but if you shoot my dog, I'll load my shotgun and come to your house and kill you."

After the gasp, the phone went dead. Within three minutes, it rang again. It was his grandfather.

"Dovidl," the stern voice said, "I want you to come to my house. *Now!*"

When David presented himself in his grandfather's den, the old man came right to the point.

"Did you just threaten to kill Mr. Greenberg?" he asked.

"Well, sir," David stammered, "let me explain what happened. You see, Mr. Greenberg. . . ."

"I didn't ask for an explanation," Isaac interrupted, "I asked for an answer. A simple yes or no."

David said, yes, he had. "But if you'll just let me tell you what happened, you'll understand why I did it."

Isaac regarded the boy coolly for a moment before he spoke. "You're a boy of 15; Mr. Greenberg is a man of 50. You had no right to speak to him disrespectfully. To threaten his life on top of that. It's unbelievable!"

"I know, but—"

"Now I want you to call him on the telephone"—he pointed to his desk—"and apologize."

To David the demand seem beyond all reason. To give in was impossible. How could he apologize for being right? And how else but by threat of violence could he save Rebel from being shot?

"Grandpa," he said gravely, "you know that in my whole life I've done whatever you asked me to do. But I can't apologize to Mr. Greenberg. I meant every word I said. If he kills my dog, I'm gonna blow his brains out."

Isaac stared at the boy incredulously, a mounting fury building on his face. This boy dared question his authority, where no one had questioned him for 30 years? This boy in whom he had invested so much of his caring?

David knew he had incurred his grandfather's wrath, had known from the cradle that one did not ever question the wishes—or orders —of the old man. Still, his reaction shocked David.

"You refuse me? You?" the old man stormed. "I won't have this, you hear. You get out of my house, right now. And until you do what I ask, you are not to set foot in this house, or let your shadow fall on me, again!"

"But, Grandpa," David said, "you don't even like Mr. Greenberg. I've heard you call him a *daitcha yid* a hundred times. Why—"

"I have nothing else to say," Isaac fumed, and snapped open his afternoon newspaper.

In a daze David walked slowly across the street to his house.

186

Rebel was waiting in the back yard. She looked at him with sad eyes as he gently stroked her back, scratched behind her ears, trying to figure out what to do.

Ben and Rachel came home together, laughing as they got out of the car. David was terribly glad to see them and in short order explained his dilemma. Rachel recommended that he simply apologize.

"You know your grandfather," she said. "He'll stick to his word, no matter what happens. It would be a pity to let a little matter of an apology come between you."

David explained that an apology would compromise his honor, that it would mean he was backing down, and that the real fault lay with Mr. Greenberg for threatening to kill Rebel.

"He oughta apologize—not me," the boy said.

Finally Ben spoke. "Look, son," he said, "the heart of the matter is your dog. And I imagine you've made your point clearly enough to slow Mr. Greenberg down. I doubt that he's going to harm Rebel now, given the thought that you just might make good on your threat whether you apologize or not. Would you?" To David, the glint in his eye signaled exculpation. "Besides, we're going on a trip next week, and you don't want to go away with any bad feelings with your grandfather to think about."

"Mr. Greenberg," the boy said into the phone a few minutes later, "my grandfather told me to apologize to you, and out of respect for him, I'm calling to do that."

David could sense him gloating as he sneered about "snotnose kids with no manners or upbringing."

When he was all through, the boy improvised.

"Like I said, Mr. Greenberg, I'm apologizing for having threatened to shoot you. But I want you to know I meant every word I said. And I still do."

David listened to him yell and bellow and wheeze and cough once or twice before he hung up. But he had done what his grandfather asked. A little more, perhaps. But in matters of honor, as his father had said many times, form is often more important than substance.

Indeed, Isaac was satisfied. David had done what he had ordered; he had apologized. When Greenberg called the second time, almost incoherent in his rage, Isaac determined that David *had* called to apologize. That was all he wanted to hear. So what, he thought, if the boy chose to add an extra sentence or two. He was secretly amused, but he mustn't let Greenberg know.

"In the south, people get very attached to their dogs," he said gravely into the phone.

187

"I don't care about no south," Greenberg sputtered. "I don't care—"

"Maybe you should," Isaac said. "You came to live here. Maybe you ought to care a little about how other people feel, too."

"I'm gonna call the police—"

Isaac chuckled. "When you do, Mr. Greenberg, better not tell them it's Isaac Shulman's grandson you're complaining about—or Ben Harris's son. And especially don't mention that you threatened to kill my grandson's dog. They're all hunters, the policemen; they'd go hard on you for threatening to kill such a good bird dog."

"I . . . you—" Greenberg stammered.

"Goodbye," Isaac said and hung up. Ah, that Dovidl, he thought, he's crazy like all the *goyim* in this town. A good, sturdy boy, though. Tough. He'll be all right, that boy.

"Isaac, who was on the phone?" Baila called from the next room.

"That Greenberg—your fine neighbor who wants to make the shul into a reform temple," Isaac said. "He just got a lesson in manners."

"You taught him the lesson?"

"I helped a little, but your grandson did most of the teaching."

David ventured into his grandfather's den in the evening, gingerly, unsure as to what his status was with the old man.

"Nu, Dovidl," Isaac called. "How are you?"

It was all right, David knew, and he sat with the old man, telling him about his forthcoming trip.

"A real gentleman's deer hunt, that's what it's gonna be," the boy enthused. "Dad's old buddy, Mr. Grady, lives in Beverly now. He's a member of a club that hunts deer in the swamp with hounds and drivers every Christmas day."

"You gonna bring me some venison?" Isaac asked. "I haven't tasted any in a long time."

"I'm sure gonna try, Grandpa," David answered gravely. "I never even saw a deer before. But just let an old buck come near me, an' we'll be eatin' venison all winter, you and me."

The week dragged by. Finally the day arrived. Ben and David packed their rough clothes, boots, shotguns, and hunting coats in the trunk of the car and were off, with calls of "good luck" and "be careful" from Rachel and Ruth.

The day of the hunt started at 3:00 A.M. with Ben shaking David and telling him to get up. The hotel room floor was cold. Momentarily David was reluctant to leave the warmth of the wool blankets. Then he remembered what day it was, and he was up and dressing quickly. A few minutes later they were out under the stars, watching a car quietly materialize out of the frosty morning darkness.

188

"Morning there, Ben," the driver said. "Good to see you."

"Morning, Gordon," Gen answered. "This is David—my son."

"Glad to have you with us, son," Gordon Grady said. "Got a bit of a ride ahead, so go ahead and grab a few winks if you're a mind to."

But David was wide awake as Grady drove through the sleeping town and out the highway toward Hell Hole Swamp.

After they had driven for about 45 minutes, David had developed a powerful need for a cup of coffee. Inwardly shuddering at the prospect of a December morning hunt without any breakfast, he finally asked Gordon Grady if they could stop somewhere for coffee.

Chuckling, Grady answered: "I reckon we'll find you about as much breakfast as you can handle—right now in a little while."

The sky was black; no lights appeared anywhere on the horizon. They rode on, with Grady telling stories about big bobcats in the swamp, the good jump hound a man he called the "Major" would have on the hunt that day, and a particularly smart old buck that had managed to get past the post line for three years running. Then they were off the highway and on a county road that led to the swamp. ". . . old bear sow had a crippled forepaw. I reckon she couldn't take much game, so she raised hell with Seab's calves and goats for a month or two," Grady said. "Finally Seab took a stand over a fresh kill and when the sow came crackling through the bushes, he let loose with both barrels of double aughts. He hit her just hard enough to make her mad, and she run him up a tree and kept him there till his hollerin' caught his wife's ear. She came out with the other shotgun and took the top of the sow's head off, and she ain't let him live it down since."

Ben chuckled with his old friend, saying he bet the farmer was more than a bit embarrassed.

"Better believe it," Grady said. "Since the story got around about his old lady saving his hide, he don't come to town at all 'less he absolutely has to."

At that point Grady turned off the paved surface onto a dirt road. As the station wagon bounced along the ruts, the headlights picked up a panorama of swamp life. A yearling doe slipped across the road ahead of them, and a big covey of bobwhites tipped off the fringe of the road and into the high grass. Once the lights caught the eyes of a big red fox as he daintily picked his way across the road.

Soon the dirt road became merely two ruts. Then, a rough little cabin loomed up ahead. It was built from what looked like scrap cedar shakes. The porch sagged under their weight. There was a light in the window, and before they could knock, the door swung open and they were invited inside.

189

The room, lighted with lanterns, was no more than 10 feet square. Against one wall was a rough-hewn table and four homemade wicker chairs.

The host, a gaunt man in overalls, with a chew of tobacco in one cheek, motioned them to sit down.

"Ol' lady already got meat a'fryin'," he said. "Have some coffee fer you right away."

The old lady, as he called her, appeared with steaming mugs of coffee and a heavy pitcher of cream. The mugs were chipped, but the coffee was strong, hot, and fragrant. The cream, David noticed, was freshly separated and still warm.

As they stirred molasses into the coffee (We don't keer much fer store-boughten sweetenin'," the man told him) the woman reappeared with a platter of hot, buttermilk biscuits and freshly baked corn bread, a bowl of freshly churned and molded butter, and a separate tray of preserves in pint mason jars.

The bread, which was hot, crumbled in their hands as they spread the sweet butter. Nodding toward the preserves, the man told David: "Try some of them, young feller. That there one is dewberry; t'other one is wild strawberry. 'Em fig preserves is good, too. Picked th' berries an' the ol' woman put'em up in the fall of the year."

They were a new experience, one sweeter and more delicious than the next. David was a little embarrassed about the gluttonous way he wolfed down the bread, but the woman reappeared with another, larger, platter.

"Y'ers some fresh bread," she said. "Hope you fellers can eat it all."

Before David could finish another hunk of corn bread, their "waitress" was serving buckwheat cakes, moist with eggs and butter. They were served with crockery pitchers of pure cane syrup and molasses, and as the trio began to spread them with butter, a large platter of country-style bacon and thick slices of home-cured ham were served.

These were unlike any buckwheat cakes or bacon or ham David had ever tasted. As they ate, their host explained that he had grown and milled the grain for all the breads and cakes and killed the hogs and cured the meat himself. His wife had gathered the eggs, separated the cream, and churned the butter just that morning. He even made his own cane syrup, he said. The only elements in the meal which had been "store-boughten" were the coffee and salt.

And the proof was in the tasting. The bacon was lean and crisp, with just the right hint of smoke in the flavor, and the ham was rich and sweet from slow molasses-curing.

Next they were served a platter of fresh eggs, fried light and fluffy in ham fat.

More fresh bread was served hot out of the oven. More coffee was poured. In the midst of all of this bounty, the man instructed his wife to quickly clean and fry some of the catfish he had taken off his trotlines.

Grady intervened. "Cal, I don't reckon we can eat anymore. Much obliged just the same."

Finally, it was over, and Grady was offended when Ben tried to pay for their breakfasts. (Ben later learned that it had come to 75 cents apiece.)

Then they were off down the double ruts again and into the swamp. The first streaks of dawn were showing over the trees as they stopped the car and joined a group around a fire. A pack of hounds of assorted lineage strained at their ropes, handled by colored men who for a long time had run the driving part of this hunt. After greetings were exchanged, the Major—an old gentleman who was president of the hunt club and therefore had the responsibility of choosing posts for each man—gave instructions to the drivers. David watched them mount their mules and head into the swamp. The hunters lounged around the fire, smoking and talking until in the distance the faint tones of a bugle were heard.

"They're in place," the Major said and then instructed each of the men to his post. The next oldest member of the hunt besides the Major was Gordon Grady; he took the last post down the line so he could position each man properly. When his whistle echoed back through the mist, signaling that all were ready, the Major took his post, the drivers were started, and the hunt was on.

And what a hunt it was. Each of the drivers had a bugle on which he blew with great fervor. The hounds filled in all of the quiet spots between bugle calls, belling after deer trails crisscrossing the swamp. Although they were several miles away, the sounds carried across the flat, quiet swamp, and each hunter could tell every change of direction as the deer, hounds, and drivers shifted first toward one of them and then another.

The excitement grew with the pitch of the noise, and finally the whole focus of the sound headed directly for David. It grew nearer and nearer. He waited tensely for the buck to burst into view. He could feel his hands sweating on the gun stock and he held it almost shoulder high, safety off, at the ready.

"Come on, baby," he whispered to the buck. "Just bust out into that clearing and give me one chance . . . just one."

Finally the noise of the hounds was sweeping in on his post and over him. "Come on, come on," he whispered urgently.

At the last moment the direction of the sound swerved to his right and seconds later the still morning was rent with a double blast of a shotgun 100 yards away. The clamor caught up with the blast, then died down. Leaving their positions, the nearby hunters rushed over to find that the big buck had at last fallen—one Christmas hunt too many for the noble old whitetail.

On the long drive back to Somerset the next day, David began to realize that it made very little difference that he had not had the shot. He discussed it with Ben, and they agreed they both would be just as happy if that smart old buck was still around to fool the Christmas hunt club members, and like as not, so would they.

"What we'll remember," Ben said, "is something other than the buck being killed."

David nodded. It would be the crisp December morning filled with the music of bugles and hounds. The good fellows around the fire, the breakfast they shared in a rough little cabin in the swamp. And most of all, being together on the Christmas hunt.

David looked at Ben, now driving fast toward home. For a moment he wanted to tell his father how much he loved him. Then he knew that wouldn't do, so he simply reached across the seat and clapped his hand on Ben's shoulder.

"It was a good hunt, Dad."

"Yeah, son, a good hunt."

David didn't have to put it in words. Ben knew.

25

In the fall, just after Jennifer left for school again, Isaac Shulman entered David's life in a new way. The old man had gone into semiretirement, giving up all of his business activities except his directorships. He had time now, and increasingly he found that he wanted to spend it with his oldest grandson. (Perhaps, he mused, he had built this big brick home and moved Baila from the old house in which she raised her children, for this reason more than any other—to be near the boy.)

Through long afternoons he and David sat in his pine-paneled den, talking quietly together.

"What on earth do they find to talk about in there," Rachel asked her mother.

"It's mostly Papa that talks, and David listens," Baila answered her. "I hear him talking on and on about the old country. About things I forgot 50 years ago."

There was purpose in the stories Isaac chose to tell the boy, a reason behind every image he sketched for him. His time was not limitless; he had already cheated fate out of many years—since the surgeons cut away his face, almost certain he would die anyway. There was an important job left to do, one for which he might have 20 years, or 20 days—who could know? It was to build in this boy, his grandson, a powerful sense of his heritage, of his role as a Jew, his obligation to carry on the skein of his people's history and destiny, and of the blood—Shulman blood—that flowed in his veins.

Isaac had watched, more carefully than David suspected, as his grandson encountered and dealt with problems throughout his childhood. In some ways the old man was glad the boy had experienced these problems. If nothing else, they increased his consciousness of his role, and perhaps of the value of protecting it. More important, David had fought for his faith and identity, and time after time had won, learning as he did so—as he smashed his fist into the mouths that said he was less worthy because he was a Jew, as he bruised and closed the eyes that saw him, not as another boy or a person or an American, but rather as some strange species of inferior creature called a Jew—a sense of victory and pride in himself for finding the strength to stand alone and win.

Isaac couldn't let the experience be lost to David. In the stories he told him he taught by example that Jews had always had troubles, but that in overcoming—in surviving—them, they had been proved and tempered, like steel in a furnace.

The old man took his grandson back through space and time to his own childhood, his own struggles and pain and fear and hunger, to his own family which he brought to life in the boy's imagination, to the people in Bogdanya, the snows, the warm spring days, the twisting streets, the businesses at which the Jews scratched out a meager living, and most of all, to the enduring, eternal faith in God and the Torah on which they feasted and which sustained their lives.

Isaac seldom questioned his growing compulsion to mold the boy's consciousness. He only dimly understood that he did so out of some instinct that the boy wakened in him; that was enough. Day after day David listened, fascinated, never tiring of the strange memories the old man had kept private for a lifetime. In the process he discovered new facets in his grandfather, who before had appeared to him as merely tough, unyielding, frightening, without any other dimensions.

"Your grandmother," Isaac said to him one afternoon. "She was my student once. Did you know that, Dovidl?"

"No sir, I didn't."

"I was so poor then that I lived in other people's houses," Isaac said, smiling wistfully at the memory. "They paid me with food and shelter for teaching their children."

David tried to imagine his grandfather young, poor, vulnerable, but he couldn't. Even as his grandfather told him of David's grandmother as a young girl, of how he loved her and almost lost her to a rich baker's son, David could not imagine it.

The story began with a *shadchen,* a matchmaker, who came to Baila's father's house to propose a marriage.

Shimon Teretsky, the matchmaker, had traveled many versts to see Chiam Donevitz, the merchant. After a dinner which Reb Chiam's

194

wife served on white linen, the two men repaired to the small sitting room to talk alone. For a while they spoke of every subject they could think of except the business at hand.

"And how is business?" Reb Chiam asked.

"Ah, I have a list of princes—merchants, doctors, engineers, even a young rabbi from a village east of here," the matchmaker said. "So many fine men I scarcely know which to suggest to fathers first for their daughters. And by you, Reb Chiam?"

"Good days and bad ones," the merchant replied. "As always, people come to look more than buy."

They spoke then of the rabbi of Dwinsk, the rabbi in Pinsk, the rabbi in Odessa. They spoke of the Tsar and the weather and crops in the fields and the merchant's wife's fish. They spoke of the matchmaker's trip, his children, his latest accomplishments.

Finally they both fell silent. The time had come, it was clear, to speak frankly.

"Honored Reb Chiam," the matchmaker began, "I come to you on a mission of joyfulness, to bring you word of a *simcheh.*"

"And what is this *simcheh,* may I ask?"

"The finest man of all in my lists has seen your eldest daughter."

"And?"

"He thinks her lovely as a pearl, a summer flower."

"Indeed, my Baila is a beautiful girl. There is none in this shtetl who is lovelier."

"He thinks her graceful as a young hart."

"There is none more graceful."

There was another pause.

"He wishes me, Reb Chiam, to discuss with you a match."

"And what of this prince, who desires my Baila for a wife?"

"He is the perfect bridegroom," the matchmaker said. "The perfect son-in-law for the honored Reb Chiam, rest assured. Learned as a rabbi," he rushed on. "To hear him read and recite brings tears of joy to the eyes."

"And?"

"He is well established; his father has a home with a polished wooden floor and five rooms to take her to."

Chiam Donevitz was known to be a devoted father. His pride in his daughters was such that his friends frequently tired of hearing of their accomplishments. When others discussed business, Reb Chiam spoke of his daughter Tybil's needlepoint. When others desired to argue the Talmud, Reb Chiam was more inclined to praise Rifkah's cooking. And of his eldest, Baila, there was more conversation than of the other two combined.

"And what is his business?" he asked the matchmaker.

Here the matchmaker's eyes lit up.

"His father owns the finest bakery I have seen in all my travels," he said. "Not in Minsk, not even in Odessa—where my business took me only last year—have I seen such a bakery. The people line up and clamor for his father's pastries before they are out of the oven. His white bread is known to every rich man in the countryside. His bagels are—"

Reb Chiam held up his hand. "Before I hear of his father or his bagels, tell me more about the bridegroom himself."

"What more is there to tell?" the matchmaker said. "He is the son of a man of means, he is learned, he lives in a fine house."

On they talked, with the matchmaker wielding his considerable powers of persuasion. When the matchmaker described his client, his words rang: "The son of a generous man, himself a man of great principle, a man of riches and respectability."

And when Reb Chiam spoke of his daughter, his eyes gleamed with pleasure. "Beautiful as a flower, a cook without parallel, a help her mother would be lost without, a girl with wisdom and education."

At this, the matchmaker showed a new interest.

"Education?" he asked. "And what kind of education?"

"For two years," Chiam Donevitz said, "a brilliant young melamed from Bogdanya has lived at our house on alternate months, teaching my daughters. And none of them, he assures me, has been the student that my Baila has been."

Later, when the matchmaker bade Reb Chiam goodnight, he knew that the merchant was weakening. After shul the next morning, the merchant's wife brought out the samovar and the two men ate small cakes and drank tea with cubes of sugar between their teeth.

Between bites of cake, the matchmaker played his trump card.

"Because your daughter is such an unusual girl, I am sure no dowry will be required. I believe my client's father will even buy all the new clothes she may wish for her wedding. You have only to grant your permission."

Chiam Donevitz had tossed and turned the night before, weighing all he had been told. The question that bothered him most was why the matchmaker only talked about the boy's father, rather than the boy himself. After all, it was not the father whom Baila would be marrying. Had the young man no accomplishments, no redeeming features of his own to recommend him? On the other hand, someday the son would own all that was his father's, and then, if he were Baila's husband, he would share it with her. On and on he had argued with himself, until he fell into an uneasy sleep almost at dawn.

Finally, when the samovar had been put away, he expressed an interest in meeting the prospective gridegroom.

The following week Shimon Teretsky returned with his client, a heavyset young man with carrot-red hair. His father, the baker, also made the journey. They met the merchant as he entered the synagogue, and appropriate introductions were made.

The bridegroom, as he was confidently called by Shimon Teretsky, hung his head and said little. But the baker was quick to demonstrate his magnanimity. He gave the rabbi two silver rubles for the poor box and another three for the cheder. Spotting a beggar outside, he sent one of the young boys out to him with a half a ruble. After the service he distributed a pocketful of groschen to the younger children who had gathered at the door.

As the matchmaker had said, the young man was learned. Throughout the service the merchant listened to him; truly, he davened like a scholar. Outside the synagogue he shyly handed the merchant a large basket filled to the brim with delicate cakes and rich tarts for his table.

"May life be as sweet for you and your family," the young man said, prodded by his father to make the carefully memorized speech.

At the appropriate time, the baker and his son found business with the rabbi, leaving the matchmaker alone with Chiam Teretsky.

"Well, honored Reb Chiam? Is he not everything I promised?"

The merchant was bothered by the young man's lack of personal presence, his seemingly total dependence on his father, and his general appearance. But he had to admit that his manner appeared gentle. He was also learned, beyond doubt. So what if he was thick at the waist and a bit homely. Was that so terrible? And if he depended on his father, so what? Someday he would inherit all his worldly goods. He would be wealthy—and so would Baila. His mind made up, Chiam said simply: "I am ready to publish the banns."

Then he added:

"Come with him to my home for dinner tonight, and we will complete the transaction."

As he walked home alone, the merchant was at the same time depressed and elated. He dreaded the thought of losing Baila, for her presence was a joy to him. Even more, he feared unhappiness for her, particularly if he should, God forbid, be the unwitting instrument of that unhappiness. On the other hand, he had found a man who could provide handsomely for her and who appeared to cherish the law.

"Ah, life forces such difficult decisions," he sighed half aloud. "There is never a sweet that does not have a tinge of bitterness to it."

At dinner that night the matchmaker, his client, and the young man's father were treated to the finest dinner the merchant's wife and daughters could prepare. Baila went about her part of the serving quietly and without comment, showing little emotion—either joy or sadness—at the occasion.

Throughout the meal she spoke only when spoken to, seldom lifting her eyes from the table. The baker praised every dish, looking constantly as he did so at his future daughter-in-law. His son said nothing, concentrating instead on stuffing food noisily into his mouth.

Whatever else he is, Baila's mother thought, he is a man of great appetite. Potatoes, *tsimmes,* fish, meat—all seemed to evaporate from his plate.

After the matchmaker, his client, and the baker had finished, they talked to the merchant for a few minutes and then were gone. The dishes were cleared, the cloth put away. The moment of truth had arrived.

Taking Baila into the next room, her father asked tenderly: "Well, my daughter, what do you think of the husband I have found for you? Have I done well?"

Because she loved her father devotedly, Baila attempted to appear happy. But in the midst of an observation on his appetite, she burst into tears and flung herself on her father's neck.

"Please," she sobbed, "I beg you to release me from your promise. I'll do anything—scrub floors, work in the fields . . ." She could say no more, so wracked was she with her crying.

Patting her hair, her father said: "I only wanted to make you happy, child. This man's father is wealthy. He has a fine house, a good business. They are both learned in the law and the Talmud. He is—"

"But I don't love him, Papa, and I never could. He is like his father's shadow, not a man who is strong—whom I could respect," she sobbed. "I have asked for very little, Papa. But now I ask—I beg—you to let me marry a man I can look up to and love, a man like—."

Her father was confused. Modern children, he thought, make life so much more complicated for a father. He had decided, as was the custom—and now?

"A man like whom?" he asked gently. "Is your heart set on another man?"

"A man like Itzrok Shulman," she blurted out between sobs.

The merchant felt as if a pail of cold water had been dashed in his face. Anger clutched his chest and rose in his throat as bitter as gall.

He had taken Itzrok Shulman into his family, treated him like a son when he came to teach. The merchant had liked him, looked forward to the alternate months he would be visiting in their home. But a husband for his eldest? Never! Never in a thousand years! Who was he, this penniless boy, to steal into the bosom of his family and make off with its greatest treasure? Baila was meant to be the wife of a man of substance, to live a life of comfort and gentility. As the wife of Itzrok Shulman, she would be lucky to eat bread; she would spend her days at work to support him while he read the Talmud.

"What does this mean?" her father asked in outrage.

"I love him, Papa. I want only to be his wife."

"Never," her father roared, "never so long as there is life in my body to prevent it."

In the next room Baila's sisters pressed their ears to the wall to hear the commotion until their mother angrily shooed them outside to fetch wood for the oven.

"Who is he, this fine Itzrok Shulman?" her father shouted. "A pauper who eats at others' tables! A tutor in patched pants! A nobody! A nobody who has nothing!"

"But he will be—"

"Don't tell me what he will be," her father roared. "Tell me what he is. No, let me tell you. He is a nobody!"

Baila Donevitz sat quietly sobbing before the uncharacteristic wrath of her father.

"A pauper steals into my house in the guise of a teacher, and suddenly he becomes a bridegroom! A *nebechel*, without a spare shirt dares to aspire to my daughter's hand! A snake crawls into my presence and—" On and on he raged. Finally his anger was spent.

"And what should I do now, Baila?" he asked.

Still she remained silent, looking down at the rug under her feet.

"I have given my word; the baker's son has been introduced at the synagogue as my potential son-in-law. The banns are being posted."

Only then did Baila speak.

"I would rather cut my heart out than bring you dishonor, papa. Let me instead run away."

"And where would you run, child?"

"To America, to Uncle Morris and Aunt Frieda," she said, hope rising to her voice.

She had anticipated this scene. She had known that her father would reject Itzrok. She had reasoned that her father would be left in an untenable position by her plea. She would throw herself in the river before marrying the fat, ugly young man her father had chosen for her. Although she had no burning desire to emigrate to America —regardless of the pictures of the new land with streets of gold that had been legend to her since childhood—it was preferable to drowning. So she pressed her case, and in the end, her father relented.

"On one condition," he said. "You must promise me that you will not see Itzrok Shulman before you leave and that you will leave no message for him as to where you have gone."

Baila quickly agreed. Although it would break her heart to leave him, she prayed Itzrok would somehow learn of the circumstances and understand.

Because of her father's predicament, preparations were made hastily. The papers were arranged, and soon she had made her tearful farewells and was gone.

"Gone, Dovidl," Isaac told his grandson. "Gone away without a word or a trace. When I asked her father about her, he raged and ordered me out of his house. The whole town was closed to me. Nobody would tell me what had happened until I happened to meet a stranger on the road. It was the *shadchen*. Not knowing me, he told how he lost a fat commission because a foolish girl had preferred a penniless teacher to his rich client. He said if he could get his hands on the teacher, he would tear his arms off, so angry was he. Of course, I had been as bitter as he until I heard his story. Then I smiled. It was a long way to America. It would cost a great deal of money to get there. But I knew I would manage, that somehow, somewhere, I would find her."

For a long moment Isaac sat smiling sheepishly; then he busied himself with his knife and plug of tobacco.

"Someday soon," he said, "I'll tell you how I found her. But not now. We've talked away the afternoon already, and I have business to attend to."

As he left the old man's den, David saw his grandmother busily polishing a brass bowl that Lucy had already polished a few hours earlier. She kissed him and smiled broadly. He suspected that she had been listening at the door when her husband recalled how beautiful she had been.

200

26

The metal ball rolled straight by the top row of numbers on the pinball machine.

"Damnit," David cried, "that seven was worth 96 games."

"Maybe I can bring it home," Bob answered.

His big hands gripping the sides of the pinball machine, Bob coaxed the ball between the 10 and the 11, ringed the 17 with it and came out, and eased it onto the bumper above the 23. The ball bounced, Bob shook the machine slightly, and it was in the ball-return hole.

"Beautiful," David said. "Like an artist. Now come on, Bob, thump that thing. You had the seven down pat last week."

Bob covered the plunger with the thumb of his left hand, gripped the frame of the machine with the other fingers, and fired. The ball hit the one side, came back and momentarily wavered on the spot between the 6 and 7. Then it fell through into the 13.

"Five in a line down the drain," David muttered, as he fed the first nickel into the slot for his own shot. "Must've had your mind on that new girl. What's her name, anyhow?"

"Uh, let me see. Virginia introduced me, but I wasn't listening too close. I think she said it was Marsha—something like that. Say, that's a pretty good shot."

The odds had taken a quick jump, and David sent the first ball squarely into the seven hole.

"See that," he said. "Any dummy can make a seven."

The next afternoon was the first day of football practice, and coach Ralph Blake, towering, former all-ACC end at the University of North Carolina, pushed his out-of-shape squad through a long afternoon of exercises and windsprints in the hot August sun.

"Come on, move! move!" he yelled. "Sweat those cigarettes outa you."

"What's the matter, Burris? Too much easy livin' this summer?"

"Kingley, don't you even think of droppin' outa this sprint, or I'll have you runnin' laps till midnight. Move it, fat man, move."

"You, Harris—I can see them smokes poppin' out of every pore."

"Move it. Ya look like a bunch a wash women, the way you're runnin'."

"McKay, get the lead outta your butt. Move."

The afternoon heat, settling like a heavy hand on the dusty practice field, weighed on them, pressured them to fall or quit. But Coach Blake wasn't having any quitting.

"You ladies better be glad I don't have you in pads," he yelled, "else you'd see what hot is."

"All right, hold it," he said finally. "I want some situps. Satterfield, lead 'em."

David collapsed to the ground, grateful that the windsprints were over for awhile. His breath was coming in short bursts, and the hot air didn't seem to satisfy his lungs. His stomach was beginning to feel queasy; he knew he couldn't run much farther without a breather.

As Alec Satterfield trotted around to the front of the group, David felt a slight twinge of envy. Satterfield was an excellent athlete, with a fine build and a shock of curly blond hair topping a square, well-made face.

In the 10th grade, Mr. Holiday, the biology teacher, had been lecturing on the muscle structure of the arm and decided to demonstrate with a live one. "Let's see," he said. "I could use a good arm to explain this. Um." As his eyes passed over them, David attempted to persuade him telepathically to select him. Nothing could have given him greater pleasure than an excuse to flex his painstakingly developed arm in front of the class. For a moment, the teacher's eyes seemed to single him out; then they traveled on to Satterfield.

Alec had a better arm than he did, David admitted to himself. Still, this didn't ease the momentary disappointment. In the seat ahead of him, Bob saw David tense slightly, and understood what was going through his mind.

"What's the matter, Roughhouse?" he asked sarcastically. "How come he picked Satterfield'n not you?"

"I dunno. Guess he doesn't know a real arm when he sees one," David whispered over his shoulder. Bob chuckled his infuriating little chuckle.

202

Whereas Alec Satterfield was a natural athlete, David was not. At 160 pounds, he was strong enough, even for the right guard position he played. And he was fast enough to run the pulling plays. But he had neither the coordination nor the natural moves of a great ballplayer. Although he never admitted it to anyone, even Bob, he didn't really care for the game all that much. Maybe, he thought, because he wasn't bloodthirsty enough. Maybe even because he had hit too many people too hard before he ever came to the game. After a slashing tackle which left an opposing halfback unconscious the year before, Billy Mack Turner, the linebacker on the right side behind David's guard position, had come back to the line with a broad smile.

"Um, um, that felt good," he said, and the others grinned and nodded.

As many times as he had heard some variation of that, and as many times as he had heard the coach praise such a tackle or a particularly vicious block, David never really understood what they were talking about.

David played football not out of love for hitting or even for enjoyment of the game itself, but because football players automatically had status in Somerset. There were football players and then there were the other boys. The girls, David had learned early on, tended to think that way, too. So he played ball, grinding out each day's practice with no particular pleasure, relying on his strength and quickness to compensate for his lack of desire and ability.

The assistant line coach, a big man name Holston, sensed the situation the year before—when David was a junior—without understanding it. In his world everyone loved football, loved to punish opposing ballplayers, loved the glory and honor of the game. David tackled competently but lightly, hard enough to get his man but never, if he could avoid it, to hurt him. The coach had watched this with growing annoyance. Finally he determined to fix it.

In head-on tackling practice one afternoon, David was in the tackling slot when Gene Peterson, a spindly, would-be quarterback, was given the ball. He ran at David (the objective being to run over him), and predictably, David hit him above the knees, picked him up, and dumped him over backward gently.

"Well, ain't that nice. Harris's got a heart," the coach jeered, as David was trotting to the back of the tackling line.

"Come back here, lady, and let's see if we can teach you something about tackling." Then he called Moorehead, the hard-running halfback; a big, fast linebacker named Bronson; and Tim Mackay, the 250-pound starting left tackle.

203

"All right, boys, you're runnin' one at a time. Harris is tackling. See if you can make him mean."

David tackled Moorehead cleanly the first time, got Bronson at the knees, and plowed into Mackay, pushing him over backward. On the next tackle Moorehead caught David on the side of the head with his knee, dazing him slightly; but he got Bronson and Mackay again. As he got off the ground, the coach pitched the ball to Moorehead who hit him just before he got his balance, and they went over together. They continued to come at him, faster than they should have. David refused to quit. At any point he could have stopped tackling. Most of the team had quit practicing to watch, and Bob and some of the others desperately wished he *would* quit. But he kept trying, going down on every tackle, but getting up again—and the coach kept throwing the ball. Finally his strength began to ebb. He caught Bronson's helmet on his left jaw, and Mackay ran right over him. But it was Moorehead who finally knocked him unconscious.

When he woke several minutes later, Bob was hovering over him, with Moorehead and Bronson looking on curiously and Pat Getty, the trainer, wiping his face with a wet towel. He got to his feet, walked a few unsteady paces, shook his head to clear it, and the fury boiled up in him.

"They can't beat me, Bob," he said. "I'll show 'em."

"Dave, come on, let's go over to the shade by the fence till you get squared away," Bob pleaded.

But David pushed away in the direction of the coach.

"I want to tackle some more," he said, the words coming out of the back of his throat in a low growl, knowing it was a crazy thing he was saying, half-expecting Holston to refuse him.

But Holston only grinned, imagining he was accomplishing what he set out to do. He called three fresh, big men over and they ran at, and finally, over David until he was unconscious again—lying on the ground with the trainer wiping blood from a cut lip and a busted nose.

David was unconscious for more than an hour. He later learned from Bob that he had stripped to the waist, wandered groggily around the field until he found big Alex Drew, who was acknowledged to be the toughest, most vicious boy in the school, and challenged him to a fight. Bob managed to pull him away.

"You're crazy, you know that!" Bob said, as they drove home after practice. "You couldn't take the whole team, so you decide to tangle with Alex. What was that gonna prove?"

David said nothing. It was not until the next day that he began to feel he had won.

204

It was at a football practice at the beginning of his senior year that he first saw Marcie. The September heat and grinding drills had turned his uniform into a sodden mass of cotton and canvas, and during one series of plays, he had eaten a mouthful of dirt, diving for a fumble. Sweat was streaming down his face, blurring his vision from time to time, until he could wipe his eyes and forehead with the dirty sleeve of his practice jersey.

In the huddle, Bob called his attention to her.

"There she is, champ."

"There who is?"

"You know. The gal I was telling you about with the big knockers."

Glancing behind him, he saw three girls in the stands; the familiar, tall Virginia Fielding, her friend Mary Chamblee, and the girl Bob had told him about the day he missed the seven for five in a line.

He was surprised when he looked at her. Even in the blistering heat of the stands, she looked cool and fresh. A full shock of deep-brown hair framed her face, and even from 40 yards away, David could see that her eyes were large and dark and her lips full. She was deeply tanned and healthy-looking—certainly the best-looking girl in town, he thought.

Picking up the football, David tossed it to Bob. "Pass me one over in that direction, Ace. I want a closer look."

He started to run, and Bob flipped the perfect spiral he always made look so easy. Running hard, David took the ball over his left shoulder. When he stopped, he was only a few feet from the girls.

"Nice catch, mister," Virginia called to him.

Turning, he smiled and waved. The other girls were smiling, too, and now he saw her teeth, even and starkly white against the lightly lipsticked lips. For the moment he was enormously glad he played football.

"David, let me introduce a friend," Mary said. He sauntered to the fence, the ball tucked casually under his arm.

The girl was still smiling slightly. He marveled again that not a hair was out of place. She wore a black, jersey shirt, cut away high on her tanned arms, and a pair of white shorts. Against the sun, the black jersey obscured the lines of her breasts, but up close, he saw that they were full and uptilted, stretching the material of her shirt up and away from a slender waist.

"David Harris, this is Marsha Stevens. She's new in town."

"Well, aren't we lucky to have her," David said, feeling heroic in his uniform.

"Thank you," Marsha said, neither blushing or in any other way appearing coquettish. Instead, she looked directly into his eyes with a level gaze. "What position do you play?" she asked.

"Right guard. Just an old dumb lineman."

"Oh, isn't that the position Tom Crawford plays?" she asked.

Goddamnit! That son of a bitch always manages to get everywhere just ahead of me, David thought.

"Yeah, we kind of alternate in the slot," he lied. Actually Crawford was the starting right guard; David played second-string behind him. Tom was better than he was, and he deserved to start. David often thought he wouldn't mind playing second string behind any other good athlete, but playing behind Crawford galled him. He had known Crawford for many years. At one point, years earlier, David had thought him his friend, but that had ended in a fight. Since then, Crawford seemed to delight in finding ways to belittle him.

Coach Blake's whistle cut the air. "Get over here, Harris. If you wanna be a hero and get all the little girls, by God, you're gonna have to earn it."

After practice David thought about her, trying to remember everything about her. There was a small mole under her left eye, he remembered. Her hair might have looked better cut shorter. But that was all he could think of that was less than perfect.

He wanted to pick up the phone and ask her for a date. But he found excuses for delaying, even though he had called the information operator for her number and carefully written it down as soon as he got home. She was the best-looking girl he had ever seen, and undoubtedly there was a line of guys waiting to date her. Crawford had already moved in; David had seen his light-green convertible pulling out of the parking lot with her and Virginia as he came out of the dressing room after practice. At the least, Alex Drew and Brad King must've already called her, too. And it would be Goddamn miserable to hear her say no.

I'll call her anyway, he said to himself. What've I got to lose? But he knew he wouldn't. He had to pick his exposures to failure very carefully.

He was relieved when his father came into the room.

"How'd practice go today, son?"

"Oh, pretty well. Nothin' special, except maybe the shovelfull of dirt I ate on a fumble."

Ben chuckled. Publicly (that is, at the family dinner table) he sided with Rachel's often-stated opposition to the boy's playing football. But deep inside he understood why David played and admired him for it.

"How does it look for starting the first game?"

"Not too good, I'm afraid. Tom Crawford has it pretty well sewed up."

"Well, the world won't end. I'm sure you'll play plenty before the season ends."

"I guess so."

Damn Crawford, probably out with her right now. If I called, she probably wouldn't be home anyhow.

At a drive-in restaurant later that evening, Bob asked between bites of a chili hotdog what the big deal was. "All right, so she's good-looking. But she's not the only good-looking girl in town." Then he added with a grin: "It's not because you've been cut out again by your man and mine, starting right guard Thomas Crawford, is it? Can't stand the ol' gaff, huh, Roughhouse?"

"Screw you, Charlie," David hurled back. "I suppose it don't eat your ass that right at this moment, Susan Harmon is being romanced by big Grady . . . only the biggest cut-out of the year."

"Nothing to it, Roughhouse. I get 'em when I want 'em." Bob chuckled back. "But you're the big lover. Least that's what I'm always hearing from you. Now we'll see how far you get with Miss Marsha Stevens."

For a moment he chewed another bite of hotdog. Then he added: "I'm bettin' you don't get any closer than the back bumper of Stud Crawford's big, green Oldsmo."

A few weeks later four carloads of football players and an assortment of girls from the high school drove up to Table Rock Park in the mountains for a Saturday at the lake. Marsha Stevens was one of the girls, ostensibly with her girl friends but clearly staked out by Tom Crawford. After lunch she brought out a ukulele and began to play and sing—extremely well—and most of the group gathered around her.

"I need a baritone who can carry the melody," she said. "Any volunteers?"

Before he knew what had happened, David had been pushed forward by Bob. Then he was singing with Marcie, and just like that, they were together, with Crawford unable to do much besides glare at him.

Later, when they went for a walk around the lake, David found an old bateau pulled up in the weeds of a pretty little cove.

"How 'bout a ride?" he asked, and soon they were out on the water. The boat leaked only a little, but David moved it efficiently along the shoreline with a board he found. The sun was hot.

"Say," he said, "you mind if I take my shirt off?"

"Of course not," she said. As he pulled the polo shirt over his head, she appraised him openly. "That's some set of muscles you've got there, sir."

"Well, I work at it. I still haven't caught up with Tom, though."

He immediately wished he hadn't said such a childish thing.

But she bailed him out. "No, you're wrong. You've got a better physique than he does."

David could scarcely believe his ears. "You really mean that?"

"Of course I do." She smiled. "Not that it makes all that much difference if you do or don't, but you do anyhow."

Just like that.

Later she said yes, she'd love to go to the movies Friday night. Then they were laughing together at the water seeping faster now through the partially rotted boards of the boat and David's frantic efforts to get them back to shore before it sank.

So, in September, it began, with Marcie making David feel bigger than he had ever felt before, with their laughter echoing across the inlet and heavy pines beyond.

And it continued. When they were together, laughter came easily to them, songs came out of nowhere, and always, David felt better because she was with him.

Every afternoon at football practice, she would be there in the stands, watching him, waiting for him to shower, just for the few minutes they would have together. They were together at dances and the movies and just riding in his car. Every Friday and Saturday night.

When he met her father the first time, Mr. Stevens called her Marcie. Later, David said to her that she looked like a Marcie. "A Marcie should be beautiful and laugh a lot."

So she became Marcie. He thought of her constantly, called her every night they weren't together. He broke Jim Sherman's nose at football practice because he asked David with a leer if he was "gittin' any of that." No one asked him again.

He played better football because she was in the stands, and in the fourth game of the season, he took the starting guard job from Crawford.

In the last quarter of the fifth game, David emerged from a pileup with a sharp pain in his right arm. He didn't mention it to the coach or his parents, but at 2:00 A.M. it was throbbing so that it awakened him from an exhausted sleep. He quietly shook his father awake, and in the bright light of the kitchen, they saw that the arm was swollen to twice its size from elbow to shoulder and was turning black.

The resident at the hospital's emergency room read the x-ray's wet and told them that the arm was not broken, but the bone was split and the muscle deeply bruised. As he bandaged the arm and tied the sling, the doctor told David there would be no more football that season. Both the doctor and his father looked for signs of disappointment but found none. David was pleased. He had the "million-dollar wound." All the credit due a football player, all the status and position, would accrue to him without his having to get his head beat in every day at practice. The arm in a sling would be a badge of honor.

"You're sure I can't play?" he asked the doctor.

"Afraid not. Not this year," the doctor said firmly. "Somerset High will just have to get along without you."

In the car, going home, David began to feel groggy from the painkiller the doctor had given him.

"Guess I'm gonna catch it from Mom," he said.

"No, son, I think when she gets over the initial shock of seeing the sling, she'll be just fine. Don't worry about it."

Then they were home and in bed again.

27

David's arm did become a badge of honor at school. He had earned it on the gridiron for the honor of Somerset High. He told the story a hundred times of how it had been injured, and each time the damage grew a bit more grievous, the pain a little more intense.

Marcie was upset when she first saw the sling, but he told her bravely that it would be all right, that it was hardly more than a scratch. What he didn't say was how glad he was that the injury would give him all the status of a football player with which to finish out his senior year and at the same time release him from the tiresome, grinding scrimmages and practice.

"Besides, this gives me my afternoons free to be with you," he said gaily.

For the next few days David went to football practice and stood with Coach Blake, watching the scrimmages. Then gradually he lost interest in the afternoon sessions.

The sling was awkward. He had trouble adjusting to it. But when he was with Marcie, he forgot about it. Because with Marcie, all reality seemed to be suspended; he seemed to float on a carpet of pure, unalloyed happiness. Not just when he held her, but when they walked down the street or rode in his car or just sat talking and laughing together before school every morning.

He had been popular with the girls since his sophomore year in high school. He had dated the brightest, the prettiest, the best of them. But none made him feel as good as Marcie did.

For hours they sat together and listened to popular music: Kitty Kallen's soft rendition of "Little Things Mean a Lot," Tony Bennett singing "Stranger in Paradise," the Four Aces' version of "Three Coins in the Fountain," and Bill Haley's raucous version of "Shake, Rattle, and Roll." Just being together was enough for them. In each other they found a new pleasure and contentment.

Soon people began to think of them as a pair. It was expected that they would be together—at dances, the drive-in, movies. It seemed as if they belonged together, that it somehow made sense that they would have found each other because they were so perfect together.

He loved her, he knew that, but he didn't know how to say it to her or—in a strange way—even to himself. At a New Year's Eve party at the lake, as they were dancing, he haltingly asked her to go steady with him, and she kissed him lightly on the lips, out there in the middle of the improvised dance floor, and said she would love to. Then she giggled, and so did he, because they both realized that they already had been going steady, and that was somehow funny.

To them, everything was funny and beautiful and delicious, because they were together and they loved each other—even if they hadn't found quite the right moment to say it to each other. The secret and the pain that nagged at Marcie dropped away when they were together, and the hurt that David had grown up with was also suspended. She was his girl—this girl, Marcie Stevens—this gorgeous, funny, talented, loving girl, and that made the tints around reality completely different shades, all silver and blue and golden. When she laughed, all of the old hurts fell away from him. When he held her, the strength of his arms told her that it was all right and that she could forget.

He wanted to be with her all of the time, to touch and hold her and reassure himself that she was his girl. So he held her when they danced and when they kissed, walked with his arm around her whenever they were together, sat touching her hand or playing his fingertips over her smooth face when he was not holding her.

All around them, soon-to-be-graduating seniors were eloping, marrying secretly because they wanted to or because they had to. He and Marcie talked about the others but never about themselves. As each new marriage was discovered by the town, Ben and Rachel anxiously watched David for signs that he might be planning to elope with Marcie. Finally, just before graduation, Ben quietly raised the question with David, who laughed and said he had a lot to get done before he could think about getting married.

"Hey, I'll be going to New York for the summer, and then to school. I can't do that if I'm married, Dad," he reassured his father. "Don't worry so much."

"My boy," Ben joked, "I've worried so much all my life that the only time I worry now is when I don't have anything to worry about. You know that." But he still felt uneasy. She was such a pretty child, so full of life, and she did seem to make David so happy.

He said goodbye to her once, solemnly, finally, sure that it was the appropriate thing to do. It was the hot June night in 1954 they graduated from high school, the night they crossed the high platform, diplomas rolled in round, white tubes clutched in their hands, sweating under their awkward black caps and gowns, the night the lieutenant governor told them to go out into life armed with the sure knowledge that the South was right, that God was supreme, and that their generation would triumph in all the endeavors where previous generations had failed.

David left the stage in a state of jubilant self-confidence. Before him stretched a summer in the Catskill Mountains of New York where, according to all reports, every nod from the glamourous guests concealed a secret invitation. And after that, college—100 miles from her and itself a brand new world that would absorb him too much to leave any time for a girl back home.

Billy Grady had a bottle under the seat of his father's red Pontiac. Bob was detained near the stage, talking to his parents. While they waited for him, Billy and David toasted each other straight from the bottle, choking, eyes stinging, solemnly promising never to forget what Somerset High had meant to them. After a second drink, they tore a dollar bill in half, each taking half to keep in his billfold until they met again, joined halves, and bought a drink together. (The next year, Billy's was a half-burned cinder in his pocket when his car hit a bridge abutment going 90 miles per hour.)

In two days the whole crowd, except for David, would be going to Myrtle Beach for a long weekend. He had to stay home and prepare for his summer in New York. So he let Marcie go on graduation night, making her sad at the moment she should have been the happiest.

"Not fair to ask you to sit home all summer waiting for me," he had blurted out. "You go on out with other guys this summer an' have a good time." He said it clumsily, and not with conviction. But when she objected, he insisted, clinching his argument with the observation that he would be undoubtedly going out with other girls.

He felt about the whole thing a certain grand nobility, more so when she cried softly and agreed. But the next day he couldn't bear the idea. So morose was he that his mother finally insisted that he go to the beach, promising to get his things prepared for New York herself.

When he arrived he found Marcie on the beach with a group of

Somerset girls. Within an hour—by cajoling, reasoning, and in one case, a naked threat of violence—he had broken all the dates she had made for the weekend.

The first night and the next, they lay together on a beach blanket until sunrise, just talking and being close. It would have surprised the town—even Bob—to know he had never had her, in fact, had never come close. The reasons were too complex to reason out: a product of the times, certainly; her fear of the possible consequences of sex; his genuinely deep respect and love for her, this and more. But on the last night, in the darkness, their lives changed forever.

For several hours, as the moon disappeared behind the clouds and left them in the privacy of darkness, they held each other very close, kissing passionately and feeling each other not with their hands but with their bodies. The sound of the waves drowned their moaning. David began to hurt from wanting her—a stabbing, physical pain in his groin that laced through his stomach and up his back. Marcie felt it, somehow knew it was happening but not knowing how, and felt in herself that, for reasons not physical, not lustful, not understandable, she needed him, too. Fear clutched her like a cold hand, momentarily froze her will, and then was pushed away by other, stronger feelings. She knew she would have to let him know, so she turned her body until her breast lay in his open hand. Never before had he held it. She could feel the hesitation in him. She pressed herself into his hand, making sure he understood that she meant him to fondle her. She had always been proud of her breasts. As the high school years had passed without their ever having been fondled or seen by the succession of boys she had dated, she had sometimes felt a momentary apprehension that they would begin to lose some of their good shape and texture before someone could appreciate them. Now the time had come. She was at one and the same time terrified and pleased. Slowly David's hand closed lightly about it, feeling its fullness and firmness. Then, very slowly, he began to caress it, to squeeze it slightly. Then he was kissing her, through her shirt and brassiere but kissing her nonetheless, then seeking her nipple through the fabric with his lips.

Now she rolled slightly toward him, feeling his swollen maleness against her leg. He had always kept it away from her, no matter how excited he became, but tonight was different.

"Oh, I love you," he muttered, now kissing the taut stomach he exposed by lifting her shirt. "What do you want me to do?"

"Anything . . . anything," she whispered. Then she felt his lips on her belly, through her shorts, felt them kissing her down to the inside of her thighs, felt the gentle nuzzlings of his face and the

213

licking of her smooth, white skin with his tongue. A feeling of electric excitement shot through her body, and she wanted more of everything.

David moved his mouth up the inside of her thighs, until he was only inches away from the triangle that joined them. At the same time, his hand was under her brassiere, now clutching and caressing her firm, full breast. He was seized, as he had never been before with any girl, with the desire to suck at her. As he kissed her thighs, her groaning and writhing only increased his desire.

There had been other girls before, the first the football team's gang bang, a girl named Carrie, whom he later felt guilty about because, like the others, he had only wanted to use her and get off in her in some dark, hidden place and then leave her. Finally he took her to a school dance, knowing that he would be embarrassed and not caring as much as he cared about her that night, daring the rest of them with his eyes to humiliate her. When they left the dance, she thanked him and cried. There were other times with Carrie, and with Dot, the waitress at the drive in, who made love not out of loneliness, not out of the need to be touched in any way she could be, as Carrie did, but because she loved it, and there was never enough of it for her.

Carrie had taught him that making love meant reaching out and touching another person. It was with Dot that he lost his innocence, because Dot could smile at him as she stripped off her clothes, not embarrassed or afraid; only wanting him, and saying things he had never heard a woman say. Every night for weeks—until the night he went for her and was told that she had moved away—he waited for her until her shift ended. She wanted only to be driven to a private place where he could take her, and her him, there in the back seat of his father's car.

She had inflamed him with her frankness and her lust, but never in the way Marcie now filled him with desire, here on the beach. Soon, desire turned to urgent need. Then the several inches of time and space had disappeared, and he was gnawing at her through her shorts, raking his lower teeth between her legs.

"Oh, David," she moaned, "what are . . . what are you doing?" But only the waves answered her, and the sound of the wind.

For a fleeting moment, terror gripped her again, even as his strong hands did. Then it was gone, and in its place, there was a strange, wild convulsion in her body, centered in sensation between her legs.

"Do it to me," she gasped, "do it to me, darling."

Then his fingers were fumbling for the button of her shorts. As

214

he slid them down over her knees, down her long, slim legs, she realized that she could still stop him, but she knew she would not. She wanted him now, wanted to feel him inside of her, to feel his weight on her, to feel their bodies closer together, to feel him reaching into her to touch the spot where the wild convulsive feeling tingled in her. She was no longer afraid.

The clouds still covered what there was of the moon that night, and later, she realized that she had been sorry it was dark and he could not see her.

As David stripped off her panties, his mind reeled with the hotness of her, the sweet smell of her, and his need. In the midst of the selfishness of possession, he managed to find one shred of control.

"Are you sure?" he asked, knowing that he loved her even more than he needed her, and that he could still stop.

"Oh, yes, David, yes, yes. I love you. I—"

Then he spread her legs, delicately and with gentleness, and took his large, throbbing penis in his right hand to guide it home.

As it touched her, he knew he would have only moments, so he hurried, hating himself as he did for having to. Then he was inside her, an inch, a little more perhaps, then half way. Slowly he began to work it in and out, slowly, slowly, trying not to hurt her, trying to prevent the imminent explosion of himself in her.

Too soon, the shuddering, compelling explosion happened, and he lost all sense of consideration and feeling, knowing only his own compelling need, which carried him into her deeply; which blacked out her sudden gasp of pain; which ignored the stiffening muscle spasm that shook her body. Then he was moving in and out of her, his way made easier by what he thought was semen but which was actually blood.

When it was over she lay quietly, feeling the pain radiate up her stomach and hips, feeling the last of the blood trickle down her thighs —wondering if he knew how sharp her pain had been and whether she should try to tell him.

For several minutes neither spoke; then David lit a cigarette. In the flare of the match, he saw blood stains on the white sand.

"Oh my God," he gasped.

"What is it?" she asked softly, her voice desembodied, floating up to him out of the darkness.

"I've hurt you," he exclaimed.

"It's all right, David. It's all right."

"No, it isn't," he said, his voice now flat. "Why didn't you stop me; why didn't you tell me? I'd have—"

"That's why, darling, I wanted you to have me. I wanted to give you everything I could before you left me."

Then he was holding her very close, stroking her hair, and almost sobbing with his own pain.

"I'm never gonna leave you, not really, not for good. I love you too much, Marcie. You know . . . I'm never—"

"Shhh . . ." she soothed him. "I know."

At that moment she felt very old and wise.

The waves were stronger now; the wind pushed the clouds beyond the slice of moon. Everything except David's conscience was quiet. For Marcie there was a strange calm, a certain contentment after the pain subsided. And as she lay in David's arms, she fell asleep.

He looked at her face, now composed and serene, and swore silently that he would never take her again until they were married. He looked away at the white lines the wave crests made against the black ocean, rising and falling in the moonlight. She slept, and for the several hours until dawn, he guarded her.

The summer was a strange, new experience for David, who joked that he was undoubtedly the worst busboy—and best paid—in the Catskills. The guests liked him, not because his memory was faultless when they ordered extra dishes or his style in pouring their coffee was graceful, but because he was an oddity: a Southern Jewish kid with the kind of moxie only New Yorkers could appreciate.

He broke most of the rules of the house that summer. At night, he hung around with the drinkers at the Tally Ho Tavern down the road from the hotel rather than fraternize with the guests, as he was repeatedly told he was expected to do. He invited an occasional guest outside when his sense of honor was offended. When one of them, a strapping salesman from the garment district in New York, accepted his offer, David sent him to the local dentist's office to try to repair three broken teeth. He learned to drink that summer, taking to boilermakers—a glass of rye dumped into a glass of Rheingold Beer.

The one area in which he obliged the management was in entertaining the ladies who claimed to be "lonely," as the Catskill vernacular had it. What that meant was that their husbands were in New York screwing their secretaries, and they—being stuck out of the way for the summer in this godforsaken dump—were horny. Whenever Herbie, the owner of the hotel, called David in to discuss another "lonely" guest, David just grinned and nodded.

Gradually he increased his tips to the point where he was earning more than Irv, his waiter.

"Look, if it bothers you, why don't you put one of these ladies

216

away once in a while?" David once asked him innocently.

Irv—fastidious, serious, dedicated to the idea of sublimating his sexual drives by writing letters every night to his fiancée in New Jersey—just shook his head. "The Gluckstern woman," he said. "Christ, she must be 45 years old, and you're laying her. She's nearly 30 years older than you are, David. How in God's name can you bring yourself to put it to a woman nearly three times your age?"

David chuckled. "To tell you the truth, Irv," he said, "I have more trouble bringing myself to do it because her name is Gluckstern than because she's 45. You know how unromantic it is to plank somebody named Gluckstern?"

Occasionally he did feel a bit sleazy about his indiscretion, and whenever he felt down on himself, he would write Marcie a long letter. Just writing her made him feel clean, and, well before Labor Day weekend when the season ended, he was almost sick with missing her.

In September he and Bob left for college. They had chosen the University of Georgia for their freshman year, for various reasons, and were pleased with their choice. The first day they arrived on campus, the Jewish fraternities began to rush David. He was, it seemed, a good catch for the fraternities. He was well built and good-looking. He was not from an impoverished home, either financially or culturally. He was personable. And most important, he was a reasonably good athlete, probably just the fellow to help TEP or Phi Ep or AEP win the intramural championship.

So he was wildly rushed: wined and dined, given cars to drive, fixed up with dates, invited to a whirl of parties.

Because of the enthusiasm with which he was rushed, he wasn't surprised to get bids from all three Jewish fraternities on pledge day. When he went to the student building to return them, he found representatives of the three fraternities behind little tables in a large room, away from the large student building social area where the other fraternities had put their anxious upperclassmen, pledge pins at the ready.

Since they were all together and away from everyone else, David found it convenient to make one speech instead of three, as he had expected to have to do. He thanked the fraternities for their hospitality and their flattering interest in him, but declined to pledge.

The reaction was one of great surprise. The TEPs figured they had him in the bag because of Lenore, the clincher they had used on him. Good ol' Lenore had come through for them in the clutch so many times; *what* were they going to do when she graduated? A prize pledge prospect would be assigned to Lenore, and if she liked him—and Lenore liked almost everybody—he was as good as laid—and pledged. But not this one.

The AEPs also figured him in the bag, because their prize athlete, Art Arnoff, had handled this one personally. Arnoff, the great SEC record-holding dash man and hurdler; Arnoff, who would not make the Olympics because of two-tenths of a second of kick he couldn't quite make. Arnoff, superjock, had worn this freshman like a second skin for two weeks. Any halfassed athlete from a small town was sure to fall for the glitter of brotherhood with superjocks—except this one.

The Phi Ep representative merely gloated. Since Phi Ep usually ended up with what was left over from TEP and AEP, they knew they wouldn't get Harris. And since all Jews joined fraternities, he was bound to fall to one of the other two. But here he was, declining to join any of them, and this was closer to victory than the Phi Eps had expected to come.

By the end of the day, every Jewish student on campus knew that David Harris, the good catch, the personable, good-looking, athletic freshman from the small town in South Carolina, was going to be an independent.

In her room, Lenore searched her mind. Where had she failed, she wondered. As she remembered the evening she spent with David, she began to feel a twinge of guilt. Maybe it was because she enjoyed it a little. She didn't usually.

Disgusted, Art Arnoff muttered that Harris was nothing but a "fuckin' *goy*" anyhow. "Let him live with the *goyim* and to hell with him."

In one way, it was the most perceptive comment Arnoff had ever made.

A month later David did pledge a fraternity. He was wandering by the Varsity, the home of the "university hamburger," after having drunk too many pitchers of beer at the Old South bar, when he was spotted by a party of TEPs out for a bucket of ice. They spirited him away to their party, and when he awoke in his bed the next morning, his head hurt and he dimly remembered saying something about belonging. Lenore had been there, and he had promised her something as she took her sweater off in the back room. Now let's see, what was it? He remembered her, how her breasts tumbled out of her black lace bra, how she smiled at him. What was it he promised? It was . . . it was . . . , oh, Christ, what the hell was it?

Aggravated, he swung his legs over the side of the bed, recoiled from the head pain, and then he spotted it: his good blue cashmere sweater, lying on the chair, with a triangular bit of metal fastened to it. Now he remembered his promise.

"Wake up, Bob," he had called to his roommate. "I think I just joined a fuckin' fraternity."

His parents were delighted at his pledging, being entirely unaware of the circumstances under which his pledge had been made. It was good, they told him, that he would have some taste of being with his own people, some Jewish experience, the comfortable feeling of being surrounded by people with whom he could relax and feel safe.

"It wouldn't hurt," his mother had said, "for you to date some nice Jewish girls for a change," with emphasis on the word "nice." The first Jewish girl David had met at Georgia was Lenore, and she was the only one he had "dated." "Funny you should mention that," he said to his parents with an unexplained grin. "It was a nice Jewish girl who helped convince me to pledge." If David's father caught the implication, he made no acknowledgment of it.

He only lasted three months. He refused to participate in any of the pledge activities, which he considered absurd. For reasons he only partially understood, the "brothers" bore his insolence in silence. He seldom visited the fraternity house, a beautiful, old, white-pillared colonial house whose stateliness was often lost under billowing "Beat Tech" banners or others noting whatever the weekly athletic aberration on campus was to be.

The first time David visited the house, he didn't get any farther than the entrance to the front walk. There, on the sidewalk, he encountered Cookie Schwartz and Janet Rosen, two freshmen he had gotten to know during rush week. Aside from a slight thickening at the ankles and a bit of superfluous hair on her face, Cookie appealed to him, so he engaged them in conversation. Hardly had he said the first word, however, when a voice bellowed at him from the porch of the fraternity house.

"Pledge," it commanded.

David ignored it, pretending not to hear it, and continued talking. Both girls looked at him nervously.

"Pledge, hey, pledge," it rang again.

Again, he refused to acknowledge it.

"He's calling you," Cookie finally interjected.

"How do you know?" David asked innocently.

"Well," she said, "he's looking directly at you and you're the only TEP pledge out here."

Turning, David looked at the senior in mock surprise.

"Why, were you calling me?" he asked.

"You know damn well I'm callin' you," the senior shot back.

"Well, next time you want to get my attention, try using my name," he said. "People call me Dave or David or Harris or Mr. Harris. But 'pledge' ain't part of my name." As he spoke, David thought to himself how snotty he must sound. "Now what do you want?"

The senior instructed him to go to the Gulf service station, about four blocks away and get him a Coke.

"I seem to remember a Coke machine in the house," David said. "Why don't you get one out of there?"

"I don't like those Cokes," the senior replied. "I like the ones from the Gulf station."

It sounded like a challenge to David, and he was never one to fail the occasion. There was about his response a large measure of immaturity, of childishness, he knew, but he was himself, and he had to live with that fact. Every little *goyish* bastard who ever called him a kike had gotten him ready for adulthood—imperfectly, violently, insecurely—but he was David Harris, so he could do little else but what he did.

"You want me to run your errands, mister, you better prove to me you're a better man than I am. And I mean right here and now. 'Cause I don't run errands for just anybody. And from here, you look like just anybody to me!"

Cookie and Janet, both nice Jewish girls from large Southern cities, were thunderstruck that a pledge would dare talk this way to a brother, much less a brother in a fraternity that could largely determine the character, success, and extent of their own social lives for the next two or three years. The senior, himself a small-town boy, understood perfectly well what was happening as he started down the steps. After the first two or three, he stopped, realizing that he might, if he continued, lose, and in front of two Delta Phi Epsilons. So he retreated with suddenly discovered—and most convenient—maturity.

"Why don't you grow up?" he asked disdainfully. "You're in college now, not on a South Carolina mill hill."

"People on mill hills got guts," David shot back. "Do you?"

It was over when the senior swore in feigned disgust—and turned into the house. David felt triumphant as he turned to the two girls. In Somerset they would be impressed; but at the University of Georgia, the ground rules were different. Cookie and Janet were already walking away.

"Hey," he called after them.

Janet called back that they had to go now, and they quickened their pace.

220

"So that's my people I've been hearing so much about," David muttered. He suddenly ached for Marcie Stevens, who wasn't his "people."

David played intramural football for the TEP team, lost three teeth in the final game of a perfect season, and burst into a forbidden brothers' meeting the next night to toss his pledge pin on the table.

"You got the football trophy," he lisped over raw gums, "and you can have this to pin on it."

His people, his mother had said. His people.

As he walked out of the stunned room, Fat Marcus waddled over.

"It's strictly forbidden for you to be in there. Don't you know—"

"Hey, Marcus," David interrupted, "why don't you go fuck yourself?"

He turned on his heel and went out into the November night. It was raining and he had no hat or umbrella; but he didn't care. He lit a Lucky, took a deep, satisfied drag, and stepped off the porch into the cold rain. He was free.

Of course, there were less social events to which he would be invited, less contact with the Jewish students at the university. But that didn't matter. Before and after his depledging, he had spent most of his time with Bob anyway. Every weekend possible, he hitchhiked home to be with Marcie.

She was a freshman at Townsend College, a girl's school in the South Carolina piedmont, a hundred miles from the University of Georgia. When she couldn't get home to Somerset, David hitchhiked to Townsend, because when she was away from him, he felt a numbing ache that no other girl could satisfy.

During Christmas vacation he told her how it hurt him to be away from her, and that he loved her with all of his heart, and that he would always love her. He whispered the words into her hair as they stood together on her front porch in the cold night air. She whispered back that she was his as long as he wanted her, because she loved him so very much. They both knew at that moment that if he asked her to, she would give him her body again. But he would not. So, filled with the sense of her giving, he kissed her once more and whispered good night.

In September David and Bob transferred together to the University of South Carolina, having concluded that it offered most of what the University of Georgia had offered, without having to pay out-of-state fees. As the new school year began, David carefully avoided any rush activities from the single Jewish fraternity on campus, making it clear from the start that he wasn't interested. That would have ended it had he not gone to the university post office when he did, the day the sororities mailed their bids.

It was 11:10 A.M. The post office was empty except for a girl—probably a freshman—who was crying. She was very much alone, standing against the wall opposite an open, empty box, her arms crossed in front of her, swaying slightly with her crying. Her dress was neither fashionable nor expensive. Her loafers were a bit turned over at the heel. She had tried to do her hair herself, and failed. Her face wasn't a pretty one, and her skin was rough.

No bid had come. Every sorority on campus, even the worst ones that took what the others didn't want, had in essence said to her: You're undesirable, you're poor, you're homely, you've got nothing going for you. You're rejected because nobody wants you. Nobody.

David imagined how she must have dreaded his moment, how she must have made excuses to herself for not coming out at 8 when all the others came over, opening their boxes, squealing as they leafed through bids and found the ones they most ardently desired. He almost choked on a nauseating wave of sympathy. He wanted to help, but he didn't know what to do.

Finally he went over to her, touched her arm lightly. She looked up at him quickly, as if he had frightened her. Suddenly she realized that she had been seen, and she brushed at her eyes with the back of her hand.

"What about a cup of coffee? Would you like some coffee?" David asked softly.

"No, I can't," she said. "I'm going home."

"Oh, do you live here in town?"

"No, I'm from Aiken."

Then she was crying again, without trying to cover up.

"I don't belong here," she sobbed. "I'm going home." Then she turned and ran out of the open door into the bright morning sun.

For a moment David stood still, watching her run, seeing her brush by other students she apparently didn't even see. "The sons of bitches," David said softly. "The no-good, dirty sons-of-bitches."

It was her complete defenselessness that nagged at David through lunch when he told Bob the story. By afternoon he felt he had to do something.

"People don't come here to be shit on," he told Bob. "What do you think is gonna happen to her now? Man, this thing could affect her whole life."

Riffling through a stack of bids from fraternities, Bob said he agreed, and for that reason, he wasn't going to join a fraternity.

"But there's not a thing you can do, Dave," he said. "That's the system here. I guess it's always gonna be."

222

David shook his head. "Not if I can help it, it won't be."

That evening he visited the offices of the university newspaper, where he announced flatly that he intended to write a column. There was a laugh from the managing editor's desk.

"Seniors who've worked on the newspaper for at least two years write columns," he said. "Not newly transferred underclassmen."

David reached into his jacket pocket and took out three, folded yellow sheets of typewritten paper. "Here," he said, "read it. If it's not the best column you've got for this issue, throw it away."

As the editor began to read, David turned on his heel and left. The following Thursday, on the lower left side of the editorial page, a column appeared, headlined "The Educational Value of Rejection."

For two and a half years David wrote that column, first attacking fraternities and sororities, arguing that they be outlawed, then gradually enlarging to other matters of social injustice, such as the Ku Klux Klan and extremist reaction to the Supreme Court desegregation ruling of 1954. People read his columns carefully, and many hated him for his lonely positions. He was called out to fight by several fraternity people a year, invitations he always accepted. Once a raspy voice phoned at midnight to tell him "some o' us over to the Lexington klavern seen yo' articles, and by God, we're gonna fix yo' ass, ya no good Jew bastard."

This had frightened David, although he hid it well.

"I know what kind of odds you creeps like," he bluffed. "About 60 to 1! You won't like it here. I got 2,000 men on my side. So come on over and try to take me, if ya' got the balls!"

Even Bob was annoyed by David's position on equal rights for Negroes. But it never varied.

"Fuck 'em," he would say about the people he infuriated, and find himself pushed into ever more liberal positions. No matter where his feelings and his growing social conscience took him, however, he always returned to the matter of fraternities and sororities, never quite able to erase from memory the girl with the turned-over shoes and bad skin, running away from the post office that morning, into the sunlight and the rest of her life.

From the moment he saw her, he had never set foot in a sorority house at the University of South Carolina, and a fraternity house only once, and then only in search of a fellow student—a former marine from New York who had spent several weeks telling people they knew in common that he was going to "shut that bastard's mouth with my fist." When David finally found him, the ex-marine, who was given to boasting about his heroism in Korea, couldn't remember ever having made such a statement.

223

That night, when the fury had worn off, David chuckled over the incident. "Either I'm meaner than the whole Red Chinese Army," he said, "or the hero of the Inchon Reservoir is full of crap. And I don't think I'm meaner than the whole Red Chinese Army."

"Yes, you are, Roughhouse," Bob had mumbled sleepily. "Now shut up and let me get some sleep."

28

Bob made a desultory note on his accounting assignment, then closed his notebook. For a moment he studied David in profile as he stood in front of the mirror, carefully knotting his rep tie.

"You're really gonna go, aren't you?" Bob asked, a heavy note of sarcasm in his voice. "Boy, you're really something!"

"Why wouldn't I go?" David shot back. "I'm invited. Maybe it'll be good for a change."

"Maybe what'll be good?"

"Aw, you know."

"You mean maybe it'll be good going to a party with only Jewish people?" Bob asked. Then he started to chuckle. "You're really something, you know that?"

"What's so funny?" David asked, an edge of annoyance in his voice.

"Nothing much," Bob replied. "Except that you've scorned these people for two years and tried to put their fraternities and sororities out of business for the longest time and now, suddenly, you're heading into the fold."

"I'm not heading into any Goddamn fold, and you know it."

"Then please tell me why you're going at all?" Bob asked with exaggerated patience. "Just explain it!"

There was no explanation that would not bring down further derision on his head, so David just muttered a jovial "fuck you" and went to the closet for his jacket. Bob was still chuckling to himself as David closed the door and headed for the sorority house across the campus. The evening was warm for late October and stars glittered in the darkening skies.

There was pleasure in walking across the manicured lawns of the campus, in wearing about him the comfort of the buildings, the arches, the trees that had bounded much of his life for more than two years. At the top of the quadrangle he saw the stolid old library and thought about its undistinguished collection of books, its uncomfortable reading rooms, its strange, outdated architecture. He liked the old library, and found himself working in it long after the new ultramodern, temperature-controlled library had been built across the campus to supplement and, in the university's long-range planning, replace it. The old library had style, he felt. Besides, it had offered him refuge the year before when the dean of women had gotten the university literary magazine offices closed because of his improprieties as its editor. His crime had been publication of a selection of oils and watercolors painted by university art students. He had argued that the magazine should not be strictly a literary publication, but rather a vehicle for creative expression for all students. The head of the art department had selected eight outstanding paintings and David had published them. As it happened, one of them depicted a boy and a girl both about 13—both nude. Nothing of their pubic areas showed, but a storm had broken the day the magazine was distributed, which culminated in a command appearance before the dean of women several weeks later. She accused David of being immoral and irresponsible. When he requested that she show him how the painting was obscene or in what way it might be damaging to the student body, she just glared at him, the severity of her wrinkled face accented by the bun of white hair pulled tightly behind her head.

"I owe you no explanations," she said. "As faculty advisor in charge of publications, I have decided that the magazine will not be published again."

David answered her quietly and deliberately. "Yes, it will."

Now anger was added to moral indignation. "I say it will not," she said. "I will see that the magazine offices are reassigned for other uses tomorrow."

"Then I'll publish it out of my room," David said. "But it's my magazine this year, and it's coming out."

The next day a sympathetic dean of the art department found office space for him in the old library, and the magazine—over the objections of the dry, old dean of women—was edited there and issued in the spring.

As David crossed the practice athletic field behind the student building, he looked east toward sorority row. It was a modern com-

226

plex of low buildings, built by the university for use by the sororities, each of which had its own dormitory facilities, as well as several public areas for social activities. This would be, he realized, the first time he had been in a sorority house since his first semester in college, at the University of Georgia. But he walked grimly on, to a party he didn't want to attend, for reasons he had not even tried to sort out. The invitation had come and he had at first laughed, then accepted, surprising even himself. Maybe Bob was right; maybe he did want to try, one more time, to find the missing ingredient in himself, the X factor in all other Jews which brought them together, which helped them need and enjoy each other en masse, which caused them to find comfort and solace in themselves when they huddled in social ghettos. And maybe, he had thought, just by some miracle, something or somebody will happen and help me find a way to love Marcie less; maybe even make the possibility of losing her less painful. Lately, he had thought of little else except how much he loved and needed her. But the thought had been increasingly oppressive to him. She is not Jewish, he kept reminding himself. The time is coming soon for a real commitment—not just words—and nothing changes the fact that she is a gentile girl. Staring into the darkness on sleepless nights, he found that the same questions kept asserting themselves, questions about his willingness, in the final analysis, to hurt his parents and his grandparents by marrying out of his faith. And about all that he had endured because of his Jewishness, and whether or not marrying a Christian girl wouldn't ignore that whole nightmare.

The social room of the sorority house was bright and gaily colored with crepe paper cutouts. In the center of the room, a large table held punch and cookies. Milling around the table were a handful of hopeful girls, while on the sofas and scattered around the room, Phi Eps talked to others whom they had already cut out for themselves.

David was greeted at the door by several girls, none of whom he knew very well, and he stepped into the room. Greetings from some of those he did know—normally quite cheerful on campus or in class—were strained and guarded here.

Several girls chatted with David for a time, including one he liked, named Mitzi Coyne. Mitzi admitted to herself that she was attracted to him. And she knew that even the ones who said they despised him, who carefully avoided even a casual greeting, grudgingly admired him for his guts, for his willingness to champion the most unpopular causes and then stand alone to take the consequences.

To most of the girls there, he was an enigma, a stranger, but still, an interesting one. Most said, from time to time, that he was socially unacceptable, an outcast who deserved whatever he got. But few would have refused him a date.

Marjorie Frankel watched him across the room for an hour before she finally decided that she wanted him. Fresh from her victory in the Miss Modern Venus contest—a beauty pageant in which contestants paraded in tight T-shirts and short shorts with sacks over their heads so their faces wouldn't distract the judges—her confidence was unbounded.

It was fortunate, David had thought the day before, that Marjorie had the sack over her head. Her body was, beyond question, gorgeous. But her face, while not ugly, was in no way a match. Her nose was too broad, her chin weak, her eyes small.

David was pleased when she took him by the arm and maneuvered him over to a couch. As she spoke to him, he remembered only the sight of her body in scanty white shorts and a tight cotton shirt. Within minutes they were chatting like old friends and within the hour were in her off-campus apartment.

There was no pretense about her, and he liked that. The prevailing ethic of the time was coyness, unapproachability, assumptions of virginity. But Marjorie subscribed to a different ethic. As he sat down on the couch, she sat down next to him so closely that they almost touched.

As they talked about David's latest column, a piece on civil rights set in New York, which she seemed to remember almost verbatim, she snuggled closer, so that her large, firm breast pressed against his arm. When he put his arm around her, she came closer still, and then he kissed her. Her mouth was open, and she sucked his tongue into it, first slowly, then urgently. His hand caressed her waist, feeling its tautness, and then the bottom of her rib cage. He expected to feel her hand stopping him as he moved it upward, but it did not. Then he was fondling her breast.

For a long moment they locked in that first kiss, then she was kissing his neck and ears. David maneuvered his body so that he was more frontal to her, so that she could feel the bulge of him against her thigh. At first she appeared not to notice it. When she kissed him again, her tongue flicked into his mouth, first questioningly, then deeply, and his hand moved to her back and the strap of her brassiere. He fumbled with the snap in his anxiety, and smiling, she pulled away slightly and released it herself. As she did so, her breasts tumbled out against the fabric of her sweater. Her gaze was level, unembarrassed, the small smile still flicking across her face, as he slowly grasped the hem of the sweater and raised it upward. David gazed at the perfection of the twin globes of full, firm flesh, white and smooth, capped with small, pink nipples.

228

She moaned slightly as he took the first one in his mouth, gently rolling his tongue over it. Then she lay back to a reclining position, so that he could lie on top of her as he sucked it harder. David started slowly to grind himself into her. She closed her eyes and moaned, grinding her hips upward to meet his.

Abruptly, David stopped and rolled away, and Marjorie understood. Waiting for several moments until he could get control, she moved her hand up his leg, over the fabric of his slacks, caressing the inside of his thighs. As she felt him, she uttered an expression of pleasure. Then his hands were on the soft inside of her thigh, her belly, and then between her legs.

He was stopped from exploring her fully by a tight panty girdle. His probing fingers could scarcely get inside it, and he asked her to take it off.

"No, please," she said, and a look of angry surprise fell over his face.

"Why not?" he asked urgently.

"I'm saving that for my husband."

"What the hell does that mean?" he exploded. "If you're saving it—"

Then he realized she was still smiling at him, still looking dead into his eyes with that odd gaze, and he stopped, confused.

"I'm not going to leave you hung up," she said. "Let me have that big hard beauty."

Within seconds she had stripped the buttons on his shirt and begun unhooking his belt. Then she was down on her knees, her head between his legs. David closed his eyes and lay back against the cushions of the couch.

"You like that?" she asked, and all he could manage for an answer was a moan.

"How about this?" she asked, as she surrounded it with the warm flesh of her breasts, rubbing them up and down on it, caressing it.

"I love it," he groaned, "I just love it."

For a while she played with him; then suddenly she was seized with a new passion.

With a little moan she said, "I want it all," and then plunged it deep into her mouth, working her head rapidly up and down. She felt his whole body tensing and she liked that too, so she sucked harder, now with her hands under his buttocks, her fingernails digging into his flesh.

Then he exploded in her. When the pain began, he tried to push her head away, but she refused to stop. Finally, it became so excruciating that he pushed her away forcibly.

"What's'a matter?" she asked.

"It hurts now, that's all," he said. "Take it easy."

"I can't. I like it too much. I want some more."

Now all David wanted was to be away from her. He didn't want to make further love or conversation. He only wanted to leave.

"That's all there is now, baby," he said. "What about tomorrow?"

As she drove him back to his dormitory, he rode in silence, trying to understand why he really wouldn't want to see her the next day. God knows, she had been sensational, and now she would be easy. Since when was he so discriminating about the girls who got him off?

It was Marcie, he realized.

When she stopped in front of his dormitory, Marjorie turned her face up to be kissed. But the memory of the last few moments on her couch made that a repugnant prospect.

"Goodnight, sweetie," he said, kissing her quickly on the cheek. "I'll call you tomorrow."

As he walked up the stairs to his room, he swore softly. "Goddamnit, Marcie, I love you but you're ruining my life."

Bob was still up, sitting on his bed in a torn T-shirt and a pair of Levis, playing head to head poker with Stanley Baxter for his NROTC check.

"Well, looka here," Bob said, "here's old Roughhouse Harris back to the land of the gentiles. How'd you make out, champ?"

"I scored," David said, and Bob laughed.

"If God loved a liar, he'd hug you to his bosom."

Before David could reply, Bob was exclaiming over the three queens that held up over two pair.

"Three pretty ladies, all in a row. Stan, be smart and quit now before I own your uniform."

As David washed his face he thought ironically that he had been with his people tonight, even been with a nice Jewish girl. Wouldn't his folks be pleased when he wrote to them?

29

Ten minutes into the history lecture David was penning sets of legs in the margin of his notebook. He had, in other dull classes over the past several years, developed a good freehand style in sketching, particularly female anatomy. That day, as Dr. Boston, the gnome-like, whitehaired head of the department, droned on about the shock waves of the Russo–German Pact, he felt like doing legs. The first pair he drew were topped with a lacy suggestion of a skirt at the thigh. But the angle was wrong; something was out of proportion; so he started over. The top line, running from crotch to knee, was drawn firmly and well, he thought, and he paused to admire his handiwork. The lower line, describing the finite shape of the right thigh, was a bit off, so he darkened it to make the leg fuller.

Dr. Boston's observations had had little impact until, in the midst of sketching a tennis skirt, David heard the word *Jews*. As always, he experienced the old, automatic reaction—the odd feeling that developed in the pit of his stomach, the hairs bristling on the back of his neck. He became totally attentive, waiting for the inevitable insult.

In his experience something had always followed, which was seldom complimentary or even bland enough to be ignored. Now it was to be different.

"When we think of the Second World War," the little professor said, "we almost automatically think of Hitler's genocidal plan to liquidate world Jewry and of the ghastly holocaust his plan served to bring about."

As Dr. Boston paused, David shot a quick glance around the

room, suspecting that some of his fellow students would be looking at him. But none were.

"What is seldom, if ever, conjured up," Dr. Boston continued, "is the remarkable damage the war wreaked on American Jews. I don't mean simply those who had relatives in Europe who died in gas ovens; I mean almost all American Jews except perhaps those living in large metropolitan areas with tens of thousands of other Jews around them."

Now David began to take clear, accurate notes. For the first time Dr. Boston was saying things about which David could care and be interested in. The professor was talking about him, and he didn't want to forget.

"Induced alienation . . . official as well as unofficial . . . pressure in schools . . . invested sense of guilt . . . inflammatory press . . . small towns in the South and West the worst . . . unaccustomed societal aberrations among non-Jews . . . bigotry begins at home . . . Ku Klux Klan in South . . . *Dearborn Independent* . . . killing of Christ. . . ." For 30 minutes David wrote frantically in his notebook. He was sorry when the bell rang. After class, as the other students filed out, he stopped by the professor's desk. Dr. Boston was reassembling his notes and for a moment didn't notice David. There was about him, David noted with surprise, or at least about the motions of his head, the bright quickness of a bird. Looking up, he noticed David waiting to speak to him. "Yes?"

"Dr. Boston, I'm sorry to disturb you. I just wanted to compliment you on your lecture. The part about the effects of the war on the Jews in this country—it was really right on the button."

The professor regarded him with interest.

"Thank you, Mr. Harris," he said. "Is this a subject that particularly interests you?" The implied question was Why?

"Yes sir, maybe because I watched it happening close up."

There seemed to be nothing more to say, and David turned to leave, but Dr. Boston's voice stopped him.

"People remember the dead in Europe because there were bodies to count or at least records of deaths. But few remember those of us here who were destroyed. We weren't statistically evaluated. That's why we ourselves must never forget."

Late that night the professor's words still filled his mind. "We ourselves must never forget." In the darkness he reached for his cigarettes. The flare of the match cast ghostly shadows around the corners of the room before it went out. Bob's deep, regular breathing sounded loud to him for the moment, then it was pushed out of his consciousness.

He lay there in the dark, remembering.

232

30

"He won't, that's all. He's too much my son to marry out of his religion," Ben told Rachel. "Hell, he fought too long and hard to be a Jew to just toss it away for a girl . . . even a pretty, bright girl like Marcie Stevens.

"I wonder," Rachel said. "He's got a mind of his own; we saw to that a long time ago. And he's certainly no child anymore."

For almost an hour they discussed David and Marcie, wondering if they should have tried to come between them somewhere back in high school or when David first went away to college.

Finally Rachel fell asleep, and Ben lay staring up into the darkness, reminded of the circumstances of his own marriage, and, consequently, of the time when he had first met the Shulman family, more than 25 years ago.

Ben Harris had never known Jews quite like the Shulmans before, although he had known *lantsmen* from many of the little towns around Augusta. Somehow, the Shulmans were different. But he had a difficult time trying to piece together the precise differences.

That they were an intensely physical family was, of course, strange to the Jewish mind, even among Southern Jews. Early on, Ben realized that, on one hand, Isaac Shulman had dealt with his children primarily on a physical—indeed, frequently brutal—level; on the other, besides the old man's rather considerable business successes, the primary distinction the family had earned was through the athletic prowess of the oldest son, Jake.

In the Shulman household the old man was treated like the Tsar

233

himself, with deference and trembling such as Ben had never before seen.

As was his way, he quickly categorized the children: Jake, a *bulvon;* Aaron, a boy of some promise, if a bit too given to eating; Irving, a sad, broken shadow who, unable to cope with the old man, had simply given up on life; Rachel, the *leberdik* one, with more life and pep than the rest of the whole bunch put together.

For their part, most of the Shulmans viewed Ben as if he had descended from another planet. To them, he was a ghetto Jew—not from some Godforsaken shtetl in Europe or even the lower East Side of New York, but rather a Southern ghetto Jew, born and raised in the large and essentially poor Jewish community in Augusta, Georgia, out of the bosom of which he ventured (at least socially) only when necessary.

There were vast differences between them. Whereas the Shulman children were essentially *goyish,* Ben was, to his core, Jewish. He spoke Yiddish fluently; he davened—at least to their untutored ears—like a rabbi. He knew and talked about a hundred different aspects of *Yiddishkeiten* with their father, discussed the Talmud with him, argued about Talmudic logic in a way that brought pleasure to the old man, so long cut off from the old ways. There was also about him a rare sense of humor, a sparkling ability to find a joke in every condition and situation, an ability to tell stories unequaled by anyone they had ever known.

Ben met Rachel at a dance in Greenville. What she first noticed about him was that he was very attractive—except for a full moustache. He was certainly the funniest man she had ever met. Before the evening was over, her sides hurt from laughing. They were together almost exclusively that evening, and the time melted away.

As she lay in bed that night, she thought about him. The next morning at breakfast, Hannah Reisfeld, the girl she was visiting in Greenville, teased her about spending the whole evening with that funny Jew from Augusta.

"I believe you liked all the attention he was paying you, Rachel."

At this, Rachel tossed her curls and made a face: "He's the most repulsive man I ever met in my life." But she hoped to see him again.

At a bar mitzvah in Augusta some months later, she looked for him. The boy, a grandson of a friend of her father's, stumbled on his haftorah and said nothing Rachel cared to hear. She concentrated on the congregation, at least that part of it she could see from her upstairs seat in the old orthodox shul. She finally spotted Ben, a tallis around his shoulder, an ill-fitting suit jacket bunched at his shoulders. At the same moment he glanced up and saw her looking at him, and before she could look away, grinned and winked.

At the reception that afternoon, she saw him again, this time surrounded by a group of laughing people.

"Why is he bothering with those stories and those mockey Jews when he should be here talking to me?" Rachel said half aloud to herself. And then, as if he had heard her, Ben excused himself and came to the sofa where she was sitting.

"Hello, *Shaineh maidel,*" he said, "can I get you a drink?"

"Thank you, I don't drink," she answered.

"Would you like to learn?"

"If I did, I wouldn't need such an accomplished teacher."

Then they laughed together and he fell in love with her.

His trips to Somerset became quite regular, and Rachel worked hard to keep him out of her mind. Who was he, after all? What had he accomplished? What did he have? What did he come from?

Months later, when she visited him in Augusta for the first time, she was shocked. His people were poor, struggling every day to put food on the table, crowded together in a gloomy apartment over a little drygoods store where his parents worked 11 hours every day to earn a few dollars. There were, she was sure, rats in the store and the apartment, and she shuddered when she thought of them.

But in his home there was one quality she liked: the laughter that abounded, a phenomenon which was outside her own experience. There was little enough in her home; she remembered more threats than jokes, more crying than laughing.

Ben's father, whom everyone called "Tot" because of his gentle, fatherly demeanor, welcomed her instantly into his heart. She thought him the kindest, most wonderfully humorous man she had ever known. Tot had a story, a joke, a laugh for every occasion. When she sat with him, the grimness of their surroundings seemed to vanish. Only the laughter was real.

Ben's mother, on the other hand, was the practical one. She was as determined as Rachel's father, and almost as stern. Miss Becky, as she was called by her friends, was clearly the boss. She had long since taken charge of assuring that the family survived, handled the ordering in the store, did much of the work there, managed the family's finances. Rachel immediately felt her an adversary.

Ben's younger brothers were also very different from Rachel's family. Despite their dim economic prospects, there was about them a bright joviality, a sense of fun. All had been working at whatever they could find to do since they were children. Marty, the oldest of the three, was a salesman on the road for a clothing company; Harry and Maxie, the two younger ones, ran a tiny jewelry store together. When they were together, the house rocked with fun.

"Tell her about this one . . . tell her about that time," was the recurring plea from the sons to Tot during her visits. And Tot would rub his hands together, smile, and begin a story.

"A little Jew with thick eyeglasses, a valise, and two geese once got off the train in Augusta. He walked down the street, leading his two geese on a string, until he saw another Jew.

" 'Tell me,' he said in Yiddish. 'Can a man get a kosher meal in this town?' The other man told him that he was in luck, that just down the street, a Mrs. Hoffberg ran a boarding house which served the finest gefilte fish and chicken soup south of New York.

" 'And might this fine woman consider swapping a meal such as this for one of these fine geese?' the little Jew asked, his mouth already savoring the chicken soup.

" 'Sure,' the other said, and wishing him good *shabbes*, went along his way.

"What he didn't mention was that in the back room of this paradise, old man Hoffberg ran the crookedest card game in the state of Georgia," Tot said, smiling broadly at Rachel.

"Well, Mrs. Hoffberg knew a bargain when one stared her in the face, so she swapped not only a dinner for the goose, but a room and a promise of breakfast as well. When the dishes were served, the little Jew all but cried for joy. Never had he seen such a meal, he kept saying, as the matzo balls disappeared in his mouth, the soup, the meat, the fresh *challeh* that nobody in Augusta to this day could equal—except, of course, Miss Becky.

"Afterwards, when the visitor was filled to the teeth with his wife's fine cooking, Reb Hoffberg mentioned that several friends were dropping over for a friendly game. Surely they would not object if such a respected visitor joined them. Sure enough, as if on signal, Hoffberg's *chavairim* appeared and they all sat down to play. As it turned out, the little Yid had a few dollars, and soon the Augusta Jews had taken off their coats and vests and gotten down to business.

"At first their visitor was cautious, betting only on hands he knew would win. But somehow, when he held a pair, someone held two pairs; when God was kind enough to deliver into his hands a straight, the other fellow had a flush.

" '10 cents on the ace,' he said.

" '20 more,' the answer came back.

"The coins clinked, the cards fell, and nothing came in the direction of the visitor. 'In cards and mitzvahs I have no luck,' he kept saying, and soon he was cleaned out. Not only had he lost his money, but his other goose had disappeared to a full house. One of the men offered to play for his eyeglasses, but the little Yid said he had already had all the pleasure he could stand for one night. As he got up to leave, Mr. Hoffberg was most polite in helping him on with his long coat.

" 'It would be a good idea to check on your valise, my friend,' Hoffberg said. 'Someone may have stolen it.'

"At this, the little Yid's head snapped around and he said: 'that can't be; every thief in Augusta is sitting in this game.' ' "

Everyone roared, Rachel the loudest. Tot rubbed his hands together and began to tell another story. But he was interrupted by Miss Becky, calling them to the table at which pungent chicken soup was already in steaming evidence.

Donning a yarmelke, Tot intoned the blessing over the bread: ". . . *homotzi lechem min ho'orets.*" Then they were eating and laughing together again.

After that trip, her own home—despite its expansive lawns and costly furniture—never seemed so grand to Rachel again.

Ben found reasons to be in Somerset more and more, and she, whenever possible, made trips to Augusta. It was no surprise to her when he proposed—nor to him when she accepted.

But getting Isaac Shulman's approval was a different matter. Ben assumed that his lack of economic prospects would be of primary concern to Isaac, and all the way to Somerset in his family's old Ford, he thought of what he would say when the old man brought up the subject. His arguments were pretty weak, he realized. But he'd have to do the best he could.

To his great surprise, the subject of financial security never came up. When he presented himself in the large parlor, the old man seemed to know what he wanted to discuss. Ben cleared his throat several times, not knowing quite how to begin. Finally Isaac opened the conversation:

"Nu?" he asked. "What can I do for you?"

Then the words tumbled out, as if he had nothing to do with them. "Mr. Shulman, I'm in love with Rachel, and I believe she loves me. I can make a good life for her, I assure you of that, and I want your permission to marry her." As he anxiously watched the old man's face for some sign of approval or disapproval, the words continued in a torrent.

"You don't have to worry about the way she'll be treated. I'm 10 years older, a lot more responsible. She'll be treated like a princess all her life. She'll—"

The old man raised his hand, palms out, as if to say, stop already; you're breaking my ears with your babbling.

Here come the unanswerable questions, Ben thought, the ones about my bank account and business prospects and the home I can take her to. He knew that Isaac was far too intelligent to ignore or overlook any such questions of substance.

To his surprise, Isaac asked instead: "How am I going to let such a puny fellow into this family?"

Ben, braced to argue economics, was stunned.

"Puny?" he asked.

"Sure," the old man said. "Look at my boys, how big they are, how strong. Next to them, you look like a boy."

Still Ben couldn't believe his ears. Since boyhood he had been called many names, but never puny. Under his white jacket, he was heavily muscled from long hours on the handball court and the weightlifting mats at the Augusta Y.M.H.A. In a flash he understood what was happening. In the unusually physical Shulman household, he was being challenged to a test of strength. And in tests of strength, Ben was almost always a winner.

"Your boys may be an inch or so taller than me," he said, "but I'm stronger than anyone in this house."

Isaac laughed the high-pitched cackle he reserved for absurdities.

"Go ahead and laugh," Ben said, "but when you get through, I'll prove it. Call the boys."

When Jake and Aaron answered their father's bellowed call, the rest of the family came along for the show.

"Aaron, go to the curb and get the weight," his father instructed.

The weight, an unbalanced hunk of iron with a handle on the top end, had been used to tie horses years before, and remained still as an ornament. Weighing about 60 pounds, it was extremely awkward to lift. Aaron set it carefully on the floor in front of his father.

Turning to his sons, Isaac told them that Ben had claimed to be stronger than any of them, and he wanted them to show him, by God, just how strong the Shulmans were.

Ben's moment had come. The thing to do was win big, he reasoned, and in the ensuing confusion, all else might be forgotten.

"Wait a minute," he said, holding up his hand. Smiles began to appear around the room. Obviously he was going to retreat, or at least, qualify his boast. But nothing was further from his mind.

"I'll lift this weight more times with my left hand than Jake with his right." This fell like a bombshell. There was quiet for a moment, then Isaac laughed again.

"Alevei! Ahf dir gezost!" he said through his laughter.

Then he turned to Aaron and instructed him to lift the weight first.

Eager, as always, to please his father, the 17-year-old stepped forward, grasped the weight firmly, began moving it toward his shoulder with one hand, then used his other hand. Once the weight was at shoulder level, the strain already showing on his face, Aaron managed to push it upward. Once, twice, three times, and then he could do no more. Not displeased as he lowered the weight, he was sure this would suffice. Meanwhile Jake clenched and unclenched his big, right hand, eager to begin. This was his cup of tea, his ball game. That Augusta Jew must be crazy to even imagine—

As Jake bent slightly to begin his lift, he found himself looking squarely into his father's gray eyes, which instructed him, ordered him, without flicker or waver, without a word, to carry the day for Isaac Shulman. Then the weight was up. Despite its awkwardness, he muscled it up several times with no signs of effort. Then the pressure slowly began to show; after the thirteenth full press, he could do no more.

Of course, it would be more than enough. If anything, this Jew from Augusta would do well to equal Aaron's lift, particularly with his left hand. As Ben bent over the weight, he was almost sure that nobody in the family recognized that although he wrote and ate with his right, he was actually left-handed.

Whisking the weight up effortlessly, Ben pressed it 19 times.

Actually that was all he could do, a fact he neatly concealed. Replacing the weight in its original position, he casually remarked that he could have done a few more, but after all, the point was already made. He hoped the fact that he had not used his right hand was fully appreciated.

Nobody answered.

Furious at being beaten at his own game, at having lost while his father watched, Jake gripped the weight and stormed out of the house. Though they would not speak of it again, Jake would never forgive Ben for the beating. Ben, of course, was delighted. Rachel merely stared, a look of sadness, rather than victory, in her eyes.

An hour later, when they had her father's consent and were finally alone, Ben was troubled by Rachel's moody silence. They sat on the big, screened porch, neither speaking for awhile, listening to the crickets sing in the flower beds.

Finally Ben broke the silence.

"Well, *shainkeit*," he said softly, "it's gonna be OK."

"Yes."

"I thought your father was going to grill me about my ability to support you. But it never came up."

"I know."

"Rachel, what's the matter? We love each other. Your father just gave us his blessing. Why aren't you happier?"

Then she turned, her eyes burning with tears.

"Why'd you have to beat them? Why'd you have to make them look bad?"

Ben didn't know how to answer. He slipped his arm around her shoulder, drawing her toward him, and felt her body tense.

"I had to beat them because I'm a man. You might as well understand that now, Rachel. That's part of what being a man is about. I never will be less than what I am. Do you understand that? I have pride too."

For a moment there was only the sound of the crickets and the soft summer breeze in the trees.

She did not understand, because she would not allow herself to understand. She loved Ben, but he had no right to come here to their house and humiliate her brothers and her father. For Ben to stand in her father's living room and beat poor Jake was unkind. In a boxing ring Jake would tear him to pieces, so Ben better stay away from him. Then she felt better.

"It's a trick, isn't it, Ben?"

"What's a trick?"

"That weightlifting. You know how to lift weights because you've done it a long time. That thing with the weight tonight, it was a special weightlifter's trick, wasn't it?"

Ben understood. Poor Rachel, he thought, raised in this *meshugeneh* house, with so little to hold on to. And now he had come along and overturned one of her most cherished idols. He started to reply truthfully, then caught himself. I've already knocked over the idol, he thought. Why step on its face?

"In a way I guess it is," he said. "Weightlifting develops a different set of muscles than other sports. So I guess you could say it was a trick."

Then she began to smile, and Ben's heart melted. His father had said only last week that Rachel had the face of an angel, with her gorgeous blue eyes and red lips. Kissing him, she murmured that she really did love him, and she was terribly glad they had Papa's consent.

Ben almost lost himself in her eyes, but a small nagging thought began to tickle his mind. What would it be like after they were married? Would she change? Or would he have to lie to her again to protect her view of her family?

But then Rachel was talking about her trousseau and their wedding, and Ben allowed himself to forget.

Upstairs in their bed, Isaac and Baila talked softly.

"He seems like a good man," Baila said. "I think he'll make Rachel happy."

240

"I don't know," Isaac answered. "He's 29 years old and doesn't have a hundred dollars to his name."

"Did you have so much at his age?" she asked.

"I was on the way, and I was working 16 hours a day to get it. What about him, your future son-in-law? You think he's gonna work like that?"

"I don't know, Itzrok. I only want Rachel to be happy. And she seems to love this man."

"What does she know about anything, that Rachel? Maybe the old ways are better, Baila. Let me ask you this: if a shadchan brought this bridegroom, would you be so eager for Rachel to marry him?"

"Ah, Isaac," she sighed, "the old way I never liked so much. If I had, I'd be in the grips of a fat, ugly baker in a shtetl in Russia instead of here with you."

In the darkness he knew she was smiling.

"I'll say this for him," he finally conceded, "he's strong as a mule. Maybe he's OK."

They talked on, Baila as Ben's advocate, although Isaac already had given his promise. It was because she wanted him to feel sure, to feel happy that his decision had been correct, that she talked. But Isaac wasn't sure. Certainly it was pleasant to have another real Jew in the house to talk with, to discuss the Talmud with, someone whose eyes didn't go blank when he brought up some stray bit of *Yiddish-keiten*. Ben was smart enough, of this Isaac had no doubt. But after all, that was only part of the measure of a man. What about his ambition, his motivation? How come this Jew, born in America with all the advantages of an American education, was still without any real material achievement at such an age? Was he, like his father, only a comedian, a teller of stories?

Not that Isaac didn't like Tot. He did, very much indeed. A good Jew, an honest man, a man you could talk to, a man you could enjoy. What bothered him was that Miss Becky, Tot's wife, carried the burden for their family while Tot told stories. He had not raised Rachel for such an existence, for keeping her hands in dishwater and her head in business matters.

Finally, as Baila began to snore lightly beside him, Isaac decided how he would handle the situation. He would keep Rachel in Somerset with her husband by setting Ben up in the mule business with Jake as his partner. It would be a good partnership; Jake only wanted to work like a mule, and Ben was undoubtedly smart with figures and other business matters. On his own, Jake would never build a business, regardless of what he had to start with. But with Ben Harris as a partner, he could do all the work he wanted to—and have the

241

benefit of Ben Harris's *yiddisher kop* to build on.

Isaac was so pleased with his plan that he chuckled out loud. Baila stirred. He said to her: "Ah, my Baila, how beautiful you are. Even now, after all these years." As he whispered to her in the darkness, he knew she was sound asleep.

"Baila, such a present I have for you tomorrow. I have decided you can keep your precious Rachel close to you, here in Somerset, instead of losing her after the wedding. I have a plan that will bring tears of joy to your eyes. But I better not explain the details to you, Baila, since you can't hold your tongue any more than a child. Instead, I'll just tell you tomorrow that Rachel will be staying in Somerset with you. That will be enough."

All of this went through Isaac's mind, and more. As always, when he thought of a plan, his mind instantly went to work on its structure, timing, and execution. He was tired of the mule business. He had enough to do looking after his properties, running the slaughterhouse, and attending board meetings at the bank and the Building and Loan. What did he need it for, the barn in town? It was more a headache than a reward anymore. So he would give the barn to Jake and Rachel's husband, to run together. Harris was certainly personable enough. He would make friends; maybe his *meshugeneh* stories would attract customers to the barn. Isaac would teach the two men the business and then step aside.

Then a thought struck him. Jake didn't like Ben, especially now, and Ben seemed to like Jake even less. Would the mule business— in partnership with Jake—be enough to hold Ben in Somerset? His mind working furiously, Isaac decided that it would not. Ben would see it as little more than a job, and one that forced him to work with a partner he didn't like.

But Isaac had decided that he wanted his daughter in Somerset with him. His mind raced over and discarded a number of possibilities and influences he might bring to bear. Then he hit it: what anchors a man like a home? Of course. As a wedding present, he would give Rachel a new brick home, built to his own specifications, and filled with furniture Rachel could select.

Isaac's mind ran on, visualizing the house, troubling over and solving details, deciding the number of bedrooms, the kind of furnace, the size lot he would buy the next day. Far into the night, he continued to build his plan, neglecting no detail, covering all contingencies. When he finally fell asleep, he was smiling.

At the Central Hotel, a mile to the north, Ben slept peacefully, unaware that the rest of his life had just been planned, his future divined to the last detail, his fate, for good or evil, decided.

"The wedding," Isaac Shulman announced the next morning,

"will not be forgotten in this town for 50 years." That, and nothing more.

Everyone at the breakfast table stopped eating for a moment when he said it. It seemed strange for him to be commenting on wedding arrangements. Even though his first child was being married, it was natural to assume that the planning and execution would be left to others, that he would, as he always did, simply give the family a blank check and suggest that he not be bothered with details.

Jake was sullen as he shoveled another fried egg onto his plate. Looks to me, he thought to himself, that Rachel could do better for himself than that show-off, quick-talking Augusta Jew. Hell, she's a pretty girl, but he ain't much of anything I can see. By God, he better not ever cross me, or he'll wish he never heard of Rachel or any other Shulman. I could kill him for coming in here and making me look bad in front of Papa. Papa was mad as hell. He didn't say nothing, but I could tell by the way he looked at me with that mean-ass stare, like he could take an ax handle to my head. And that son-of-a-bitch from Augusta just standing there gloating! By God, I should have landed him on his ass right then and there and gotten it over with. And Rachel, she seemed glad to see me get beat, too. Well, she don't know what's good for her if she thinks she can turn against her own for the likes of Harris. Because she'll be back before too long, when she gets tired of old clothes and a beat-up, cheap car and no maid to wash her underwear. And then where in hell's she gonna be? I reckon she'll come back on her hands and knees. And I'll laugh when she does. What the hell's the matter with her, anyway, siding against her own? Now Papa ain't saying nothing to me, hasn't spoken all morning. Just like I never done nothing to make him proud, just like I never won the conference boxing championship and held it for 17 fights, just like he never come to 16 college games in a row when I played 60 minutes. Just like I never played the whole Maryland game with a broken hand rather than let the coach know and come out. It ain't fair. But he don't care. And that Goddamn Ben Harris is up there at the Central right now laughing at me. He better not tell the story around or I'll have his ass. Just let me hear one son-of-a-bitch in this town talking about what happened, and I'll tear him down. If I had a good excuse, I'd do it anyway.

Jake's reverie was interrupted as Rachel walked sleepily to the table and plopped down next to him.

"G'mornin', Papa. Morning," she mumbled. Lucy came in with a fresh platter of biscuits and offered one first to Rachel, who shook her head. "Just coffee, please, Lucy," and yawned broadly.

"You oughtna spent all them hours sitting on the porch," Jake barked. "What the hell you think the neighbors are gonna think about you?"

Rachel smiled. "Now, Jake, aren't you a fine one to talk. From what I hear, you'd be a lot better off sitting on front porches than jumping out of back windows every night."

Jake started to answer, but Isaac cut him off. With an angry glare, he told Rachel to shut up. "As long as you put your feet under my table, you'll talk with respect!"

Rachel was about to say she was only teasing, then thought better of it. When Papa gets mad, she knew, it was best just to leave things alone. Actually she was proud of Jake's exploits with women, what she knew of them. Big and handsome, she knew Jake fluttered pulses, married and unmarried women alike, when he walked down the streets of Somerset with his rolling, athlete's gait. She also knew of several close scrapes her brother had had, and one time when he had found it best to leap from a second-floor bedroom window.

Isaac's anger was directed more at Jake's behavior than Rachel's allusion to it. He, too, knew about his son's escapades. Little in Somerset escaped his attention, and men in the town talked about Jake's women and his narrow escapes and the way he was in a different bed every night. To the *goyim*, this was a mark of manhood, a thing to be admired. But Isaac saw things quite differently. Although he had lived among these people for 30 years, had come to like some of them, to understand them, to speak much as they did, even to eat their food, his moral values had never been altered even remotely by his association with them. Right was right, wrong was wrong. And Jake bedding every *shikseh* in Somerset was wrong and a source of disappointment. Such a young man needed to work off his juices, but that's what loose women were for.

He gave Jake all the money he could spend. Why didn't he buy himself a whore when he felt the need for a woman, instead of ruining decent girls all over town? Isaac had a position to maintain in the town—and Jake had some moral obligations to maintain. Every night now, Jake jeopardized both. What kind of a *chi-eh* had he raised, with him jumping into beds and out of windows?

Isaac felt a sour taste in his mouth. He pushed back from the table, threw his napkin across his plate, and got up. Jake wanted to talk to him, to see if he was still angry about his failure the night before.

"Papa, I wanted to ask you if—"

"I have nothing to say," Isaac spat back at him over his shoulder. And he was gone.

For a moment Jake toyed with a piece of buttered toast in his big hand, then crushed it and threw it into his plate.

244

All because of that Goddamn mockey from Augusta, he thought. He started to say something to Rachel, failed to come up with words, and finally left the table, in the opposite direction that his father had gone.

"What was that all about?" Rachel asked nobody in particular. "What on earth's everybody so angry about?"

Aaron shrugged his shoulders. "Papa must really have some shindig in mind," he said. "He said the town won't forget your wedding for 50 years."

Since she knew her father was given, if anything, to understatement, Rachel began to imagine the most lavish celebrations. But even her wildest imaginings didn't compare to what would, in September, be reality. The first preparation was made later that morning.

"The *whole* hotel, Mr. Shulman?" The desk clerk's jaw fell open in amazement.

"For a week—the week of September third," Isaac replied. "I want every room."

"But how many guests are coming to the wedding, if I may ask, sir?"

"I don't know yet, but I want to be sure that everyone has a room."

31

David was shaken out of sleep by his father, his hand rocking his son's shoulder four or five times as he steadfastly clung to the thread of a dream.

"Hey there, Dave," he whispered. "Get up, wake up, now. We got quail to hunt. Come on, boy—"

Then David was awake, sitting up against the big bolster pillow and rubbing his eyes.

"What time is it?" he asked, yawning mightily. "Must be the middle of the night!"

"Nope," his father said with a grin. "Farmers already up and had breakfast four hours. Come on, now. I've got some water boiled for coffee."

Still rubbing his eyes, David walked to the kitchen table, his white shorts showing in marked contrast to his lithe body, still brown from the summer sun. Ben looked at his son with obvious satisfaction. He's a fine boy—the best, Ben thought, as he buttered a piece of toast. The boys will be mighty glad to see him again today.

"Got in a little late last night," David said sleepily.

"I know what time you got in. It was 2:07, and I was wide awake, like always. You know I can't fall asleep until you're home."

David grinned over his coffee cup. "Now isn't that something! Me a grown man and you still waiting up for me. How do you know what time to fall asleep when I'm at the university?"

"I usually don't," his father said. "You know me; I need something to worry about."

Ben wanted to talk about Marcie. Perhaps when the hunt was

246

over. He knew they'd find plenty of birds, that T.S.'s dogs would work them well, and that after the hunt and a nip or two, they'd both feel warm and relaxed. Then they would talk.

Ben had been dreading the conversation, but now there was no more putting it off, for every day, he knew, brought the boy closer to the brink of a painful, maybe even self-destructive, decision. He had talked to Rachel for hours, then lain awake and thought about it for hours more. How could he make David understand?

Other Jews of his generation disowned their sons, even sat *shiva* for them like corpses, when they married Christian girls. But he would never do that. He wouldn't lose his son. But in an even subtler way, wouldn't David be leaving him anyway if he married Marcie?

He looked across the table at David—now awake and alert, hurrying his coffee—and sensed that he would give him fine, strong grandsons to carry on his name. But where would they carry it? To church, maybe. Little *goyim*, holding their mother's hand as they walked down the aisle to their pew?

The morning was fresh and bright, with an early frost on the ground. The .12-gauge felt good in David's hand—cool and solid— when he carefully placed it beside his father's .16 pump on the back seat. They would hunt the back side of the farm, which, in the way of the region, was still called the old Fowler place because his father had only owned it for 24 years, and since people and their hopes came and went and only the land stayed, it—the land—changed names very slowly.

They met on the hill. T.S. was already there when they arrived —a half-hour ahead of time—his dogs tied in the back of his pickup, whining to get into the broomstraw and lespedeza and on with the hunt. The winter sun cascaded down through the cold onto their necks and shoulders. The air was winesap-apple sweet. David sucked large draughts of it into his lungs, tasting it in his mouth.

"Well, looka here," T.S. said, pumping David's hand in the strange pump-handle greeting of the rural South. "Ol' David's come home to show us how to shoot birds."

David grinned and pumped back on his friend's work-hardened hand. "No," he said, "I'm here to learn something. You know I can't hit a partridge."

"Seems to me you hit six birds with eight shells last time we were over here," T.S. shot back. "That ain't bad even in cotton country."

"Wad'n nothin' but luck. I couldn' do that again on a bet," David replied, slipping easily into the slurred talk of Somerset County.

Moments later, a panel truck appeared, a grizzled, overalled Otis Mayfield at the wheel. Greetings were exchanged all around, then Mayfield unhooked his pump gun from the clips behind the driver's seat where he always kept it. Mayfield was a member of the Ku Klux Klan and a leader in the local White Citizen's Council, yet he saw nothing incongruous in his friendship with Ben and his boy, and they chose not to, either.

Then they were in the fields, the dogs trembling with excitement. T.S. worked his big setters with practiced skill, talking to them unceasingly as they stepped through the undergrowth.

As he had for the past two seasons, David watched Belle with a mixture of joy and sadness. Since the awful morning they found Rebel, broken and dying beside the driveway—the victim of a careless driver who apparently never even stopped to see if she was dead —David had experienced an aching, empty feeling that no other dog could ever fill. Every time he saw a classy English setter working a covert, he remembered her with pleasure—recalling the pride he felt in her performance and the unalloyed joy at her belonging to him and him to her. But he was also reminded that she was gone, never to romp ahead of him into a field again, never to freeze into her faultless point, never to sit with him quietly, nuzzling his hand to be patted or licking his face, as she did all the times when he was troubled and needed to talk to a friend.

No setter reminded him of Rebel more vividly than Belle, the pup from her first litter, which he had given to T.S. Her configuration was almost identical, as was her grace in the field. She reminded David of Rebel most when she began to make game, worked out the scent, and then froze on point. Just for that moment, he was hunting his own dog again, and his heart swelled with the happiness and the pain of it.

He felt it now as he watched Belle and Blackie, and listened to T.S.'s voice as he expertly worked them.

"Hyuh, hyuh, come in here, Belle . . . easy, now, slow down . . . come in here, Blackie . . . birds in that field . . . huyh, Black . . . easy, easy . . . where you goin', come in here . . . hyuh. . . ."

Grinning, his pulse racing with the dogs and the morning and the hunt, David looked at his father as they walked.

"Isn't this sum'thin'?"

"Yessir, David, it can't get much better than this."

Suddenly, they heard the tone of Bragg's voice change. David whirled to see Belle stiff-legging up on a point, with Blackie easing behind her to honor.

"Easy, now," T.S. whispered to Belle. "At's a good gal, easy."

The men stood in a rough semicircle behind the dogs, tensing for the booming, terrifying rise of a covey. The birds would be holding tight on the frost-wet ground, so T.S. sent Ben around one flank and Mayfield around the other. He and David walked up to the dogs and stopped, peering into the cover ahead of them, shotguns at the ready, waiting for the brown rockets to explode.

At T.S.'s signal, David stepped tentatively in and on by Belle, noticing without concentration how beautiful she looked, her head up, nostrils quivering with the hot quail scent just ahead of her—concentrating instead on the grass just ahead of each step.

The first bird shot out from near his right boot, thundering its wings, scaring him as quail always did. As he brought the Savage .12 to his shoulder, a second bird was up, closer and easier, and then a third. A shotgun somewhere to his right punctuated the covey rise as more birds went out, and David, smiling at himself for falling for the oldest and least intentional of quail tricks, stopped waiting for the next bird and leveled his sights on the third quail up. It was a climbing shot, going away. He held a bit over the hurtling form and squeezed the trigger. Even as he saw the feathers puff, he was swinging on the next bird, making sure he had a clear shot. But he squeezed off too quickly, and the bird kept flying—into a load of number 8's from his father's .16.

Belle fetched his bird to T.S., who handed it over to David and sent the dog out to pick up another.

"Quail still scare me to death," David admitted, grinning.

"Quail supposed to. That's all part of it."

Then the dogs were moving again, working laterally across the broomstraw and through the briars, heads up, tongues lolling as they ran, their noses testing the morning air for bird scent. David felt the life tingling through him, and for the moment, only the clean air and the good dogs and the thrill of the next covey mattered. And one more thing: being in the field with good men—most of all, his father.

He slowed his pace a bit so he could walk closer to his father.

"You like this, boy?" his father asked happily.

"Fine, Dad, just fine."

There were no words he could use—in Somerset, South Carolina —to tell his father he loved him very deeply. This was proscribed by the code. But being there, the joy they had together, walking close in the gold-and-gray field, said it all.

"Blackie's making game," Mayfield called, pulling David out of his reverie. The big, black-and-white, setting dog had slowed his pace now to a delicate crawl, crouched slightly, his good head swaying in the hot scent to pin it down. Then he froze on a single that flushed under Ben's feet. Reflex action brought the gun up and against David's cheek, brought the bead on the bird, brought his finger to the trigger guard and in on the cool metal of the trigger. Tense, he held the shotgun there, waiting for his father's shot to hit or miss. But all he heard was stillness until it was too late to fire.

Glancing over his shoulder, he saw his father looking at him sheepishly.

"I wanted you to have the shot," he said. "I never drew down on him."

One way for a man to say to another that he loved him in Somerset, South Carolina.

"You boys better git together," T.S. said, "else the dogs gonna get discouraged."

"Sorry, T.S.," Ben called. "Just got our signals crossed, that's all."

Now the morning breeze began to freshen, pushing the straw tops over in long, undulating patterns before them. The dogs found two more singles out of the first covey and then two more large coveys before the hunt ended.

Back at the car, after the dogs were watered and tied, Ben pulled a pint of whiskey and paper cups out of his glove compartment.

"How 'bout a little something to wet down your whistles, boys?" he asked. Without pausing for answers, he poured stiff shots into cups, as was their tradition—with one difference. There were four cups today, where before there had been only three.

A bit surprised, David took the last of the four, raised it slightly, and bit off a chew of the bourbon. Ben saw his quizzical look and answered it.

"You're a man, now, David. No reason you shouldn't drink with men."

David's taste had been spoiled by scotch. The bourbon tasted mean and raw in his throat. But the drink was a statement, an invitation for him to join these men as a man now, a graduate of sorts; so he drank it to its last drop.

"Another?" Ben asked.

Mayfield held out his cup for a refill, but T.S. said "Naw, I got to git home. You know the old lady don't hold with no drinkin'."

The bourbon felt warm and good in David's stomach.

When T.S. and Mayfield had driven off, David and Ben stood on the hill, their shotguns broken and unloaded, five bobwhites on the fender of the car. David studied the old foreman's house—maintained when there was need for a foreman, now run down by the sharecroppers who lived in it—standing as a reminder of another time before the tractors rolled over the hopes of the little farmer and the land, chewing up and spitting out in a day what a farmer with a good pair of mules couldn't do in two weeks. Down the road, the other cropper shacks stood in weatherbeaten gray, as old as time and the sweat of black men who had worked those fields for 200 years. Behind him, trees rose up surprisingly out of fallow fields, framing the creek which stank now and ran colors, the shades depending on

250

what goods the Agnew Mills were dyeing that day. In between the creek and the shacks along the road was good, rich soil which gave David a sense of belonging in this place.

"I'm sure glad this belongs to us," he said to his father.

"Me, too." Ben said quietly. "It's what I'll have to leave you and Jennifer one of these days—and your children."

There was much left unsaid in that, and even as David demurred, even as he willed his father another hundred years to keep and enjoy the land, he sensed more would come on the subject of his birthright.

Ben had prepared what he would say, how he would ease into the subject, the arguments he would use. He had gone over the details in his mind time and again even as he followed the dogs earlier that day. Now it all left him, not because he couldn't remember, but because it was of no value between them. The thought was there, hanging in the air, not really needing to be articulated. They were too close for that. They had discussed it before, casually, almost cursorily. Now there was urgency, and Ben knew it, although he did not know how or why he knew it. The boy was close to the time when he would choose; Ben knew that without having to be told. And it needed to be talked about.

"You ever thought much about children?" Ben asked.

"Yes sir, a good deal."

"What do you want them to be?"

"I dunno. Honest, I guess, most of all. And decent and bright. Kids you and Mom would be proud to call your grandchildren. A boy first, if I'm lucky."

"I'd be mighty happy if I had a grandson to carry on our name. Our family has been through a lot over the last 200 years just to keep it alive."

"Yes sir."

"Son, there's something else," Ben went on. "When you have that boy, I want to come to a *briss*. And if I live, I want to see his bar mitzvah. I can't tell you how much I want that."

Somewhere behind them, along the creek, a crow talked shrilly to other crows. Only the cawing filled the silence, which was long between them, but no more than a few seconds in real time. David shook his head slowly, letting the thoughts form in his mind.

"Life's not an easy business, is it?" he asked.

"Not ever, son. It tries to force us to be different from what we really are or want to be, and that's the hardest part."

Then David turned to face him, looking directly into the small brown eyes which usually crinkled at the corners with humor or the anticipation of it.

251

"Would it be so terrible if I married her and kept on being a Jew myself?" he asked, his voice tortured, restrained. "Would the world end?"

"No, it wouldn't end. And I wouldn't disown you or sit *shiva* for you like the old ones would have done, either. Your mother and I love you too much to lose you that—or any other—way. But it wouldn't bring me any joy. Maybe not you either, in the long run.

David slowly broke off a piece of stick he was holding and distractedly began to peel the bark.

"In a way," Ben continued, "marrying out of the faith is like turning your back on all Jewish history—on your own heritage. The world has always dumped its hate, like garbage, on the Jews, and we've held up. That has to mean something to us, David. We can't just discard it as if it had no value."

"I don't know anymore," David said. "God knows, I had my share heaped on me, too."

Ben rubbed his hand slowly over the worn stock of his shotgun, caressing the junction of metal and wood.

"I know, son. I know. Many's the night I laid in bed when you were a kid and wished to God I never came to this town because of it. But that's all over now; one of these days you'll be out of college and headed for a city where you'll be able to meet your own kind and—"

"Wait a minute," David interrupted. "I don't have any 'kind.' I've just spent two and a half years in colleges loaded with Jews I couldn't stand and who couldn't stand me. I didn't fit in with them. Never did. I come home and I don't really fit in my own town either. And I don't imagine things are gonna be any better anywhere else. Don't you see, Dad, that's the whole point: I don't have any *kind* anywhere—except for you and Mom and Jennifer and a couple of other people. And Marcie's one of 'em. She asks for nothing. She gives me love. Now you tell me, doesn't that mean anything?"

Ben's look was tortured as he spoke. "Of course, it means a great deal. I know that. But it doesn't have to mean marriage. It's something you can walk away from and still always have in your heart. But if you marry her, Dave, I believe you'll be making a mistake for both of you, one you'll both regret. There are so many strains and pressures on a marriage as it is. One more big one like a religious difference might destroy it."

"I know that can happen, but believe me, that's not what keeps me from marrying her, Dad. If it were only that, I'd be married to her right now."

252

Ben shook his head in understanding. "Can you tell me what's holding you back?"

"Well, part of it is that I don't want to hurt you and Mom. And then there's another part that's all mixed up with every kid who ever tried to beat me up because I'm a Jew, and with Grandpa, and, I guess, with the mystical mumbo jumbo about his father and the old country and being Jewish. I don't know. If I could put it in words, I could deal with it better; but I can't. It's like some big hand wrapped around me, squeezing me all the time."

David picked up one of the dead quail, its dark eyes no longer bright, a single drop of blood drying at the tip of its beak.

"This little guy doesn't have any problems anymore, does he? No hawks to worry about, or foxes or people. All the problems are over for him."

Ben shook his head slowly. "Let's go home and have some coffee," he said.

Just after eight that evening, David drove out of the driveway toward Marcie's house. As the tires of the Buick crunched on the gravel, Rachel asked Ben how their talk had gone.

"All right, I guess," he said. "In the end, I believe he'll do whatever he believes is right."

He did not mention the bobwhite with blood on its beak, although far into the night, it was the bird that filled his thoughts.

32

"Ruth, would you serve Mr. Harris some more butterbeans, please?" Rachel called.

Across the table, Ben was distractedly toying with a piece of fried chicken.

After Ruth had left the room, Ben looked across the table at his wife.

"Whatever happens now is our fault. That's all there is to it," he said. "We brought 'em up like *goyim*. It's our fault."

Rachel was silent for a moment, staring into her glass, swirling the ice cubes.

"Well," she said finally, "if we were starting over with them today, I don't know that I'd want to do much different. I mean, what would we change?"

"I don't know," he said. "Maybe I'd try to teach them a little more *yiddishkeiten*. Up till now, I thought we were right all the way, but maybe some of the old ways were better."

Although the room was warm, Rachel felt a shudder run up her back. For her, the "old ways" meant the ways Isaac Shulman had raised her and his other children—ways transported directly from his shtetl in Russia, unchanged, and imposed on the family. The old ways meant respect built not on love but on fear, physical and psychological brutality, a constant unwillingness to bend, to listen, to change. The old ways meant a razor strap across the legs and back; they meant the back of a man's hand across a little girl's face, which left red marks to be embarrassed about in school.

For Ben, it was different. The old ways held an entirely different meaning: the excitement of Channukah, the good smells of his mother's kitchen at Purim, the scrubbing and dressing in all new clothes for the first night of Passover, the feeling of pride at his grandfather's position in the shul. And laughter, always laughter, at the distinctly Jewish wit and humor in his home.

Of course there was discipline, sometimes heavy-handed. When Louis kicked the *cheder* teacher, Reb Farbstein, in the stomach and fled, his father and his grandfather had beat him half the night. Miss Becky was stern; she had to be, or the family would have collapsed. But so what? They didn't starve; all the boys grew up to be happy, healthy men. They loved and respected their parents. They clung to their Jewishness. What could be so bad?

All of this flashed through his mind as he stirred sugar into his tea. Since Rachel was silent, he traced small patterns on the side of the tall, frosty glass with his finger.

Finally she looked up from her plate. "We don't live in a ghetto in Russia or Hungary, and what you call the 'old ways' aren't worth a damn anymore," she said deliberately. "Our children have to make lives for themselves in this world, a different world. I just hope they can survive it."

A match now flared in Ben's hand, touching and igniting the tip of his cigar. Pushing back from the table, he said he was going to the Elks Club for awhile.

Rachel remained at the table for several minutes looking off into space without focusing her eyes or her mind, drumming her fingers on the tabletop. Why is it, she wondered, that men always make pronouncements on life and then leave women to worry about them?

Then she noticed Ruth's presence.

"Ruth, have you eaten?"

"No'm."

"Sit down here and eat, then."

As Ruth poured her tea, Rachel looked at her closely, at the pretty, tan face, the straight, black hair, the ageless gracefulness of her gestures. A warm feeling flooded Rachel as she watched her, now daintily buttering a biscuit. There was a great deal she had taught Ruth, but then Ruth had been the family's teacher, too—particularly David's. She had taught him respect, pride, and restraint. She had, as much as anyone, instilled in him the sense of values that drove him to protect weaker people, to care about them and their feelings.

"What do you think, Ruth?"

"Bout what, ma'am?"

"About the problem with David?"

For a long moment Ruth regarded the biscuit she still held in her

255

hand. Then slowly and deliberately she answered.

"You need'n worry none, Miz Harris. Davey's gonna be OK."

"Do you mean that you think he'll wind up with a Jewish girl?"

"Not 'xactly, ma'am," Ruth answered.

"Then what do you mean, he'll be 'OK'?"

"I mean he'll wind up with a good girl."

Rachel was perplexed. "Does that mean he'll be OK?"

"Yessum. Might not mean you and Mr. Ben and Mr. Shulman'll be all right, but *he* will."

"Well," Rachel said, a bit petulantly, "I believe David is the only member of this family you care anything about at all."

"No'm," Ruth said simply and then was silent. In her heart she knew she did love David best. All the others were important to her —Jennifer with her kindness and gentleness, Mr. Ben with his teasing, Mrs. Harris, too. But David was hers, had always been hers. If he found a girl he loved, that was more important than the way anybody, including Mrs. Rachel, felt about it.

"Don't you worry none, Miz Rachel. That boy'll be all right. You see."

Wouldn't Rachel be surprised to know that years ago, she had made it her business to know everything about Marcie Stevens, that she had sought out and gotten to know the Stevens maid, had befriended her by getting her out of a scrape, and over a period of time had extracted detailed information about the girl, her father and her mother (a drunken whore who had deserted them)? She knew about Marcie Stevens' personal habits, her limitations as a cook, her housekeeping (what little of it she had to do), her relationship with her father. She had been told about her schoolwork and her popularity, and that now, she was dating some "Jew boy dat she say she goan' marry, an' dat don't set quite right with her daddy, but he 'bout give up on it, seems lak to me." All of this Ruth had heard from the Stevens maid.

She had also seen Marcie long before Mrs. Rachel had. She was a pretty girl—every bit as pretty as Jennifer—and a nice one, too. Ruth had contrived to be strolling by the Episcopal Church one Sunday morning when Marcie, whom she recognized from her picture, and her father walked by. In the manner of the Southern Negro, Ruth had lowered her eyes as she approached them, but Marcie had spoken to her. Even as Ruth smiled shyly and returned the greeting, she was thinking the girl refined, despite what that trashy Lila had said about her mother.

256

If Davey wanted her, Ruth decided, he ought to marry her, and that's all there was to it.

Having said her piece and finished eating, Ruth began to scrape the dishes and run the hot water.

33

Almost as soon as she awoke, Marcie Stevens remembered that this was a day she had not wanted to come. A part of her wanted nothing more than to stay in bed, to forget the appointment, to play sick. As she stretched her long, tanned legs under the light coverlet, her mind played over the possibilities. But finally, she knew, she would go.

She had made the appointment with the rector, Johnathan Martin, several weeks earlier, and, if only out of courtesy, she would keep it. At first, the prospect of talking to him had seemed quite natural, perhaps even pleasurable. He was a youngish man, rather good-looking, she thought, and she had enjoyed their several earlier conversations. Today would be different, though. Inevitably he would tell her things she didn't want to hear; perhaps even try to use his considerable persuasive power to convince her that she was wrong.

Water began to run in the sink just outside her door. With a final stretch, she swung her legs over the side of the bed. The room was small, with only enough space for her bed and clothes. It opened onto a larger room, pine-paneled, with built-in desks and bookshelves running the length of one wall. It was the most comfortable dorm on campus, and a privilege of seniors only.

At the sink, Joanne Marshbanks was scrubbing her face. For a moment Marcie watched her. She was a pretty girl, with long, honey hair that ordinarily cascaded over her heavy, tightly brassiered breasts. In the green chair near the sink, Alice Woods sat waiting her turn, toothbrush, soap, and towel in her lap. Alice was a shy, quiet girl. Joanne had once said that Townsend College had been the best choice for Alice and the worst for herself. Alice wasn't unattractive, but her attractiveness required close examination and thought, just as her friendship did. In both areas, Joanne required neither. Her eyes were big and blue, her mouth slightly overlarge, her lips full and sensuous. Even when she didn't mean to be, which was seldom, she was a miracle of sexiness, her pear-shaped bottom wiggling at every step, the slim waist emphasizing her ripe breasts.

Marcie worried about her. To Joanne, life was a joke to be lived as if tomorrow were an abstraction. Her psychiatrist father and diamond-studded, busy mother had launched her past adolescence with the values of an alley cat.

"You know that ugly, pimply boy at P.C. everybody laughs at?" she had asked Marcie the year before.

"Yes, I remember him. He's the one who had an epileptic seizure at a party in Grayson?"

"Right," Joanne nodded. "Well, last night, I believe I rescued him from a miserable life of shyness and inferiority."

Marcie scarcely dared to ask her how.

"Well," her roommate said, "I saw him at a ball game and talked him into driving me home. He seemed afraid to even do that. Poor kid . . . must have been rejected all his life. On the way, I started feeling sorry for him, so I got him to pull off the road in some trees, and I laid him."

Marcie was shocked.

"You what—?"

"What difference does it make to anybody but him?" Joanne asked. "Now he feels like a man, like a somebody, for the first time in his life. You know what it feels like to be a nobody? It feels worse than having a disease!"

Marcie could only shake her head. Of course, she admired the purity of her friend's intent. But her morality, or her lack of it—that was something else again.

When she made no reply, Joanne upbraided her. "Oh, don't be such an old prude. Making people happy sexually is a victimless crime at worst. Besides," she laughed, "maybe it'll clear up his pimples."

With that, she threw her eyebrow pencil aside and walked toward the door. "I got a class now in ethics," she giggled. "See ya later."

Joanne was, in other contexts, a model of decorum. During the frequent weekends she visited Somerset, she was restrained and virginal, particularly in Marcie's home and at the Episcopal Church where she sat demurely, hands white-gloved, a small hat on her head, listening to the service with unaccountable solemnity.

One small area of difficulty had arisen: Joanne and Bob, Dave's friend, had naturally been thrown together. Bob was, Marcie knew, a pretty slick operator with the ladies. He was also one of her very favorite friends. The first time they were together, Joanne was conscious that Marcie was watching, so she reined in her natural, sexually superheated instincts. But the next night, just as she was dozing off, Marcie had been awakened by a tapping on her door.

It was Joanne.

"Look, Marcie, I'm having a hard time falling asleep and it's your fault. Either keep me away from Bob or convince yourself that he's discreet."

"What does that mean?" Marcie asked sleepily.

"It means I'm going to get in his pants," Joanne said, tossing her long hair. "Goodnight."

As she fell asleep, Marcie was thinking that no girl she had ever known talked or acted like Joanne. On anyone else, it would seem dirty and immoral. But on Joanne, it was just Joanne.

Her appointment with the rector was at 2:00, but she arrived 20 minutes early. She had been careful to select her most modest outfit —a dark-blue dress with a high, white Peter Pan collar. As she waited in his study, she became mildly annoyed with herself for having felt the need to set the stage for her conference. She walked around the room, or rather, fidgeted around it, finally stopping in front of some bookcases. The lower shelves were jammed with scholarly, theological texts, histories, and works of philosophers which made her vaguely uncomfortable. Somehow they presented, in their dark bindings, the picture of a rigid, somber man without compassion or understanding. Then her eyes traveled to the top three shelves, and she immediately felt more comfortable. She recognized many old friends: Milton, Thackery, Shakespeare, Browning, Blake, Flaubert, Dumas, Henry James, Faulkner, Wolfe, Robert Penn Warren, Poe.

"Who's your favorite?" a deep voice boomed behind her. Startled, she turned and saw Johnathan Martin. His eyes were bright and cheerful, and suddenly she was glad she had come.

"Milton, I guess, or Faulkner. I'm reading *Absalom, Absalom* now, but he's really got me confused."

The rector was smiling, an even smile over white teeth. "I'm afraid you may not like the way the love affair ends," he said. "I didn't."

For a moment her mind dwelled on Charles Bond and Judith Sutphen. Then she realized that Martin knew why she had come.

"Sit down, please," he said, his hand sweeping over several heavy-leather chairs. "It's always a pleasure to have my young people

260

coming by. Freshens up my point of view, and goodness knows, it can always use it."

The rector looked very much like the marine he had been 15 years earlier. He was tall, deeply tanned, and well built. The lines that were beginning in his face only made him look more rugged. Marcie thought he looked out of place the first time she saw him in the pulpit. Then when he spoke, she recognized how remarkably well placed he was. His sermon had blended strains of Episcopal orthodoxy with clear undertones of compassion and humanism. His voice was deep—nontheatrical but powerful. There was a gentleness about him, a compassionate understanding that had for years attracted troubled girls, Episcopal and non-Episcopal, from the college to talk in his study.

For a few minutes he chatted lightly about the new dean of women, about his undergraduate years in a small, secular college in the Midwest, about several people they knew in common in Somerset.

Naturally, easily, without her even realizing that it was beginning, he soon had Marcie talking about herself and why she had come. It felt good to talk to someone who, she was sure, would not answer her with negative clichés or psychological claptrap.

Martin looked at her as she spoke, nodding occasionally or smiling a half-smile of encouragement. When she had said all she came to say, he encouraged her to say more, and to her surprise, she did so, including even a confession of her one sexual indiscretion and the guilt she carried for not feeling guilty. As she said this last, she had begun to wish she hadn't. She had said too much, given too much away, left herself with too few defenses. Suddenly the room, so cozy before, felt stuffy and uncomfortable. The theological texts seemed to press in on her.

"Are you all right?" the rector asked.

"Yes, sir," she answered. "I just felt a bit dizzy for a moment. I don't know why."

The rector opened the window behind his desk, then called the maid.

"Marybeth, please serve us tea and bring in a glass of icewater."

Gratefully Marcie took the glass and drank deeply, all the while avoiding his eyes.

After tea was served and the door closed softly behind the Negro woman, Martin spoke.

"You know, Marsha, lots of people come to a priest or pastor or rabbi or even a psychotherapist to confess, in a way—or at least to get rid of some guilt feelings. And what we always find is that the guilt is much greater than the supposed crime.

"Take you, for example. Your great crime is love. You've come here and told me that you're deeply in love with another human being, and that all kinds of problems are arising because of that love."

He smiled. She began to relax.

"Now you know that next Sunday morning, I'll be up in my pulpit delivering a sermon urging people to love each other. But still you're feeling confused and maybe even a bit guilty about—in a way —following that very piece of advice."

"But you—"

He interrupted, holding up a large hand and smiling again.

"Now, listen, young lady. I'm going to insist on sharing this stage. After all, I'm part of this act, too."

She smiled and sank backward in her chair.

"So," he continued, "let's take this thing in some kind of order. First, on one occasion, you expressed your love for this young man in a physical, a sexual, way. I suppose you expect me to rant and rave about sin and fornication and all of that, but I usually can't find it in myself to do that. The church is against fornication, has been for many centuries. But personally, all I'm against is meaningless and permissive sexuality, more because it's destructive to people than because it violates the dictates of our faith. To be honest, though, I hope you will refrain from further premarital sexual experiences, only because they lend themselves too easily to endless, perhaps even promiscuous, repetition."

Marcie felt relieved at this, more because it indicated the reasonableness of the man than because she was "forgiven" in the "Catholic" sense.

After a sip of tea, he continued. "As to your mother, my heart goes out to you and your father. I know it must have been just horrible for you, that somewhere inside, the scarring is still raw and deep. But you simply have to forget, to trust that there is a reason for it in a much larger scheme. Who knows, maybe God intended it as a lesson to you."

Marcie had seldom spoken of her mother since that night she died. Telling the rector was purely accidental. Subconsciously she was terrified that somehow, she might become her mother, might hurt others as her mother had hurt her. Now she began to understand this, began to sort out the pieces. He talked softly on.

". . . marriage is a sacred institution but, in truth, a difficult relationship at best. There are so many stresses that ordinarily occur that one must be careful not to beg extra ones without the best of reasons. And Marsha, a deep religious difference is an extra stress— sometimes . . . an inordinately difficult one. Of course, the situation

262

will be alleviated considerably after your young man leaves the Jewish faith and joins the church. Even so—"

He stopped in midsentence, startled at the way she snapped her head around toward him.

"You don't understand," she said. "There's no way in the world that would ever happen. What we're talking about here is my living with a Jewish husband, not a convert to Christianity. He'd *never* change."

As she said this, she could sense an unexpectedly powerful reaction in the rector, even before he spoke again. His gaze seemed steely now. Suddenly she didn't want to hear anything else he might say. She had expected a theological argument and then perhaps some advice. But not this.

The rector crossed the room in long strides, pausing at the window for a moment before turning back to her. "Have you considered just what your life might be like, living among Jews?"

The question shocked her. "What?" she asked.

"If you marry this man and if he remains true to his faith, you will find yourself living essentially among Jewish people," he said evenly. "Your children's grandparents will be Jews, so will their uncles and aunts and cousins. But beyond that, much—if not most—of your social life will be shared with Jews."

"So what?" she said, angrily. "Would that be so terrible? Are all Jews such reprehensible people?"

The anger felt good. It was a defense of David, a sensation that made her feel noble.

The rector threw up his hands. "Oh, be realistic," he said. "I'm not saying Jews are reprehensible. What I *am* saying is that they're different from you, and you had better face that fact now instead of later. Their heritage is different—their values, their family life-style. Not awful, enormous things in themselves, but cumulatively, they add up to pressures on you and your marriage."

Still she said nothing. She simply stared at him, looking more confused than angry. A nagging thought began in her mind. Different? it asked. Maybe. She forced it back into her subconscious.

"I dislike stereotyping as much as anyone," he said. "But Jews are, in many cases, more different from you than you might like to admit."

She was about to remonstrate, so he hurried along, not wanting to be left at this juncture.

"But all of this is really understandable from even the most cursory knowledge of European and American history. They've just really gotten into our culture, only one or two generations back.

Complete acculturation takes time. Of course, there are some lovely reform Jews, particularly among the Spanish and Germans who emigrated to this country hundreds of years ago. In fact, I've had any number in my congregations. But on the whole, they are not really socially representative of the Jewish population. And that's the simple reality you have to face."

Marcie was angry and disappointed. But the nagging reasserted itself again, demanding that she consider the possibilities.

"Is that the biggest part of the problem, in your way of thinking?" she asked.

"Yes, I believe it is. I believe it is the part too often left unexamined, unconsidered. Maybe because of that, it's potentially the most damaging. Look, don't answer me or yourself now. Just consider what I've said and what you already know. Then ask yourself if they are the kind of people with whom you're prepared to spend the rest of your life."

"I can't look at it that way," she said. "I just can't."

"I think you'd better, for your own sake and for your young man's."

As she emerged into the sunshine outside, Marcie realized for the first time that she did not know David's parents at all.

34

When Isaac began to die in earnest, he wanted "the boy" with him more than he wanted any of his children. Every afternoon that August, the two of them would sit in the air-conditioned den on Jackson Square, the old man in the green leather chair with the hassock, acknowledged as "his" chair, David on the red leather couch across from him, listening.

The old man felt a special urgency during these hours, for reasons he never stopped to question. His mind was still sharp, logical, clear, and if he had wanted enough to pin down the feeling—if anything but the feeling itself had been important to him—he could have done it, could have arrived at the conclusion in his consciousness, as well as his subconscious, that he knew this boy, David, his oldest grandson, was his best hope for his own replication. It was in this boy, he felt, that his own morality and intelligence and drive might be merged . . . a generation skipped . . . but providing, nonetheless, a chance that he, Isaac Shulman, might live on earth after he had passed beyond the shadows of life.

What had he done? he would ask himself bitterly between their visits. Amassed a moderate fortune. Bought property. Raised children. Made a name in a little town. Built a synagogue. Given to charity. It wasn't enough. He had raised no significant monuments to himself, either in deed or granite to keep his memory alive, or in flesh and blood among his sons.

To him death was an abstraction, a trifle he had already cheated out of more than 20 years, a chance to rest. It was not death he feared, not in the least, but rather the thought (in fact, the almost certain eventuality) of being forgotten.

Outside the casement windows, two mockingbirds were chasing a gray cat, swooping down at him in mock attack, sending him rolling on his back to swipe at them. The rose bushes beside the garage were full of flowers now, and huge, white blossoms dotted the magnolia. Life was everywhere outside the windows, but in his study the old man talked to the boy about death.

The old ways, he said, were finally better. When a respected Jew died in Bogdanya, the family sat *shiva* in their oldest clothes, beating their breasts, properly grief-stricken and abandoned. Every day for a year, the sons, relatives, and friends were waiting by the synagogue door for the shamus to bring the key, so they could go inside to say the *Yortseit* in his memory, and by so doing, to plead and ease his way into *Ganaiden*. After the year, the sons still made the Kaddish for their father during every holiday service in the shul.

It was the right way, he told the boy. A Jew died more easily knowing he would be remembered.

"Now what?" he asked ironically. "My sons can't read enough Hebrew to say the Kaddish. Oh, they'll go to shul a few days and mumble the English translation, and then they won't be able to get a *minyan* so easily, and that will be it."

His eyes looked yellow and feverish as he spoke. Although the matter had been bothering him for months, this was the first he had spoken of it.

Outside, the mockingbirds shrieked at the cat in imitation of its own voice, and David was distracted for the moment. Crazy birds, he thought, what does that get you? Then he turned to his grandfather. "What do you want me to do?"

The old man smiled. "You, Dovidl? You'll know what to do."

This puzzled David, and he pressed the old man to explain, but there was no explanation he could put into words, so he simply retreated into a strange silence. His eyes looked through and beyond his grandson, who imagined he might be seeing through the mirror of his life, through 70 years of time to a crooked alley, a hut with a dirt floor, a stern old man at his books, in a place far away from David's knowledge and understanding, but a place, nonetheless, which was known to him, deep in his subconscious where his dreams and nightmares began.

Slowly, dreamlike, the old man reached for the small, black case knife, then carved a tiny plug of Brown's Mule tobacco to put in his cheek. The snap of the blade closing seemed to bring him back to the present, to the room of green and red leathers.

"What shall I do, then?" David asked again.

"Have courage and wisdom," the old man said. "Believe in God and your Jewishness. That will honor me enough." A look of bemusement played at the corners of his eyes.

"Soon my bones will be rotting in the ground. No, don't interrupt me . . . my bones, like the bones of all who have gone before me, will be rotting in the ground, and a little bronze plaque will say that Isaac Shulman lived and died, and that will be all. Nowhere on the plaque will it say that I was lame and then I walked, that I had hard times and overcame them, that I sweated and hurt and bled and tried and sometimes won."

"It's not true," David began halfheartedly, but Isaac stopped him: "Of course it's true. Nothing is more true than the fact that people are born and live and die."

Then he talked of Bogdanya, of his brothers and his mother but mostly about his father whom he watched at his books with wide eyes as he lay, a tiny, crippled child, behind the stove in their hut. As Isaac talked, the rabbi of Bogdanya came to life in David's mind, as he always did when his grandfather spoke of him, reaching across the long expanse of time and distance to lay an icy hand on the boy's heart.

Months before, Isaac had begun to dwell more and more on Bogdanya—especially when talking to David—his memory chilled by its cold winters, his heart gladdened, as a child's would be, by its green, spring meadows, his spirit haunted and tortured by the memory of his father.

Despite his material successes, his position in the community, his large brick house and considerable holdings in land, he knew he would be a failure in his father's eyes, and these days, he thought more and more about that failure. He had abandoned the Talmud. He had eaten fish without scales a hundred times with the *goyim*. He had abandoned the ways of his people. He had lived an honest life but not a Godly one. As he told his grandson now about another of his father's arbitrations, he longed to be at a rough bench himself or reading by the stub of a candle in the cold synagogue of Bogdanya, wondering again at the wisdom of the Commentaries.

Late that afternoon, as David left the house and walked into the fading Carolina sunshine, the spectre of the rabbi of Bogdanya walked with him, and he felt cold.

35

Early the next morning Baila was awakened by a thrashing in the twin bed a few feet away in the darkness.

"Isaac . . . Isaac," she called softly. "Isaac, are you all right?"

The sound continued, but he did not answer her. She sprang out of bed and snapped on the light. The sight she saw made her feel faint. She gripped the side of her husband's bed to keep from slipping to the floor.

He was thrashing against the mattress with his left arm, his mouth open, his eyes bulging with the effort to speak, his face red, the muscles and veins in his throat and neck distended.

"Itzrok!" she screamed, frozen herself, terrified at the sight of him. She touched his face, wanting to comfort him and not knowing what to do. But something brought her out of her shock, forcing her away from him, to the phone.

Ben hardly understood a word she said, but he knew from the moment he sleepily answered the phone that something was terribly wrong with the old man. He tried to get through to her, to reassure her that he and Rachel were on the way, while at the same time yelling for Rachel to wake up.

In the emergency room of the hospital the resident quickly examined Isaac, gave him a shot to calm the anguished, awkward jerking of his left side, and sent him to intensive care. Ben spoke with the doctor briefly and was told that Isaac had apparently suffered a massive, paralytic stroke. When Ben asked him about the old man's chances, the doctor shook his head slowly. It was the answer Ben expected.

In his hospital bed, Isaac lay quietly, his mind clear, frustrated by being trapped in a body that would not respond to any of his commands. Even more than when part of his face had been cut away, Isaac knew now what death was like, for then it was a toss-up whether he would live or die—and that would be the end of it. But now he lay thinking that in all substantive ways, he had already died except for the formality of his heart stopping and his brain ceasing to function.

He wasn't in pain, in the usual sense, but the terrible frustration of not being able to speak or move freely was worse than physical pain. He would not get better—he knew that—even if the doctor had told him he could. The time had come for him to die. So, what of it? All of us come onto this earth and live and try a little while and then die. It is the natural order of things.

Jake came into the room, a frantic look on his face, out of breath from running across the parking lot.

"Papa . . . Papa," he whispered, bending over the old man. Isaac rolled his eyes open and feebly raised his good hand to let his oldest son know he was awake and that he could hear him.

"You're gonna be all right, Papa," Jake said clumsily.

If things had been different, Isaac would have laughed his high-pitched cackle. This Jake, he thought . . . he's a good man, and part of it is that he never has been able to tell a lie worth a damn.

"We sent for Aaron, Papa. He's comin' now."

Isaac moved his eyes again, wishing that he could reach out and touch Jake, just to clasp him on the arm—even if he couldn't say it in words—to let him know that in his own way, he had made Isaac proud and that it was all right.

The nurse now had Jake's arm, pulling him away from the bed, but Jake told her gruffly that he would go in a moment and to leave them alone. Silently she left the room.

Jake bent over the bed again, choking on his words but saying them because it was terribly important to him that he get them said. "Papa . . . I . . . I . . . did the best I could, Papa," he said. "I couldn't do no better. . . . Couldn't do no better for you than what I did. You understand, Papa? It was all for you . . . every bit of it."

The old man rolled his eyes again to try to say that he did understand and that it had been enough. Then he slept for a few minutes. When he awoke, the room was still dark and Rachel was sitting in the chair next to his bed, her face resting lightly on her hand, looking at him. She saw his eyes blink open and spoke to him softly, murmuring that he was so much loved and respected that he would have to get well and come back to them and to Somerset.

Good, strong, bright Rachel. Had he given her back even a part of the love she had given him? The caring? Had he ever told her about his feelings for David, her gift to him?

Suddenly he wanted desperately to see David. He began to struggle to say it to her. Straining with all of his strength, he tried to say the word. The sweat poured down his face from the effort, and saying the word was all that was important to him. At first, no sound came. He tried harder, trying to form his lips, trying to make his larynx respond to the order. Rachel wiped his face, staring intently at him, fearful that he was dying at that moment. Then a sound came —not much more than a low grunt, unshaped and unformed.

"What, Papa? What are you trying to tell me? What is it?"

It wasn't good enough. He tried again and again until finally the insignificant sound took a semblance of shape, not because it was medically realistic that he could communicate, but because he was Isaac Shulman, and he had a last thought to convey. So, by God, he would force it out of this now-dying, paralyzed body that frustrated him so miserably.

The sound was hardly more than a whisper, coming deep out of his diaphragm, starting higher and then collapsing into a lower sound, so that it sounded like a word rather than a grunt.

Rachel tried to make out the word. Then in the darkness behind her, Jake called out quietly:

"Are you tryin' to say *boy*, Papa? You want to see David?"

Isaac didn't hear him clearly, so Rachel repeated what Jake had said.

"The boy, Papa? Is it David?"

Isaac was thrilled that they had understood. He rolled his eyes excitedly to tell them that it was indeed the boy he wanted to see.

"I'll get him, Papa," Rachel said and left.

The darkness settled over him now—and the quiet. Jake was there in the room somewhere, and he tried to think about Jake, but suddenly, Jake's face began to change in his mind. Then Jake was his brother, Avrum, standing tall and straight in his army uniform, saying goodbye to his father, Mordecai Shulman, the rabbi of Bogdanya, and to his mother and to Uri and Motel, and last of all, to tiny Itzrok, staring out at him through wide, shining eyes.

When David hurried into the room a few minutes later, Isaac was dead.

36

Look at 'em, David thought bitterly, all here to see the show. Come to see the final punctuation mark drawn in on the old super-Jew's life.

The family was seated in a small room, facing the lectern. The others sat in a larger room on the other side of a fancy grillwork screen. Before the funeral service had begun, David had distractedly watched the unctuous attendants lug in all the extra chairs they could jam into the room, but there were still not enough, and many people stood at the back of the room.

Look how self-righteous and concerned and grieved they're acting, he thought. Can you believe it?

His eyes moved slowly over the first few rows, visible to him through the screen. There was old Mrs. Louella Pringle, who would die if she knew the whole town knew she sipped gin all day out of a prune juice bottle she kept in the refrigerator. Look at her gawking through the screen, hoping to see somebody break down or scream or faint. And would you look next to her. Jimmie Lee Hall, trying to keep a straight face. I must have knocked him on his ass 15 times when we were kids, he hates Jews so much. And Charlie Baxter and his wife over there, aren't they something. Her sitting there in a ratty-looking dress and him buying clothes at Straws and Cooper every week for that big-assed blond waitress in Wakeley, and his old lady too dumb to know he's too sorry to kill. Who the hell let them in here?

God, look at all of them. Who needs them here? Fucking creeps, most of 'em. How about Harlow Cooper a few minutes ago, trying to nag an insurance policy out of Mr. Trager, right at the foot of the coffin? Or Marsten Green . . . him half-drunk and his wife wearing dark glasses from where he musta beat her last night. One of these days, that boy of theirs is gonna take an ax and split old Marsten's head clean down to his Goddamned neckbone, and if a jury so much as reprimands him, there's no justice.

Look at 'em, he thought again. In their starched shirts and silly, white gloves and black shoes and good suits. All here to see the show, to hear the Jew preacher mumble foreign words and see old lady Shulman collapse or whatever other good stuff might happen, and all for no admission.

As he watched the last few file to their places along the sides of the room after the last seat was taken, David's mood became increasingly bitter. He thought of the old man again and his death and death itself.

Jennifer squeezed his hand slightly and nodded as the rabbi mounted the platform and began to arrange a few pieces of paper on the lectern. "Who is like unto thee, oh my God," he began. The words flowed easily, theatrically, from his thin lips, rising up and curling in crisp currents around the heads of his listeners, the tones foreign in their precision even as he spoke in English. The rabbi liked to hear the words, liked the full, rich resonance of his voice, allowed himself this, his greatest vanity. As he slowly raised his hands, the large tallis flowed in just the right attitude, created, he knew, just the right impression on the Jews and *goyim* whose rapt attention he now held.

But even as he enjoyed the richness of his own voice, he was troubled. Soon, after these essentially routine opening words, would come the eulogy, and he wasn't entirely satisfied with it. The old man had been so complex, so contradictory, so strange in his own way, that the pat, easy words that sufficed for most funeral orations didn't apply here.

The floor in his study had been littered with crumpled papers the night before, as one piece after another failed miserably. There were few absolutes about Isaac Shulman except his absolute control and absolute conviction that he was right. A kind and loving father? It had looked absurd, staring bleakly up from the typewriter at him. A man who never wavered from his traditions and his religious convictions? The old man had eaten his weight in catfish on the riverbanks of Somerset County, had satisfied his tastes for ham and bacon and shellfish a thousand times over. And his *tefillin*, the rabbi knew, had gathered dust until just before he died. A man with a gentle and forgiving nature? There would be at least one or two people in the room who might laugh outright. A man of tenderness and compassion? He had killed his own favorite horse for rearing at his wife 50

272

years ago, had beaten his children without mercy.

A man of brilliance?—Absolutely. A man driven to win?—He had no equal. A man who had overcome obstacles and accomplished, where others—weaker ones—failed? Again, beyond doubt. A man devoted to the truth? Isaac Shulman's dedication to honesty had been legendary.

The eulogy concerned these things, then; but still, they seemed not to be enough. Finally, at 3:00 A.M., he had turned out the light and gone to bed. The sun that awoke him the next morning brought no new inspirations, so, with a sigh, he had let the words stand.

Now he was into a Hebrew portion of the service, and the words were automatic. From his lips came *boruch atoh adonoy elohenu*. . . . But in his mind, the Shulman family whirled. There before him was Rachel Harris, the most *leberdik* of them, her face swollen with crying, in the front row with Ben and their children. She stared up at him, hollow-eyed, captured by the moment and what he was saying. Beside her was her son, David, a senior in college now. Was it eight years already since he had bar mitzvahed him?

Down the pew, he saw Jake, the oldest son—his sleeve pinned up at the shoulder, a better, more gentle man than anyone thought he could ever be—with his wife and daughters. Jake's jaw was set firmly, his eyes down. The rabbi wondered what Jake was feeling at that moment. Probably some terrible kind of numbed aloneness.

Aaron, the bright one, sat with his family behind Jake, seeming more interested in the service than crushed by it.

Irving, the third son, sat slightly apart, his eyes downcast, reaching into his heart for tenderness and loss, but finding confusion and questions he dared not ask or try to answer.

As the rabbi progressed into the service, he wondered about the children. The old man, he knew, had brought the old ways intact from some tiny village in Russia, ultimately superimposing them on life in his home in Somerset. Where others had moderated their ways to accommodate the new culture, the old man had not given an inch. Undoubtedly this had been hard on his children; it had twisted them in dark and unfathomable ways. How much love, and how much fear —how much respect and relief—is the old man's portion there in his coffin, the rabbi wondered. And he looked to the children's eyes for clues.

In his waning years, Isaac had become as much myth as man, the sum total of his accomplishments more than flesh and blood, flinty courage and strength more than father and human being. For the mourners, where did the man begin and the myth end, the rabbi wondered. Even for himself?

Isaac Shulman's wife—small, frail, and very much alone—sat in the front beside Rachel. She was thought of by everyone the rabbi knew as the wife of Isaac Shulman, not as Baila Shulman, a person competent even to exist without the man who now lay in the bronze coffin. She would have to live, and she would live, the rabbi had decided late the night before. Maybe there was more substance to her than anyone had thought. Now we and she are going to find out.

David wanted a cigarette badly, but he momentarily forgot it when the words of Dylan Thomas, brought to life by the resonant tones of the rabbi's best delivery, rang out through the room. "Death shall have no dominion," the rabbi said, making four syllables of the word *dominion* as Thomas himself did in a reading David had heard. "Death shall have no dominion . . ." the rabbi continued, reciting a fragment and developing it into his text.

"A man lives by what he is, for what he is, and for that, Isaac Shulman remains alive and will continue to live—a spark carried in the minds and consciences of those who knew and loved him. And they were many—"

David might have become bored at this point, for the service had begun to sound like the eulogy of any man, except that it triggered a question that nagged at his mind. "A man lives by what he is," the rabbi said. What am I?

"The measure of most men is that they live, perhaps they beget more life, they give some, take some, and they die. But for a few there is more. For Isaac Shulman there was more. His determination transcended most understanding, his courage most human imagination. As the prophet said. . . ."

The rabbi's voice rose now, developing one thought he had particularly liked in the eulogy. He had them now, he knew, all of them, as he glanced out over the rapt faces in the larger room. Automatically, without concentration or conscious thought, he picked out the Jews in the room. One face puzzled him, however. A girl, apparently alone, who could be Jewish, a *shaineh maidel* with dark hair and eyes, but he did not remember having seen her. He suspected that she was Christian.

Why, then, he wondered, was she crying?

37

As David backed the Buick out of the driveway, two thoughts were jumbled in his mind. The first was what the world would be like for him without his grandfather, and the second was what it might be like without Marcie Stevens.

The streetlights were already lit, glowing white against the late-summer sky along Main Street. Stopping at a succession of red lights, he forced himself to concentrate on the lights on the poles, on cars going by—anything to distract himself. There's Osborn's car over at Cowan's with nobody in it; probably out in his girl's car getting laid. The line for ice cream is longer than usual at the Dairy Queen. They ought to do something about the lights there; it's pretty damn unappetizing to have a moth fly in your milk shake. The tennis courts are full at the Rec Center. Christ, Bob and I sure beat hell out of all comers there last summer. The square is deserted; must be the heat.

When he got to Greenwood Street, he eased into the left lane and turned, passing the high school.

How easy things were for us there, he thought. How easy and uncomplicated. There were no commitments that couldn't be gotten out of, no decisions that had to stand; only laughs to laugh. The worst that ever happened was a split lip or a board across your butt in the principal's office.

But now? Shit!

When he turned into Ford Avenue, his eyes immediately picked out the Chrysler she drove, parked out in front of her house. He hadn't called, hadn't said he would be by, and he was relieved that she was home. This night, particularly, he needed to see her, to talk.

Her father met him at the door, the evening newspaper in his hand. "Evening, David," he said evenly. "Come on in. I'll let Marcie know you're here."

Even as he smiled and shook hands, David wondered what Mr. Stevens was thinking. He seemed to look at him oddly, maybe remembering the yarmulke on his head that afternoon, maybe remembering the Jews of Somerset, particularly his family, all huddled together in their spiritual ghetto, maybe remembering his grandmother's lack of restraint as she cried out in her pain and grief.

David glanced around the familiar living room, at its light-green walls, the heavy, patterned furniture, the photographs on the walls. On the chair arms he noted the dainty, crocheted doilies, white and fluffy with starch and ironing. He was suddenly seized, as he had been at other times, with the feeling of being a stranger, the Jew boy in a Christian home, who didn't belong.

He crossed the room and stood looking out the front window at the old water oaks that lined the street. The streetlights played odd shadow tricks through the network of branches and leaves, barely illuminating the trunks. Then he heard her behind him. As he turned around, a thought rocketed painfully through his head: Question: where do I belong? Answer: nowhere.

Marcie was only slightly surprised to find him calling for her. She knew everything would be strange between them. She understood much more than he imagined—even that on this night he would feel estranged from her. There was about him a small corner where he kept hidden away the pain and scarring of a childhood of being different, kept it always like a ghostly presence, to be remembered, repressed, brooded over.

There was much he had allowed himself to tell her, never understanding that it was safe to tell it all. For the five years they had been together, she had quietly tried to make him understand that it was safe to take her into the worst moments, the darkest corners in which he had always seen himself alone. She had given of herself all there was to give, tenderly, and lovingly. She had raised the curtains on one hideous moment in her childhood, the moment that had left her with a sense of reality ordinarily reserved for older people who had, because they had dealt with the world before, been better prepared to cope with it.

She was nine years old, a silly, skittish child with long, skinny legs and chopped-off bangs, as she described herself. As so often happened, her mother had not come home by 8:30, so her father put her to bed with a reassurance and a kiss. A bit later, as she lay somewhere between awakenness and sleep she heard loud voices downstairs. Groggy, she made her way to the head of the stairs, there to behold her mother in the hall below—her eyes and mouth heavily painted, her flimsy dress hiked over one thigh—as she pulled away from her husband.

"For the love of God," she heard him say, "stop behaving like an animal. Come back in at least till you sober up."

"T'hell with you, an't'hell wi' God," her mother said. "Don' need any of you! Leggo my Goddamn arm, you sissy sumbitch!"

With that, she jerked her arm clear of his grip, weaving across the hall, dropping and fumbling to recover her suitcase.

"I got a real man wai'n th' car," she jeered. "An' I'm not comin' back this time, ya hear me?"

"No, Momma, please," the cry had torn itself from the little girl's throat as she rushed down the stairs. Throwing her arms around her mother's tightly corseted waist, she begged, sobbing into the thin fabric of her dress. "Please . . . don't . . . leave . . . us . . . Momma . . . please."

For a moment, her mother stopped, her free hand falling on the child's head and stroking the long, chestnut hair. Then she pushed her away, against the child's frantic clutchings.

"Nice kid," she said. "You're a nice kid, bu' your father's not. Gotta leave. Someday you'll understan'. Bye, honey. Bye, now."

There was a finality in the way she shoved the child aside. Marcie understood it, if she understood nothing else in the nightmare that was happening to her. The final punctuation marks of the grotesque episode were the slamming of the car door at the curb and the screeching of tires as the car wrenched away from the curb. The girl and her father stood hypnotized at the sounds echoing in the still summer night, until they faded and finally disappeared.

Her mother was no good; everyone who knew about her in Macon said so, but Marcie did not know, as children never seem to know. All she knew was that her mother had deserted her; her *mother*—not the slut, as the lady next door referred to her, or the fancy whore, as she was called down at the pool hall. For weeks Marcie walked the corridors at school like a ghost, showing no evidence of even hearing the cruel whispers or seeing the gestures of the other children. Her eyes empty and staring, she seemed to have withdrawn entirely, a little girl without animation or spirit, without will, interest, or appetite, a little girl lost.

Long after the first time she told David she loved him—only when she finally felt it safe, when they were sophomores in college —she told him this story. She had not wanted to, but finally she felt it dishonest not to tell him, not to give him the opportunity to recoil from her in revulsion, from the sordid inheritance, the possibility that she, Marcie, quite beyond her own control, might turn out no better, because she was her mother's daughter. Unless he was strong enough to prevent her from being no better, she might not be. And in her mind, there was more. Only by knowing this could he understand that part of her—the terrified little girl part who still heard the whispers echoing in the halls of her grammer school—that forced her to cling to him so fiercely, that sought out all the strength and reassurance and affection he could give her. But it was mostly the strength she sought, for it told her it couldn't happen to her because David wouldn't let it.

At the end of the story, she was crying, for it had long been hidden, and now it was out—and that was also painful.

"I promised myself I would never really love anyone else again," she sobbed, "and now I . . . I . . . I've gone back on my promise."

He smoothed the long, silky hair, running his hand over her head as one might a child, and gently kissed her eyes.

"Shhh, don't cry, baby. You know I love you. You know that, don't you? That I love you?"

Suddenly she bolted upright. "David, are you going to leave me, too? Tell me now if you are, David. Please. Because if—" She could say no more.

He was glad she didn't finish the sentence. Touching his fingers gently on her lips, he murmured that love was not something he could turn on and off, that he loved her now and he always would. It seemed to be enough for her. Poor baby, he thought, she asks for so little. Poor baby, poor baby, poor baby. . . . He discovered that he was saying it aloud.

Like a physical sensation, he felt the bitterness gripping his chest. Life is some no good son-of-a-bitch to use this poor kid so badly! Some no good son-of-a-bitch!

He never shared her secret with anyone. He carried it around inside him, always close to his consciousness, glad to have relieved her of it. After that evening she never pressed him again about what might be. But at night, when the world was still and black around her, she would peer into the vault of darkness that covered her and pray that nothing would ever come between them, that he would never walk away from her.

Now she felt the presence she had feared, a wall of some kind separating them. When he walked her to the car, she had brushed his lips with a kiss as always, but tonight it was different. She might never have noticed it had she not been expecting it, but it was there, nonetheless, terrifying her because it was pushing her away.

The heat had passed. A small breeze had come up, moving the needles of the pines slightly, cooling the evening. David drove east.

Marcie knew he was heading for Braden Lake and the spot in the trees overlooking the water, where they had spent some of their happiest times together, laughing or talking or just holding each other.

When he turned off the engine, she looked at him hopefully, but he made no move to turn toward her or to speak. Instead he stared ahead at the dark lake. For some time they sat without a word, sunk in the night symphony of the crickets and deep-throated bullfrogs and catydids and occasional splash of a heavy fish—a bass striking on the surface, perhaps, or a carp throwing roe.

Finally she spoke. "Was it so hard for you?"

Slowly he turned to answer, and she could only half see his face in the dappled moonlight.

"Sure it was hard. He was quite a guy, my grandfather."

"But there's more, isn't there, David?"

"Yes, Marcie, there's a good deal more."

"And it has to do with us, doesn't it?"

"Yes, it does."

He looked away again. The bright stars seemed very near in the summer sky. For a moment he let his concentration wander over them. Out in the lake he heard another splash, a particularly heavy one, and knew that a night-foraging bass had found prey, perhaps a frog skittering across the surface, itself looking for a victim. The breeze had freshened more, and he heard, above the songs of the night creatures, the rustle and moaning of the giant water oaks, pines, and hickory trees.

Then her hand was stroking his arm.

"Poor David, so sad tonight. Can't you let me share it with you?"

"I don't know, Marcie. I really don't know."

"Well, at least tell me about us. I mean, what was it about today and us?"

He took a long breath, began to speak, stopped to find a better way to say it, then began again.

"Marcie, what were you thinking during that funeral service?"

"Well," she said softly. "I was thinking about you and your family, mostly, and how sorry I was that your grandfather was dead."

"Is that all?"

"Well, I'm sure I had some other random thoughts, but that was most of it."

"But what were the other thoughts? Try hard to remember them."

"Let me see," she said. "I remember thinking how beautifully the rabbi spoke, and how dignified the service was. And . . . oh, yes, I remember thinking about a dress a lady had on across the aisle from me, a blue dress that was quite pretty. I wondered if she had gotten it in town. And I thought about you a lot, about how handsome you looked and how much comfort you must be to your mother. That's about it."

"Nothing more?"

"Nothing that I can remember, David. Why?"

He didn't even hear her question so intent was he on trying to make her impressions fit the pattern he was looking for. But they did not fit. Finally he spoke again.

"I didn't think about any of those things. I sat there trying to figure out what my grandfather's life had meant, and no matter which direction I came at it from, it kept adding up to how very far apart my world and yours are."

She started to speak, but he didn't let her.

"I sat there thinking about how you must be reacting to the Hebrew part of the service and to the yarmulke, the little skullcap, on my head. I sat there thinking about how we all must look to you, all the family and the rest of the Jews on one side, huddled together like we always are when the going gets rough."

"David, that's not fair—"

"Yes, it is fair, because it's real," he said. "We carry our own ghetto around with us. We're conditioned to crowd together in it at appropriate moments, like when we smell trouble or death. We've got a real instinct for death, we Jews," he added harshly.

As the words tumbled out, David realized that he had always avoided this kind of talk with her. Of course, over the years, they had spoken of religious differences, but always politely, gently, in a theoretical, abstract way. Tonight was different, in ways only he could understand.

In high school and college he had been permitted to forget somewhat. He had been accepted, had even become a leader. But today, in effect, he had come back home to Somerset, to be reminded that here he would always be different, an outcast, a dirty Jew, whether anyone bothered to articulate the words or not. He knew the lesson well, for the town had been his teacher and the course of instruction had begun early.

280

38

An Oldsmobile roared by, kicking up dust.

"Wonder why they didn't stop?" Bob asked.

"Must be that old raggedy-ass suitcase of yours," David chuckled. "Musta been afraid to stop. How about hiding that old thing in the ditch until we get a ride?"

Bob stood shaking his head. Traffic was light. A mockingbird began to sing in its odd, warbling notes. For a few minutes both stood listening to the bird's song.

"That old bird sure sounds lonesome," Bob said.

"I know just how he feels," David answered.

Bob glanced at him. "Surely you don't miss that gal already. You were with her two hours ago."

"It's not that I miss her now. It's tomorrow I'm thinking about, and after that."

"What's that supposed to mean?"

"Oh, hell, Bob, you know better than anybody."

"You're crazy as a loon, Harris, just crazy clear out of your head if you let her get away from you. I'm tellin' you—"

"Thank you, Dorothy Dix," David said.

Bob didn't say anything. Instead he stood listening to the mockingbird, now trilling another melody different from the two-note song before.

"Did you know that's the only Jewish bird in America?" David asked. "It's called a mockey bird."

Bob failed to see the humor, bitter or otherwise, in the remark.

"What's been eating you, Roughhouse?" he said. "I mean, why

all the Jewish stuff? That's all I been hearing the last few weeks."

"I don't know. I guess the funeral. I guess it's because the whole damn town seemed to be on the other side of that little wall, looking through it at me and my family. I could almost feel them thinking how strange we looked in our skullcaps, how different we are."

"I was there with Mom and Dad. You think we were thinking that?" Bob asked with a slight show of impatience. "Cause if you do, you're full of shit."

"Wait a min—"

"No, you wait. You think the whole world revolves around David Harris. Believe me, it doesn't. Most of the people didn't even know you were there—couldn't have cared less, if you want the truth. Your grandfather was a big man in Somerset, a popular man. It ever occur to you that some people were there to attend his funeral and not to stare at you and think how Jewish you were?"

Disgustedly Bob yanked at a weed and bit off the bottom of the stem. The disgust was deliberately exaggerated. He knew that much of what David was feeling was very real indeed, not so much that the town was staring at him but that many people individually were staring at the family, seeing them not as a grieving family but as a grieving Jewish family somehow taking comfort from a bunch of weird mumbo jumbo their rabbi was saying to them. Most of them, including Bob, had never before seen a Jewish service of any kind— and Bob had to admit uneasily to himself that he had found it strange. As he thought about it, he began to realize that he, too, had reacted somewhat like David had said. He did view the family and the other Jews of the town, who sat together some distance from his seat, as the "Jewish people." For a brief moment Bob had felt embarrassed, but the feeling passed. Hell, they are Jewish and they do stand out, he thought, but that doesn't mean there's anything wrong with my noticing it. Then he remembered that Marcie was in the room, and he began to understand.

"It wasn't that the town was staring, was it?" he demanded. "It was that Marcie was there and she saw your little hat and heard the rabbi and saw your people all together, and you didn't like being exposed that way. Wasn't that it?"

For a moment David didn't answer. Instead he picked up a stone and threw it at the insulators on a telephone pole across the road.

"I dunno. Maybe that's it."

"You know that's it, David, and so do I. And that doesn't speak too well of your opinion of Marcie."

David's head snapped around.

"What's that supposed to mean? What kind of bullshit is that?"

"The truth hurts, right, Roughhouse? You never want things put to a test because you're not so sure of yourself after all. Down in your gut, you figure Marcie really doesn't care as much as you say she does, and that any little excuse will send her running for the nearest exit."

David had to admit—at least to himself—that Bob had hit on part of it. He never had allowed himself to believe that Marcie was really his, no matter how events worked to prove to the contrary. After all, she was the best, the prettiest, the smartest, the most desirable. And he was David Harris, the Jew from Somerset, South Carolina. But it was more than that. Mostly it was that the funeral had reminded him that time was passing rapidly, that all things—even institutions like Isaac Shulman—eventually come to an end, and that he and Marcie, because of their difference, would probably come to an end, too. Over the years, that difference had been largely ignored by them, passed off, hidden from view. But the funeral had brought it all home to him.

"You ever hear Marcie talk about her grandfather, Bob?" he asked.

"No."

"Well, let me tell you. Marcie's grandfather was the son of a Virginia planter who was also a lawyer and a member of the House of Burgesses. When Marcie was a little girl visiting up in Richmond, her grandfather used to take her for strolls over the Civil War battlegrounds where his father and his uncles fought under Lee. Her grandfather was born in an 18-room plantation mansion loaded with crystal and imported shotguns and Queen Anne furniture."

"So?" Bob asked.

"Well, some time remind me to tell ya a little bit about my grandfather," David said, "and his father. Just remind me."

But now wasn't the time, and David was glad when a station wagon braked to a stop and he and Bob were climbing inside.

39

The alarm clock jangled away, jarring David out of sleep. "Goddamn it, Bob, turn that thing off," he growled sleepily, and Bob finally managed to grope it quiet.

What was his first class today, David tried to remember. Was it Wednesday or Thursday? If it was Wednesday, he could go back to sleep for an hour, but if it was Thursday, he had Spanish.

Then he remembered that he had no classes at all. It was the first day of Rosh Hashonah. Later that day he would be going to services. As Bob swung his long legs over the side of the bed, David turned his pillow over, punched it, and lay down on it to return to sleep.

Bob had forgotten, too.

"Hey, Ace, you better get up."

"Not gonna get up," David mumbled.

"Don't you have Spanish at eight?"

"No."

"Yeah, you do. This is Thursday. You better not cut that class anymore."

"Would you let me go back to sleep, for Christ's sake?" David implored. "Today's the high holidays. I'm going to the synagogue."

"Oh, OK. Sorry, champ."

As the door closed behind Bob, David was already asleep.

The hot water felt good as Bob soaped his face and neck. Next to him was Jeff Allen, a buddy more of David's than Bob's. David liked Jeff's reputation as a hard ass, and the respect he got from the other guys from his hometown. Jeff was small, no more than five feet six, and thin. He had fought in Korea and was undoubtedly mean as hell. Bob never quite understood why David liked and admired that. In the shower Jeff looked even smaller than he did in his clothes.

"Where's your roomy?" he asked.

"Still in the sack," Bob answered him over the noise of the shower.

"He better get his ass up if he's gonna make his first class," Jeff said, shutting off the shower.

"Not going to class," Bob said. "He's going to—uh, he's got some things to take care of."

Bob had caught himself just before he said *church*, as if he had been at the brink of revealing some terrible secret about his friend. Maybe, in fact, given the circumstances, he was.

"Isn't he about to cut out of his language class?" Jeff asked.

Bob, lathering his face to shave, decided it would be easier just to lie.

"I think he's got two left," he said. "He's all right."

Jeff was shaving, too. In the large mirror they shared, Bob saw him stroke the straight razor up his neck and over the tip of his chin. In four years of college, Bob had never seen any other student but Jeff use a straight razor, which he had commented on to David.

"He carries that Goddamn thing all the time," David said. "Right in character; he's a mean little bastard. He believes in evening up the odds when he has to. Willie told me the other day he cut two airmen from Shaw last year with that thing."

The razor glided deftly over the protruding jaw and cheek bones, over the pock marks, then up the neck, slowly, slowly. As he finished his own shave, Bob reflected on the fact that he didn't like Jeff for the same reasons he didn't like the razor he carried in his pocket.

At 9:30 David reluctantly opened his eyes and reached for a cigarette. Taking the Lucky Strike in the corner of his mouth, he struck a paper match once, then again, and again, without lighting it. Finally, placing the matchhead more directly under his finger, he dragged it hard across the matchbook striker. As it flamed, a piece of the phorphorous stuck to his finger, burning it.

"Ow, damn it," he exclaimed, dropping matchbook and still-lighted match on the blanket. After knocking both of them to the floor, he lay back on his pillow, sucking his injured finger.

He didn't want to go to shul, but he would go. As he lay there in the morning brightness, he thought about how much he didn't want to go. Mostly because it was such an incredible bore to sit there listening to some stranger drone on in Hebrew, singing off-key chants David didn't understand and wasn't interested in enough to follow the English translation. To make matters worse, he knew he would leave the service after only an hour, maybe less—stepping outside, he would tell himself, to smoke one cigarette, and then not going back inside; and then he would feel guilty about it for days. Eight days, to be exact, until he found himself doing the same thing on Yom Kippur, except probably faster, because if the Rosh Hashonah experience was bad each year, the Yom Kippur service, with all its severity and sadness, was infinitely worse.

Rosh Hashonah was a big day for the Jews, he thought, as he ground out his cigarette. The beginning of the high holidays, the beginning of another year, which meant that somehow, perhaps by oversight, the world had let them live another year; the holy day on which Jews everywhere supplicated their (and his, he supposed) God, to inscribe them for another year in the book of life. Had he not been taught to revere God and especially to keep the High Holy Days? Or was it that in three more days it would be the weekend, and his father would be asking him about *shul* on Rosh Hashonah, and he couldn't lie to his father and say he had been if he had not, any more than he could hurt his father by saying he had stayed away.

Sitting up, he lit another cigarette and headed for the shower.

For the past two years, he had attended the conservative synagogue, riding over with a fellow journalism student. Today, however, he hadn't made any arrangements for a ride, so he walked—to another *shul* he had seen, which was closer to the campus.

When he entered the vestibule, a choir was singing, accompanied by an organ. For a moment he considered the possibility that he had somehow walked into a church. Then he realized that for the first time in his life he was in a Reform Jewish temple. The interior of the temple was beautiful, with lush tapestries adorning the walls, the light broken into a million jewels by the heavy, stained-glass windows, the altar decorated in handsome velvets, brocades, and golds. Above and to the right of the altar, the choir sat together in purple robes. The men in the congregation wore no tallises, and only a few wore skullcaps.

"*Daitchen Yidden,*" he muttered with contempt, and, turning on his heel, walked out of the synagogue into the light. As he walked he found himself muttering—not out of logic but out of conditioning, not out of reason but out of unreason—the words *Daitchen Yidden* over and over again.

He was sweating slightly when he finally reached the conservative shul three miles away. A yarmulke box and a rack of tallises were at the door, and he felt easy with them—not that he had spent so much of his life with them at hand, but because they represented old, comfortable values.

After donning both, he made his way to a back-row seat, where

286

he was instantly bored, as he knew he would be. No boredom was so complete and so instantaneous for him as the one he always felt in shul. Seeking relief, he opened his siddur and read a few pages—roughly at the place in the service where the rabbi was reading in Hebrew. Then he closed the book to listen for awhile. The pew was uncomfortable. He wanted a cigarette. And the voice droned on and on. The people around him were boring, too: the man davening softly beside him was gray-haired, gray-suited, gray-tied; the young man sitting across the aisle scowling at his brat kid who wouldn't sit still; the old woman, fat hanging like wattles on a turkey's neck from her arms, fanning herself with some papers.

Just then David was struck by the irony of his walking out of the Reform temple with such sure conviction. Right now, he thought, the rabbi over there was talking to his congregation in English, maybe even saying something interesting, and the choir music, which he had always liked in churches, was filling in the dead spots in the service. The organ was playing beautiful, rich, quavering notes, filling the room. And here he was, sitting in this stifling room, bored to death, listening to a bunch of people muttering and grumbling Hebrew—most of them poorly and without comprehension—his collar sticking to his sweaty neck. And he had walked out of the other place almost angry. Now what kind of bullshit is that, he wondered, but he knew the answer all too well. It was the blood of the rabbi of Bogdanya, three generations removed, pulling him out of there; the prejudices of his grandfather and his father, his heritage; the old lore to which he, a modern, should not be heir. It was that he had not stayed, for even a moment, to think or wonder. *That* annoyed him the most.

The young man across the aisle walked up to the *Bimah* now, smiling at the congregation, and the rabbi indicated the place in the Torah. Touching the words with the corner of his tallis, and then kissing it, in the age-old symbol of love and awe for the Word, he said the first part of the blessing: *"Boruhu es adonoy hamvoroh."*

A feeling of loneliness came over David. If he were home, he would have an *aliyah* now, he would be blessing the Torah, looking out at all the familiar faces smiling up at him, nodding approval.

Then Marcie entered his thoughts, almost subconsciously. He felt a tightness in his stomach. Sitting in this strange place, alone and unwelcome, he longed for her, not for her to be with him here, but just to be with him.

Then he thought about God. It was only fair, he thought. He was here, in God's temple, on the High Holy Days, where he had been every year at this time for all his life that he could remember, yet during which he had never remembered addressing a single real word or thought to God, merely muttering the unfamiliar, meaningless words. It was only fair that he should get some benefit, some spiritual uplift, some dividend—and he thought more of God and Marcie. For the first time in a synagogue, he thought about God in a real way and felt that maybe God was aware of him, if indeed, there was a God, and if, indeed, given there was a God, that He ever listened—not for words but for thought-words. He felt his mind slowly filling up with God and Marcie.

I love her, God, he thought. What about that part of it? I love her and she needs me. Does that count for anything?

"*Boruh adonoy hamvoroh leolum voed,*" the young man intoned over the Torah.

I'm in a trap. I'm in a trap and I can't get out. . . .

"*Boruh atoh adonoy, elohanu meleh hoalum. . . .*"

It's killing me. . . .

"*. . . asher boher bonu mekol. . . .*"

The blood in my veins, God—it calls me a traitor because I love her. Isn't that what it's about, God? Isn't that the whole thing? Why is this happening to me for loving? I mean, all this pain? It's hating that's supposed to be wrong, not loving.

"*. . . vanosanlonu es Torahso. . . .*"

Marcie!

"*Boruh atoy adonoy, Nosen a Torah.*"

The *aliyah* was finished and the man was returning, smiling contentedly to his wife who was going to beat hell out of her kid when she got him outside, mad not so much at the child as the price her husband had paid for the honor of making the blessing, poised to leave now that it was completed.

"*Boruh atoh adonoy, Nosen a Torah.*"

Ben Harris smiled as he finished his *aliyah*, as he completed the blessing that was being made over Torah the world over that day— in the same words the ancients had used—since the beginning of Jewish consciousness and memory.

Were he home today, Ben thought, David would have an *aliyah* of his own. As he started back to his seat, beyond the shaking of hands, he pictured his son, alone, in a strange synagogue, surrounded by strange people. For a moment Ben thought—with great discomfort—that maybe David had not gone to shul, but the thought quickly passed. As he slipped into his seat beside Rachel, he smiled and winked at her. Of course David would be in shul. How absurd to even think it.

Three hours later Marcie was doing her nails, quite oblivious to the fact that around the world, Jews were celebrating the new year. Then the call came on the bitch box: "Marsha Stevens . . . Marsha Stevens . . . you have a visitor in the lobby."

Moments later one of the girls who had ducked out of her room when the call came reported back. "It's David. You'd better hurry."

Quickly Marcie stripped the curlers from her hair, her mind on which dress she would wear.

In the lobby David crushed out his third cigarette, then he saw her, swirling down the staircase in lavender. He sucked in his breath at the sight of her.

They couldn't kiss in the lobby, so they simply squeezed each other's hands as they met.

"Hi, beautiful girl," he said to her.

"Hi, beautiful man," she giggled. As they walked out of the building, her voice assumed a mock seriousness.

"It's Thursday afternoon, sir, and you have a geology lab from two to four, and you're here instead of there. Explain, please—"

"Well, see, I wasn't going to the lab anyhow," he said. "I was suddenly seized with the most powerful urge to see this girl I know. So I walked a mile or so to the highway and started thumbing, and here I am."

She laughed then, her white-toothed, throaty laugh.

"Oh, David, how wonderful. Let's go to "the Oaks" and sit on the grass and I'll tell you how beautiful you are."

For awhile they just sat in the shadows of "the Oaks," an old stand of trees to which girls had been taking their boyfriends since the college was built, oaks that summoned up images of other times, so old was the stand, so massive the boles. The images were correct, for many goodbyes had been whispered under their branches, and fewer reunions had taken place there. In the darkened rooms of many sagging, old, once-white house in the county, "the Oaks" were remembered as a sad place. But they were beautiful to David and Marcie.

He held her very close to him, smelling the faint roses (or was it gardenias?), the scent that always clung to her, that rose up from somewhere under her blouse. He felt the smoothness of her neck under his lips, and loved her—with a tightening, purring sensation in his chest, with a strange, physical sense of satisfaction and pleasure she aroused in him.

He lay for a while, then, with his head in her lap, listening to her talk, saying little himself, for the pleasure now was in feeling her, hearing her, smelling her, having her near him, rather than bragging or being witty.

In the grass somewhere he heard the murmuring buzzing of bees. Suddenly he was aware that time had somehow slipped, passed too quickly.

"I'm so sorry, baby," he said, jerking awake. "How impolite of me—"

But then her fingers were on his lips, hushing him.

"It's really all right," she said softly. "I had a whole 15 minutes to sit without having to say a word, and just be with you and touch you and look at you."

"Yeah, but—"

"Yeah, but nothing," she said, a smile playing on her lips. "I never saw you asleep before, did you know that? And for those few minutes, you looked so peaceful, as if—"

"As if what?" he asked, but he knew the answer, and he hoped she wouldn't say it.

"Well, never mind," she said softly. "What's important is that you're here. It's not every day a girl has a fellow hitchhike a hundred miles to see her for an hour or two—particularly a fellow a girl happens to love an awful lot."

He looked at her eyes then, and they told him what she had decided not to put into words.

"There's a song being played a lot now," she said. "Frank Sinatra sings it. It's called 'Don't Worry About Me.' Have you heard it?"

"No, I don't think so."

Quietly, in a hushed voice, she began to sing it to him.

Don't worry 'bout me,
I'll get along . . ."

Then she stopped singing, her lips trembling ever so slightly, and she turned her face away from him.

Gently he put out his hands, gripped her shoulders, and turned her around. At first she tried not to look up. But finally she had to, not because he forced her to, but because the time was right for crying between them. The tears welled up and spilled over in her big eyes, and coursed down her cheeks.

"Honey?" he said.

"I'm sorry. Sad songs always make me cry."

They both knew that wasn't it, that she was crying because she believed that somehow a songwriter somewhere had managed to catch a moment in their lives and freeze it for everyone to hear; that it was the way—that somehow the songwriter had known it would be the way—for them; that when it was all done—all the struggle and tension and rationalizing and his fighting with ghosts and biases and real life—that he would walk away from her. And maybe more, because he would have to fight it out alone, even though the battle was for her, and there was nothing she could do to influence the outcome. All she could do—as women had always had to do—was wait.

Glancing at her watch, she saw that two hours had passed. He would have to leave soon to have enough daylight for hitchhiking back to school. She was about to tell him, but he interrupted her.

"Marcie," he said, "you do know that I love you, don't you?"

There was something fierce in his voice. For the first time that she could remember, she was almost afraid of him, so intense was the fierceness, so demanding the tone.

"Tell me what love is, David," she said. "Tell me."

Then he smiled, and she felt him relax.

"Well, lemme see. Love is hitchhiking 100 miles to see a girl smile once."

"What else?"

"Well, it's feeling so crazy happy and contented that you fall asleep with your head in a beautiful girl's lap."

"Anything else?"

"Yeah, one other little thing or two. Like wanting a girl so much you ache down in your bones for her and not taking her . . . feeling like you're only half alive when she's away from you. Most of all, Marcie, it's getting up for either letting her go instead of stringing her along, because letting her go might be the only kindness he can finally do her, or marrying her and turning his back on the rest of his whole world . . . and watching her get caught in the crunch as the whole Goddamn thing falls apart."

The last words were almost spat, with a bitterness she had never before seen in him.

They had never gotten to the point this directly before: she because she preferred to hope things would somehow work out for them if it went on long enough, and because talking about it frightened her more than crying about it alone; he because he didn't know how to say it, or maybe because he knew how to say it all too well, but saying it would make it bigger than it already was, which is to say that it would make it real.

She didn't want to make it hard for him. She knew silence would do that, so she struggled for the right words to say to him, but they wouldn't come. Now, finally, it was out in the open, and even though she knew it had to come and had told herself she was ready (and, of course, she was, more so than he, because she was a woman, and

291

women are stronger and less vulnerable than men). Nonetheless, a cold, numbing feeling spread in her stomach, and she suddenly knew a despair she had not known since her mother pushed her away that night, away from her legs and the clutching at her skirt, and disappeared in laughter and a squeal of tires. Oh God, oh God, oh, God, oh God, please, she thought desperately. Then she was crying in heavy sobs.

All her life she had walled out the potential for being hurt again, but now the walls were down, and she was being pushed away.

He held her very close, feeling her grief. She tried to speak, but the words came in pieces.

"Da . . . vid . . . pl . . . pl . . . please, don't don't le . . . leave . . . m . . . me. Pl . . . please," she sobbed. "I'll do . . . do . . . any . . . thing . . . please."

She tried to stop, but she was a little girl again, feeling the strong hand push her . . . firmly, inexorably . . . away into loneliness.

He was kissing her, hushing her, pleading with her not to cry, but she was nine years old. She was being pushed into the darkness. She couldn't hide behind the walls anymore.

For a long time they remained there, the darkening shadows of the oaks reaching beyond them and onto the rolling lawns beyond. Bullbats marked the hour with their wheeling overhead, slender forms diving down on night insects in the air. Somewhere behind them a catydid began its rasping. In the distance, they heard a tree frog's night song.

Finally she had cried herself out. Exhausted, she lay still, the last shudders passing her shoulders. There was nothing for them to say, so they huddled together in silence, listening to the night sounds.

A second tree frog opened up on the other side of the stand of trees, and David thought how uncomplicated its life must be. Every night at the right time, it had a responsibility to announce that darkness had come again—that and nothing more.

They should talk it out, right now, he knew. But there seemed to be no way to do it without hurting her more or frightening her more. She had said everything she could say: that she would do anything. She had begged him not to leave her. As for himself, everything meaningful had to be argued out within himself. Only after it was over would there be anything more to say.

The lights twinkled in the distance, and the ground grew cold. He took his last cigarette from the pack, fumbled for a match. She moved slightly, but he held her close to him with his other arm. He finally found the match and with his free hand, folded and struck it. The first drag was bitter. He began to feel an odd sensation, like a rumbling deep inside him, a resentment as bitter as the cigarette, except that he felt this physically, felt it flowing in his guts and knew that soon it would have to erupt or it would destroy him. It could have erupted in tears for him and been gone, but he couldn't cry. The most destructive part of his Southern heritage insisted that a man endures the worst pain, the deepest sorrow, the most violent emotional and physical losses, in silence; with dignity, with strength. And if it happens to destroy him, well, that's all right, because it's better to die than to be a human being who feels deeply and thus is weak.

So he sat like a stone, feeling the fury mount inside him.

Her back began to feel stiff from the chilled ground. To Marcie this was the first real thing she had recognized since the nightmare of truth had begun an hour earlier. Then a menacing crack of thunder split the night, followed by a long, ragged lightning streak to the west. She remembered again that David still had to get back to school. He did not want to move, but she urged him, and finally he released her. As they brushed themselves off, David uttered one choked sentence: "I couldn't love you any more than I do. I—" Then he had to stop. The rain came down, and they were running to the dormitory.

For a long moment, he faced her at the door. Then without a word, he kissed her and turned away in the darkness. A wind had come up now, driving the rain harder. Without hat or coat, he walked in the darkness toward the center of town and the sleazy bus station on the square. The wind whipped the oaks and hickory trees and the rain stung his face, quickly soaking his clothes. Not caring, hands thrust deep in his pockets, he walked on. Suddenly the force inside him erupted, and he wildly looked for something to strike out at. But the street was empty, so he thrust back his head and hurled his hands upward into the rain.

"You're killing me, God, and her . . . is that what you want?" he screamed over the howl of the wind. "You're ripping my guts out of me and you're breaking her down, too, and she didn't do anything . . . you hear me . . . she didn't do anything!"

He was becoming incoherent, his control gone at last. If he had been fighting a man, he would have killed him because he would have been unable to stop, but it was God he was fighting, because there was nobody else to fight, and because it was God's fault anyhow.

"You're no damned good to do this, God, you hear that! But I'm David Harris, and you can't beat me. I'll win, you hear that? You can't break me. I'll win and you'll lose—you know that, God?"

Tears were streaming down his face now. He was sobbing as he yelled, howling like a wild thing screaming out its pain at the empty sky as it tries to avoid dying or gives in to death.

"You wanta kill me, go ahead! Hit me with a fucking lightning bolt. Go ahead. I'm not scared of you or anybody. But you won't beat me, God; you won't beat me—you hear me?"

All he got for an answer was the sharp crack of thunder, riding the tail of a lightning bolt to the ground. Then it was over, and he walked on in the rain, alone.

40

Somerset's Main Street was already festooned with Christmas decorations. Stores had Santa Clause and nativity scenes in their windows, and merchants were engaged in their annual struggle to get their share of the Christmas business.

As David passed the movie, all the Christmas lights suddenly snapped on, and he smiled. On the square the Confederate soldier stood in all his gray, marble stateliness, leaning on his musket, facing east—watching for a marble soldier of Union sympathies, David imagined. The benches at the base of the statue were empty. After all, they were summer benches for people who thrived on heat, the ones who made up that ragtag outfit of summer squatters on the square, men who had worked in the mills or plowed behind teams of mules until they were worn out. Now they could only sit around the base of the old soldier when the sun was hot enough, swapping tired old stories in July and August and September, and lying a little about the cotton they had made, the girls they had had, the fights they had won before bursitis or arthritis crippled their joints.

A sparrow, nervous in the first cold winds of winter, flitted along one arm of the bench, then down to the ground to spear a minuscule bit of bread crust in its beak. Stopped at a red light, David watched the sparrow absently, thinking about Allen Tate's poem he liked so much. How did it go? He tried to remember—the part about the gray spider ticking across the leaves in a Confederate graveyard, over the graves of boys long since dead who had been, as Tate put it, "hurried beyond decision." In the poem, a green garter snake also slithered under a bush. The whole point was that being alive is better than being dead, that it's even better to be a snake or a spider if it's alive than to be a dead human creature.

The sparrow was alive, vital, unlike the humans who would have been on the bench had the sun been hot enough to bring out a little sweat under their hatbands and give them relief in their old joints.

The car behind him honked its horn politely, almost apologetically. David moved on under the light. The sparrow made him feel good, somehow, perhaps because he, like the sparrow, was very much alive.

He felt even better when Marcie met him at the door. She was wearing a brown, woolen shirtwaist dress that hugged her good, full body; he knew she had put it on because it was his favorite. Her father wasn't at home. She had made coffee. Sitting at the kitchen table, watching her serve, made him feel married and warm and comfortable, and he reached out for her.

"I'd rather hug you in the kitchen than any room in the house."

"That settles it. You're just after me for my coffee."

Tonight they would laugh, he knew. Tonight they would think back on five years of silly, funny things and laugh together, laugh not with hollowness but heartily, as they could when they were together. She would scold him for some misadventure he would describe, and he would like that, too, for it meant that, if only for a minute, he belonged to her.

They had planned to go to a movie, but instead they stayed in her kitchen, hers because she had been the woman of the house since the night her mother died. She had come home with the disease eating lines into her face and darkening her eyes, not to the sounds of squealing tires and shrill laughter, as she had left, but with the smell of death about her and a plea for forgiveness on her pale lips. When her waist had broadened, when her large breasts had begun to sag and the honky-tonk lights didn't hide it anymore, the first man, the one who had squealed his tires in the night, had left her. There had been another and another, and finally, the cheap booze dragged her into a whorehouse near an army base in Georgia, where she worked night after night to pretend she was enjoying the five-dollar trick she could still manage, because she needed the next drink so badly. Until one night that finally gave out, when not even the drunken kids wanted her anymore, and she was sick anyhow, so she came home to Somerset. A few months later Marcie was with her in the dark hospital room when she finally got out of life. But Marcie never told David exactly what happened.

They gave her a decent funeral, and her daughter cried, standing in the rain next to her father, who merely looked morosely into the grave. A maiden aunt was there, and a few men with whom Stevens worked and their wives, and David.

David remembered the scene fleetingly as he sat in her kitchen and drank good, strong coffee and ate fresh chocolate cookies while Marcie went in to change the records.

"Ling ting tong, now hear my song, called hi sa mo kum but I ai, hi sa mo kum bu . . ." the lyrics went. David reached for her.

"Don't mess around with the cook," she giggled. "Why, boss man, hit'll git roun' de neighborhood."

Later, the night air bit at their ears and noses as they walked together, holding hands in the darkness, singing songs. She sang the harmony, he tried to sing the melody. The world was a good place to be.

The next day he took her hunting, even persuaded her to carry the light .20-gauge shotgun which had been gathering dust since he had graduated to a .12 gauge years before. As they walked through the wheat stubble he told her about how quail startled him and how doves fly on one wing at a time and about the whispering noises the wind makes on a wood duck's wings. The lambskin at the throat of her jacket emphasized the redness of her cheeks and her lips. He loved her very much.

"Say," he called, "what're you gonna do if an old bobwhite gets up in front of you, lady?"

"Well, sir," she said, grinning, "I'm gonna do just what you told me. I'm gonna put the gun up, close my eyes, pull the trigger, and hope I miss. Isn't that what you said?"

"Well, not quite, but close."

The sun had sunk into the trees behind the creek when he opened the car door for her, carefully taking the unfired gun and unloading it along with his own.

"I can just hear it now," she drawled. "Ol' Pap's gonna say, 'Pearl, whur yo' been?' and I' gonna say, 'Pap, out in the wheat straw with this here city feller,' and that's when the shootin's gonna commence."

"Yo Pap's got a mean look about him, Pearl, ain't no doubt about it."

Rich laughter broke over them again. It was still ringing in his ears that night when he went to sleep. Time was running out; tomorrow he'd be back in school. But the sight of her and the sound and the good, clean smell of her put that back in the recesses of his consciousness, and he only heard the tinkling laughter as he fell asleep.

41

The brief Thanksgiving holiday rushed by, and then David and Bob were back at school.

He had promised that he would decide by Christmas. Although he preferred not to talk about it, Bob reminded him several times of his promise.

The more he thought about it, the more intolerable the decision seemed to David, so he worked to distract himself and put the thought out of his mind. As never before, he threw himself into his school work and editorial chores with the magazine and newspaper. And he drank.

Drinking was an easy way for him to forget momentarily, so he drank prodigious amounts of beer every night. Bob disapproved of his drinking and refused to accompany him to the bars he frequented, instead, worrying about him in the dormitory room alone.

One morning, when the first light awakened him, Bob glanced at David's bed and realized that his roommate hadn't come back. For a minute he considered calling the police, then decided David could take care of himself and rolled over and went back to sleep.

Even before he opened his eyes, David knew he was in a strange place. The bed was soft; the cover was silky under his touch. It smelled good, like roses or maybe carnations. His head hurt. For a moment he lay still on the softness and silkiness of the bed and smelled the flowers.

He stretched his arms and legs, feeling the soreness that came from sleeping on a soft bed. Then slowly, cautiously, he opened his eyes. The blinds were pulled, so the room's details were lost in shadow. His mouth was cottony; a pain slipped like knife points behind his eyes and through the back of his head.

Rubbing his hands over his face and then rotating his thumbs in the slight depressions of his temples, he began to try to piece the evening together. He had started to drink beer early in the day with John Miller at the Stage Door. Then he had moved on alone to that gritty place on Granite Street where the soldiers drank. He remembered listening to war stories for awhile and then going with a sergeant to an after-hours joint out on the highway where the bartender made a big production out of slipping you a half-pint of cheap bourbon under the bar for seven bucks.

There was an argument, he remembered—with the sergeant, maybe, or somebody—

"Christ," he mumbled, "Christ sakes—"

Then he heard the sound across the room—a low chuckle—and when he turned in the bed, she was sitting there watching him.

"Hi," she said, smiling at him.

"Hi, yourself," he said, trying to remember where she fit into the picture.

"I've got some coffee on. Be back in a jif," she said. Then she left.

She returned with a tray containing orange juice and steaming coffee. David gulped the juice, took a long drink of the coffee, and then from habit reached for a cigarette. As he rolled, the cover raised over his hip. He was naked.

"Here's a cigarette," she said and handed him the one she had just lighted.

"Thanks, uh, thanks—"

"If you're wondering what you're doing in my bed, naked as a jaybird, with a fearsome headache and a strange chick lighting your cigarettes, maybe I can clear up some of the mystery."

"Yeah, that'd help."

"Well, you had a lot too much to drink last night, and you wandered over to my table and started to talk. My date was a mean jock; when he came back from the men's room, he got pretty obnoxious. You decided to be a hero."

At this, she laughed lightly, a soft, tinkling laugh like a Chinese bell in a breeze.

"The reason you don't have any cuts and abrasions is because I stopped him. He got mad, so I told him to get lost. Then I was stuck with you."

"Jesus, I'm really sorry—"

"Don't be. Somebody had to take care of you. Your buddy Bob wasn't around this time."

"How do you know about him?"

"Oh, I know a lot about you. Your name is David Harris, and you're from Somerset, South Carolina, where you singlehandedly took on the whole male population. You're 20 going on 35, you write groovy poetry, you edit the school magazine, your best friend is named Bob and you'd go to hell and back for him. You're about to graduate in journalism and—shall I go on?"

"I dunno. Did you leave anything out?" he said, grinning.

"Yes, maybe I left out the reason you were doing all that drinking. You're really hung up on a girl. Somehow, in a way I still can't make out, she's all tied up with your parents and your grandfather. Maybe you can straighten that one out for me sometime."

"I told you all that last night?"

"No, just most of it."

David took a long sip of his coffee and slowly collapsed back onto the pillows.

"Want to sleep some more?" she asked.

"No, no please. I just wanta let the pounding in my head ease up a little. How 'bout tellin' me who you are."

"My name is Mary Beth. I specialize in helpless males and lost causes."

"That's all?"

"Well, it's not all," she replied, "but it's enough for now."

As he ground out his cigarette, she went out to bring him a second cup of coffee.

"By the way," she started, as she handed him the cup.

"By the way, what?"

"In case you're wondering, you didn't get in my pants last night. I slept on the couch."

When he looked up at her, she was grinning. "Well, did I at least try?" he asked her.

"Are you kidding? You were out like a light by the time I got you here. I had a real struggle just getting you out of your clothes. And believe me, you didn't have the faintest idea of trying to get me out of mine."

After he had showered and brushed his teeth with her toothbrush ("Go ahead," she said, "when you're rich and famous, I'll tell everybody we once shared my toothbrush") and dressed, they drove to the Steak Joint for sandwiches.

She wasn't beautiful, he decided, as he sat looking at her in the restaurant. But terribly attractive. Her skin was healthy and smooth as satin. Her eyes were large and extraordinarily expressive. She was small and narrow-hipped. There was a fine delicacy about the way she moved.

After lunch they drove to the lake. By the time they arrived, he knew only a little more about her. She was completing her master's in cultural anthropology, had done her undergraduate work at Sarah Lawrence, had come to the university to study under a particular professor who had done his field work among the plains Indians in Arizona. Her father and mother were divorced, and she had spent much of her life shuttling from boarding schools to Europe to a stiff apartment in a place called Sutton Place in New York.

It was warm for November, and David suggested a walk around the lake. As they walked he told her about the lake, about the times he had fished and hunted there, about the way he could smell out a big bass, about the way flighting ducks hunker down into the coves in December, whistling in on the wind, setting their wings into the gusts coming off the water and settling down as light and pretty as a feather. There was something about the day—actually about her—that made him feel fine. He wanted to tell this strange girl everything. He wanted her to laugh with him and wonder at what he knew. He wanted her to care about him. The more he wanted that, the lighter he felt, the giddier, the freer. He knew somehow that it was a special day, that when it was over, there wouldn't be another just like it. They walked slowly, as if walking fast would rush the day. When they finally sat down, it was on the still-green grass in a cove he loved the best on the lake. A small flight of wood ducks were feeding in the high grass of the cove. When they neared the bank, a rush of wings startled them as the ducks jumped, skittering across the water toward flight. She fell back on him slightly, and he tightened his arm around her.

"Hey, it's just a little flight of puddle ducks," he said quietly. "They're the smallest and prettiest ducks you'll ever see. Nothing to be afraid of."

He felt her soft against him for a moment, and then they were sitting on the grass.

"You owe me something, David," she said.

"Oh?"

"Well," she said softly. "It isn't really that much. But I want to collect it anyhow. I want to know about whatever it is that's eating you."

At first he tried to toss it off as unimportant.

"Hey, just because I had a few drinks too many and tried to pick a fight with your date last night doesn't mean anything. Let's talk about Europe. Where did—"

"No, David, that's not good enough," she said quietly.

"Look," he said "why should you be burdened with my crazy problems? To hell with it. Let's just enjoy being together for a little while."

But even as he spoke to her, he realized that he wanted to talk about all of it, to get it, once and for all, out of his system, maybe to put it in some new kind of perspective that he could deal with.

So he talked. He told her all of the things that bothered him and stirred the deepest sadnesses and consternation in his heart. She listened, seeing him through all his life: first small and alone, bruising his hands and crying out wordlessly for a better chance than he got from the other children; saw him continually torn in the conflict between his grandfather and the world, saw him struggling finally to make his choice and yet keep all the love he could—the love he was afraid to lose—either Marcie's, the whore's daughter who herself needed everything and more of love and strength, or of his parents, whom she knew he wouldn't lose regardless of his choice. She saw the ghost of his grandfather, brooding, lurking, taunting him with tradition and an inarticulated sense of treachery if he betrayed his memory.

He talked until the sun dropped below the treeline, and still she listened, snuggled now against him as the breeze off the lake freshened and chilled and the nightbeats of the bullbat's wings cut the air above them.

As he talked, she caressed him, drew him to her to make him warm. Finally, as the moon rose over the water, it had all been said, and they got up together and left the cove.

They drove along the highway toward town in silence. David felt his face burning with embarrassment for having talked so personally and so long. Several times he tried to justify what he had done, but she wouldn't let him.

"What's wrong with it?" she asked, her voice firm and positive. "Is it wrong to want to survive, to be human, to let it out before it consumes you?"

She paused; then before he could speak, she added softly. "David, don't you see? It makes you human to reach out. Maybe it's all that makes us human."

She knew this all too well, she thought, for she too had been alone. Out of the depths of her loneliness, she could reach out to him and understand; she could find the central meaning and interconnection of things in his life from what he said and did not say.

After dinner she put a stack of records on. First a Dylan Thomas reading and then some soft jazz. Then she was very close to him.

They danced and she kissed him. Then she led him to the bedroom and pulled him down to her.

"Just this once, David Harris, we're going to forget everything together."

The satin sheets felt cool. Then he melted into her. She was hot like fire and cool like ice and her mouth was sweet as the roses or gardenias he smelled. The only reality was him—David Harris—plunging deep into her, and her—Mary Beth Chamberlain—who had come out of the mist to love him for a day, moaning and pulling him deeper, to the places where loneliness lived like a gnawing animal. Even as she knew he would be gone soon, all that mattered was that she could give everything to him at that moment and get everything—and it was good, oh so good—and she was filled with him and he was filled with her.

When it was over they lay together, spent, exhausted, liking each other and themselves. Then she spoke to him, her voice quiet in the darkness.

First she told him how good it was, how good *he* was, how *good* she felt. Slowly, her fingertips playing lightly over his chest, she talked about life and happiness and the best and the worst things she knew. He whispered back in the darkness, lighting cigarettes for them. Finally she was saying the things that needed to be said.

"Your grandfather is dead. Buried and gone. You don't have to drag his corpse around anymore in your heart. His traditions . . . they have the smell of death about them, too. They're clutching at you, pulling you away from life. I think I know your mother and father, David. I came to know them at the lake today. What they want for you is what I want. That's life. *Life.* It's waiting for you—somewhere away from here, away from death and rot and old promises.

"That girl, Marcie, David, let her go. Let her find her own life. It's not with you, don't you see? It's somewhere else for her, too. It's not so hard. Not really. All you have to do is shake the smell of death off you, kick away the pain and turn another chapter that reads life."

Then she snuggled close to him, and they were asleep.

42

For a few days David stayed in Mary Beth's apartment, leaving in the morning for classes and hurrying back as soon as they were over. Then, as suddenly as she had appeared in his life, she disappeared. He found a note on the apartment door that said simply: "Darling, gone on a field trip. You have the answers now. Goodbye, Mary Beth."

He tried to see her again when she returned, but she said firmly that she didn't think it would be wise. It was finished.

It confused him. He tried to put the pieces together, but he could not. Maybe he did have the beginning of the answers, he thought. Still—

A rainstorm lashed the windows of their dormitory room. David and Bob talked late. As he fell asleep, a dull ache gnawed at his stomach, and he tossed uncomfortably, still trying to make logic out of Mary Beth and the rest.

Then he was running as hard as he could, sweat pouring down his forehead and into his eyes, calling for them to stop; chasing after one of them and then another. But each time he got close, they pulled away.

"Wait . . . please . . ." he screamed at them repeatedly, but no one would wait. Only their voices remained behind.

Not just the sounds; the words hung in the air, echoing and written, in fat, dripping sausage letters.

"I don't understand!" he yelled. "Why is it?"

But no answer came, just more words that hung fat in the air.

". . . never been to no Jew funeral . . ." a voice said.

". . . blood's gonna run up to the wagon rim . . ." said another ghostly voice, the letters dripping red.

". . . tell Avrum . . ."

". . . kind of holiday?"

". . . it ain't pretty . . ."

". . . a man . . ."

His head hurt with hearing them, with seeing them, so loud and bright were they, and his lungs hurt from running.

". . . kike . . ."

". . . *und sollst de varen getrunken . . .*"

". . . I need you . . ."

Now the sounds grew shriller, hurting his ears; the words ran together, the fat letters pushing each other for room.

". . . can't turn . . . her virginity . . . she needs . . . all for nothing . . . Jew, Jew coward, Jew . . . different no matter what . . . mamma . . . Bogdanya . . . a debt . . . to be decent . . . Shulman . . ."

He wanted to stop, but he saw Marcie and he had to reach her, so he kept running, his lungs bursting and gasping for air. Then she was close enough for him to lunge at her. He caught her hand, but his fingers went through the skin and flesh and the bone cracked and there was nothing in his hand except a spreading red stain. She was ahead of him again, trying to get away, and he was crying because he had hurt her. He slowly collapsed to the ground, falling backward into the smoke. The stain wouldn't wipe off his hand, and he was too tired to work at it. The sobs wracked his body and he yelled after her that he hadn't meant to hurt her, but she couldn't hear him over the screeching.

Suddenly he was sitting bolt upright in his bed. For a moment he couldn't shake off the sights and sounds. The sheet was soggy with sweat. He got up, threw a towel over his bare shoulder, and headed for the bathroom.

The water cascaded over his head and down his face, stinging him. Gradually he turned the big chrome handle counterclockwise until the water was very cold.

The bathroom was cold, too. He shivered as he toweled dry and headed back to his room. He sat on the edge of his bed, listening to Bob's even snoring, looking at him in the darkness and wishing he would wake up so they could talk. Morning was a long way off, and he knew he couldn't sleep. He felt strangely clearheaded and alert, moreso than he had ever remembered feeling. But he was restless, so he pulled on khaki pants, a sweatshirt, and a heavy jacket. The storm was over, and soon he was walking in the new moonlight on the campus.

Coleridge woke up like this one time, he mused, and wrote *Kubla Khan*. In the full light of the moon he could make out the few leaves remaining on the nearest trees with great clarity. Everything seemed to have a sharper dimension, a clearer definition, than he had ever seen before.

He paused to light a cigarette. The match sputtered in the gentle wind and died before he could cup his hand around it. He struck another, and the taste of the smoke was rich in his mouth.

For awhile he tried to reconstruct the dream, then decided he couldn't, so he tried instead to reconstruct what the voices had been saying to him.

All of them—the voices and the words—seemed to have exploded out of his dilemma. He tried to make some order out of them. He thought about the words and about his choice, and somehow everything gradually began to fall into place for the first time. Then suddenly he grasped what he had never understood before.

Right from the beginning, everyone had been right. Marcie. Bob. His folks. Even the rabbi of Bogdanya. Every one of them. For themselves. But none of them had ever been right for him, because he had been overlooked, somehow, in the equation, and that's what had made it all so confusing. For he had listened, caring, wanting so desperately for all of them to love him, trying so hard to hang on, that the edges of the question had blurred, and the central question had long since disappeared.

It was clear now—suddenly and without any logic or reason— and he could see it. He started to laugh now out loud. He had only been part of the symbology, a witness. It was all an abstraction. There the words were, right in the Goddamn dream. Blood up to the wagon rim. Never going to leave. Kike. *De varen getrunken*. Debt. Fight. She needs you. Decent.

Bullshit! he thought. Bullshit!

Because they didn't add up to the right total, which was he himself, David Harris, a person, a man, a living human creature with a life to live, who had managed to get himself forgotten in the rush by all of them, not out of malice, because they were the people who loved him, but out of some larger, more compelling, imperative.

History and culture and heritage must be served. Weakness must be hidden in yourself, protected in others, just like everyone's feelings must be hidden or protected.

It's all symbology, he thought, and I'm the biggest manipulative symbol of all.

I need you because you are strong; therefore you are bound to me. You need us, so it is situationally incorrect for you to be different; we know what the correct answer to the problem is. It's what's right.

306

It is the only morally correct way to go. You're flesh of my flesh; I, who stooped to care about you, and so the debt is inscribed indelibly. It's the only right thing . . . the fair thing. You can't forget what you are, can't be something you aren't. And she is something else, so that answers everything. How can you think of turning your back on us, on her, on him, on me, on history? Thousands of years of suffering— it means nothing? You owe it to us . . . all of us. You are the son of Ben and Rachel Shulman Harris, lover of Marcie Stevens, best friend of Bob Brock, grandson of Isaac and Baila Shulman, great-grandson of the rabbi of Bogdanya, brother to Jennifer Harris, student number 51287 at the university, 1-A in the draft of the United States government, number 251–46–0023 in Social Security's registration, member of the class of 1958, a Jew, a southerner, a mean son-of-a-bitch in a fistfight.

Is that all?

No, you have physical dimensions, social standing, some intellectual attainments, creative stirrings. You are five feet ten inches tall and weigh 160 pounds. It says that much right on your driver's license. Not bad-looking, at least to some girls, and other people do seek you out. Your newspaper column is read by people who throw the rest of the paper away; you carry a B-plus average and write good Negro dialect poetry. You've read enough to bullshit your way through most conversations and sound brighter than you are; you've been on the dean's list three straight semesters; you can work almost anybody right into the ground, even in a cotton mill. You have a rather considerable capacity to love, particularly your family, and Bob and Marcie.

You see, a voice somewhere deep in his head seemed to say, there's more to you, to it, than the bravado and bullshit. That's what got forgotten, somewhere, somehow, by other people, sure, but also by yourself, David Harris. The equation had been too perfect. When you weren't sure of anything, she appeared and said you were the strongest, the best, and that made it so. All the rest was coasting behind the first strong push down the hill, out of control because to put your hand on the wheel was to risk waking up and finding out it hadn't been so—ever—and she had just made it feel that way for a little while.

You and Marcie don't make any sense for one another, but not for any of the reasons anybody had ever come up with. Not the religion thing, God knows. That was always just a load of crap. But because you had both just hung on because you were afraid to let go, and that can't last very long, certainly not long enough to make a life out of.

You see, there's more to you than you ever thought, more to life than that even. You add up to more than a lot of guts, a hollow leg, a cock that gets hard when you want it to, a quick mouth and a pair of fists. Jesus, there's more, there really is, and you haven't begun to nick the surface of it.

And Marcie. Well, she's the best, no two ways about it, and she gave you a hell of a lot, but you paid it back in spades. There's no debt there, not a nickel's worth, because she never gave you a thing you didn't give her back, except her virginity, and that's not enough to build a life on or destroy one for, because it wasn't any more or any less than saying "I love you" at that moment on the beach. Once she gets away from you for a few days and finds out that every man in the world except you isn't weak like her father, at least the kind of weakness that scares her so—the kind that lets a wife walk out into the night with some drunken stumblebum and lets her keep walking till she winds up on the balls of her ass in a whorehouse somewhere —when she understands that, you won't be all that important to her anymore, because she won't need you the way she thinks she does now.

For the first time David was conscious that rosy streaks were appearing on the horizon, and that he had walked more than four miles.

He felt good, light, as if he could run all the way back to the dorm without stopping if he wanted to. The morning air smelled sweet. It was a good feeling just to be alive and out walking by himself in what was going to be a glorious day.

He picked up his pace, walking quickly by dark houses and carefully manicured lawns, under streetlamps that winked out as the sun came up. He lit a cigarette and tossed the match in a neat arc into the street. His folks would be happy; Christ, would they be happy. It wouldn't matter to them why he had decided as he had— even though his reason was better than theirs.

The chill in the air made him think of bass fishing and bird hunting. He'd go home this weekend, he decided, and walk up some quail on the back of the farm with his father. Maybe he'd tell his father then; maybe he'd even begin to understand it better himself then, out there in the lespedeza and Johnson grass.

It would take awhile to explain it to Marcie, to make her see why it was best not just for him, but for both of them. She'd cry, he knew; but he also knew that after it was over, the tragedy would be gone, the uncertainty, the painfulness of the whole Goddamn thing, and she would feel light and free, just like he did at this moment. It would be good.

A squirrel scampered up a tree ahead of him, running up the

trunk. Then from the safety of the first big branch, it chattered at him.

"Now aren't you something?" David called up to the squirrel. "A little bit of a fellow like you chewing out a big, mean son-of-a-gun like me?"

Then he chuckled and thought about a cup of coffee.